The Longing

BEVERLY LEWIS

The Longing

BETHANY HOUSE
MINNEAPOLIS, MINNESOTA

The Longing
Copyright © 2008
Beverly M. Lewis

Cover design by Koechel Peterson & Associates, Inc., Minneapolis, Minnesota

Scripture quotations are from the King James Version of the Bible.

Published by Bethany House Publishers
11400 Hampshire Avenue South
Bloomington, Minnesota 55438

Bethany House Publishers is a division of
Baker Publishing Group, Grand Rapids, Michigan.

Printed in the United States of America

Library of Congress Cataloging-in-Publication Data

Lewis, Beverly.
    The longing / Beverly Lewis.
        p.   cm. — (The courtship of Nellie Fisher ; 3)
    ISBN 978-0-7642-0584-2 (hardcover: alk. paper) — ISBN 978-0-7642-0312-1
(pbk.) — ISBN 978-0-7642-0585-9 (large print pbk.)
    1. Amish—Fiction. 2. Amish women—Fiction. 3. Lancaster County (Pa.)—
Fiction. 4. Domestic fiction. I. Title.

    PS3562.E9383L66   2008
    813'.54—dc22

                                                                    2008027994

By Beverly Lewis

ABRAM'S DAUGHTERS
The Covenant • The Betrayal
The Sacrifice • The Prodigal
The Revelation

⸎

THE HERITAGE OF LANCASTER COUNTY
The Shunning • The Confession • The Reckoning

⸎

ANNIE'S PEOPLE
The Preacher's Daughter • The Englisher • The Brethren

⸎

THE COURTSHIP OF NELLIE FISHER
The Parting • The Forbidden • The Longing

⸎

The Postcard • The Crossroad

⸎

The Redemption of Sarah Cain
October Song • Sanctuary* • The Sunroom

⸎

The Beverly Lewis Amish Heritage Cookbook

www.beverlylewis.com

*with David Lewis

BEVERLY LEWIS, born in the heart of Pennsylvania Dutch country, fondly recalls her growing-up years. A keen interest in her mother's Plain family heritage has inspired Beverly to set many of her popular stories in Amish country, beginning with her inaugural novel, *The Shunning*.

A former schoolteacher and accomplished pianist, Beverly has written over eighty books for adults and children. Her novels regularly appear on *The New York Times* and *USA Today* bestseller lists, and *The Brethren* won a 2007 Christy Award.

Beverly and her husband, David, make their home in Colorado, where they enjoy hiking, biking, reading, writing, making music, and spending time with their three grandchildren.

PROLOGUE

~

Spring 1967

Like the steady thaw of snow and ice on field and paddock, undoing winter, my sadness has begun to melt away. Six weeks have come and gone since Caleb and I said our last good-byes, and it's nearly time to plant peas and carrots, once the soil is soft enough to take a footprint and be tilled. Time to press on in other ways, too, as I look ahead to joining the New Order church this fall.

Honestly, a great yearning has entered my heart, lingering there in the deepest part of me . . . warming me as I learn to live under the mercy of amazing grace. There are moments, though, when I think of the love Caleb Yoder and I once had and what is now lost to us. At such times, I simply knead the bread dough harder, trying not to fret. With God's help and my family and friends, I'll move forward.

There's no denying it has been a long winter here in Honey Brook, with far too much heartache all round. *Ach,* but I feel as if I'm holding my breath sometimes, waiting for the change of season to bring new life.

As for heartache, my dearest friend, Rosanna King, seems to be doing all right after relinquishing her twin babies, Eli and Rosie, to their birth parents. She's as kind and cheerful as always, but there is unmistakable pain in her eyes, especially when she works on the little cradle quilts she gives away to local midwives. Truly, she longs for her own baby to care for and love. God has certainly allowed some awful hard things in this life, and even with my newfound faith, Rosanna's loss is beyond my understanding.

Not only does Rosanna's plight puzzle me, but my oldest sister's desire for fancy things does, too. Rhoda's made a beeline to the modern world and has herself an English beau, who treats her to fine restaurants and drives her around the countryside in his sporty car. And sometimes in *her* car, according to the grapevine.

Not even Mrs. Kraybill, Rhoda's part-time employer, will shed any light on the rumors when she stops in at the bakery shop. I admit to worrying that Rhoda will get herself hitched up with this *Englischer* and bring new sorrow to Mamma's heart . . . and *Dat*'s, too.

For now, at least, Rhoda's still staying with our brother James and wife, Martha, new members of the well-established Beachy Amish church, not far away. As such, they're enjoying a good many modern pleasures. To think that Rhoda *and* Martha are learning to drive!

And they aren't the only ones. More than a third of the People who originally left the old church have already followed a similar path. My oldest brothers, twins Thomas and Jeremiah, have both purchased cars, unable to agree on the same make and color so they could share one between them.

They managed to scrape up the money for a down payment on a tractor, too, which they'll both use.

No telling where all this buying and whatnot will take folk. Truth be told, such a mighty strong pull the world has on us all.

Frankly, I don't boast when I say I have no interest in the fancy life. Thus far, there's little temptation in that direction. How can I miss what I've never had? I do miss Rhoda, though, and long to win her to the Lord one day.

Nan has become my closest and dearest sister now, and I've shared with her the whole prickly story of my courtship with Caleb. She quietly says, "Soon your pain will lift, Nellie Mae." Since she has suffered her own recent heartbreak, I suppose she should know.

I do still wonder if Caleb ever thinks of me. Does he wish things had turned out differently?

I, for one, won't let his determination to adhere to the Old Ways stop me from praying that his eyes might be opened. Often my prayers are mixed with tears, but I refuse to put my hand to the plow and then turn back. I believe I'm called to this new way of living, and nothing will change my mind.

Preacher Manny said last Sunday, in order to be a true follower of Christ, you must allow God to mold you—to remake you—hard as that may be at times. So I read the Scriptures and contemplate the fork in my road, wondering what sort of young woman I'm becoming since I knelt in the sawdust of Dat's woodworking shop nearly two months ago. I know one thing: I'm free from the bondage of the past . . . and the expectations of Caleb's father. I live to honor God, not my uncle Bishop Joseph and more rules than I can possibly remember. And I don't believe it's wrong to talk to the Lord in prayer, like I would to a close friend.

Hopefully the passage of time and the still, small voice of

God's Spirit will soften Caleb's heart, too. I'd like to think I pray that not for my sake, but for his alone.

It's strange, really. Even though I carry a lingering tenderness for Caleb, sometimes I have to look down to see if my feet are touching the ground. I feel so light and free and ever so clean that it wonders me how a person can be filled with both joy and a sense of sadness at the same time.

Uncle Bishop, who still oversees our New Order group, and Preacher Manny Fisher, my father's cousin, have decided it's time to add a deacon and a second preacher to help with our growing house church. So the divine lot will be cast twice in a few weeks. Some have already gone to prayer and fasting . . . to be in one accord. I wish I were already a voting member. Not that I have anyone in mind for either office, but it would be wonderful-good to feel more a part of the new fellowship of believers.

These days the *Bann* is back in force and the months of easily switching churches are over. Those who remained in the old church are settled and a bit self-satisfied, too—or at least Dat has hinted as much. It's sad to think they are so closed-up to the notion of salvation through grace, but Mamma says we might be surprised at what's happening deep in their hearts, just as we were surprised about Suzy.

I do ponder such things when I look at her picture, given to me by Christian Yoder, her Mennonite beau's older brother. I gaze at the forbidden image more often than I should, probably, wondering what my parents might say if they knew. I am thankful, indeed, for Suzy's life, short as it was, and for the words of faith and love penned in her diary. Words that have helped to guide me.

All in all, there is peace in knowing that my future—and my salvation—doesn't depend on me. It never did. I'll continue to pray for Caleb and trust I'm not being selfish in that. Meanwhile, I know I can cling to my new faith and to my precious family, come what may.

Speak to Him thou for He hears,
and Spirit with Spirit can meet—
Closer is He than breathing,
and nearer than hands and feet.

—TENNYSON

CHAPTER 1

The debris of winter lay in a messy mat over the ground as the earth beneath groaned to life. Caked mud and the mire of old leaves, dried-up twigs, and downed branches, all tangled together in the chaos left over from the coldest season in recent memory.

Indoors, where embers in the woodstove warmed the kitchen, Nellie Mae scrubbed the green-and-white checked oilcloth. A smudge of cherry cobbler had stained it red near where the edge of Dat's dessert plate had been. She worked on the blemish while Nan washed Mamma's best dishes in the deep sink. Meanwhile, Mamma made quick work of the few leftovers at the counter, commenting again about the "delicious dessert," as if the simple baked dish was extra special.

They'd had an especially fine feast on this Easter Monday noon, even if it was only the four of them seated around the table. They'd sent a written invitation to Dat's parents over in Bird-in-Hand but, not surprisingly, *Dawdi* and *Mammi* had quickly declined. Things had been that way since her parents, Nan, and Nellie, too, had chosen to embrace the teachings of the New Order church.

Resurrection Day, their father now referred to Easter, with a broad smile. Both he and Mamma seemed keen on celebrating the day in a different way than before, though they and the rest of Preacher Manny's New Order group had observed prayer and fasting on Good Friday, just as in the old church. But Nellie had noticed from the very start of the weekend that a certain radiance permeated the observance. Easter was more meaningful than it had ever been in all of Nellie's eighteen years.

Oh, the wonder of it, she thought, wiping down the entire oilcloth even though they sat just at one end of the table now that Rhoda had moved out.

Missing Rhoda and Suzy—one sister gone to the world and the other to heaven—was becoming more bearable. "Life is all about change," Mamma often reminded her, but it didn't make things any easier . . . especially where Nellie's heart was concerned. Even so, Nellie knew that the sooner she got over missing her former beau, the better.

Nan tossed her a tea towel as Mamma left the kitchen. "*Kumm* dry."

Nellie reached to catch it. "Ach, I ate too much. Didn't you?"

"Will you have room for some supper later on?" Nan glanced her way with a curious look.

"Only a smidgen, maybe. We'll have plenty of leftovers, *jah*?"

Nan shook her head. "I was hopin' you'd go with me to the Honey Brook Restaurant, maybe."

"To see Rhoda?"

"Jah . . . I can't help but think our sister must be homesick for us."

Yet Rhoda hadn't bothered to contact them, not even Mamma, for all this time. A sore point, to be sure, and Nellie could have been miffed about it if she let herself. For the most part, she found herself whispering a prayer for Rhoda nearly as often as she did for Caleb.

Hesitating, Nellie asked, "Have you ever been there?"

"Only once." Nan frowned. "With my old beau . . ."

The last time Nellie Mae had talked with Rhoda, she'd taken Suzy's diary to her. Since Rhoda seemed to love jewelry, she'd also given her Suzy's gold bracelet, engraved with that sister's favorite verse. "Sure would be nice to see Rhoda again," said Nellie.

Nan brightened. "Well, I know she's working tonight, since it's Monday. She's there till closing on Tuesdays and some on weekends, too." Nan seemed quite certain of their sister's schedule. "Mamma doesn't mind. I already asked."

"Well, I wish you'd told me before I took my second helping of mashed potatoes and gravy, then." Nellie smiled. "Sure, I'll go with you."

Nan nodded, her hands deep in the suds. "*Denki,* sister." If Nellie wasn't mistaken, tears glistened in Nan's eyes. "Seems odd that she'd be satisfied with her life," said Nan, "out there in the world. . . ."

"Well, she does have James and Martha . . . and the children," Nellie said. "Plenty of family round her."

"Just ain't the same, though."

Nellie agreed. How *could* it be, as close as Rhoda and Nan had always been? For so many years, this house, their father's home, had sheltered them from every possible storm, except those brewing under their own roof. Everything they loved was here—the grand old farmhouse itself; Dat's barn and the horses he raised and trained; the surrounding acreage of fertile land. And the bakery shop. Nellie's Simple Sweets was a haven of sorts in the hollow, between two treed knolls that rose on either side of Beaver Dam Road like protective barriers against the outside world. For now, at least. Nellie sometimes sensed how temporary her own stay here was—she longed to marry and have her own family someday. *With a husband like Caleb. But with a passion for life . . . and the Lord.*

She thought again of Rhoda and wondered how she could be truly happy being courted by a worldly man. Someone foreign to the Plain community. Surely she would tire quickly of the enticement and long for home.

"I wonder what Rhoda did for Easter." Nan looked at Nellie Mae. "Do you think she dyed eggs and ate chocolate bunnies, like the English do?"

Nellie had wondered, too. "You'd think she would've missed goin' to Preaching yesterday, jah?"

"Would seem so."

She wasn't sure if Rhoda continued to attend the Beachy meetinghouse with James, Martha, and their children. Martha rarely visited since Rhoda's leaving. Such a painful wedge now.

Nellie wished Rhoda might have come to visit for Easter, or sent a note, at least. But maybe her absence was her way of saying she was quite content as she was.

Nan continued washing the last of the dishes, staring down at the water, daydreaming. Suddenly she looked up at Nellie Mae. "I've been wanting to tell ya something," she said softly, glancing toward the doorway.

"Jah?"

Nan brightened. "I've met someone," she said, but her lower lip trembled.

"Ach, Nan . . . you're sad?"

Nan shook her head. "It's my joy I struggle with, sister. Truly, it is. I'm so happy, but . . ."

"But what?"

Nan paused. "Well, to be honest, I'm afraid to be disappointed again. Will this beau hurt me, too?"

Nellie leaned her head against her sister's. "Oh, Nan, I'm

worried for ya, honestly." She sighed. "But you mustn't let the past spoil the present . . . nor should you keep mum because of what's happened 'tween Caleb and me."

Long into the afternoon, while Nellie wrote her circle letters and read from the New Testament, she pondered Nan's news. She couldn't help but wonder who the young man could be, hopeful Nan might confide in her in due time. Surely he, too, was of the New Order church.

Nellie let her mind wander, imagining what it would be like to share the same faith as a beau. *Maybe someday I'll know.*

———

The cry of a siren rang out in the distance. That, accompanied by a sudden gale, caught Caleb's attention and he raised his head. Several cows bawled at the sound, shifting in the stalls of his maternal grandfather's barn. Unexpected noises, especially high-pitched ones, disturbed the livestock. He'd observed this even when he'd lived at home, working for his father.

Those days are long gone, he thought, dismissing the far-off distress signal as he emptied the fresh milk into the pumping tank.

He had another hour or so of milking before he returned to the little *Dawdi Haus*, his home these many long weeks while he worked off his "debt of sin"—or so his father called it.

The second urgent wail assailed him as he stood near the last milking stanchion, tired and hungry, as he often was at this hour. This time, the siren sounded closer, but here in the barn, with no way to look out, he couldn't be certain of the direction.

Eager to stay on task—not wanting to delay his grandmother's supper—he dismissed the siren once again. *Best to keep busy.* The thought was a constant refrain since Nellie Mae Fisher had called off their engagement.

What was she thinking?

Lest he fall into discouragement, he refused the defeating thought. He was free now to court a girl from his own church district—someone who gladly held to the Old Ways and appreciated their strict tradition. No longer would he have to plead with Nellie to stay far away from Preacher Manny's group, nor the more liberal Beachy Amish church.

So Caleb was back to looking for a mate while the very girl he'd proposed to was moving in a new direction—away from him. He was miserable working for his grandfather, cut off from his immediate family by his own hand. Even if he could convince someone to marry him, he would have nothing to offer a bride, now that he'd given up his claim to his father's land.

He moved about the milking parlor, comforted by this twice-daily routine—knowing what to expect. The familiar barn smells and sounds relaxed him, just as his older sister Rebekah had often reassured him with her kind words when they were young. But now he was cut off from her, as well, since she'd moved over to Mill Road with the Ebersols. Downright peculiar. How was it they, being Old Order, could tolerate her attending the New Order meetings—even her planning to join that church come fall—but *Daed* could not? Truly, Rebekah had been as harshly ousted from *Daed's* house as Caleb had been, but for very different reasons.

Things just didn't make sense—not Rebekah's arrogant declaration of "having salvation," nor Nellie Mae's bold claim of redemption. Yet despite the church split and all that had changed because of it, he was as determined as ever to live out his life in the old tradition. *Where I was meant to be . . . even though my loyalty's gotten me nowhere.*

So the gray days continued, and he found no joy in this new life of hard work and loneliness. Still, Caleb had yet to completely regret the ill-fated night with Nellie Mae in the very Dawdi Haus where he was sent to reside. The night he'd crossed a delicate line with the woman he so loved and had planned to marry, asking her to let down her hair for him. *A loving act meant only for her husband's eyes . . .*

Though that night was long gone, he clearly recalled their sweet affection. He hadn't heeded his own inner warning, nor dear Nellie's, to wait for lip-kissing till their wedding day.

The cows were lowing contentedly now, and he moved among them, talking softly, as was his grandfather's habit. He was accustomed to emulating those with more experience and wisdom, the way of doing things passed down by imitation. That's why Nellie's abandonment of their tradition kept him awake at night. It was so foreign . . . not the way of the People, especially not for a woman. Yet, if he let his mind wander back to their earliest dates, her ability to think for herself had been one of the things that drew him to her—and he missed talking to her. *Ach, I miss everything about her.*

It was during his grandmother's skillet supper of sausage, onion, green pepper, stewed tomatoes, and macaroni, that Caleb discovered the significance of the siren's wail.

His grandfather had just commented on the recent rise in feed prices when a startlingly loud rap came at the back door. His older brother Abe burst into the kitchen, red-faced. "Caleb! Kumm *schnell*!—come quick!"

Immediately he leapt from the table, dashing out to the utility room for his coat and hat . . . leaving Dawdi and Mammi to wonder what sudden calamity had befallen them.

———

A light rain had begun to fall, melting the remaining snow on either side of the road as Nellie Mae and Nan made their way to the Honey Brook Restaurant.

21

"Do ya think Rhoda will be surprised to see us?" asked Nan, holding the reins.

"Well, she said she missed us when I visited her some weeks ago." Nellie wondered if Rhoda had ever considered the verse inscribed on Suzy's bracelet: *Not by works of righteousness but by His mercy He saved us.*

"I hope she won't think we're spyin' on her."

"Well, I doubt she'd admit that." Nellie forced a smile, hoping they weren't making the trip to town only to be rebuffed, if only for Nan's sake.

"Might be best if we don't seem desperate for her to come home, jah?"

Nellie sighed. This was going to be hard, no getting around it. "If she's aloof, I hope you won't take it to heart, Nan."

"Oh no, I'm beyond bein' hurt over her leaving. Honest, I am."

Nellie heard the slight waver in her sister's voice and knew better.

———

"Oh, Caleb . . . Caleb, you're here." His mother's face was ashen as she greeted him and Abe at the back door. "Your father's been hurt," she said, wringing her hands. "I should've gone along in the ambulance," she added as they moved into the kitchen.

"What happened?" Caleb asked.

His sisters Leah and Emmie hovered near *Mamm*, looking right peaked themselves, and their oldest brother, Gideon, seemed mighty grim at the head of the table.

"Ach, the chain broke on the plow hitch," Mamm explained, "and while your father was down fixin' it, one of the mules kicked him in the head." She faltered, openly weeping. "Your poor Daed . . . so terribly wounded."

Caleb's heart broke as she attempted to describe the accident, and he made her sit down because she seemed like she might just teeter over.

"Abe was out in the field with your father—saw it all—and ran for help to our Beachy neighbors . . . used their telephone to call an ambulance."

"Was Daed breathing?" Caleb asked, sitting at the table with Mamm and the others. A cluster of panicked souls.

Abe nodded. "I checked his breathing and his pulse . . . awful weak. And he couldn't stop shaking."

"Will he pull through?" asked Caleb.

Abe's face fell. "It . . . it's hard to know."

Gideon leaned forward, his voice all pinched. "The medics didn't say one way or the other. But Daed was struggling, that's for sure."

Leah began to cry, and Emmie, Caleb's youngest sister, put her arms around her. "Daed'll pull through . . . he will," Emmie said bravely, but she, too, shed tears.

"One of us must go to the hospital," Caleb spoke up, looking at his mother.

Abe glanced at Gideon. "I should be the one to go. Caleb can stay here with Mamm and the girls, once you head home."

Gideon got up from the table, saying he ought to get back to his own family. "I'll stop in at Jonah's on the way," he said, referring to their other brother. "Maybe he's returned from his errand by now. Sure would hate for him to hear this from anyone but us." He went to Mamm and leaned down to say good-bye, then left.

Abe prepared to leave, as well. Trembling, their mother rose and followed him to the door, pleading with him. "Bring word back as soon as ya know something . . . anything!"

"I'll see what I can find out." Clearly eaten up with worry, Abe nodded and darted out the door.

Caleb led Mamm into the kitchen once again and pulled up the rocking chair for her. "You mustn't fret. We must keep our wits about us."

Trying to be brave, no doubt, she blinked her sad eyes silently, and then with a great gasp, she buried her face in her hands. "Ach, what'll we do if—"

"Mamm . . . Mamm." Caleb stood near her chair, leaning over her now. "Try to remember how strong Daed's always been. Not much can hurt a man like that."

She nodded slowly, wiping her tears. And he wished he believed his own words.

Sobbing loudly, Emmie reached for Leah's hand and they hurried out of the kitchen, toward the stairs.

"Plenty of men have been kicked by a horse and died on the spot," Caleb reminded his mother. "But you heard Abe, Mamma. Daed's alive . . . let's cling to that."

She bowed her head. "Ach, why didn't I go with him? Oh, Caleb." She could no longer speak as she softly cried.

"Everything happened so fast," he said, his heart pounding. He tried to ignore the stranglehold sensation on his chest and throat that fought his every breath.

CHAPTER 2

The interior of the restaurant was bright, with ruffled white curtains adorning the windows. One end of the enclosed porch area made for a cozy dining spot. *For courting couples.* Nellie Mae caught herself and cast away the niggling thought.

Nan spotted their oldest sister first. "There's Rhoda," she whispered, bobbing her head in that direction.

Wearing a pale aqua dress with cap sleeves and a knee-length white apron tied at the waist, Rhoda scurried to deliver a tray of food to a table of four young men.

Nellie forced a smile, fascinated by whatever Rhoda had done to herself. Noticing Rhoda's new eyeglasses and the arc of her eyebrows, she realized their sister had plucked out a significant number of hairs to alter the shape. She wore makeup, too, and was even so reckless as to display much of her legs—the daring hem of her waitress dress just grazed the tops of her knees. *And she's lost weight.*

Rhoda did still have her light blond hair twisted back at the sides and pinned up in a bun, but her prayer *Kapp* was missing—another startling surprise.

Nan twittered nervously, "Did ya think she'd change so quick?"

"Well, people do when they wander away." Nellie glanced at Rhoda again.

Once they were seated, Nan reached for the menu. But Nellie couldn't keep her eyes off Rhoda. A long-ago memory took her back—she and Rhoda as young girls, tugging hard at a faceless doll made by Rosanna's frail mamma. Rhoda had been determined to hang on to that precious doll, no matter what. *"It's mine! Let go! I had it first!"*

Rhoda's little-girl voice rang in Nellie's ears. "She was a bit stubborn even then," Nellie Mae muttered to herself.

Nan lowered the menu, peering over the top. "You all right?"

Quickly she blinked. "I s'pose so."

"Then why do you look so . . . aghast?"

She bent forward, her voice a whisper. "When Rhoda comes over to take our order, you'll see why."

Nan nodded, squinting her eyes in apparent agreement. "Oh, I can tell from here. She's deep into the world, ain't so?"

So Nan had noticed.

As uncomfortable as Nellie felt, she and Nan were here now. And Rhoda had just spotted them across the room, where she waved and smiled before taking another order.

Several more people entered the restaurant—a young couple, then a family of four, who sat down at a table a few yards from Nellie and Nan. A light-haired young man, evidently the older of the family's two sons, caught Nellie's attention. His profile was rather familiar. Goodness, but it was the fellow she'd met so unexpectedly out on the road weeks ago—Christian Yoder, one of Suzy's Mennonite friends.

"Now who are you lookin' at?" Nan was eyeing her, her menu closed and on the table.

"That family over there. Well, don't look now, but I honestly think the younger of the two boys—the darker-haired one—might be the *Mennischte* Suzy dated. I'm pretty sure the older one is the same person I met on the road last February."

Nan's eyes brightened. "Ach, really?"

"Don't stare!" she whispered.

Nan seemed all too eager, literally gawking over her shoulder. "So that's Christian Yoder . . . the one who gave you Suzy's bracelet."

"Nan."

"Oh, all right." Reluctantly Nan turned, and just then Rhoda came over, licking her thumb as she flipped the page over on her order tablet. "How are you *ladies* this evening?"

"We're hungry," Nan said right away, reaching to touch Rhoda's waitress dress. "It's so good to see you!"

"Denki—er, thanks." Rhoda blinked her eyes, her cheeks rosy under her face powder. "I never expected to see yous. . . ."

"I had a hankerin' to come," Nan admitted, still fingering Rhoda's dress. "Hope that's all right."

Seeing that Nan was about to cry, Nellie spoke up. "We thought it'd be fun to visit you here at your work."

Rhoda nodded awkwardly, glancing over her shoulder toward the kitchen. Just as quickly, she turned back to them. "How's Mamma? And Dat?"

"Dat's got some driving horses trained and ready to sell," Nan said. "And Mamma is helping Nellie in the bakery shop quite a lot."

"Still goin' to Preacher Manny's church?" Rhoda looked at Nellie.

"Both of us are. And Nan and I plan to take baptismal instruction this summer."

"Oh, really? When did ya decide *this*?"

Another waitress breezed past, briefly saying something

to Rhoda. Rhoda told them she'd be right back, and the two waitresses promptly hurried away.

Nellie wished she might have shared with Rhoda all the wonderful-good things happening deep in her heart. Sighing, she decided to order a bowl of vegetable soup and a grilled cheese sandwich, and when Rhoda returned, she and Nan placed their orders.

Moments later, Nan excused herself to the washroom, and Nellie felt terribly conspicuous and almost wished they'd stayed home. Staring at the salt and pepper shakers, she fidgeted, moving them around. She'd never found herself in such an uncomfortable situation, not that she recalled. Well, perhaps the day she had been out walking, minding her own business until suddenly encountering Christian Yoder in his tan car.

Remembering that day, it took her a moment to realize someone was standing next to her table. Looking up, she saw Christian himself smiling at her, with his presumably younger brother at his side.

"Nellie Mae . . . nice to see you again. We thought we'd come over and say hi." He turned. "This is my brother Zach."

Zach offered his hand, looking a bit bashful. "Nice to meet you, Nellie Mae." He studied her as if searching for a resemblance to Suzy.

Feeling embarrassed, she looked for Nan, wondering what was keeping her. "My sister Nan's here with me." She tried to avoid Christian's gaze. "It would be nice if she could meet you, too."

Zach was nodding, and Christian asked if they'd come to celebrate something special.

She wouldn't say they were here for the sole purpose of visiting their wayward sister. No, she wouldn't divulge that prickly tidbit. "Well, it is Easter Monday, after all."

Christian's face lit up. "And my dad's birthday."

Zach glanced back toward their family's table, and Nellie's gaze followed. Their parents appeared curious, and no wonder.

Christian's eyes remained on her. "Good seeing you," he said again, more softly this time.

Christian and Zach's parents were looking her way again, which made her feel too tense to talk. Unsure of herself, Nellie merely nodded.

Just when she thought she ought to offer them a seat, Nan returned. She looked surprised to see Christian and Zach there and cast a quick frown at Nellie, who introduced her. "This is my sister Nan."

"Hi." Christian reached to shake her hand, as did Zach, smiling.

"Nan, these were some of Suzy's friends," Nellie explained. "From last summer . . ."

Nan nodded with affected courtesy and directed another sharp look at Nellie.

"Would you mind if my parents say hello sometime before we leave?" Zach asked.

Nellie could just imagine her sister's questions, once they were alone again. "Why, sure . . . if they'd like to," she replied, her neck stiff now with tension.

When Christian and his brother headed back to their own table, she reached for the dessert menu right quick, hiding behind it.

"Nellie Mae?"

She sighed; there was no avoiding Nan.

"Nellie, look at me."

Slowly she peeked over the top of the menu.

"Those two fellas looked real pleased, talking to you."

Ach, here we go. . . .

"Honestly, what took you so long in the washroom, Nan?"

"You're ignoring my point." Nan leaned closer.

"Which was?"

Nan shook her head. "You're hopeless." She looked across toward Rhoda, who stood near the table of four young men, obviously flirting as she refilled their coffee cups.

Nellie saw it, too—Rhoda smiling and joking, like she was quite at home. Ever so peculiar.

This is her life now.

Nan frowned and absently touched the end of her fork. "Oh, Nellie . . . I wasn't goin' to say anything yet, but Rhoda just told me something awful troubling in the hallway."

Nellie raised her head, noticing Nan's solemn face. "What?"

"I best say it somewhere in private . . . don't want to burst out cryin'."

"Jah, don't do that."

Rhoda was headed their way now, carrying a round tray of food. When she set it down in front of them, both Nan and Nellie smiled at her. "Denki, Rhoda," they said in unison.

There was a brief glint of welcome in Rhoda's eyes. Maybe seeing them again brought back happy memories. Nellie hoped so. She was counting on them to bring Rhoda back to her senses soon. *Memories . . . and plenty of prayer.*

Once they were alone again, Nellie offered a blessing for the food. Then silently they began to eat. But all through the meal, Nan picked at her food, clearly distracted. What had Rhoda said to make Nan so glum?

Several times during the evening, Christian glanced over at them. Usually it was about the time Nellie looked *his* way . . . but only to ponder his brother. Surely if Suzy hadn't died, her friendship with Zach—and Christian—would have been short-lived. The boys seemed so . . . *English.*

Nellie tried to engage Nan in conversation about other things—even the weather—but to no gain. And then, about the time Nan seemed more herself again, the whole Yoder family rose and walked over to their table. Nellie gulped inwardly.

Her mouth was dry as yarn as Mr. and Mrs. Yoder offered their kind condolences. Christian's steady gaze rested on her all the while. Truth be told, she felt quite relieved when the Yoders finally turned and headed for the door.

"Aw, c'mon, Rhoda, tell us when you get off work," the most flirtatious of the four men said. Running his finger around the lip of his water glass, he looked her over but good.

Rhoda should have been put off by their attention. A fleeting thought crossed her mind: *What would Ken think if he saw me laughing and talking with these men?* But she was not the instigator. They'd struck up a casual conversation, asking what was her favorite entrée on the menu . . . making harmless small talk. Still, she hadn't discouraged it, nor was she flustered by the attention.

A friendly waitress, older and wiser, had warned her: *"Remember how men act around waitresses."*

Even so, she'd gone from no male attention to this—why not enjoy herself? It wasn't like she was engaged to Ken yet, although she would turn off the charm to others the minute that happened. *When* it did.

Hurrying back to the kitchen to check on an elderly couple's order, she glanced at Nan, noticing the way her closest sister leaned forward at the table as she talked to Nellie Mae. Was Nan telling Nellie what Rhoda had shared?

She suddenly felt sad, missing Nan, especially. How long

had it been since they'd curled up in their room, confiding their hopes for marriage and babies?

Fact was, Nan looked downright dismal, and no wonder. *I shouldn't have breathed a word. . . .*

Nellie Mae seemed preoccupied—and much too apprehensive. Had something changed at home in the time since Rhoda had quarreled with Dat and left? What was wrong? For a moment, Rhoda regretted the distance between her and her two remaining sisters.

Not wanting to cry, she headed to the washroom and stared at herself in the mirror. She removed her glasses, washing a few smudges off the lenses and drying them on the skirt of her uniform. Oh, how she loved her new things . . . her growing wardrobe of for-good as well as casual clothes. She'd even considered buying a pair of dress trousers, the nice-looking pants that English women wore for shopping or for a more relaxed outing.

She washed her hands, letting the warm water run. She'd considered painting her nails—wouldn't that look pretty for the days she put on her waitress dress and half apron?

Heading out the door, she thought again of Suzy's diary. She'd read the surprising last half twice already. In fact, for the second time just last night. She'd had to hide the journal quickly this morning, fearful Martha would discover it. She found it strange that Suzy's wild days had led her to something quite different than she'd set out to find. *She got religion,* as Rhoda had heard it described. *Same as Dat, Mamma, and nearly the whole family.*

"But before all of that, Suzy had gotten herself a fella," she muttered.

Slipping her hand into her pocket, Rhoda felt Suzy's bracelet there, thinking she ought to start wearing it. After all, she was as gussied up as any fancy woman who'd never been raised to know better. *Why not?*

———

Waiting for some word on his father, Caleb was captive to his own imagination. In his drowsy state, he replayed his final visit with Nellie Mae in her bakery shop, unable to put the dreadful day behind him. He wondered how he might have steered the conversation toward a happy outcome. But no, Nellie had been determined to have her way, unlike any young woman he knew. She'd spurned his love for a newfangled faith that could never endure. He scoffed at the very idea of the new church—the New Order, or whatever they called themselves. Yet somehow, they'd gotten to his beloved.

"She's brainwashed." He hurled his angry words into the stillness of his mother's kitchen. There was some consolation in knowing he had tried to talk Nellie Mae out of joining the new church. Given time, he would have done anything to get her to see the foolishness of her choice. If only she'd agreed to run away with him. If only the church split hadn't ripped the People apart . . . hadn't ripped *them* apart, destroying their hopes for a future as man and wife.

How was I to know it would come to this?

Thoughts of his former sweetheart pressed hard on his mind as he got up and went to the sink for some cold water. He'd lived with this frustration each day since their absurd farewell.

Caleb had no recourse now but to dismiss Nellie completely. Yet, hard as he tried, it was impossible to think of his darling being courted by another man. He clenched his jaw as grief and rage filled him.

It was close to midnight when Abe startled him, shaking him awake. Caleb had fallen asleep near the woodstove, in Daed's old kitchen rocking chair. Rousing himself, he sat up. "How's Daed doin'?" he asked.

"It's bad news, Caleb. Awful bad. He might not even survive the night."

"Ach, this can't be."

"Listen, we can't give up just yet," Abe chided. "There's still breath in him."

"Shouldn't you have stayed?" Caleb asked softly, concerned his father might die alone.

"Believe me, I wanted to, but I thought it best to return right quick for Mamm. Take her back with me . . . just in case. The driver's waitin' outside."

Caleb agreed that Mamm should be at their father's side at this dire time. "You'd best be getting Mamm up, then, jah?"

Solemnly, Abe nodded. "If she's even asleep. No doubt she's up there stewin'." He removed his black hat, brown eyes shadowed in the dim light. "Perhaps that's the hardest thing of all. Not knowing what the mornin' will bring."

Caleb had many questions, but he sat as still as the great stones in his father's field. Shouldn't he go to the hospital, too? Try to make peace with his hardhearted father?

Abe placed a hand on his shoulder. "Go on back to Dawdi's now, Caleb. Get some more rest—you'll need it for what's ahead, no doubt."

Caleb shuddered. *He doesn't think Daed will pull through. . . .*

"Remind Mamm how determined our father's always been," he told Abe. "Don't dash her hopes."

Abe gave a nod and trudged toward the stairs, saying no more.

Slowly Caleb rose and headed into the utility room for his coat and hat, aware of the effort of pushing one foot in front of the other. His tired mind raced with uncertainty—concern that his father's death would leave so much undone between them. And his heart went out to Mamm for all the years she'd stood by the most stubborn man Caleb had ever known.

On the cold ride back to his grandparents' place, he considered the possible changes ahead . . . the harsh reality of his family's predicament. At this dark hour, his father's very life hung by a thread.

CHAPTER 3

Reuben Fisher was surprised when his oldest brother, Bishop Joseph, arrived from the next farm over early the following morning. Reuben was grooming the new foals when Joseph came plodding into the barn, a look of apprehension on his face. "There's been a terrible accident."

Anxious about his aging parents, Reuben braced himself for bad news, the hairs on the back of his neck prickling.

"One of David Yoder's mules kicked him yesterday afternoon—like to have killed him, but it seems he's got himself a hard noggin."

"Will David live?"

Joseph pushed up his spectacles, his eyes serious. "Too soon to say. I expect to hear more from Abe today."

Reuben listened as his brother gave a few more details about the accident. Then Joseph sighed. "Well, I best be goin'. I've got to get word to a few more folks yet this morning." He offered a wave as he departed.

Rushing to the house, Reuben relayed the news to Betsy, who looked as stunned as he felt.

"Oh, Reuben, more sorrow?" She spoke in a whisper as she reached to embrace him, her Bible pressing against his back.

He held her near, aware of her trembling. "You needn't fret, love." He stroked her long, beautiful hair, still down from the night. "Leave all the worry to me. I'll see what can be done to help the Yoders."

She looked up at him ever so sweetly, eyes filling with tears. "I'll do my part, too."

"You're a wonderful-*gut* woman, you are." He leaned down and kissed her. "Take care of yourself today, hear?"

Before leaving, he snatched up his own Bible, wanting it with him in the buggy. There was a quiet confidence in knowing he had God's Word within his reach.

Then he headed out to the barn to get his driving horse, planning to make a quick trip to Preacher Manny's to solicit help from a few of the New Order men. He would also go to each of his sons to request their assistance with David's farming duties—milking, hauling manure, sowing alfalfa seed in the former wheat field. Such work was never ending, especially during the warm months. He also assumed David and his sons were in the process of sterilizing their tobacco beds with steam, tobacco being one of David's major cash crops. Reuben didn't see how his conscience would allow him to help with that particular job, but he knew plenty of progressive farmers who wouldn't mind pitching in. Even some of the older men were mighty strong in their hands, due to years of working with "the 'baccy."

Last of all, he would stop by to see Elias King. Perhaps Elias would ride with him to visit David at the hospital—a trip Reuben felt compelled to make, no matter the bleak reception that might await him.

Betsy slipped on her bathrobe and hurried downstairs to tell Nan and Nellie Mae of the tragic accident, her voice shaking as she did. To think such a terrible thing could happen—and without warning. She could scarcely bear to think of poor Elizabeth Yoder, who must be heartsick, beside herself with worry. *Ach, what the whole family must be going through.* . . .

"I'll bake a nice, hot dish or two," Nellie said, blinking her eyes.

Nan slowly nodded and leaned on the kitchen table. "And I'll start breakfast . . . then bake some more cookies."

Betsy, too, was eager to help Nellie finish baking the day's offerings for Nellie's Simple Sweets. It was impossible for Nellie alone to keep up anymore, what with the crowd of customers. In fact, she'd thought recently the cozy bakery shop had outgrown its name—Nellie, Nan, and Betsy's Simple Sweets seemed a better fit these days, though the selection was no longer so simple.

Quickly Nan and Nellie Mae decided how they might manage their regular baking with the added meals for the Yoders, and soon the numbing shock of David's accident gave way to purposeful action.

Will the Yoders accept our gift of food . . . and Reuben's offer to help?

Betsy knew it would take a miracle for the Yoders to abandon their so-called shunning of New Order and Beachy folk, even in the midst of their great need.

A thoughtful glance at Nellie's ashen face revealed how deeply the news had affected her now-youngest daughter. Betsy sensed not only Nellie Mae's deep sympathy but her understandably great caution where the Yoder family was concerned. As if it was hard even to speak their names.

It's hard to change horses in midstream, she thought. After all, David Yoder was to have been Nellie's father-in-law.

"I'll cook the food, but I'd rather not take it over there," Nellie admitted softly.

Betsy breathed a prayer of gratitude for Nellie's merciful heart, doing this hard thing. *To show the love of the Lord Jesus . . .*

All the while Nellie chopped potatoes and made small snibbles of a large yellow onion, her thoughts were on Caleb. *How horrid he must feel.*

Oh, his poor, dear mother and siblings . . . and his father, whose life hung in the balance. As she greased the pans for the beef-and-potato casserole and buttered-noodle dish, she wondered what she might be doing differently today in response to this tragedy if she and Caleb were still courting. Wouldn't she rush to his side to offer comfort?

Sliding the baking dishes into the oven at last, she wished there might be something more she could do. But no, she was doing exactly what she ought to—making an anonymous meal.

Her throat was tight with dread. David was a man of conviction and of action, too. Even though he was as sincere as the next man, she believed he was sincerely wrong in the way he'd treated Caleb—and in his firm stance against the new church.

Yet Nellie did not hold even the slightest grudge, though she couldn't help but wonder if Caleb still did, after everything he'd endured at the hand of his unyielding father.

In any case, Caleb surely needed the support of his friends . . . and his extended family. "But it's not my place," she caught herself saying aloud.

She glanced back at Nan to see if her sister had noticed the slip, but Nan appeared lost in her own thoughts. Her usually joyful countenance sagged; doubtless that had more to do with the private chat with Rhoda last night at the restaurant. So far, she hadn't yet divulged what had prompted her concern, but

Nellie assumed it had something to do with Rhoda's plans to live a fancy life. What else could it be?

Soon Nan headed out to help feed the livestock, in Dat's absence. Most likely, he was on his way home to wait for the hired driver. Numerous other farmers would surely drop by the Yoders' to offer farming assistance, as word spread. And Uncle Bishop would open up the benevolence fund to help with medical bills, as usual.

Nellie crimped the edges of the crust on one of her many pies as the sun shone hard against the gleaming windows. Dawn was bringing daylight earlier each morning, another vital sign of spring. And with the change of season, there would be much more to do outdoors—tending their own vegetable and charity gardens, weeding flower beds, keeping the lawns well trimmed and neat, and whitewashing fences. She was ready to work outside again, feeling like a cooped-up hen in a chicken house. Eager to keep busy, too. During slow times in the shop, she had even begun writing down favorite recipes. Anything to keep her hands and mind occupied—and her thoughts away from her lingering loneliness for Caleb.

I wish I could be the one to soothe his pain, she thought now, picking up her pace. Deep in her heart, she knew she was grasping for excuses to offer kindness to Caleb. But she must act as though she had never been courted—or kissed—by handsome Caleb Yoder, no matter how desperate or hopeless his father's condition.

———

With Reuben's help, Elias King made swift work of feeding and watering his goats. The younger man seemed pleased to be invited along to visit David Yoder. He slipped briefly into the house to let Rosanna know where they were headed before stepping up into Reuben's carriage. They would wait at the Fishers' for a hired driver to take them to the hospital in town.

Elias was rather solemn in Reuben's buggy. "Such a shame 'bout David. I hope he hangs on." He shook his head. "Denki for askin' me to join ya."

Reuben nodded. "Visiting him is the least we can do."

"Any real hope of us seein' him?"

"Even if not, our goodwill gesture will mean something to Elizabeth, no doubt."

"If she hears 'bout it," Elias said with a knowing look.

"You'd think his children would let their mother know we offered to help with farm work." He informed Elias that he'd gone to see his cousin Manny in hopes of gathering a group of folk to assist the Yoders. "A good way to demonstrate God's love to a stubborn soul," he added.

Elias agreed. "Hard to put ourselves in their shoes just now." Not saying more, he lowered his head, as if in prayer for the unwavering man, now so severely injured.

Reuben joined him silently. *O Lord, bless David with divine mercy and your great compassion. Preserve him so that he might come to know you. And may we be an encouragement to that end.*

Truly, there was little chance of two New Order church members being permitted to visit with David, regardless of how seriously wounded he was reported to be. If the man could think for himself . . . and speak, too, there was no way either Reuben or Elias would step foot in his room, such was the ill will David displayed toward them. Even so, Reuben was glad to make the effort, still faithful to his former friend. He wouldn't think of giving up on David Yoder, no matter.

———

The steady melting on the road had caused a muddy mess out front and all the way down the road. Betsy recalled Reuben saying how caked up the horseshoes on their driving horses had become. She and Reuben were both fond of the horses, especially those used for pulling buggies. Betsy had known some families who thought of their driving horses as dear pets, even going so far as to give them special nicknames like Josie-girl or Ol' Gertie. She smiled, glad for such reliable transportation this day, the carriage laden with Nellie Mae's delicious meal and several pies, too, along with sweet breads and other pastries. Nellie had been ever so eager to include a broad assortment in the hamper of food.

As if she's making up for something . . .

Betsy could speculate, of course, but she wouldn't go so far as to presume to know what had transpired between her daughter and Caleb Yoder. It wasn't her place to pry. But since Nellie was staying close to home on weekends, most likely she wasn't seeing anyone, including Caleb. To think the young man had been cast out of his own house by his father and sent to live in his grandfather's Dawdi Haus, of all strange things.

Children are such a worry. She thought back to all the fretting she'd done over Suzy. One day she hoped to read her youngest daughter's diary, though she'd not asked Nellie Mae about doing so—nor would she just yet. Nellie had enough on her mind now, without wondering why her mamma was still interested in reading Suzy's private thoughts.

As she rode, Betsy settled back against the front seat, noticing the rise of trees on either side of the narrow road. She envisioned the fiery dahlias she and Nan would plant when the weather was warm and the grass green and soft beneath their bare feet. Such bold flowers looked especially pretty bordered by goldenrod and Queen Anne's lace.

Suzy had loved flowers, wild ones in particular. She

remembered her often talking of "their woods," chattering about the many varieties of flowers that bloomed there in all but the deepest parts. The chaos of the forest, the intertwined branches and underbrush that threatened to confuse the casual visitor—all of it delighted Suzy, most of all in early spring. There was something about today, with its fresh, raw smell, that kept Betsy's mind on Suzy, who had once planted wild flowers in the forest with Nellie Mae.

Chuckling softly at the memory, she knew something had lifted in her in the past months. She was free of the heaviest grief. It wasn't that she didn't yearn for Suzy any longer. Oh, she certainly did. But she also envied her girl in a sense, too. Her youngest was sitting at Jesus' feet, soaking up answers to her oodles of questions as readily as she'd spent hours reading Scripture after her conversion.

"What would it take for all of us to hunger for truth?" she whispered.

Closing her eyes, she prayed for a way to reach Elizabeth Yoder. *Let your loving grace shine on her, dear Lord.*

———

Alone with Nan in the bakery shop while Mamma rode to the Yoders', Nellie wondered how long before her sister might open up and share with her. She glanced up from her little recipe notebook, but Nan was concentrating on embroidering a new pillowcase. Nellie returned her attention to the cake recipe she was adding to her growing collection. She had started by writing down the recipes customers requested most often and already had filled up half a notebook.

The bell jingled on the door, jarring the quiet of the shop. She looked up from the counter as three customers stepped inside, obviously excited. "Hullo," Nellie greeted them, recognizing Mrs. Kraybill and two of her neighbors, all nicely dressed.

"How're you today, Nellie Mae?" asked Mrs. Kraybill, sporting a long turquoise coat.

"Just fine. A perty day, jah? How can I help you?"

Nan glanced at Mrs. Kraybill, smiling even though she must surely resent her for taking away Rhoda.

The women purchased one pie each, and Mrs. Kraybill lingered, asking for the recipe for gingersnaps. Opening her notebook, Nellie found the correct page and offered her an index card and pen to jot down the recipe for herself.

Meanwhile, the other ladies discussed the pleasant weather and the social occasions coming up. Some reference was made to the local high school's events associated with May graduation, and Christian Yoder flickered across Nellie's mind.

Not long after, Rosanna King dropped by, asking for five dozen cookies. "Three different kinds, if possible."

Seeing her friend sitting alone in the carriage as it pulled up, and now in the bakery shop, made Nellie want to go and wrap her arms around her. She didn't dare ask how Rosanna and Elias were doing without their twin babies, because that would only prompt the raw emotions to surface. Rosanna was obviously struggling to keep her tears in check.

"I'm having a big quiltin' bee soon. Would you like to come?" Rosanna asked, a small smile appearing. "A Sister's Day—a week from this Saturday."

"Sounds like fun," Nellie was quick to say, and Nan nodded her agreement. "Maybe Mamma would tend the store."

Nellie thought of Rhoda, wondering how to persuade her to come, too. *Unless she has to work at the restaurant.*

Rosanna brightened. "If you want, you could invite your cousin Treva from Bird-in-Hand and her sisters."

Nellie liked the idea; she had been hoping Treva might come visit for some time now. "Jah, I'll see if they can get away."

Nan spoke up. "They could spend the night, maybe."

"A good idea." Nellie smiled. "Maybe Rhoda would join us, too, if she knows about it."

Rosanna agreed, as did Nan, though neither said more. It made Nellie wonder if they both assumed Rhoda was lost to the People. She hoped not. Surely Rhoda's strange behavior would be short-lived.

Some time after Rosanna left with her dozens of cookies, Nellie noticed Nan staring down at the counter, leaning forward on her hands and brooding. "What's wrong?" She went to her side.

Nan's eyes glistened as she looked up. "Oh, I best be tellin' ya, or I'll burst."

Nellie Mae held her breath.

"Rhoda's decided to quit goin' to the Beachy church," Nan said, her lower lip quivering. "She says it's precious time she could be makin' money to pay off her car . . . and other things she's itchin' to do on Sundays."

"Workin' on the Lord's Day?"

"That's what she wants to do."

Nellie had no idea what to think. How could her sister even consider such a thing? She hated the thought of anyone putting money over the Lord God—and Rhoda in particular, anxious to hurry up and buy all the luxuries she appeared to be craving. If you were bent on doing things your way, there was only one cure, according to Mamma—to simply go and experience what you thought you were missing. That was precisely what Rhoda seemed intent on doing. Of course, still being in *Rumschpringe*, the running-around years before baptism, she could do pretty much what she wanted. *Hopefully, she'll get all that out of her system soon.*

"Rhoda's movin' further away from us all the time, seems

like." Nan wiped away her tears before continuing. "Ach, there's more."

Nellie wasn't sure she wanted to hear.

"She's getting rid of her hair bun . . . wants a short hairdo. A shag, she calls it."

Groaning, Nellie reached for Nan's hand. "What can we do?"

"Believe me, I tried to change her mind. But she wants to go fancy. You know how Rhoda is when her mind's made up."

"Do ya suppose . . . did she mention a beau?" Nellie asked. "Maybe he's muddled her thinking."

"She did hint that Mrs. Kraybill's nephew is sweet on her."

"Ach, she's not thinkin' straight if she's letting an Englischer court her."

"Her heart's deciding what her head oughta. And, just so you know, she didn't say not to tell ya, so I'm not breakin' a confidence."

Nellie was actually glad Nan had shared this news, hard as it was. "We'll keep prayin'." She reached into the display case and began blindly rearranging the pies and cakes, distracted by the thought of Rhoda forever leaving the Plain life, seeking out the world.

"What if she dislikes her short bob?" Nan blurted. "What then?"

"Well, once her hair's off, she won't be able to paste it back, now, will she?"

Nan tried to hold in her snicker, and soon they were both laughing. Nan reached to hug her. "Maybe something will keep her from choppin' off her pretty locks, jah?"

Nellie Mae couldn't imagine what.

CHAPTER 4

Betsy took care unloading the food hamper, gingerly carrying each item to the Yoders' back stoop. When everything Nellie Mae had cooked and baked was set in place on the cold steps, she rapped on the back door.

Fourteen-year-old Emmie came to the storm door, a slight frown on her pretty face.

"I'm so sorry 'bout your father's accident," Betsy began, realizing from the girl's slack jaw that she was either hesitant or worried.

"My parents ain't here. . . . Mamm's with Daed at the hospital." Emmie's voice faltered as she looked longingly at the row of hot dishes and pastries. "Ach, Betsy, it's awful nice of you, but I ain't allowed to . . ."

It was obvious the poor girl had been given strict orders not to accept benevolence from the hand of the New Order folk. "I'll be goin', then." Betsy forced a smile, wanting to make things easy for Emmie, whose mouth was watering, no doubt.

"Here, let me help you." Emmie opened the door and stepped out.

"No, no, that's all right. Really." She didn't want to get Emmie in trouble.

But fair-haired Emmie, more like her mother than her father, offered her a hand with the food anyway, while Betsy silently beseeched the Lord to intervene on behalf of this hurting family. She prayed especially that they might come to an understanding of God's abundant grace, perhaps through Rebekah.

She wasn't so audacious as to dictate her wishes to the Almighty, but she had been kneeling and praying so frequently that Reuben said she'd be wearing out the tops of her shoes even before the soles.

May David and Elizabeth and their family—each one—find this great joy, too, she prayed, lifting the reins as she directed the horse forward, back to the road.

———

Not wanting a soul to know what she was up to, Rhoda carefully placed three new magazine clippings about distant lands—Africa, India, and Brazil—in her newly purchased accordion file. She longed to travel someday, to fly far away in an airplane. She hadn't told Ken or anyone else of this dream as of yet. For now, though, she would settle for faster land transportation. And if all went well, this coming Friday she'd have her driver's license and go out for her first solo spin in her lovely car.

She slid the file beneath her bed, close to the wall—the same place where she kept her youngest sister's eye-opening diary. The account of Suzy's running-around time was ever so revealing. To think her life had taken a sharp turn not long before she drowned.

My life's turning, too. Quickly she brushed aside thoughts of Suzy's "saving grace," much preferring to think of Ken now. It was uncanny how Mrs. Kraybill seemed to have known that Rhoda and Ken would be so well suited as a couple.

Stepping back, she checked to see if either the file or Suzy's journal was evident from where she stood near the door. The bed quilt wasn't quite long enough on the side to camouflage her hiding place. She'd suspected one of Martha's four children—possibly two-year-old Matty—of having scooted under her bed, since someone had bent the cover of the diary. Matty was certainly one to get into everything, unlike his sister, Emma, nearly six. But of all the children, Emma was the one to watch, since she seemed the most interested in *Aendi* Suzy—"gone to Jesus," as she sometimes said.

Rhoda closed the door securely behind her as she left her room, wanting to talk with Martha. Surely James and Martha were instructing their little ones to respect other people's property.

If only I had a closet with a high shelf.... Rhoda made her way through the main-level sunroom and out to the kitchen. She found Martha setting down a plate of warm cookies in front of the children, already at the table. Matty wriggled in his wooden high chair.

She smiled at Jimmy and Emma, who looked up from the table, bright-eyed at the prospect of the treat. "Can I talk to you right quick, Martha?" she whispered. "I'd like to buy a doorknob . . . for my room."

"Oh. Something wrong with the old one? James can repair it if—"

"No . . . it's just fine."

Martha looked confused. "I don't understand."

Rhoda stammered, "Well, I need one . . . with a lock."

"Whatever for?" Martha glanced at the children.

"I'd give you the spare key, of course." How was she to explain her need for more privacy? She'd craved a place all her own even back when she lived at her father's house, tired of sharing a room with Nan.

"Would ya mind?" she persisted.

"James never locks anything. No reason to."

Sighing, Rhoda could see this approach wasn't working.

"Seems to me we need to discuss some things. James, for one, is concerned about you playing hooky from church the past few weeks, not going to Preaching with the rest of the family. And you've been out awful late, too." Martha's eyes gave her away: Both James *and* Martha were peeved but good.

It wasn't like Martha to speak up about such things, but she continued. "You've been spendin' a lot of time with that English fellow."

"He's the sweetest fella, honest he is," Rhoda defended.

Martha shook her head. "Best be takin' it up with your brother."

"All right, then. I'll talk to James later on." Rhoda turned to go, anxious to be done with this conversation. No matter what Martha thought she knew, her sister-in-law hadn't the slightest idea what was going on in Rhoda's personal life.

"When will ya be home tonight?"

"I'm scheduled to close up at the restaurant . . . so it's hard to know." She didn't dare admit she was going out with Ken afterward and that she might not make it back till midnight or later. One of the best things about dating an Englischer was she could see Ken as often as she wished—no waiting for Singings and youth gatherings on the weekends. And since Rhoda didn't have to be at the Kraybills' for work till around noon tomorrow, she could sleep in.

"I hope you know what you're doin'," Martha said.

"Not to worry." Rhoda went and kissed chubby Matty, squeezing his soft cheeks. *I can't wait to have my own little boy.* She could just imagine how cute Ken's and her children would be someday.

Pushing away any feelings of rejection, Betsy Fisher pressed on, not allowing the slightest bit of discouragement to rankle her. She stopped off at James and Martha's, hoping to see Rhoda before she headed off to work at the restaurant.

Wiping Matty's face, Martha told her that Rhoda had just left. She picked Matty up out of his high chair, the tray catching on his pant leg.

"Here, let me take him." Betsy reached for her youngest grandson as he giggled, all smiles, while Martha continued to wash his face, cleaning cookie crumbs off his earlobes.

"Such a messy eater you are, jah?" Betsy kissed his cheek and set him down on the floor to toddle away.

"James isn't too happy with Rhoda lately," Martha said, keeping her voice low. "She's out all hours . . . on weekdays, yet. And she's quit goin' to church, too." She shook her head. "Not sure what's come over her."

"Wasn't Rhoda happy goin' to the Beachy meetinghouse?" Betsy asked. She glanced around, noticing the small radio on the kitchen counter. "If it's the worldly life she's after . . ."

Martha rinsed out her washrag in the sink. "There's more to it, I'm thinkin'."

Nodding, Betsy assumed Rhoda was under the influence of an Englischer, but she wouldn't go as far as to mention that.

Busying herself in the kitchen, Martha said no more and Betsy remembered the many food items out in the buggy.

"Would ya like to have the day off from cooking? I've got a whole hamper of food out in the carriage. I'd hate to see it go to waste."

Martha gladly accepted, undoubtedly putting two and two together, since Betsy had already said she'd stopped off at the Yoders'. "Who'd be crazy 'nough to turn up their nose at Nellie Mae's cooking? She'll make a mighty gut wife someday."

Keeping mum on that, Betsy did not so much as move her head.

"You need help bringing it in?" Martha offered.

Betsy waved her hand. "I can manage." She was glad to leave the extra food with Martha, what with four little ones to feed and Rhoda's living here, not paying room and board, most likely. Besides, bringing the food back home for Nellie to see would only be a reminder of the Yoders' turning up their noses at her heartfelt gift.

When she returned with the last of it, she asked, "Where's Emma keepin' herself?"

Martha called to her daughter, "Mammi Betsy's here to see ya."

Putting the pie on the counter, Betsy heard the patter of feet. She knew that sound anywhere, and here came little Emma, bright as day, running into her arms. "I want to see your latest sewing project," she said after they hugged. And Emma scampered off to show her.

"She'll start school next fall." Martha wiped the table clean. "It'll be mighty quiet round here . . . 'least during the day."

Betsy noticed a sad glint in her eye. "Little girls are hardest to let go."

"I'm finding that out."

No matter how old they are, thought Betsy.

She recalled the long strip of saplings Reuben had planted as a windbreak on the northeast side of the house when their first sons, Jeremiah and Thomas, were born. She had held her newborn babes, one in each arm, as she watched Reuben and his brother, then Preacher Joseph, from the upstairs window. How fragile, if not temporary, those wispy trees had looked without their leaves.

And she wondered, *How deep into the world will my Rhoda put down her roots?*

What struck Reuben most was the starkness of the hospital. The long, sterile hallways. The lack of decoration was almost a comfort, really—like home somehow. *Yet still mighty foreign.*

The nurses looked awfully young where they sat at a long desklike table with papers around them and stacks of patients' files. There were several telephones and a vase of flowers, too. One of the nurses did a double take as he and Elias walked past.

Then, seeing the words *Intensive Care*, he and Elias located the room where Elizabeth Yoder and her two older sisters kept watch over David, hovering near the bed.

Reuben paused at the door, catching Elizabeth's eye. She seemed to crumple at the sight of him.

"Elias King is here with me," he said, sensing Elias behind him.

David's head was all wound up in white cloths, and his puffy eyes were closed. He lay flat in bed on the near side of a pale blue curtain room divider. Elizabeth straightened, nodding for Reuben to come closer.

"He's under heavy medication for pain . . . and other things. Now that he's survived the night, they say blood flow to the spine is the biggest worry," she explained, looking smaller than he remembered. "David prob'ly won't even know you're here."

Reuben stood motionless at the foot of the bed, aware of the length of David's body taking up the whole of it. Various tubes ran in and out of him, and the effect made the shrewd farmer look even more helpless. All the men in David's family were strong dairy farmers—his grandfather, father, brothers, and every one of his uncles. In the years Reuben had known them, he'd never once heard a Yoder complain about being tied down to the twice-daily milking or any of the other demanding work required.

"He's had lots of tests—X rays and whatnot—to find out more about his brain injury," Elizabeth said. "He isn't able to move his legs at all. The doctor says the longer his legs are paralyzed, the less likely he'll be able to walk again."

Reuben absorbed the news—such a tremendous blow to this proud man. "It's still early yet," he said, wanting to offer hope.

She bowed her head silently.

"Is there anything we can do for you, Elizabeth?" he asked.

The two older women looked at him suddenly, as if he'd misspoken.

"What I mean is . . ." He paused as David's eyes fluttered and then blinked open.

All heads turned, and Elizabeth bent low to speak softly, "You have visitors, dear."

David frowned, his gaze falling first on Reuben and then on Elias before returning quickly to Reuben. "Did ya say . . . you want to . . . help out?" David's voice was raspy, and he struggled to breathe.

"That I did."

David lifted his hand to his forehead and held it there, eyes squinting shut momentarily. Then he said painstakingly, "Have someone get word . . . to Caleb."

Reuben nodded, not sure what David meant.

"Tell him to return home," David added.

Elizabeth looked pained suddenly but never took her eyes off her husband.

With that, David lowered his hand, placing it on his chest, and his eyes closed once again.

Reuben wished he might lead out in prayer right here in the quiet of the dim room. He was fairly certain Elias was already praying silently yet fervently, even as Elizabeth reached for David's hand.

———

Chris Yoder leaned both elbows on his father's desk in the landscaping office late that afternoon. He twirled his pencil over the ledger—the week's garden sales. But he couldn't focus. How could he dismiss his attraction to Nellie Mae Fisher? There was no denying it; he liked her more than he should. She was, after all, Amish. *Like Suzy.*

True, Nellie Mae was different from Zach's girl in that she appeared more conservative than her younger sister, who'd seemed eager to push beyond the boundaries of her Old Order traditions.

Nellie must be dating someone . . . or even engaged, sweet as she is. She was also pretty, though not in the obvious, dolled-up way of most of the girls in his high school.

Thumbing through his father's receipts, he considered the upcoming graduation events at both school and church. The banquet sponsored by their church youth group to honor the high school grads was the most interesting.

He leaned back in the chair to stretch his legs and thought of several girls he could ask—even the pastor's daughter might agree to go with him. Or a seemingly nice girl like Joy Landis from school. Letting his imagination soar, Chris wondered what it would be like to take Nellie Mae as his banquet date.

Of course he would never know, since she would never give an "Englisher" a second look. That was the word Suzy, as well as his Amish cousins, had used to refer to him and his family, but only at first. In time, Suzy in particular seemed to forget that he and Zach weren't actually as Plain as *she* was.

Knowing better than to mention his crush to Zach or anyone else, Chris shrugged the ridiculous idea aside and returned to his work.

———

Puzzled yet obedient, Caleb packed his things. He loaded his buggy, organizing things on the floor before hurrying over to the main house to let his grandparents know he was returning home at his father's request. This, according to Reuben Fisher, who had stopped by for the few minutes it took to relay the message. Seeing Nellie's father made him wish he might talk to her, too. But a clean break was far better after courting. And since it appeared Nellie hadn't changed her mind, he wouldn't try to win her back. Time might bring some relief to the pain of rejection.

For now he stood in his grandmother's kitchen, where Dawdi was reading *The Budget*, a Plain publication, at the table.

"Well, I'm all packed up," Caleb announced.

Mammi wiped her eyes, nodding her gray head, and Dawdi rose from his chair to clap a hand on his shoulder. "You're doin' the right thing by your father, son."

He agreed but was still conflicted about his father's decision after being cast out so harshly some weeks back.

"Don't worry 'bout us. The neighbor boys'll come help with milkin' and shoveling out manure from the barn, just as before." Dawdi paused, his bearded chin quivering. "Your Mamm needs ya now, and when your Daed returns home, he'll be needin' you, too."

Caleb put on a smile for his grandparents' sake. There was much to forgive and be forgiven for, and he would give it his all. Meanwhile, he must work hard, caring for his father's livestock, overseeing the milking, and plowing the land that had once been intended for his inheritance.

Having refused his birthright to prove his love to Nellie Mae and to be free of Daed's say-so, the land would now bypass him and go to another brother. Or possibly to one of his courting-age sisters' beaus, provided they married and remained in the old church. And what baptized soul would be foolish enough to leave the church now, with the shunning reinstated?

"Be thankful for this chance to serve your ailin' father, Caleb." His grandmother's voice sounded feeble.

A bitter pill to swallow.

"Don't keep your Mamm waitin'." Dawdi rose and walked with him to the door.

His grandfather had come to regret telling on him to Daed. Caleb had seen it in Dawdi's eyes during the time here—the pain of having to report his grandson's indiscretions, however slight, with Nellie Mae.

"Denki, Dawdi . . . Mammi." He appreciated their hospitality, and especially his grandmother's good cooking. "Thanks so much."

"Anytime, Caleb." Dawdi shook his hand. "If ya ever need anything . . . just give a holler."

He nodded, grateful for the offer. Unsure what was ahead of him, he pushed the door open and headed outside to his waiting horse.

No need for a courting buggy now, he thought as he climbed in. *I'll have my hands full taking care of my father.*

CHAPTER 5

Rhoda whispered good-night to Ken outside James and Martha's kitchen door, feeling giddy. He reached for her, kissing her squarely on the lips.

"I'll see you soon." He gave her another quick squeeze.

She waved and watched him head toward the car, her heart beating fast as she opened the back door quietly. Recalling their exciting first date following the introductory dinner at the Kraybills', Rhoda relived how awkward, even embarrassed she'd felt. The oddity of spending time with an attentive man, let alone an outsider not a single person in her life would approve of—aside from his aunt and uncle, of course—unnerved her when she contemplated it. She was still bemused as to why her employer was so keen on getting them together. Or at least it had seemed that way at the time.

Ken had made reservations for that first date at a fine restaurant in Reading, a thirty-minute drive northwest of Honey Brook. The food was delicious and everything as perfect as she'd ever imagined, but it had just seemed so peculiar to be out in public with a beau. Far different than the Amish custom of dating under the covering of night, alone in a courting buggy with only a horse as a chaperone. But she'd quickly learned to delight in the difference, rejecting the memory of the Amish bumpkins who'd passed her by, and by the third or fourth date, she began to acclimate, accepting Ken's fancy way of doing things.

Of course he knew Rhoda had been raised Plain, but she answered his questions about her background only in the vaguest of terms. She avoided talking about her family and the disappointment and discord that would certainly arise if she and Ken were to marry. She did wonder in which church they would raise their children, but the subject had never been broached. They could work that out later. Keeping things simple—even streamlined—was the surest way to matrimony.

She left her muddy shoes inside the door and proceeded to tiptoe toward her room, one of two former spare rooms just off the sunroom. Holding her breath, she wanted to avoid disturbing the household. Her brother had opened his home to her nearly without question at the outset. He and Martha had been ever so kind, yet here she was defying James yet again.

Moving lightly down the hall, she darted to her room. With a great sigh, Rhoda closed the door and leaned back against it, her heart still pounding.

Good. She'd been as quiet as a field mole. She reminded herself to breathe as she removed her lightweight shawl. Such a wonderful time she'd had again with Ken, who was smart and made her laugh, besides being the most handsome fellow ever. To think he owned his own real estate company, too. She had the Kraybills to thank for meeting him in the first place, but she had herself to thank for attracting and keeping his attention all these weeks.

She hung her wrap on the back of the door, then removed her stockings. The feel of the hardwood floor beneath her bare feet brought to mind Ken's carpeted house. He'd invited her to his lovely historic home on two separate occasions, both times cooking a delicious meal for them in the luxurious third-floor "suite," where he lived. *Imagine Dat or my brothers fiddling about in the kitchen!*

On the first visit, Rhoda had inwardly fretted about not feeling comfortable enough to relax in the tantalizing privacy of the place—like she was doing something wrong and feeling guilty about it. But the second time, this very night, it was slightly less nerve-racking, and she sensed she was beginning to let go of her earlier notions and enjoy Ken's fancy world.

And everything about it was wonderful-good—his choice of music, exotic foods, well-made clothes, and the subtle aroma of his cologne. Even the musky scent of Ken's occasional cigar appealed to her.

Suddenly a single knock came at her bedroom door, and she jumped, startled. "Rhoda . . . are you still up?" It was James.

"Uh . . . jah."

"You decent?"

She looked down at her bare toes and grinned. *All but my feet,* she thought. "Jah, I am."

"Open the door, then."

She did, and there stood her older brother in his pajamas and long blue bathrobe, his hair all *schtrubbich.* "Ach, it's late," she said quickly, hoping to ward off a confrontation.

"Late it is." He leaned on the doorframe. "Why is it you can't seem to abide by my house rules, Rhoda?"

She should've known he'd ask.

"You knew from the start I expected church attendance when you asked to stay here. That and your comin' in before midnight . . . on weekdays, yet." He stared at her, waiting for an answer.

"I'm in Rumschpringe."

"That's the old-time ordinance." He inhaled slowly. "The

Beachys are more strict with their young people, and honestly, I think it's mighty gut."

"You're askin' to know where I go and who I'm with?" Such a strange, new way.

"I never said that, but dating's best left to the weekends . . . there's sleep to be had and work to be done during the week, ya know."

She knew, all right; the late nights were catching up with her. "It's not up to me how late I get in. Not really." She was thinking of Ken, who wouldn't be any too pleased at an imposed curfew. He didn't care much for her tying up her Sundays at Preaching service for hours, either. "And I've changed my mind about goin' to church."

"Oh? Returning to Preacher Manny's?"

She paused, feeling almost embarrassed. "I'm goin' nowhere. For now." Once she and Ken were married and didn't have to see each other so late at night, she might start attending again. *Maybe.*

He frowned. "So this is how you got yourself kicked out at home, jah?"

Rhoda felt her face flush. "I'm twenty-two," she said. "Shouldn't I be able to live as I see fit?"

"Why, sure, as long as you find someplace else to do it. And I'll give you a couple weeks to look." He shook his head and turned to leave, muttering about not standing for rebellion under his roof.

Rhoda felt chagrined, even sad. But moments later, as she contemplated the new adventure before her, she secretly felt glad to soon be free of James's expectations.

A small apartment is all I need, she thought, both excited and terrified.

Nellie made her way out to the road for the mail Wednesday afternoon, carrying a letter for Cousin Treva to invite her and her sisters to Rosanna King's upcoming Sister's Day. She'd also taken the opportunity to ask about her grandparents, Dawdi Noah and Mammi Hannah. Nellie had been tempted to write, *Do they seem to miss us?* But it was best not to open that all up again since her parents' last face-to-face attempt to convince them to move back home to Honey Brook. So long ago that January visit seemed—one Nellie had missed out on altogether, having stayed too long after the common meal to dote on baby Sadie, her brother Ephram's infant daughter. The babe was already ten weeks old now.

Perhaps she should write to Mammi Hannah herself. She could begin by asking for a few of her best-loved recipes. There had been no need back when she saw her dear grandmother every week and could simply ask if she used butter crackers or biscuits in her cracker pudding, or pecans or walnuts in her morning glory muffins. But now that Mammi was clear over in Bird-in-Hand . . . Nellie sighed at the thought.

She was sure her mother especially missed seeing Dawdi and Mammi Fisher once a week, as was their typical pattern prior to the church split. They'd always sat together following Preaching, during the common meal of cold cuts, bread, and pies. She recalled sometimes slipping over to the table where Mammi Hannah and Mamma chatted with aunts and older cousins. Often Mammi Hannah talked of the "olden days," when boards were put in bundling beds and girls never so much as raised their eyes to a fellow at Singings. Mammi Hannah told stories at quilting bees and canning frolics, too. Once, when she was in Rumschpringe, she sneaked off with a pony cart into town to visit an antique shop, where she'd bought an old, glittering brooch. She'd secretly worn it to bed on her cotton nightgown, taking it off when the sunlight peeked under the window shades, only to hide it beneath her mattress.

Nellie longed to hear Mammi's stories once again. She missed her sweet, crooked smile and her soft laugh. But most of all, she felt less alone about having missed the mark with Caleb—her past sin all washed clean now—when she thought of Mammi Hannah's girlhood pranks.

The Good Book said her heart was white as the driven snow, and deep inside, where no one could steal it away, Nellie had the promise of salvation. The knowledge brought her such joy she wanted to tell everyone.

Opening the mailbox, she discovered letters. Already! So she'd missed getting Treva's letter out. *It'll go tomorrow, then.*

She looked through the mail and was happy to see a letter from Cousin Treva herself. "Well, look at this." Thrilled, she hurried up the drive, toward the bakery shop.

"Anything interesting?" asked Nan when she entered.

"Treva wrote." She handed the letters to her sister.

"Anything for Mamma?"

"Didn't bother to look." Nellie pushed Treva's letter into her pocket, relishing the thought of reading it later.

"I'm afraid Mamma's not feelin' so well. I sent her to the house to lie down."

"Oh? Something she ate?"

Nan shrugged. "Hard to say."

"Maybe it's because of Emmie Yoder's response to the food Mamma took over there. Sure would be upsetting to be turned away. . . ." Only someone as stubborn as the Yoders would turn down Nellie's cooking. But Nellie dismissed the thought.

"Jah, rejected by folk who used to be our friends," Nan added. "The Yoders haven't heeded Uncle Bishop's plea not to shun the New Order folk who left during the grace period." Nan came to sit down at one of the small round tables with Nellie.

Nellie knew this all too well. "How's Rebekah doin', since she moved out?"

"Well, I know it's awful hard living away from her family." Nan glanced out the window, a faraway look in her eye. "And now this sad thing with her father. She must not know what to think. Or do."

"Won't she want to move home to help?" Nellie asked.

"Dat says David Yoder summoned Caleb to return home yesterday."

She blushed suddenly. "He did?" This was the first she'd heard it.

Nan smiled kindly, reaching for her hand. "Honestly, Nellie Mae, you act like a girl in love."

Embarrassed, she looked away. *Guess I still am. . . .*

"Truth is, I believe I'm fallin' in love myself. Little by little." Nan began to share about her new beau—a fellow she'd met at Preacher Manny's church—and Nellie was glad to listen. "He's such a hard worker and bright as can be. Treats his driving horse so wonderful-nice—"

"And you, too, Nan?"

Nan nodded, her face rosy. "Ach, you just don't know."

"Well, I can imagine." Nellie was more than happy for her sister. "I hope he keeps on bein' kind and loving."

"He is that." Nan was nodding emphatically. "I have a feeling he's the one."

"So you'll be tying the knot come weddin' season?"

Nan's eyes were bright with excitement. "Thank the dear Lord, is all I can say." She put her hand on her heart. "I would never have believed a new love could nearly erase the sadness of the old."

"Does this wonderful-gut fella have a name?"

Nan looked at her shyly all of a sudden. "I'd best be waitin' to say."

"Keepin' secrets from your own sister?" She laughed; she'd expected as much.

"Jah, 'specially." Nan gave her a mischievous smile and squeezed her hand. "I do love you, Nellie Mae. I'll tell you in time, I promise."

"Well, as long as you've promised . . ."

With that, Nan turned right into Nellie's arms and gave her a joyful hug. Even so, Nellie couldn't help but worry. *Will this one be Nan's husband someday?*

An hour later, after the bakery shop was closed and supper was laid out on the table—while they waited for Dat to come in from the barn—Nellie read Treva's letter silently.

Dear Cousin Nellie,

I have so much to tell you.

First of all, we've built a new, smaller Dawdi Haus onto ours, and my great-grandparents are moving in. I couldn't help but think of your grandparents this week, with all the hustle and bustle of getting my elderly relatives settled there. We do see Noah and Hannah every other Sunday at Preaching, and Mamma invites your grandmother to quilting frolics, too.

But I have something else even more important to share. Mamma's told me of three expectant women—two in our Old Order church district, one New Order—who've heard the sad story of your dear friend, Rosanna King, and been moved to act. Each of them is offering to give her baby to your childless friend. Can you believe it? It does seem odd for me to be the one passing this news along, but Mamma assures me it's all right to mention. In fact, she'd like for you to tell Rosanna yourself, close as you two are.

None of the women knows yet about the others, so I would think Rosanna could talk to each of them individually and then decide without anyone else ever needing to know. Mamma and I will keep this news quiet here.

Oh, I do hope it is right for me to tell you this, Nellie. See what your mamma says, though. There's always safety in wise counsel.

Nellie groaned. If Treva had a mind to talk with Rosanna herself about this, Nellie would want to protect Rosanna, not sure her friend was ready to attempt to adopt another baby. She sighed, considering the amazing news. To think *three* mothers-to-be felt enough compassion for heartbroken Rosanna to bear a child for her and Elias!

Same as her cousin Kate Beiler . . .

Nan came over and stood nearby. "You feelin' all right?"

She hated the thought of Rosanna's going through what she had with her cousin again—first being promised a baby, then having the twins taken away. "Did I make a sound?"

"Jah, like you might be sick."

Nellie smiled. "Well, I didn't mean to." She folded up the letter. No sense bringing Nan into this yet. "Is Mamma goin' to eat supper with us?"

Nan turned. "I'll check on her."

Nellie resumed her reading, finishing her cousin's remarkable letter. But the rest of the news—the division of a nearby church district due to growth, and farmers already seeding the oat crop—couldn't compare to the notion of the Bird-in-Hand women wanting to give Rosanna a baby. And two of them were members of the old church. What on earth?

Do I dare tell Rosanna?

Long after dishes were done and Dat had read the Scriptures and led them in prayer, Nellie waited for a private moment with Mamma in the kitchen. At last Dat obliged by making himself scarce, going upstairs to retire for the night. Nan had already gone up.

"I'd like to ask you somethin'," Nellie said before her mother could follow the others.

Mamma motioned for her to sit at the table.

After relating the contents of the letter, Nellie asked, "What should I do? I mean, think of it: This puts poor Rosanna in an awful place . . . you know, if something should happen and things fall through."

"And things just might." Mamma's face was serious. "Sometimes the answer to our prayers isn't always clear. Sometimes it's 'no,' or 'just trust.' "

Nellie smiled. Naturally her mother would think this. And the more Nellie learned from Manny's sermons and her own Bible reading, the more she, too, would approach things similarly. "I'm most concerned for Rosanna's frail state right now. She still cries, missing Eli and Rosie."

"Well, it's prob'ly too soon, then."

"So I best keep mum on it?"

Mamma sighed, rubbing her neck as she thought it over. "You'd just hate to see her get thrown more sorrow on top of what she's already suffered. Maybe just wait a bit . . . see if these women are truly serious."

Nellie Mae fiddled with her cousin's letter, considering Rosanna's fragile heart. "If Treva and any of her sisters accept my invitation, they'll be here next Saturday for Sister's Day."

"My goodness. I can't remember the last time we saw her. Can you?"

Nellie shook her head. "We exchange letters so often it doesn't seem that long ago, but I think it must be at least several years."

Mamma stretched and yawned. "Too long, I 'spect."

"Well, I best be headin' for bed . . . there's a little gathering at Rosanna's tomorrow, too. We'll quilt some of her cradle quilts to give away."

"She sure keeps herself busy, ain't?"

"Maybe too busy, really."

"Oh, but bein' so is a real blessing when you're grievin'," Mamma said with a small smile. "It's a real gut thing, truly 'tis."

Nellie looked at her mother and knew she was speaking of herself.

Chapter 6

Nellie was surprised to see Rebekah Yoder at Rosanna's work frolic the next morning, given her father's frail condition. Nevertheless she and six other young women had come for a few hours, all of them sitting around Rosanna's kitchen table and working on separate cradle quilts of pale yellows, greens, and blues.

Rosanna's sister-in-law Essie was not in attendance, nor were any of her other relatives from the old church. Nellie felt a twinge of sadness for Rosanna, who had once spoken of this very possibility—close relatives avoiding her and Elias because they'd embraced the New Order.

A hard price to pay . . .

Nellie had been visiting Rosanna each week since the return of her twin babies to their biological parents, John and Kate Beiler. And although Rosanna appeared strong, Nellie knew from the things her dear friend had shared that Rosanna still struggled terribly with the loss of little Eli and Rosie.

Such a brave and thoughtful thing for Rosanna to do, making baby quilts, Nellie thought, sitting across from Rosanna, whose eyes were fixed on her quilt. Her slender fingers worked the fabric, the needle rapidly moving up and down. Rosanna donated the small quilts to Amish and Mennonite midwives, who presented them at the birth of a new baby. Though the quilts were meant to be anonymous, the grapevine suspected Rosanna, and if anyone asked, she did not shy away from acknowledging the truth.

Nellie pondered again Cousin Treva's letter. *So surprising.* Still, she couldn't imagine opening up that precarious door only to have it slam shut again, as she and Mamma had discussed last night. Rosanna's cousin Kate had broken her heart, and Nellie did not want to be a party to a repeat of any such thing.

Nevertheless, there was the niggling thought in the back of her mind that perhaps she was making a mistake in not telling Rosanna the astonishing news. If she did keep it quiet and her dear friend got wind of it later—perhaps from Treva herself—would Rosanna be hurt to discover that Nellie had known?

Shifting in her chair, she forced her thoughts to Rebekah, who sat next to Rosanna at the table. Seeing her made Nellie wonder if Rebekah was permitted to help her dear mother, who must need her now more than ever.

What about Caleb? Surely he, too, is suffering under this new burden.

Nellie felt downright tense, with a hint of a headache. She tilted her head back and forth before returning her attention to stitching up the rest of the baby quilt.

As time passed, the talk around the table became surprisingly cheerful. It was as if they were making a conscious effort to avoid the painful topic of David Yoder's accident.

Looking about the table, Nellie realized that each one present called herself a saved believer. The awareness brought her joy, and she took pleasure in the feel of the needle between her fingers and the pretty colors in the fabric, all remnants from other quilting projects. Some as old as four years, back when Rosanna was a young bride of only seventeen.

The chatter slowed some, and when all that could be heard was the pulling of thread through fabric and the snipping of scissors, Rosanna spoke up, inviting all of them to her planned Sister's Day. "Bring along your sister or a close friend and *her* sister, of course. We'll have us a *wunnerbaar-gut* time with a light lunch at noon and plenty of pies." Smiling, she looked right at Nellie, who nodded and let her know she'd be happy to bake a half dozen or so different kinds.

Rosanna's smile broadened. "We all know how delicious our Nellie's pies are, ain't so?"

This brought a round of smiles and bobbing heads, and Nellie felt a bit embarrassed, though her heart warmed anew for Rosanna. Such a precious friend deserved the happiness of many children. *Just as Mamma had—nine in all.*

Nellie wondered if anyone had ever offered a healing prayer for Rosanna—the kind Preacher Manny spoke of in his very practical sermons. Nellie wouldn't be so bold to ask Rosanna unless the subject came up naturally . . . and only if they were alone, just the two of them. Yet in her heart, she felt impressed to add Rosanna's healing to her growing prayer list. The Lord God could strengthen her friend and enable her to carry a baby to term. Prayer was the best gift Nellie could offer.

———

Chris Yoder headed outside to the school parking lot to his car, especially enjoying his off-campus privileges during lunchtime. Today he was hungry for a big juicy hamburger and some hot French fries with salt and pepper. While he ate, he planned to scan the paper for his current events class this afternoon, since he hadn't had time to catch up last evening.

Physics, he groaned inwardly, wondering why some teachers had to pile it on.

On the way out for some fast food, he passed the Honey Brook Restaurant and the idea taunted him again—was he bold enough to ask Nellie Mae Fisher to his graduation banquet? Why this nagging thought, despite his every attempt to brush it away?

The whole situation was strange. *First Zach falls for an Amish girl . . . and then I meet her sister.* How wise was it to even consider getting to know Nellie better? He could imagine what his father would say, but not Zach. He didn't need his younger brother to remind him that his interest was laughable. Actually, Zach might even be troubled by any reminder of the girl he'd lost. It didn't help that Nellie Mae was Suzy's sister.

Settling in with his lunch, he scanned the front-page headlines. Escalating soldier casualties in the Vietnam War and the upcoming Eastern Division finals between Philly's 76ers and the Boston Celtics got top billing.

Chris flipped over to the local-news section and stopped to read an article about an Amish farmer who'd survived a kick to the head by his mule. Longtime dairyman David D. Yoder of west Honey Brook had been left tragically paralyzed by the freak accident.

"David Yoder?" he said aloud. *Dad's cousin!* He scanned the column again. It had been some years since his family's last trip to the Amish farm, but he hadn't forgotten their many Saturday afternoon visits. Staring out the window, he remembered flying through the barn on the rope swing with Caleb and his older brother Jonah. He had forked hay into the stable area for the new calves, too, and helped with milking chores, much to the amazement of the boys—and their parents. Cows were very sensitive to strangers, but they'd taken to Chris like he was one of Caleb's brothers.

He'd been nine or ten the last time, a Saturday before the Yoders were to host Preaching service. He remembered the excitement as the Amish bench wagon pulled up to the house. The men had removed all the walls on the main floor of the Yoders' house before hauling in long wooden benches to set up a temporary place of worship. The wagon contained piles of Amish hymnals, too, and dozens of extra dishes for the big meal afterward.

Chris and his own brothers quickly became as caught up in the fun of the preparations as his many cousins. The Yoders had provided popcorn and cold apple cider for everyone who helped, and he and Caleb—the cousin closest to him in age—had enjoyed more than their fair share. While Chris's older brothers pitched in to help, he and Zach had played hide-and-seek with Caleb under the benches as they were stacked in the yard.

Chris wondered how much had changed since the days of his own Grandpa Yoder, who'd left the Amish to marry an English girl. Because Grandpa hadn't joined the Amish church, he had not been shunned, and Chris's father's family could visit their Plain relatives whenever they pleased.

Suddenly curious to drive out to the Yoder farmhouse, Chris also felt compelled to offer his help during this trying time. *And I wouldn't mind seeing Caleb again, either.*

He wondered if his father's cousins had a strong faith to draw on.

Yeah, I think it's time I got in touch with my Amish roots. Chris grinned, and Nellie Mae popped into his thoughts yet again.

———

The day had been plentiful with sunshine and clear skies since her brother James dropped Rhoda off at the Kraybills'.

She had admired the big clapboard house, the detached garage, and the stretch of land behind the Kraybills' property, but mostly, she was eager to see her Buick again. *My ticket to freedom.* She had driven it with Mrs. Kraybill instructing her at least a dozen times now, and with her brother James—before he'd laid down the law to her.

She'd come a long way since January's snows, when she'd accidentally backed into the Kraybills' front yard, running over the children's snowman. Yet she wanted to be fully prepared for both the driving test and the written one.

Ken was urging her to take the test soon, so she could drive independently to meet him places and drop by his house for supper, too. Her heart pitter-pattered whenever she thought of Ken . . . and his beautiful house. Although they hadn't been dating long enough to be quite that serious yet, she wondered when he might pop the question, as the English often referred to a proposal of marriage.

Hurrying now to finish dusting the downstairs rooms, Rhoda dismissed her romantic notions and set about doing a thorough cleaning. In a while, she hoped to take a few minutes to look over the apartment ads. Smiling to herself, she recalled it hadn't been so long ago she was poring over the ads in search of a car. *That turned out just fine,* she thought, congratulating herself as she carefully moved the many knickknacks, one by one, on the old desk in the living room.

I'm getting my dearest wishes . . . and tomorrow I'll have my driver's license. If all goes well.

Numerous times since having first met Ken here, in this very house, she'd stopped and pinched herself to see if this was all a mere dream. Working for the Kraybills was indeed providential. She still embraced that mind-set, though she wondered if Ken might be right. He viewed things differently—that life

was more about what you made of it in the long run. That's
what counted, he said.

It's all up to me, she reminded herself.

With that in mind, she eyed the newspaper, ready at last
for a coffee break. Feeling good about striking out on her own,
she opened to the ads and noticed several apartments available immediately. One not so far away caught her attention,
though she wondered if she could afford it.

Mrs. Kraybill wandered into the kitchen. "What are you
looking to buy now?"

"Well, I'm being shown the door, so to speak." She explained
that James was much too strict for her liking. "Ken's not terribly pleased about his rules, either."

Upon hearing her nephew's name, Mrs. Kraybill tilted her
head, eyebrows raised. "Oh, the two of you are becoming
serious?"

Rhoda wasn't used to discussing private matters. "I think
it's safe to say we like each other."

"And your brother's opposed to your seeing someone outside the Plain community?"

"That's putting it mildly." She'd heard Ken say this before
and liked the ring of it. "So now I'm hunting for an apartment." Mrs. Kraybill leaned down to look where Rhoda was
pointing. "What do you think of this one?"

Mrs. Kraybill read the ad. "Well, if it's as nice as the description, you could be very happy there." She straightened, eyeing
her curiously. "I'm sure Mr. Kraybill wouldn't mind if you'd
like to rent the spare room from us, Rhoda. Until you get on
your feet."

Does she mean till I'm married?

"Oh, nice of you to offer," she replied. "I'll let you know
soon."

She wasn't too keen on the idea, but she didn't want to be

impolite, either. Truth be told, she wondered if it was such a good idea to live under her employers' roof, no matter how kind.

Thankfully, Mrs. Kraybill didn't press further. Perusing several more ads, Rhoda realized she was actually excited about looking for a place to call her own—never mind that James was forcing her out. Perhaps Ken would be willing to take her to see the apartments listed in the paper after their supper date tonight.

And if not, maybe I'll discover how serious he is, she thought, wondering if this turn of events might even spur him to ask her to marry him.

CHAPTER 7

His favorite radio station blaring, Chris took in the sights as he continued on Beaver Dam Road past the narrow bridge, near the spot where he had first met Nellie Fisher. He noticed, for the first time, a small sign posted along the road—*Nellie's Simple Sweets*. Could it be her shop?

Not giving in to the temptation to slow down, he headed toward the stone mill. He knew better than to let his mind wander back to the two times he'd talked with her. Suzy's sister was off limits to him. Anyone knew that.

But what was he supposed to do? Wash her from his mind— those appealing brown eyes, her sweet innocence?

The afternoon was bright as he passed the old stone mill. His mother had often pointed out the historic building, with its millpond and the wide creek that ran parallel to the road. Though not far from his own neighborhood, this stretch of countryside felt strangely removed from the familiarity of town. Few trees obstructed the sun's rays, which splashed gold onto the road. Everywhere he looked, nature seemed to be springing back to life.

Squinting, he reached up for his sunglasses, sliding them off the visor. The deeper into the country he drove—a place of grazing land and the silhouettes of silos and barns—the more clearly he pictured David Yoder's farm. A long swing dangled out front, hanging high from the tallest maple.

He'd once snuck off to a water hole with Zach and Caleb, leaving their clothes strewn along the trail—all but their undershorts. They'd climbed high into a sycamore tree to leap off the thick middle branch into the cold, clear water below.

What adventures we had!

So many memories of their country visits were racing back that Chris had to purposely slow down, his excitement fueling his speed.

———

Reuben was put off by the Yoders' refusal of his most recent offer to help—"*We'll stick to our family's aid*," the oldest son, Gideon, had told him—and he relinquished his frustration to prayer. He was not alone in his predicament; a good many other New Order farmers had been turned away, as well. Prior to the church split, the People had always united when a tragedy struck, regardless if the victim was family or not—in or out of the old church—with the exception of the Bann.

But now? The Yoders seemed to be making a point of the division, and just when they needed the most assistance.

Overwhelmed with concern, Reuben knelt beside the love seat in the upstairs bedroom. "O Lord, make my heart soft toward the Yoders . . . come what may." He prayed for salvation to come to David's household, for physical healing, and for divine help for the whole family. Claiming the promises of God, he stayed on his knees.

After a time, he rose and felt the familiar urge to extend himself yet again to David. *I'll do your bidding, Lord.*

He hurried outdoors, going to the horse barn to trot his two best driving horses around the training track. Two farmers from Chester County would be arriving soon, interested in dickering. Reuben needed to sell more than two horses this spring if he was to keep his head above water, but as he now endeavored to do in all aspects of his life, he would trust God for the outcome.

———

Before starting the afternoon milking, Caleb headed to the house for some ice tea. He'd seen his sister Leah making some earlier as he'd brushed past her, adding oodles of sugar, just the way he liked it. He entered the kitchen; with both Mamm and Daed away, the house felt too quiet. He wondered how Daed was holding up, lying in a hospital bed, unable to shift or even feel his legs.

My brothers have all been to see Daed. . . .

Truth was, he couldn't bear the thought of seeing his father waste away, being cared for by English folk he merely tolerated. Yet they were undoubtedly making him comfortable with pain medication . . . and keeping him alive. He didn't know all the ins and outs of his father's condition. Mamm said little enough when she returned home, and none of his older brothers was given to talk. Of the three, Abe was most often around, overseeing things as best he could, though like Gideon and Jonah, he had his own farm to keep going, and a growing family.

Caleb was aware of a small shadow gathering inside him, taking up residence in the middle of his chest, threatening his very breath at times. He must not give in to it, must not let those big black crows nest there.

Not wanting to get bogged down with thoughts of his harsh father, he drank the sweet tea straight down and then headed back to the barn. It was already close to four o'clock, and Daed had the whole herd of dairy cattle on a strict milking schedule, with one milking at four in the morning, and the second at four in the afternoon. *"Like clockwork,"* Daed had once stated. And his father usually had to state things only once.

Caleb's right arm had taken a beating today, during a difficult birthing early this morning. In an attempt to limber it up, he waved it around and around, like a pitcher preparing to throw a ball. He smiled momentarily. He hoped to slip away to play some softball come summer, if he found any spare time while Mamm and his sisters were busy shelling, snapping, and pickling the produce from their vegetable garden—an acre or more, which he needed to till up before long. Attending Singings and other youth gatherings was already out, no matter that he was courting age. Despite her past smiles, Susannah Lapp had snubbed him after Preaching service recently. No doubt she'd heard he had given up his father's land and had nothing left to offer a bride now. "Not that I care," he muttered, rubbing his bruised arm. The poor calf had been turned wrong and taken hours of labor to birth. He was thankful his arm had withstood the near bone-crushing contractions long enough to move the valuable calf deep within its mother. He'd nearly lost the beautiful creature.

Hurrying across the wide backyard, he almost welcomed the thought of the strenuous days of work stretching before him. He still had several tons of hay to unload, hay that had been hauled in from neighboring barns, since the drought had wreaked havoc with dozens of local hayfields last summer. He recalled Nellie's talking at length about it, too. Goodness, but he remembered in vivid detail every conversation he'd ever had with Nellie Mae. Was that how it was at the end of things . . . you remembered too clearly the beginning?

Just as he reached the barn, Caleb heard a car creep up the lane. An unfamiliar tan sedan slowed and then stopped near the back walkway.

A fellow about his age jumped out, hair like shocks of wheat. "Hello, Caleb!" he called, waving.

Caleb recognized him immediately as his second cousin. "Hullo, Christian!"

Grinning, Christian approached him, his gaze taking in the entire area. "Looks just like I remember."

"All but the barn . . . that needs a good paintin', I daresay." He put out his hand. "Good to see ya."

"Same here. Last time was . . . where?"

"In town at the hardware store, seems to me. A jingle, as you called it, was playin' on the radio behind the counter." Caleb stepped back to appraise his cousin, all spiffy in dark jeans and a brown suede jacket. "What brings you here?"

Christian pursed his lips, displaying the first hesitancy since he'd arrived. "I'm real sorry about your father's accident, Caleb. I read about it in the paper."

Caleb's back stiffened, uncomfortable with sympathy. "We don't get the English newspaper. Never have."

Christian looked over at the house. "I wasn't sure I'd find your place. It's been a while. . . ."

Suddenly impatient, Caleb was eager to start milking. "Well . . . I'd show you around," he said, thumbing toward the barn, "but we're kinda shorthanded these days, what with Daed in the hospital. So I'd better—"

"Could you use some help?"

"What?" He stuffed his hands in his pockets. "Actually . . . no."

"Seriously. I've got some free time, and I *have* milked before."

Caleb did recall his father's showing Christian how years ago. *How old was I then?*

"I'm sure I still remember." Christian grinned again. "Besides, it would give us a chance to get reacquainted."

Reacquainted? Caleb was befuddled again. Normally, Caleb would have sent him on his way, just as he had the new church folks who'd frequently come by since Daed's accident. Men who were thought to be too keen on converting them, like the whole lot at Manny's church had done to Nellie Mae and her family. Like them, Chris seemed entirely too friendly, yet what could it hurt? He *was* family, though English, and milking was a big chore for one man.

He found himself shrugging. "S'pose if you really want to. You remember how to approach the cows?"

Christian nodded with evident confidence. "I never forget!" Christian walked along with him to the barn.

"Well, let's see how the cows respond to you, okay? They're quite wary of strangers, ya know."

It turned out Christian really did remember, and after only a few tips he was working his way between the rows of the heaviest milkers.

More than an hour had passed by the time Caleb took his cousin over to the milk house for a short break.

"You weren't kidding." Caleb showed him the bulk milk tank. "You didn't forget much at all. Actually, kind of a miracle, seems to me."

Christian slapped his pants free of straw. "Hey, I forgot how much I like it here."

"Smells nasty." Caleb chuckled. "At least that's what city folk say."

Christian shook his head. "I must be crazy. I've always liked the smell of manure in the springtime."

They laughed and then Christian turned to Caleb. "So when do you milk again?"

"Four o'clock tomorrow mornin'. You comin' to help *then?*"

Christian chuckled. "No, but seriously, I could come after school several times a week."

Caleb stared at his long-lost cousin, mulling over his unexpected offer. The fellow was as likable as the day was long. There was something disarming about him . . . something refreshing, too. *What could it hurt?*

He glanced at Christian's shoes. "Next time, tennis shoes might not be so good."

Christian lifted his right foot; dried manure was stuck to the bottom. "Yeah, I see what you mean."

"You'll need work boots."

"Is that a yes?" Christian asked, breaking into a broad grin.

Caleb slapped him on the back. "We'll make a farmer out of you yet, Christian."

"Fine with me . . . and please call me Chris."

Caleb hoped he'd done the right thing by John Yoder's boy . . . hoped, too, that Daed wouldn't get wind of Chris's helping anytime soon.

———

Rhoda wanted to skip for joy, but she demurely walked down the steps of the Department of Motor Vehicles. She'd worn her floral cotton skirt and tan sweater set, with a long single braid hanging down her back and her hair parted on the side, instead of the traditional middle part. Above all, she did not want to be thought of as Plain. Not today!

A colleague-friend of Ken's had followed her and Ken here to the town of Reading, the closest location for her driving test. Ken and his friend had already returned to the real estate office in Strasburg. Secretly, Rhoda was glad, eager to enjoy her first solo drive now that she'd passed both her written and driving tests with what the official had said were "flying colors."

Flying colors. What a peculiar idea!

Hurrying to her car, she opened the door and slipped into the driver's seat. "I did it!" she said, leaning back and laughing.

Feeling confident now that the tests were a thing of the past, she pulled out of the parking lot, relieved not to have had to parallel park, as she'd done earlier. Her only slight weakness, the testing official had said, explaining that many new drivers improved that skill over time.

Heading south on Business Route 222, she was anxious to get back to rural Honey Brook before going to work at the restaurant. She'd brought along her change of clothing, still marveling that she'd landed the waitress job while wearing her Amish garb. *Must've been providential,* she thought, catching herself. Did she believe that anymore? She wanted to go fancy in every way, but try as she might, it was hard, if not impossible, to dismiss that part of her upbringing.

Rhoda came to a stop sign. She actually welcomed the sight, but not because she enjoyed slowing down or stopping. Rather, she enjoyed shifting gears, having gotten the rhythm of the clutch and accelerator down as smooth as vanilla custard.

After another twenty minutes, the landscape began to open up, but she did not allow herself the luxury of looking out the side windows. She was focused on the road ahead . . . and on her future, as she saw it unfolding in her mind.

"First, I pay off this car . . . then I save up for my travels. *Our* travels," she corrected herself, thinking of Ken. He was, after all, the perfect choice for a husband.

At the intersection of Route 10 and Beaver Dam Road, she slowed, looking both ways before accelerating again. She noticed several farmers out doing early plowing with teams of mules, and she thought of Dat and her brothers. Ephram would wait awhile longer to start plowing, because he liked the soil to be softer, but Thomas and Jeremiah—James, too—could plow anytime now with their new tractor. She felt a brief pang of sadness. She missed seeing her parents and her sisters, too, but her new, fully modern lifestyle was far more exciting than theirs could ever be.

As she neared her father's farmhouse on the left, Rhoda noticed a family of ducklings close to the road. She slowed the car, waiting for them to toddle across to the other side. "Be careful, little ones," she warned in the voice she used with her nieces and nephews. "Be ever so careful. . . ."

When the familiar horse barn and house came into view— her father's house—she purposely did not look. She was determined to keep her gaze straight ahead. No good reason to look back; even the Bible said as much.

———

During a short lull at dinner between the salad and the main entrée, which required a few more minutes in Ken's oven, Rhoda folded her hands tightly in her lap beneath the white linen tablecloth. She looked at Ken, all spruced up, as he sometimes described himself—and her—when they dressed up. What should she say about her dilemma, if anything?

His eyes searched hers. "Are you all right, Rhoda?" He slid his hand across the table, palm up, but she continued to press her hands together.

"I'm moving out of my brother's house."

Ken's eyes widened and he frowned. "After such a short time?"

His response put her even more on edge.

"I just need to leave, that's all."

He sighed, withdrawing his hand. "Well, if you need a place, one of my renters gave me notice yesterday. I'll have a vacancy downstairs, on the second floor. It's a spacious place with its own bath but won't be cleaned and ready for another three weeks."

Second floor?

"Nice of you to offer . . . but I haven't decided what I'll do just yet." She considered what her mamma might say about living in the same house as her beau, although a floor apart. *Avoid the appearance of evil.*

No, her mother wouldn't understand. Neither might the Kraybills, especially as Mrs. Kraybill had been so kind to offer their spare room. Now Rhoda was flummoxed, unsure what to do.

James would ask why I don't just abide by the rules, she thought, shrugging that aside.

"I think you'd be very comfortable in that room," Ken said from across the small table. "But seriously, no pressure."

After dinner, Ken insisted on making ice cream sundaes. "Do you want the works?" he asked. "Chocolate syrup, nuts, whipped cream . . . and the cherry on top?"

"Sounds good. Denki . . . er, thanks."

When he brought her bowl around and placed it on the table in front of her, he leaned down and kissed her. "Congratulations, Rhoda. You're a licensed driver now."

She blushed, happy about passing her test, and nearly as happy with his sweet kiss. Truth was, the written test had gone quite smoothly, after studying the booklet so many times with both Ken and his aunt.

She smiled too broadly and Ken caught her eye and grinned. "You know the Pennsylvania rules of the road better than most high school students taking driver's training, I do believe."

He was humoring her and she loved it. She relished the attention Ken gave her. She loved him with no real gauge of such emotion from the past, never having had someone so interested in her before.

And now they were spending time once again in his wonderful house. She assumed he must love her, too, because his kisses seemed to say as much, although he hadn't declared it with his words. But then, Mamma often said, "Actions speak louder than words." Maybe that applied when it came to falling in love, too.

For no apparent reason, Ken winked at her. Then he reached for her hand, and this time she accepted. "You seem tired."

"I've been thinking. What would you say if I had my hair cut?"

He scrutinized her with a mischievous expression. "I would never presume to tell a lady what to do with her hair."

She didn't want to say she'd already arranged the appointment for tomorrow morning, before she had to be at work around noon. "All right, then. But it'll be short."

"A drastic change?" He paused. "I've never even seen it down."

You probably shouldn't.

"How long is your hair, Rhoda?" His eyes had softened to the point she felt he might be sorry if she followed through with the haircut.

"Past my waist."

"Really?" His eyes lit up.

"But not for much longer."

He smiled thoughtfully. "No matter what you have done to it, you'll always be pretty to me."

Ach, pretty . . .

She felt like dancing, even though she'd never danced a step in her life.

CHAPTER 8

Saturday morning held an air of expectation as Rhoda drove herself to the beauty shop. Even the sky seemed a deeper blue, and the song of robins had awakened her—a right good sign.

Today was her special day, and she knew precisely how she wanted her hair to look, like that of a movie star she'd seen in a magazine left behind at the restaurant. She'd discovered it while closing up one night recently. She had been struck by how long and graceful the actress's neck looked with such a short bob, complete with wispy bangs.

Unlike the actress—Suzanne somebody—Rhoda was not a brunette. Nor was she at all interested in dying her blond tresses a dark brown.

She only hoped she would not regret this bold move today—her hair was the final link to her formerly Plain appearance. Knowing Ken was in agreement with her decision encouraged her.

An hour later, Rhoda stared at herself in the beauty shop mirror, touching her hair repeatedly, surprised at how short and bouncy it was. Not only was the weight of it gone—and the weight of what her bun had signified—but she felt an overwhelming sense of defiance. She gave the beautician a nice tip and stepped outside to her car, parked at the curb.

She relished the breeze blowing through her short 'do and realized her life had already changed completely. Cutting her hair was only one more step toward her hope of becoming a fully fancy woman, a life that had begun with her purchase of this wonderful car.

Slipping into the driver's seat, she somehow felt even freer than the day she'd left Dat and Mamma's house. Moving her head from side to side, she adjusted her rearview mirror to admire herself once again.

She pushed her glasses up and slid the key into the ignition, never tiring of the sound of the engine starting up. *Ach, what power.* She signaled and looked over her shoulder to check for oncoming traffic, then pulled into the street, rejecting thoughts of tedious horse-and-buggy travel. *All of that's behind me now.* She was headed directly to Ken's house, eager to see him—and for him to see her new look, as well.

At the first traffic light, she noticed a scruffy fellow wearing tiny "granny glasses," standing on the curb, holding out his thumb, his hair long and stringy. She knew from listening to Ken talk that this young man was a hippie—"a flower child." The name struck her as peculiar, yet another English term that made no sense to her. Feeling sorry for the man, she considered picking him up, but something hazy and odd about his eyes made her think better of it.

The light turned and she focused on the road ahead, enjoying the drive. She glanced now and then at the speedometer, as both Ken and James had instructed her. Thinking of her brother again, she felt a sudden mix of emotions. James had asked her to leave his house. So many sacrifices she'd made for her new life, though surrendering two feet of burdensome hair was not one of them.

The sight of Ken's big house inspired her as she parallel parked on the street. The stonemasonry work made her think of the houses on Beaver Dam Road, near her father's own sprawling farmhouse.

Glancing up, she saw Ken standing in the doorway, waiting. She ran her hands through the back of her hair, checking the mirror quickly, liking what she saw, and then got out of the car. She called to him as she hurried up the flagstone steps. "Well, I did it . . . what do you think?"

"It's nice . . . really cute." He cocked his head humorously. "You look like someone in the movies."

"Oh?" she said coyly. "Who's that?"

"She starred in a horror flick—an Alfred Hitchcock movie." He snapped his fingers. "Not the lead actress, but a pretty brunette. . . ." He looked at her, studying her again as she angled her head demurely from side to side. "Ah yes—Suzanne Pleshette. She was in *The Birds*." He leaned over and kissed her cheek. "You're simply dazzling, darlin'."

She had no reason not to believe him, and let out a little laugh, nearly frightened at this latest victory. "Thanks ever so much," she said when he repeated how pretty she looked. "Well, I'd better head off to work."

"It's definitely you, Rhoda." Ken was nodding as he waved, all smiles. "I'll drop by in a while, if you'd like."

She smiled her response.

"See you later," he called.

Everything she'd longed for was coming true.

———

Rosanna King had awakened extra early to redd up the house the morning before Sister's Day, scrubbing the floors in the kitchen, sitting room, and front room. More than a dozen

95

women were coming, including Nellie Mae and her sister Nan and their Bird-in-Hand cousins Treva and Laura.

She needed this time to sweep the dust bunnies out of the corners, dust the furniture, and wipe down the windowsills. If she'd felt up to it, she might have washed all the downstairs windows—inside and out—but she must conserve her energy.

Before it was time to make the noontime dinner for Elias, Rosanna felt drawn to go to the nursery upstairs, where Eli and Rosie had slept. *All those many weeks they were ours.*

She stood there, taking in the cozy room with its single dresser and blanket chest filled to the brim with receiving blankets and baby afghans she'd made. The lump in her throat turned to sudden tears, and she sat in the middle of the floor in a heap. The matching oak cradles made for their twins soon blurred as she wept uncontrollably.

Hugging herself, she rocked forward and back, thinking of her babies in Kate's and John's arms now. She remembered the last time she'd seen precious Eli, nestled in Kate's embrace across the room from her, where she'd held little Rosie for the final time. It had been the day the bishop had called the two couples to his house—the day Rosanna had relinquished both babies back to their original parents.

She could not erase the images from her mind. Hard as she tried, she kept seeing her sweet babies . . . Eli, Rosie . . . even all the nameless ones she'd lost since her first failed pregnancy.

And silently she promised herself not to let on to Elias what she now knew to be true: Another wee babe lived within her. But for how long? The knowledge brought her no joy. "Is this my lot in life, Lord?" she prayed, knowing she must somehow prepare herself emotionally and physically for the likelihood of yet another miscarriage.

She cried out to God for grace to bear the impending loss,

loving her baby for the few short weeks it was safe in the haven so near her heart. Her very soul felt bound up in this life, just as it had been with each of the others, and she felt she might simply break apart. Oh, the desperate way she loved her forming child, though she was never, ever to see him or her, or to hear her little one's cry for nourishment and love.

"How many more times, dear Lord?" Rosanna sobbed. "How many?"

———

Over the lunch hour, while the pies for Sister's Day were baking, Nellie asked Nan to help her make up the bed in the spare room. Nan, who had been darning several of Dat's socks, hurried upstairs with her. "I ironed the bedsheets and pillowcases yesterday, so they'll be extra nice," Nellie said.

Nan's face shone. "Treva must be looking forward to comin' to our neck of the woods, jah?"

"She's curious 'bout the bakery shop, too, I think."

"Is that why she's comin'?" asked Nan.

Nellie suspected the reason had more to do with hoping to find a baby for Rosanna than with the shop. "Well, we've been writing letters all these years, so it's certainly time she visited."

"Seems odd, really." Nan scrunched up her face. "To think we have cousins we know mostly through circle letters and whatnot."

"Well, when there're more than a hundred of them—and they don't all live round here—it's hard to keep up."

"Even so. Family's family."

She looked at Nan, who was making square corners on the bottom sheet, and suddenly thought of Nan's best friend. "Do you think Rebekah Yoder will come tomorrow . . . with a friend or a cousin?"

"I'm sure she won't bring her sisters Leah or Emmie."

"I hadn't thought either of them would go." She wondered how poor Elizabeth was getting along, traveling back and forth between the house and the hospital, as she was rumored to do daily. Her husband's survival was no longer in question, but his paralysis remained. "Any news on David Yoder?"

"Only what Rebekah told me yesterday—that her father's comin' home today or tomorrow."

She couldn't imagine what a sad reunion that would be for the whole family, and especially for Caleb. She assumed he was working the dairy farm, since he was back at home. He would be seeding the tobacco beds real soon, as well. His father, like quite a few others, depended on that cash crop, which required the help of nearly the whole family and a "dark-to-dark" work schedule. Anymore, though, Preacher Manny was speaking out against growing tobacco, and plenty of farmers were agreeing with him that it was just "feedin' the devil's crowd."

Plumping the pillow on her side of the guest bed, she waited for Nan to do the same. Then together they pulled up the old quilt—the bold Bars pattern, in shades of deep blue, red, and palest pink—and tucked it beneath the pillows. She stepped back to appraise their work.

"Too bad Mamma didn't let Rhoda move into this empty room," Nellie said softly. "Maybe she would've stayed put."

"Ach, you can't know that." Nan leaned on the foot-board.

"Rhoda's her own person, and she's makin' that mighty clear."

Nan hung her head. "Maybe we should talk less 'bout it and pray more."

"Jah," Nellie agreed. "Well, s'pose it's time to check on the pies."

Nan went ahead, and Nellie stayed to open the window to let the room air out a bit. She looked to the west, drinking in the view of the meadow, hoping it would please her cousins, too. It wouldn't be long now till Treva and Laura arrived.

Nellie sighed. She half wished she'd told Rosanna that her wait for a baby could well be over.

No, I can't do that to her, she decided. But what could she tell Treva was the reason she'd held back such astonishing news?

———

Caleb felt strangely like two different people, standing in the barn looking through the milk house window as the van pulled into the drive—bringing his father home. There was the Caleb who'd been tending to the brand-new calf, coaxing it to nurse from its mother, wanting to hurry to the house to help Mamm—and the others—get his father settled. His wounded father was home after eleven long days in the hospital, although he would have to return regularly for rehabilitation.

The other Caleb kept himself in check, lest he rush outside and look like a bumbling fool in front of Daed and the family. *That* Caleb knew the right thing to do but was nearly frozen with fear and frustration . . . even guilt. *If I'd been home, would the accident have even happened?* he'd asked himself a dozen times. Yet it was his father's doing that he'd been absent that evening, living over at Dawdi and Mammi's place.

Cast out for loving Nellie Mae.

He watched his sisters hold the door open for the wheelchair to pass through, and surprisingly, it cleared. Mamm's face was as solemn as he'd ever seen it. He knew from observing her jerky movements that she was as frightened as he was. This wasn't the usually confident and poised mother who could weather any storm.

If only he could describe how wretched he felt, knowing his father was severely injured . . . and frail as could be. If only he could utter his deepest fears to someone, whether they understood or not—just saying them might bring some sense of relief. But he was reticent to breathe a word, especially to his brothers, and Mamm had worries enough of her own. Rebekah, now, she was a different story—the smart one, long gone as she was and staying away, just as he sometimes wished he had. Yet now he was back, running the farm for Daed, under Abe's oversight. That brother most likely stood to inherit everything someday, since he was renting his farm and their older brothers already owned theirs.

How foolish I've been. Yet Caleb felt powerless to change the circumstances. At night he dreamed maddening dreams where he was ensnared in a pit, unable to move or get out.

He would have much preferred to dream of Nellie Mae, despite knowing she was forever lost to him. At least then a hope of some beauty and goodness could be evident in his recurring nightmares. She, of all people, might understand how he felt today.

Caleb heard the sound of Chris's car rolling up the drive later that afternoon, right on schedule. It was nearly time for the second milking of the day, and Caleb had yet to make it to the house to welcome his father home. *Just as well,* he decided. "Hullo again," he greeted his jovial cousin as he pushed open the barn door.

Chris grinned. "Time to extract milk from the milk makers."

"You're far too excited about this." Caleb laughed and led him to the milking parlor.

"It's great to be back." Chris took a deep breath and held it, catching Caleb's eye. They broke into guffaws.

"We've got nose plugs on hand for English folk."

"Seriously?"

"No," Caleb admitted, instigating more laughter.

They shoved open the back barn door, and the cows began to move toward their assigned stalls. Quickly, Caleb started latching them into their individual stanchions.

"It's restful here," Chris said, moving between the rows of cows to wash down udders in preparation for attaching the milkers.

"Well, the roosters are raucous at times, cows complain, dogs bark—"

Chris chuckled. "So you'd compare them to blaring horns, squealing brakes, and the endless hum of the city?" He patted the bulging side of a cow.

"You've got me there," Caleb replied.

"Coming here is about as peaceful as it gets, other than early morning, when I have my devotions."

Caleb nearly groaned. So Chris was one of *those* Christians. He should have suspected this of his Mennonite cousin; he'd heard this about Preacher Manny's group, too. *The trouble-makers* . . . He still despised what they'd done to his Nellie— feeding her such nonsense.

"What about you, Caleb?" asked Chris, disappearing beneath the cow. "Where do you find peace?"

He felt his chest tense up. Instead of answering, he shrugged and then steered the topic to the mild weather. He brought up the growing season and tobacco seeding just around the corner, anything to avoid Chris's question. "Still catchin' up, really. Hadn't been home for nearly two months." He glanced at the row of heavy milkers on the other side of the barn, aware that Chris was looking his way.

"Two months is a long time," his cousin said.

"Just workin' for my grandparents, is all." He opened his mouth to say more but thought better of it.

"You weren't needed here?"

Caleb rubbed his lower back and stretched. "We don't see eye to eye, Daed and I."

Chris paused. "When I was little, your father used to play volleyball like his life depended on it."

Caleb guffawed. "That's how he does everything."

Chris squatted to reach under the cow again. "Sure hope his health improves."

"No one seems to know what'll happen." Caleb hesitated to mention what he feared. "Doctors say he could be paralyzed for the rest of his life. But with his rehabilitation sessions . . . maybe those'll help get him back on his feet."

Chris nodded and turned his talk to the past, asking Caleb what he thought of having such fancy cousins. Fact was, Caleb had never given it much thought, having little interest in the outside world. Yet despite their obvious differences, including Chris's keen interest in "God's Word," Caleb was surprised by how comfortable he felt with him. He appreciated his tenacity and hard work, too. Chris had come twice already since his first visit last week, when he had stayed a good two hours, keeping close tabs on the feed for the cows and helping to put on the milkers. Chris was strong from working for his father at their family-run nursery and landscaping business, something he did several hours during the week and all day Saturday. Even so, he'd made it clear he was available to help Caleb with some afternoon weekday milkings, provided he was able to keep up with his homework.

Chris had a real special way with the herd. Yet as surprisingly well as this little arrangement was working out, Caleb couldn't help but wonder what would happen once his father got wind that an outsider was lending a hand.

Most likely my days with Chris are numbered.

CHAPTER 9

Cleaning up for supper, Caleb heard his mother calling. He quickly dried his hands and hurried through the sitting room to the bedroom just off the front room, where Abe and Gideon were helping lift Daed from his wheelchair to the small bed on the far wall.

The wound on the right side of his father's head was still bandaged, and the rest of his face seemed somewhat swollen. Fading bruises marked his temples.

"Steady the wheelchair, won't ya, Caleb?" asked Mamm softly.

He squatted down and set the brake. *They should have done that sooner,* he thought, wondering why Mamm had called for him. Soon enough he knew, and it was just as he might have guessed. Daed's gaze fell on him momentarily before his father looked away, never acknowledging Caleb at all. Then, turning toward Gideon and Abe, Daed spoke quietly . . . slowly thanking Caleb's brothers for all they'd done.

Caleb experienced a jumble of emotions, but he straightened and pushed out his chest, daring his father to ignore him once again.

When Daed finally did acknowledge him, he offered a brief nod. Nothing more.

Is this how it's going to be?

A few minutes later, when Mamm was setting the table, she offered a quick apology. "Your father's out of sorts, ya must know, son."

Jah, well, he's always been that, thought Caleb.

———

"*Willkumm,* Treva . . . and Laura," said Mamma as Nellie Mae opened the back door to greet their cousins. "We've been expectin' you."

"Hullo, nice to see ya," Treva said with a big smile, removing her black outer bonnet. Her face was flushed with excitement.

Mamma ushered them inside, and Nellie took their long shawls and hung them up on the wooden wall pegs. "How was your trip over?" asked Nellie, taking the shared suitcase from Treva and setting it in the kitchen.

"Well, we did get stuck in some traffic, but overall the car ride went by quick," replied Treva, glancing at her younger sister. "Laura, here, was a bit nervous, though."

"First time?" Mamma asked.

Laura nodded somewhat bashfully.

"Oh, go on, you were *so* nervous . . . holdin' on like we were doomed." Treva shook her head in pretended disgust and then smiled.

Mamma glanced at Nellie and suggested she take them upstairs to see their room for the night.

Nellie Mae nodded, motioning for her cousins to follow. Treva chattered away all the while, and Nellie understood better why it was she was such a frequent letter writer—Treva loved to express herself, no getting around that. Maybe she'd ask Treva to rattle off some of her favorite recipes, too.

Smiling politely, Nellie couldn't wait for the wonderful-good supper Mamma had planned. And for Rosanna King's big quilting bee tomorrow.

———

Saturday breakfast was plentiful, with blueberry pancakes, scrambled eggs, bacon, and German sausage—a typical early morning meal and not just putting on the dog for company. Dat made a comment about how "extra light" Nellie's pancakes were, and everyone agreed.

Once at Rosanna's, it was clear how well she had planned for the special frolic. She had already spent numerous hours doing the piecework and appliqué, stitching the many rings down till they were as pretty as a picture. The middle, a thin layer of cotton batting, was already in place, and the plain tan backing had also been skillfully fitted.

Twelve chairs were positioned around the large quilting frame, and everything necessary for the quilting was on hand, including the cardboard templates for the intricate figural motifs designed and passed down through the generations. There were even two tin templates, heirlooms from Rosanna's quilter grandmothers.

"You've done a beautiful job with all the piecework," Nellie said, pointing to the array of pastel colors. "When on earth did you find time for all this?"

"Oh, there's plenty of time, believe me." Rosanna laughed, but she looked a bit peaked. "I enjoy the work."

"You feelin' all right?" Nellie whispered.

"I'm fine."

Nellie noticed the gray shadows under Rosanna's eyes. *She needs more distractions . . . like today's frolic.*

"Well, I'd be happy to help serve the pies at noon. Or do anything else to help you today."

"Denki, Nellie Mae . . . I appreciate it." Then Rosanna hugged her unexpectedly, a short little embrace.

"You sure you're—"

"Nonsense." Rosanna waved her away and headed into the kitchen.

She's not herself. Nellie turned to see Treva and Laura standing and talking with Nan and Rebekah Yoder. "Would ya like to all sit together?"

Laura looked at Treva as if awaiting her lead. "We'll sit wherever you say," Treva spoke up quickly. She smoothed the auburn hair that peeked from beneath her Kapp and touched the rings in the quilt. "Downright perty, jah?"

Laura nodded and followed, and Rebekah stayed put, still talking in low tones to Nan.

After a time, they settled down to work. Treva had brought along her own thin needle, brass thimble, and a cloth measuring tape in a small packet, as had several others.

The prattle rose and fell with the rhythms of a lively sermon. And Treva filled the occasional lulls with her own chatter—just like her letters, she was newsy and interesting.

Later, during the noon meal, while Nellie Mae cut each pie into eight helpings and dished up ice cream, Treva singled out Rosanna. "Did Nellie say anything to you about . . . well, something a bit personal?" Although Treva had lowered her voice to a whisper, the question was loud enough for Nellie and anyone else present to hear.

Nellie Mae cringed. *No, don't bring that up!*

Treva continued. "Did she tell you 'bout my neighbor, next farm over, and two women in our church district . . . what they're hopin' to do?"

Rosanna shook her head. "No."

Nellie cast a warning glance at Treva, who asked Rosanna and Nellie to go with her into the empty sitting room.

Rosanna agreed, frowning at Nellie. "What's she talking 'bout?"

When all was clear, Treva leaned in close to them both. "All three women have offered to give you a baby, Rosanna." Treva nodded, as if to punctuate her declaration. "None knows 'bout the other, but they each want you to visit. You could go and meet them—decide which woman should be the one."

Rosanna's eyes dimmed suddenly. She stared at Nellie as if in disbelief.

Nellie reached for her friend's hand. "Ach, Treva," she said, glaring at her cousin. "Come, Rosanna, we best be talkin' this over . . . alone."

Quickly they headed for the front room, leaving Treva behind. "Are you sayin' you knew of this . . . and said nothin'?" Rosanna whispered, her tone tense.

"Oh, Rosanna . . . I just learned of it last week. I was frightened, honestly. I didn't want to open the door to more sadness for you and Elias." She shook her head. "Please, believe me."

Glancing over her shoulder, Rosanna trembled. "Is your cousin ever so sure?"

"'Bout the women's intentions?" Nellie nodded. "Seems so."

Rosanna leaned into her and wept.

Before the final quilting stitch was made midafternoon, Rosanna had decided to indeed travel to Bird-in-Hand to meet the women. Nellie worried that Rosanna might suffer further heartache just from the visits, let alone agreeing to receive one of the babies once he or she was born.

Treva leaned forward to ask, "Would you want to come along with Rosanna?"

Nellie offered a smile. "If that's what she wants."

Rosanna's tears sprang up again, and she nodded silently, her lips pursed tightly together.

Bless her heart . . . does she even know what she's getting into?

Knowing Rosanna as she did, Nellie was somewhat surprised her friend hadn't said she'd wait to discuss the idea first with Elias. And surely she would, as close a couple as they were. *Far closer than any husband and wife I know . . . 'cept Dat and Mamma.*

Rebekah Yoder and Nan offered to help Rosanna take the quilt off the frame after the guests began to leave. Then, come Monday, they would drop by to finish off the edges by adding a colorful, contrasting one-inch border.

Nellie offered to sign and date the wedding quilt in a chain stitch, one of her favorite kinds of stitching. "Do you have a bride-to-be in mind?" she whispered.

"Let's leave it as is—just today's date for now." Rosanna's face looked nearly gray.

"Oh, Rosanna, you've overdone it." Nellie touched her elbow. "Here. Sit and relax, why don't ya?"

"*Nee*—no. I best be keepin' busy."

Nellie wondered why she wouldn't let the rest of them remove the quilt and dismantle the frame. "Just for a minute?" she pleaded.

Rosanna shook her head, going straight for the quilt and frame, almost as if she were miffed. This hurt Nellie no end, but she tried not to let on and volunteered to help her and the others with the quilt while Laura headed to the kitchen for another piece of pie.

———

Turning off the road that Monday afternoon might have been crazy, but it was too late now. Chris was already headed into the drive leading to the country bakery shop. Not normally given to impulsive decisions, he knew only one thing as he stepped out of his car: Strange as it seemed, he wanted to talk to Nellie Fisher again. Besides, he hadn't tasted shoofly pie in a long time, and he was pretty sure his parents and Zach would enjoy something homemade *and* Amish. Who wouldn't? And anyway, he had plenty of time before he had to be at David Yoder's for milking. This new connection to the Plain community was a great idea—something he'd overlooked for too long—getting reacquainted with relatives, learning about his own heritage. *Getting a peek into Nellie Mae's world, too.*

Pushing open the door, he was startled to see five Amishwomen standing behind a counter, three of them smiling a glowing welcome. Two he recognized as Nellie Mae and her sister Nan, whom he'd met at the Honey Brook Restaurant. The other two young women looked like they might be related somehow, but he knew Suzy had talked of having only three older sisters. The last woman was much older and quite plump, with wisps of gray hair mixed among the blond visible beneath her prayer cap.

"Hullo," she said, her blue eyes reminding him of Suzy's. "May I help you?"

Nellie and her sister glanced at each other shyly, as if to say, *What's he doing here?*

When he asked to purchase a shoofly pie, the older woman—Mrs. Fisher, he guessed—pulled out a deep-dish pie. "Wet bottom's the best, I have to say." She offered another big smile. "And we also have two fruit pies today. Do ya like Dutch apple?"

Eyeing the shoofly pie in her hands, he hesitated—Dutch apple was one of his father's favorites, and both smelled fantastic. Suddenly he was unsure which to buy.

"Both are just delicious." She tilted her head.

Nellie Mae surprised him by speaking up. "You could take two pies and decide which one you'd like to buy another time, maybe."

He looked at her, taking in her fresh beauty—her clear-as-silk complexion and kind and sensitive eyes. "Sure, why not?"

He smiled at her specifically, and she smiled back, her eyes brightening as she did.

He felt his face redden. *She's on to me,* he thought. Then, reaching for his wallet, he said, "I'll take both pies, please."

Nellie's friendly manner made his heart beat faster. While he waited for them to box the pies, he looked around at the shop, which wasn't as stark as he might have guessed. The tables and chairs scattered around were a nice touch, and the uncurtained windows let the light pour in.

Feeling all sets of eyes on him, he turned and paid for the pies. "Good-bye," he said. "And thanks!" He headed out the door, aware of the jingling bell as he left.

Chris didn't dare glance back toward the shop as he approached his car. *Guy time straight ahead—afternoon milking.* He laughed at himself, thinking of all those Amishwomen in one place, gawking at him. "Man, do I need to get a grip."

Nellie Mae hardly knew what to say, embarrassed as she felt. The bakery shop was much too quiet now that Chris Yoder was gone, even though Treva and Laura now sat at one of the round tables, flipping through Nellie's recipe notebook and chattering a blue streak about the bakery business.

Mamma was looking out the window at Chris, who was putting the pies in his car on the passenger's side before getting in on the other.

Ach, that was awkward, thought Nellie Mae.

It crossed her mind that he might have come here hoping to talk with her again. But why would that be? He was clearly an outsider—and quite a befuddled one at that. *Uncomfortable with so many of us helping him, that's for sure.*

She smothered her urge to giggle and watched him back the car up slowly. He took the driveway at a snail's pace, glancing over at the house a couple times.

What the world? She felt a bit nervous as he slowed even more out front, where the long porch stretched across the house and met the sidewalk. Then Chris made his way to the road, finally turning east.

Betsy sighed and sat down to rest a bit. Nellie and Nan had gone to the house with Treva and Laura to help them prepare to leave for home, and here came Fannie—Jeremiah's wife—with her youngest, Jeremiah Junior, looking to purchase a big batch of cookies for a sewing bee she was having tomorrow. "A whole group of us Beachy churchwomen are getting together," she made it known to Betsy. "I heard Rosanna King had herself a doin' over there last Saturday."

Nodding, Betsy checked to see how many dozen cookies were left. "Jah, Nellie and Nan went with Treva and Laura." Picking up a box, she asked, "Would ya like a mixed variety?"

"Whatever Nellie has left will be wonderful-gut," Fannie replied, hoisting her son on her hip.

"How've you been, Fannie?" asked Betsy as she gathered up the many cookies, glad her daughter-in-law was cleaning them out so there'd be no day-olds to sell tomorrow.

"Just fine . . . and you?"

"Oh, as busy as ever."

Fannie pulled out a wad of dollar bills from her pocket. "Here, take what you need." She kissed the toddler's head.

"It's so gut to see you. And you, too," Betsy playfully wrinkled her nose at her grandchild. Then she counted out only a few dollars and carried the cookies around to the front of the counter.

"Nice seein' you, too, Mamm." Fannie leaned up and gave her a kiss on the cheek. "Sure miss you and Reuben at church . . . since we pulled up stakes from Preacher Manny's."

"Come over anytime. Yous are always welcome." She

reached out a finger to tiny Jeremiah, who grasped it. "Here, let me walk you out."

Fannie accepted. "How are you and Daed takin' the news about the Yoders? I just feel so terrible 'bout what happened. Poor, poor Elizabeth. I know ya used to be fairly close."

Betsy sighed. " 'Tis a shame all around, that's for sure."

"I heard they've got themselves a new fellow workin' with Caleb. And he sure ain't Amish, neither."

"Are you certain?"

"Well, Jeremiah was over there last week, offering help. Jonah turned him down flat—that one's got a bit of his father's edge to him. But when Jeremiah went out to the barn to talk to Caleb awhile, there was a blond-haired young man, dressed all fancy—well, not in fine getup, I don't mean that—but he surely wasn't Amish. Even so, he was washin' down the herd for milking while Jeremiah was there, chewin' the fat with Caleb."

"Blond, you say?"

"Jah. Jeremiah said his name was Christian, and he could've passed for Caleb's twin."

Betsy pondered this as she set the cookies in the buggy. She took her grandson from Fannie, holding him while she got settled. "Ya know, this very fella might've dropped by here earlier. Just a few minutes ago, in fact."

Fannie looked surprised. "Well, now, that's mighty odd. Wonder what he wants, comin' here."

Who's to know, she thought. "I'll ask Reuben and see what he thinks."

An Englischer helpin' the Yoders? A more peculiar piece of news Betsy couldn't imagine.

CHAPTER 10

Since long before dawn, Reuben had been praying for unity among the brethren, whether Old Order, New Order, or Beachy.

His prayers had deepened for David Yoder, a mere shell of a man. It pained Reuben to recall David lying there so helplessly in the hospital, Elizabeth nearby. Wanting to trust the blessed Lord for all his concerns, he headed outside to sit with the Good Book in his makeshift office, a small area at one end of the barn.

After reading for a good half hour, he reviewed his notes on the particularly fine Morgan that he hoped to sell today. *That's three now this spring,* he thought, mighty thankful.

When the sun slipped over the horizon, he went out and hitched up his best mare to the buggy. Then he went back upstairs to tell groggy Betsy that he planned to go and have breakfast with Ephram, wanting to keep in touch with him. *My only son still in the old church. . . .*

Several magnolias were already thick with buds and loaded down with robins in Ephram and Maryann's side yard as Reuben reined the horse into the lane. He was coming for breakfast unannounced, which he knew was fine with his son and daughter-in-law. The young ones, too, would make over him, and oh, how he enjoyed that. He planned to build some more martin birdhouses in a few weeks, inviting a different grandson to help with each one. But that could wait—he had other things on his mind this morning.

When Maryann glanced up from the stove and saw him, she smiled and came to open the door. "Ach, come in, Dat. Awful nice seein' ya!"

Soon toddlers Katie and Becky were tugging and pawing at his pant leg. "Up, Dawdi . . . up!"

Ephram rose from the table. "*Guder Mariye,* Dat! You're just in time for breakfast."

"Smells wonderful-gut," Reuben said, carrying little Katie to her place at the table. Becky ran over to Maryann, fussing till her mother reached down and kissed her curly head and set her in her high chair.

"*Kumm esse,*" Ephram said, waiting for Reuben to pull out a chair and sit at the opposite end. *Down here at the foot of the table, reserved for us old folk,* thought Reuben with a chuckle.

The silent prayer was short, and soon Maryann was passing a platter of scrambled eggs made with cheese, and then a plate of home-cured ham, some French toast, sticky buns, and blueberry jam. There was black coffee and cream right from the cow, as well as fresh-squeezed orange juice.

"Goodness, were you expectin' company?" Reuben asked.

"Well, Dat, you're hardly that!"

"Mamma cooks like this every mornin'," said one of the school-aged boys.

"That's right." Ephram looked at Maryann.

Her pretty face turned several shades of red. "Awful good of you to come," she said softly.

The children ate without making a sound, except for smacking lips and an occasional burp. Maryann had trained them well—to be seen but not heard. He wondered how long before they might come to realize the differences that so painfully existed between the old church and the New Order.

When offered it, he took a second helping of Maryann's cheesy eggs, ever so delicious, and another cup of coffee, this time with a dot of cream, which made the children snigger. Ephram did the same, clear up at the head of the table, as if imitating, although he was not one to go along with others for the sake of pleasing them. Reuben had been reminded of that stubborn trait during the contentious days of the church split, when Ephram had remained fixed in his resolve to stick with the old church. *I've got my work cut out for me in the coming years, getting him to see the light.* Still, Reuben believed in the power of prayer. The mightiest force of all.

After breakfast, they moseyed out to the woodshed, and Ephram mentioned being tired of the drab, brown colors that lingered on, reminders of the hard winter. He picked up an ax and handed one to Reuben. "I tilled the wife's vegetable garden yesterday . . . she's already got lettuce, peas, carrots, and her parsley planted." Ephram made small talk as he set up a log. Then, bringing the ax down with a mighty blow, he split it in half.

"Soon we'll be tilling the fields for potatoes and corn." Reuben made quick work of his own log.

"Thomas and Jeremiah will be using their tractor, no doubt," Ephram muttered. "So many new freedoms, anymore." He paused for a moment. "And lots of folk have used them as license to branch out to other things."

"When freedom comes, one must use good judgment," Reuben said.

Ephram pushed his straw hat down hard and slammed his ax into the tree stump nearby. "That church split you and

Preacher Manny got started, well, it's opened up a whole bunch of doors that should've stayed shut, Dat."

"Are ya sayin' give them an inch and they'll take a mile?" Reuben quit chopping, too, wiping his brow with the back of his arm. "Listen, son, I didn't come here to squabble." He picked up his ax again.

"Well, then, tell me: Where's God's will in all this disjointed mess?" Ephram asked. "If I can be so bold, I believe the Good Lord gave me a sensible head on my shoulders."

"Won't deny that."

They locked eyes. "That's why I've stayed put in the church of my baptism."

Reuben reached for another log. "I understand why you'd want to stay."

"And why's that, Dat?"

"For one thing, it's all you know. It's familiar."

Clearly put out, Ephram quickly changed the subject. "Did ya hear David Yoder's boy has himself some fancy help?"

Reuben shook his head. "Doesn't sound like him a'tall."

"I saw the young fella myself the other day, forkin' out the muck with Gideon and Caleb."

"Who is it?"

"No one said." Ephram shrugged. "But he ain't Amish, and that's all *I* need to know."

"Sure wish I could help David during this time." He scratched his head. "He's not keen on having New Order farmers over there, doing chores."

"I guess if David doesn't want your help, you'd best walk away."

Reuben wondered if Ephram was suggesting the same was true for him. Things had gotten rather tense all of a sudden. He set his ax aside. "Well, I have horses to tend to, so I s'pose I should be sayin' so long."

"All right, then." Ephram waved.

Reuben lifted off his hat for a moment to fan his head. He walked to his horse and buggy, mentally putting Ephram in God's hands. *Best place for him, Lord . . . for all of us, really.*

———

Rhoda helped Martha clear the breakfast dishes until she caught sight of little Matty's messy face. "Oh, look at you, sweetie." She got a clean, wet washcloth and wiped his cheeks and mouth as he grinned up at her. Then she set to work on the table, wiping it off and catching the crumbs in her hand. Tossing the crumbs into the dishwater, she leaned close to Martha. "Just wanted you to know, uh . . . I'll be movin' out real soon."

Martha looked surprised. "So you've found a place?"

"Well, nothing's for sure yet, but I have two possibilities."

"And is one of them to return to your father's house?" Martha's eyes probed, piercing her.

I won't go back, Rhoda promised herself anew, glancing at Emma and Matty playing together, and suppressing her sadness.

"Makes good sense, doesn't it?"

"Honestly, I just can't." Sighing, she wished things could have been different and that she'd been given the freedom she longed for while living there. But that was all water under the bridge, even though she missed Nan and Nellie Mae terribly. "S'pose I should get to work."

"Have a gut day, Rhoda."

She blew kisses to the children and thanked Martha for breakfast; then she hurried to get her coat. The phone rang and Martha answered.

"Rhoda, don't leave quite yet. It's for you." Covering the receiver with her hand, Martha whispered, "It's a man."

Ken? Oh, she hoped so, but she felt awkward accepting his call in front of her sister-in-law. Thankfully, the children were nicely occupied in the next room, and Martha was polite and excused herself after handing her the phone.

"Hullo?"

"How's my girl this morning?"

My girl . . .

She peeked around the corner to see whether Martha was out of earshot. "Well, hi, Ken. You just caught me."

"I wanted to talk to you before you left the house."

Maybe he was calling to ask for another date. How she loved the convenience of the telephone and the feel of it in her hand! Not to mention having Ken's voice so close to her ear.

"I was thinking about dinner tomorrow night. How about prime rib?" he asked.

She leaned against the wall, enjoying the sound of his voice as he talked about wine and all the delicious food they would enjoy. She herself had only had one small sip of a very sweet wine in her whole life, but if Ken felt it topped off a meal, she didn't mind trying some.

"You know, Rhoda, you never said why you're leaving your brother's place," he surprised her by saying.

"Oh, you know how older siblings can be."

He chuckled. "Well, would it help if I got you in earlier at night?"

He's a sharp one.

Secretly she'd hoped her leaving James and Martha's might move things along more quickly toward her ultimate goal. So far, though, Ken had not even hinted at marriage—this in spite of Rhoda's attempts to make herself into the sort of modern woman she assumed he'd want in a wife.

Really, she could scarcely believe how well she was pulling off the transformation. She'd steadily lost close to a pound every four days by eating only fruit and juice at breakfast, and a big salad at noon—thanks to the chef at the restaurant on the days she worked there, and Mrs. Kraybill and Martha. While she still craved lots of fattening foods, she was ecstatic about her evolving shape.

But when it came to thinking about weight and her overall appearance, Rhoda remembered back to her delight at Ken's having chosen to date her even when she was beyond pleasingly plump. And that made her smile.

CHAPTER 11

Having deliberated long enough, Rosanna was ready to make plans to travel to Bird-in-Hand, hoping to meet the women behind Treva's astonishing revelation. She'd shared with Elias what she wanted to do, and although he brightened a bit at the prospect of another child, he was also tentative. *"I don't want to see you endure more heartbreak, love,"* he'd said.

She walked down the road and noticed the meadow grass trying its best to green up, and the bursting buds on trees. Spotting the small communal telephone box hidden by a large oak tree, she hurried to it and placed her call to a driver to set up a trip for tomorrow, thinking she might first stop in at Treva's and then go with her to meet the women. The feel of the telephone receiver in her hand always made her nervous, and today was no different.

While she waited for an answer on the other end, she thought how nice it would be for Nellie Mae to go along tomorrow. Sighing, she recalled how hurt Nellie had seemed by the way things had unfolded on Sister's Day. Rosanna felt bad about that. Part of it was due to her own struggle, knowing she would soon lose the baby growing within her. Yet that was no excuse for treating Nellie so.

If only I'd told her the truth . . .

But there was no need to tell a soul, really. No need for anyone else to experience the too-familiar pain.

After calling for a driver, she strolled back toward the house. She resisted the urge to cradle her stomach, to somehow comfort the fragile life growing inside. She cherished every day it continued. At least now Rosanna trusted she'd know this child in heaven if not here on earth.

She thanked God for bringing the light of Scripture to her heart and to Elias's. Its truths had led them out of past bondage and into the liberty of such things as feeling free enough to talk to her Savior in prayer.

Because of this, more than any other springtime, Rosanna observed the aromas of April's freshening landscape and the clusters of songbirds, each with a unique call. And the way the sky appeared increasingly blue as each week passed . . . the way the sun came to rest in the mulberry trees at sunset. The neighbors would soon turn their heifers out into the grassy meadow, and woodcutters would scout out the woods for dry timber.

Spring's never been more stunning.

She hoped she was doing the right thing by going to meet Treva's acquaintances. She'd asked for a divine warning, for something to stand in her way if she was not to go. So, moving ahead cautiously, Rosanna felt her way through this painful maze, her bittersweet memories of Eli and Rosie still lingering.

———

Betsy laid out her dress pattern with some help from Nan while Nellie looked after the bakery shop. She planned to cut out a new dress and sew most of it today, since her for-good dresses had seen better days.

Reuben came in the back door just then, looking for another big mug of coffee. She stopped everything and poured some for him as Nan finished pinning her pattern to the blue fabric. Then, with a quick smile, Nan headed out the door to the shop.

"Well, such gut timing," she admitted to her husband.

He reached for the coffee, nice and black, the way he liked it. "You have a kiss for me, Betsy . . . is that it?" He leaned forward and puckered up.

"Oh, you silly." She bent down and kissed him soundly. "I wondered if you'd heard 'bout Caleb Yoder having an outside fella helping with milking of an afternoon."

" 'Tis mighty curious, I daresay. Just heard it from Ephram."

"So it *is* true." She moved back to the table and picked up her scissors, leaning over to cut out the dress. "I think the same young man might've stopped in here . . . bought himself some pies."

Reuben glanced out the window. "Here?"

"Jah, Nellie sold him two of her pies yesterday afternoon."

"Well, now . . . wonder what David thinks of all this." He shook his head and made his way toward the back door again.

Betsy picked up her pace, determined to cut out the dress before it was time to lay out the noon meal.

———

With Abe's help, Caleb lifted his father from his wheelchair onto the downstairs bed, where he preferred to rest, following the noon meal. Like clockwork his father slept each day for more than an hour, something he had never done, at least prior to his accident.

Abe stepped out of the bedroom, leaving Caleb alone with Daed, whose face was still marred with fading bruises. Caleb was careful to move his father's legs just the way he'd requested, even though Daed could not feel anything from his waist down. But he could speak his mind without wavering—his tongue wasn't paralyzed.

Daed leaned his head up, bracing himself with his long arms. He scowled down at his rumpled trousers. "Ach, straighten them, Caleb," he barked.

Nodding, Caleb lifted first one foot, then the other, pulling the pant legs down. He remained calm as he untied and removed the heavy shoes to place them at the bottom of the double bed, stumped as to why Daed didn't simply wear his bedroom slippers. After all, he never left the house and stayed mostly in the kitchen near Mamm, where he read *The Budget* or watched her bake and cook and clean all day.

Then, before Daed could remind him to get the quilt that was folded over the blanket rack near the bureau, Caleb reached for it and spread it over his father's legs with great care, almost forgetting there was not a speck of feeling there.

"Don't leave me alone for too long." Daed closed his eyes. "Like the other day."

Caleb stared at the floor, grinding his teeth. Was it ever possible to meet Daed's expectations?

"Are you listenin' or still mooning over that Fisher girl?" Daed's words gnashed at him. "Don't leave me here to rot," he repeated.

His brothers and Leah and Emmie were in and out of the room all the time. Why was Daed picking on him? But no, he wouldn't let his father's sharp remarks discourage him.

Caleb felt strongly that his older sister Rebekah could be of some good help indoors when Gideon, Jonah, and Abe were too busy with farm work—especially on days when Leah was away working at the neighbors'. Even if Daed wouldn't allow Rebekah to live here, wouldn't it make sense for her to help sometimes with everything all topsy-turvy?

"Well, what're you waitin' for?" Daed said, one puffy eye open. "Start sowing all them tobacco seeds. Won't be long and you'll need to transplant, ya know. You, your brothers, and all their families. As many as you can get to help."

Caleb nodded, but resentment hung like armor around his shoulders. "Anything else you need for now?"

Daed waved his hand, still big and strong from all the years of raising tobacco.

"I'll check on you in a couple of hours, then."

A guttural grunt was the response.

Now's not the time to bring up Rebekah. . . .

He was glad he'd kept his cousin Chris's visits quiet, too, wondering why neither Mamma nor any of his brothers had said a word to Daed. If anyone had, surely his father would have mentioned his disapproval by now.

As he left the room, he pulled the door partly shut, leaving it open a crack, as Daed insisted. He felt mighty sorry for Mamma, who was at his father's beck and call even more so than before. Caleb had even helped with the heavy part of spring housecleaning, washing down walls and windows with his mother and sisters, since it was their turn to hold Preaching service—all of this while Daed looked on, seemingly disgusted that his son would stoop to women's work. But Caleb didn't mind; he had to fill up his hours somehow to avoid thinking too much about Nellie Mae.

At times, he could kick himself for not leaving town when he'd had a chance. With *her* . . . if she'd agreed. But he'd made the mistake of staying on and waiting for Nellie to come to her senses, hoping she'd realize she was mixed up in the wrong church. To no avail. And the longer she stuck it out in that new church of hers, the more unreasonable she was sure to become.

———

Nellie was so delighted to see Rosanna turn into the lane, she ran out of the shop and waved. "Hullo, Rosanna!"

Her friend was slow to climb out of the buggy, and a fleeting thought crossed Nellie's mind that she might still be under the weather. "I'm not here for pastries this time," Rosanna told her.

"No need to buy a thing."

Reaching for her hand, Rosanna asked, "Would you consider goin' with me to Bird-in-Hand tomorrow?"

This did Nellie's heart good. "I'll see if Mamma or Nan can manage the shop without me. Maybe both."

"Goodness, you must have lots of customers."

"You have no idea." Nellie hugged her. "Oh, I'm glad you're not mad at me."

"Well, why would I be?"

They grinned in unison, and Nellie led her inside to sit at the table nearest the window. "Care for some warm tea . . . or coffee, maybe?"

Rosanna shook her head right quick. "None for me."

This was a surprise. Since when had Rosanna given up her favorite hot drinks? Nellie joined her at the table, wondering what she could offer her instead. "How 'bout some juice, then?"

"Apple juice, jah—sounds good."

Nellie nodded. "I know we have some. Just wait here."

Quickly she made her way to the house, returning back to the shop with a small pitcher of the juice. But she was alarmed to see Rosanna brushing away tears. "Dear Rosanna, whatever's wrong?"

"I'm ever so frightened . . . just like you were when you read Treva's letter."

Nellie patted her hand. "Of course you are."

"What'll I say to them . . . I mean, think of it: How do I

pick the mother of my baby?" Rosanna's face was streaked with tears, and her Kapp was off-kilter.

"God will give you wisdom." Nellie took her friend's hands. "Just ask." She bowed her head and began to pray softly. "Dear Lord in heaven, you see into our hearts—both Rosanna's and mine. You know how unsure Rosanna is just now. So I ask for help tomorrow, as Preacher Manny says we ought to pray. And may your will be done. Amen."

When they opened their eyes, Nellie saw her mother walking from the house toward the bakery shop. "Mamma knows of Treva's letter—I shared it with her. Is that all right?"

Rosanna nodded, sighing. "Denki for the prayer, Nellie Mae. I like the way you're comfortable talkin' to the Lord like He's sittin' right here with us."

"Well, He is . . . ain't so?"

Rosanna smiled now. " 'Where two or three are gathered,' jah?"

Mamma came in the door, and Rosanna motioned for her to sit with them, asking if she'd mind watching the shop tomorrow so Nellie could travel to Bird-in-Hand.

"Are you ever so sure 'bout going, Rosanna?" asked Mamma, her face pinched with concern.

Rosanna looked at Nellie, smiling again. "Nellie Mae prayed 'bout it . . . and, jah, I'm mighty sure."

"Well, then, who am I to say differently?" Mamma reached over and gently squeezed both of Rosanna's hands.

Nellie bit her lip, fighting back her own tears.

CHAPTER 12

Sheryl Kreider hadn't exactly caught his eye, but the junior *was* pretty, a girl Chris had known in the church for nearly all his life. The graduation event was six weeks away, and he figured he should ask *someone*, since the entire youth group turned out for these things, seniors or not—like one big, encouraging family. It did worry him that Sheryl might think he was interested in going out with her more than once. In reality, there was no one he cared for like that. No one in his world, at least.

Thinking back to his spur-of-the-moment stop at Nellie Mae's bakery shop, Chris felt ridiculous. He knew he wasn't crazy enough to ask her out, interesting though she was. Zach had been quizzing him about where he disappeared to several afternoons a week, but Chris refused to own up, saying only that he was helping a friend in need. All the same, it was getting harder to dodge Zach's questions without raising even more. No sense throwing him back into missing Suzy all over again, with talk of their Amish cousins.

He spied Sheryl at her locker between fifth and sixth period as she was spinning through her combination, her brown shoulder-length hair pulled back in a loose bun beneath the formal Mennonite head covering. He did a double take; her profile reminded him of Nellie Mae's.

Enough of that, he told himself, heading down the hall to ask Sheryl to the banquet.

———

Rosanna hoped each of Treva's acquaintances would like her and see her as a good choice to raise a baby. *Lord willing,* she thought while walking across the side yard with Nellie Mae as Treva tied up the horse.

Soon the three of them were entering the large brick farmhouse to meet the first woman, a faithful member of the Old Order Amish church. The young mother of four preschoolers was named Emma Sue Lapp, and the way she said her first two names pushed them together into one.

Rosanna listened as she chattered about her lively children, enjoying the woman's delicious chocolate chip cookies. As they visited, Rosanna held Emma Sue's youngest boy—a towheaded one-year-old—thinking all the while how terrible it would be to take away his baby brother or sister. Visions of Cousin Kate's other children making over Eli and Rosie hit her ever so hard, and she shivered and looked away from the tot still in her arms. Seemingly untroubled, the little boy leaned into her, close to where her own wee one grew.

Rosanna tried to keep her focus on Emma Sue. The cheerful woman was making it overly clear that her husband was in favor of giving Rosanna this next baby, "as long as it's a girl."

Feeling out of sorts and terribly presumptuous, Rosanna was relieved they couldn't stay long. Right now, when she considered again why she'd come today, she felt nearly heartsick.

"We'll have us a light meal at the next house," Treva said,

glancing at Rosanna, who sat sandwiched between her and Nellie Mae in the front seat of the buggy.

Thank goodness neither asked what she thought of Emma Sue. It was all Rosanna could do to sit still and not suggest that they turn back.

Even so, she'd come this far. Why not go ahead and meet the others?

By noon, Rosanna was all in. She wanted to be more grateful, or at least show it. But she felt sad as they pulled into the lane where Rosie Miller lived.

Rosie met them at the door. The thoughtful yet rather outspoken woman had already been blessed with eight children, four boys and four girls. With another baby on the way—the little one she was willing to give to Rosanna and Elias—her home would certainly be full. Treva pointed out how interesting it was that her name fit so well with Rosanna's, evidently forgetting that Rosie was also the name of the baby girl whom Rosanna had dearly loved.

But Rosanna wouldn't allow herself to make an emotional connection between the adult Rosie and the baby she missed so much that she sometimes awakened in the night, her face wet with tears.

Yet something didn't set well with Rosanna about this Rosie. Perhaps it was her too-aggressive way. She worried Rosie's baby might have a similar temperament, when what she desired was a tender-hearted child. Something she knew Elias would cherish in a little one, as well.

The third mother-to-be, Lena Stoltzfus, was a quilting friend of Nellie's grandmother Hannah Fisher, who also lived nearby. Rosanna wished there might be time to stop in and visit with Nellie's Dawdi and Mammi. Lena's connection to

Nellie Mae's family immediately caught Rosanna's interest, and she hung on to the woman's every word.

Lena's face glowed as she spoke of "the Lord's guiding hand," and Rosanna wondered if she was trying to say that God had impressed on her to have a baby for Rosanna, just as Cousin Kate had claimed. With the memory of that still too fresh, Rosanna became increasingly tense. Lena was not as young as either Rosie or Emma Sue, and she wanted to know that this baby—her seventh—would be "raised up in the knowledge of the Lord." At that, Treva let out a little gasp, and Rosanna nodded quickly in agreement.

On the buggy ride back to Treva's parents' house, where Rosanna and Nellie Mae were to meet their driver, Rosanna thanked Treva. "I appreciate you so much."

"Glad to be of help." Treva smiled. "If anything gut should come of it."

When they arrived at the house, they waited inside for the driver, sitting at the kitchen table while Treva's mother poured a glass of lemonade for them.

"If I might be so bold, do you have a preference out of the three?" Treva asked.

Rosanna didn't want to appear ungrateful. "I need time to ponder the day," she managed to say. *And more time to grieve over Eli and Rosie . . . and my own sweet babe right here,* she thought, letting her hands rest on her lap. "All this has come up so fast, ya know."

"Well, sure it has," replied Treva, looking somewhat disappointed. No doubt she'd hoped to be involved in making things better for Nellie's friend.

Nellie Mae spoke up. "It's such a big decision after all you've been through."

Rosanna reached for her lemonade. "Nearly too much just

now." She suddenly felt like she was slipping away, like she wasn't actually here in the flesh. *Or maybe I only wish it.*

"No one's sayin' you have to decide today," Treva said, glancing now at Nellie Mae.

"Given Rosanna's recent heartache, why don't we let all this settle for now?" Nellie Mae suggested.

Treva seemed to understand, slowly nodding her head. Then Treva and her mother began to discuss quilting bees, asking Nellie Mae when she'd be attending the next one in Honey Brook.

Not feeling very sociable, Rosanna merely listened and was glad when she heard the driver pull into the lane.

———

"You've gone *ferhoodled*, Ken!" Rhoda let the word slip; then, eyes wide, she clapped her hand over her mouth. Leaning back in her chair, she smiled apologetically across the table. "Ach, I didn't mean it."

Ken leaned forward, blue eyes soft in the candlelight. "What did you say?"

She laughed a little and wiped her mouth with the napkin, attempting to compose herself. Dare she say he was both crazy and mixed-up? After all, he'd just poked fun at her wonderful secret—her dream to travel one day—adding he had no intention of ever hopping a plane himself. "What's so wrong about wanting to fly in an airplane?" she asked.

"Don't get me wrong." He paused, regarding her with a bemused smile. "You just don't seem, well . . . like a jet-setter to me."

"That's precisely why I want to, though. Don't you see?"

"But why not be yourself instead?"

"Well, I am. This is who I *want* to be." *Though a far cry from who I was raised to be.* "You know, my bishop uncle would call me hell-bent for wanting to fly."

He squinted across the table. "Seems rather disapproving."

"Some might think so." More and more she believed that much of what the bishop said—and some of the preachers, too—was hard to take. Not so much what Preacher Manny had shared from *his* heart, though—those sermons, for some reason, had struck a chord in her. But she didn't want to talk about church, since Ken wasn't interested. And, too, she didn't want to spoil their time together—this special dinner, complete with candles. Just what was her boyfriend up to?

"So, are you going to tell me what ferhoodled is?" He winked, and her heart felt like it might melt.

"What's it sound like?"

"All mixed-up?"

"Sure. That's it, then," she teased.

He rose and went to her, taking her hands and pulling her to her feet. "I'm mixed-up, all right. You do that to me, I'll admit."

She smiled, enjoying the attention she'd come to expect.

He glanced at her hair again. "You look so different, Rhoda," he whispered, reaching up to touch it.

"You like it, then?"

"It's pretty . . . so smooth—like silk."

They laughed together. Then he cupped her face in his hands. "You're perfect, Rhoda . . . just the way you are."

Reluctantly she pulled away, unsure how to respond. Should she say he was the most handsome fellow she'd ever known?

He surprised her by speaking first. "If you'd like to see the room for rent, I'll show you now."

"Oh . . . all right." But her heart sank a little. Did he want her to rent from him instead of thinking ahead to marriage?

"The tenant's gone for the evening. We'll just take a look, if you'd like."

"You sure it's all right?"

"He knows I need to find another renter."

Ken slipped his arm around her waist, and they walked down the hallway to the long, gleaming staircase to the second floor.

———

Mammi Hannah had seemed so delighted to see them, she'd talked Nellie Mae and Rosanna into staying for supper, much longer than they'd intended. Thanks to the community phone booth, Rosanna had managed to reach nearby neighbor Linda Fisher, Jonathan's wife, who was glad to tell Elias she'd be home after supper.

Rosanna relaxed a bit as she enjoyed the tasty beef stroganoff and buttered peas, warm dinner rolls with strawberry-rhubarb jam, and applesauce cake. Mammi Hannah gladly shared her recipes with Nellie while they lingered at the table over coffee and second helpings. Meanwhile, their driver had other folk to pick up, so it worked out for him to return later.

"Sure was surprising to hear of David Yoder's accident," Dawdi Noah said, stirring sugar into his coffee. "But a body never can tell what's ahead."

Nellie Mae nodded.

"Such a sad thing 'tis." Mammi shook her head.

"Well, David's a fighter, no question on that," Dawdi said, his beard twitching. "He might just surprise everyone and walk again . . . who's to say?"

Nellie knew that what distressed her grandparents most

wasn't David Yoder's paralysis—it was the choice her parents had made to join the new church. This was the reason they were living clear over in Bird-in-Hand instead of next door in her parents' Dawdi Haus, as planned. She hoped something she might say, or do, would make them think twice about the religious stir in several areas of Lancaster County, and in other states, too. Some called it a "move of God." Others shook their heads in utter confusion, like Dawdi and Mammi. She hoped they'd soon know the amazing things she and her family—and many others—were learning from scripture and from the pertinent sermons preached each Lord's Day.

"Lots of prayers are goin' up for David Yoder," Nellie said softly. "Healing for his body, for one thing . . . and his spiritual healing, too."

This brought an immediate hush to the table.

Nellie felt a sudden boldness. "If the truth were known, David Yoder just might be pondering, deep down, all the talk of a personal relationship with the Lord. Lots of folk seem hungry for it."

"Now, now, Nellie Mae." Dawdi's eyes pierced hers.

"I'm serious," she continued. "Why squelch the questions . . . the longing?"

"How's your sister Rhoda doin'?" asked Mammi. The effect of her grandmother's stroke was still evident in her slightly slurred speech.

Nellie knew she was being shushed in a kind sort of way, but Rhoda was not the most pleasant subject. "I don't know much about her these days."

Both Dawdi and Mammi nodded.

Surely they've heard she's living with James and Martha. . . .

"We saw Mrs. Kraybill the other day over at the General Store. She mentioned something about her nephew and Rhoda.

Sounds like your sister has an English beau." Dawdi set down his spoon and folded his knobby hands over his coffee cup. "First Suzy, now Rhoda?"

Feeling awkward, Nellie looked at Rosanna and sighed. None of this was a secret. "Rhoda's finding her wings, I daresay. But Suzy . . . well, honestly, she found hers in the Lord Jesus." She began to recite some of Suzy's favorite Scripture verses, sharing the things Suzy had prayed about . . . all of it. When she was finished, Mammi's eyes were moist, but Dawdi seemed unaffected.

"No one's ever mentioned this side of things 'bout your sister," Mammi said. "I just don't know what to think."

Rosanna nodded. "Suzy was in love with the Lord, that's for sure."

Dawdi frowned, his brow knitted tightly under his thinning bangs. "Talkin' like that about the Almighty? Ach, that's *unsinnich*—senseless!" He shook his head.

"I used to feel the same way, Dawdi," Nellie dared to say. "But now I see that the truth is set before us . . . in God's Word. It's impossible to turn away." *At least for some . . .* Her heart broke to see her grandparents struggle so with the whys and wherefores.

Rosanna reached for Nellie's hand. "Elias and I, too, believe we have been saved by the grace of the Lord." Tears glistened in her friend's eyes. "You can be, too."

Dawdi frowned, and Mammi mumbled under her breath.

Verses Nellie had memorized sprang to mind, but now was not the time to speak them. The resistance was ever so strong here, where the old church still reigned.

Chapter 13

"This is one of the largest bedrooms in the house." Ken pointed to the high ceiling as Rhoda stood beside him in the doorway, peering in, conscious of Ken's arm around her. "The windows face the southeast, so if you have indoor plants, they'll do nicely along that wall." He motioned to the windows, draped in a tweedy gold fabric. The views of Strasburg were nearly as lovely as those from Ken's upstairs suite.

Rhoda attempted to place herself in the room in her mind, wondering how it might be to wake up here each morning, knowing Ken was living on the floor above her. Would she hear his footsteps early and late, be aware of his comings and goings? The modern space was so different from the farmhouse where she presently resided with James's family. She thought of her darling niece and nephews. *I'd miss them so much if I moved here.*

Ken looked at her. "So, what do you think?"

"It's nice and roomy." She couldn't help admiring the present tenant's arrangement of furniture.

"Don't forget there's a private bath—with a tub and a shower."

The television in the corner caught her curiosity. How exciting it would be to own one. *Someday,* she thought, looking now at the pretty pole lamp and other pieces of furniture. Would she develop a style of her own? Since she didn't have many things, she'd have to invest in a bed and a chest of drawers, as well as a small sofa or love seat to entertain guests. *Will Ken visit me here?*

Sighing, she stepped back. She'd had her heart set on living upstairs with Ken as his bride, sharing the larger space of rooms. She mustn't let on how disappointed she felt, or she would seem presumptuous.

"When the room's vacant, you're welcome to see it again. Maybe by then you'll have a better handle on what you'd like to do." He closed the door, locking it with his master key.

If they married, would they ever have the entire house for themselves, for their growing family?

It was then she realized he'd never talked of having children. Was he as fond of them as she? There hadn't been any playful times with the Kraybill children—Ken's own young cousins—that first night she'd met him for dinner there. No talk of them from his perspective, either.

He reached for her hand when they came to the landing at the top of the long flight of stairs. "I'll pour us some after-dinner wine to go with the surprise dessert," he said. "Would you like that?"

Wine . . . during dinner and after?

Well, who was she to interfere? This was Ken's way, and she welcomed even the most foreign aspects.

"Do you accept tenants with young children?" she asked as he pulled out a chair for her at his table. The dining room seemed too dark, and she smiled when he pressed the dimmer switch and raised the light a bit before lighting the candles once again.

"There." Stepping back, he smiled. "Much better." He

went to the kitchen, where he pulled out two dessert plates and two small glasses. "What was the question?"

"Are children welcome here?"

He grimaced. "Dogs and kids are liabilities for investment properties."

"What do you mean—a liability?" she asked.

"To rephrase it, they're a pain in the proverbial neck," he stated flatly, carrying the two dessert plates with a generous slice of pie on each. "Most kids are more bother than they're worth." He placed the cherry pie and single scoop of ice cream in front of her. Then, picking up his fork, he looked across the table without batting an eye.

She felt nearly ill. She thought of his own relatives' children. They were entertaining and smart and responsible. In short, lots of fun. "Are you fond of your young Kraybill cousins?"

"What's this? Twenty questions?" He stared at her across the candles.

Realizing she was on the verge of spoiling a perfectly good evening with a wonderful man who seemed to dote on her, even love her, maybe, Rhoda picked up her fork and made herself take a bite of Ken's cherry pie. Even though she had absolutely no appetite now.

Dat says children are a blessing from God.

He rose to pour the dessert wine, and she nodded her thanks as he handed her a glass with a small amount. Holding her breath, she slowly sipped it, as she'd seen him do. She felt terribly tense, like she was falling with no way to stop herself.

———

Betsy felt chilly and wanted the afghan she sometimes draped over her lap while Reuben read the Bible to her. Quickly she made her way upstairs to the blanket chest at the foot of the bed. Opening the lid, she stepped back, surprised at the sight of the small sachet pillow—the "headache pillow" Suzy had made for her—lying on the top of the quilts and crocheted afghans.

How'd this get here?

She recalled having gone to sleep with it one recent night, only for it to have fallen to the floor by morning. Of course, that's where Reuben must have found it, and he'd slipped it back into the chest.

She stared at Suzy's delicate handiwork. Did Reuben have special mementos or memories of their Suzy? He scarcely ever spoke of her. Was the pain of loss still too raw . . . too tender? Or had his grief found solace in the knowledge their youngest now resided at the feet of the dear Savior?

Finding Suzy's favorite spring quilt several layers down, she tucked the sachet pillow into one of its folds and left it safely stowed in the blanket chest. Then, locating the small afghan, she closed the lid and headed downstairs, looking forward to the scripture reading . . . and time spent alone with Reuben later tonight.

———

The boys seemed exceptionally fidgety during Wednesday evening class, and following the Bible study—geared to junior boys—Chris asked only three questions to test their attention level. After more bantering, he asked for prayer for his father's cousin, mentioning that a mule had kicked David Yoder in the head. In typical boyish fashion, several bucked their own heads.

To his surprise, Billy Zercher, usually the loner, hung around after the others left. "I've never heard of a mule kicking someone." His eyes blinked rapidly. "How'd it happen?"

"He was fixing the chain on the plow."

Billy was fiddling with his fingers. "Is he Amish?"

The kid was pretty perceptive. "Yeah. Why did you ask?"

"Well, they use mules out in the fields, don't they?"

He smiled. "That's right. Have you seen them?"

"Sometimes, from a distance."

He watched Billy head for the door. The boy stood there, as if waiting for Chris to say more. That's when an idea hit. "Say, Billy, how would you like to visit a working Amish dairy farm sometime?"

The boy's eyes lit up. "For real?"

"Ask your mom."

"Oh, she'll let me go . . . if you're taking me." His eyes registered near-glee.

Chris was heartened.

Suddenly turning shy again, the boy waved and left.

Chris gathered up the Bibles and stacked them in the cupboard, hoping Caleb might agree. He'd been amazed by how much he looked forward to spending time with his cousin, and he hoped to make more connections with Caleb, to influence him toward the Lord. Befriending him was simply the beginning.

If only it were just as easy to get better acquainted with Nellie Mae. Maybe he'd actually get over his crush if he knew her better. *Only one way to find out.* Was it possible to win her confidence enough to ask her for ice cream sometime, or to go for a walk? How weird would it seem for her? For him?

Was it time to tell Zach what he was thinking? He was reluctant to do anything that might plunge his brother back into the pits of depression.

On the way toward the church lobby, he spotted Sheryl with a girl friend. Thinking it was time he became more friendly with his future date, he smiled, waiting until she finished her conversation. Sheryl's eyes lit up as she made her way to him, and he struggled with guilt for having set things in motion.

"Hi, Sheryl."

She smiled prettily, her eyebrows arched slightly with apparent delight. "How are you?" She spoke so softly he had to lean close to hear her.

"The school year's winding down," he said, even though small talk was the last thing he wanted.

She nodded. "Another month till the banquet."

"Six weeks, yes."

Smiling, she glanced at another friend who waved to her as they passed.

"What color dress are you planning to wear?"

"Pale blue," she said.

He made a mental note. "All right . . . sounds nice." He smiled, wondering how other guys did it, making conversation with a girl they knew but didn't *really* know. For all the years they'd grown up together in this church, he'd never bothered to become better acquainted with Sheryl . . . till now. Why, Zach probably knew her better than he did. His younger brother had always been more outgoing, more comfortable with girls.

Maybe that's why Zach and Suzy clicked. Both were more extroverted than he, which wasn't saying much. *Outgoing like Nellie Mae,* he mused with a genuine smile. Instantly Sheryl brightened, probably believing that his joyful expression was meant for her.

All during the drive home, Chris felt lousy. He could kick himself for putting Sheryl in such a pitiful spot. He sure had a lot to make up for. *Her corsage better be extra special,* he decided.

But wait—if he went all out on flowers, wouldn't that send a too-encouraging message? He groaned aloud as he drove toward home.

CHAPTER 14

Rosanna took her time laying out a half dozen large quilts at market day on Thursday. Thanks to Elias, she'd arrived early enough to claim the display table closest to the sweets, a popular stopping place for shoppers. This way she also wasn't very far from several other women from Preacher Manny's church who were selling pickled green tomatoes, beets, and peppers.

She spotted some women from the Beachy church already setting up, as well. "Hullo!" She waved quickly and smiled, thinking how thankful she was Elias had changed his mind about tractors and cars—and about joining the more liberal Beachy Amish. Such a push and pull that would have caused in their home, just as for any couple divided over beliefs. For now, she felt sure Elias was quite satisfied to attend the New Order church, where the ordination of a second preacher was to take place this Sunday, following the sermon and songs of worship.

She had been praying in earnest for God's will in the selection of this preacher. As with the old church, the man chosen by drawing lots need not be a learned man, nor one trained in speaking. The greatest difference in the New Order church was that all candidates nominated by the membership had to be willing to study scripture and spend time preparing sermons. Memorizing God's Word was also emphasized, which was encouraging to Rosanna, who felt like a thirsty sponge during Preacher Manny's sermons.

She anchored the display table with the quilts' color schemes, placing the bold-colored ones at each end—a red and royal blue Bars pattern and her Sunshine and Shadows quilt all done in plums, blues, and golds. The softer, more muted colors and designs were for the center of the table. She'd learned this from her aunt, an expert quilter and her mother's oldest sister.

Usually Rosanna sold out of everything by around noon. She wished that might be the case again this week. Elias had an errand to run over near White Horse, and she was hoping the timing of his return might coincide with her being ready to head home.

Feeling sluggish again, Rosanna sat behind the table, satisfied the quilts were marked and situated nicely. In her frequent daydreams, she often thought of the many lovely baby things she could make, should the Lord allow her to birth a son or daughter. She would gladly use her quilt money for plenty of yarn and fabric.

Following yesterday's visit to Bird-in-Hand, she found it nearly impossible to stop thinking about Emma Sue, Rosie, and Lena—such considerate women. But was she ready to take another woman's child as her own?

A bright-eyed young lady stopped by the table, and Rosanna dismissed her earlier musings. She hoped the general weakness she felt now might dissipate so she would not have to reassure Elias again that she was going to be all right. Each morning lately, he lovingly inquired. Yet she wanted to protect him, so she still kept this pregnancy to herself.

"Oh, isn't this a striking quilt," the customer said. "Is it the Log Cabin pattern?"

"Jah, 'tis." She pointed to the large square quilt.

"Is it definitely Amish-made?" the woman asked.

Rosanna nodded. "I laid it out myself."

"Your work is exquisite." The woman fingered the edge of the quilt. "Do you ever do custom work?"

"I'd be happy to make something for ya." She reached for her tablet and a pen, accustomed to sewing quilts to suit a buyer's fancy. She delighted in the process of choosing patterns and colors and laying out the unique designs, as well as the quilting itself. Every aspect was wonderful-good, including bringing the finished quilts to market. "Which pattern would you like?" she asked.

"Can you make an Album Patch for me?"

"What color scheme?"

The woman thought about it for a moment. "As long as there is some green in it—as a background, perhaps—and yellows and pinks, too, any mix would be fine."

"Sounds perty," Rosanna said, envisioning the many pieces within each of the twenty-five squares—as expensive to make as the lovely Dahlia pattern, with its individual gathered petals.

"I once saw one at an antique quilt sale and it went for nearly seven hundred dollars," said the customer.

"Well, mine won't cost you near that." Rosanna explained that the fine wool batiste and wool cashmere of the old days were no longer available. "Now we use polyesters and scraps of old dress fabric, pieces from men's for-good shirts, and other odds and ends. I even purchase quilt squares just for my work. Does that sound all right?"

The woman's smile spread across her face. "Oh, this is so exciting." She took out her wallet and made the down payment in cash, saying she'd pay the rest with a personal check.

Rosanna agreed to the method of payment. She had been told she was too trusting, but that's how her mother was and her grandmothers, too. And they'd never run into a snag with Englischers, that she knew of. "I'll give you my address, and you can come pick it up either at my house or here—at market—three weeks from today. I'll do a nice job for you."

The woman wrote her own name, address, and phone number on another index card Rosanna handed to her. "Thank you so much. You just don't know how you've made my day."

Rosanna glanced at the card. "I hope you'll be pleased, Dottie," she said, a twinge of pain in her middle. She smiled through the impulse to flinch as she handed the woman her own address. "Have a nice day."

After that customer, there were several more sales, including two sisters—Julie and Wendy—who wanted custom-made quilts, as well as crib quilts. Rosanna offered to make a baby quilt in the Ocean Wave pattern at no charge. The sisters were quite surprised at this, but Rosanna insisted and they told their friend Bonnie to purchase the most expensive quilt there, "to make up for it."

By eleven o'clock, when Rosanna reached under the table for her lunch sack, she felt so hungry and dizzy, she was glad to be seated. She'd thought of going to see a doctor, but she knew such a visit would be sure to worry Elias.

As she slowly ate, she happened to notice her cousin Kate with her niece Lizzy, standing at the far end of the row. They were each holding one of the twins as they talked to the young Amishwoman best known for her jams and jellies, Rebecca from nearby Hickory Hollow.

Try as she might, she could not keep from staring at Kate and Lizzy . . . and the babies. Goodness, were they growing! She stopped to think how old they'd be now. *Born Novem-*

*ber seventh and today's April tenth . . . so they're already five
months old, bless their dear hearts.*

She began to cry, unable to stop the flow of tears.

"Ach, Rosanna—you all right?" the woman at the next
table asked, coming to lean over her.

She could not speak, shaking her head and patting her
chest, trying to compose herself.

Indicating the half-eaten sandwich in her hand, the woman
asked if there was something spicy in it. "Do ya want a drink,
maybe?"

Rosanna nodded, relieved when the woman marched off
to get a cup and some water. By then, Kate and Lizzy had
evidently moved around to the other side, because Rosanna
could no longer see them. *Just as well.* She had to pull herself
together, or she might begin to really sob. *And oh, would I
ever, if I caught sight of the twins' sweet faces.*

Then she was getting up, compelled by an irresistible drawing. *I must see Eli and Rosie . . . must touch their little hands.
Ach, I can't help myself.*

The woman carrying the water intercepted her journey,
taking her arm and leading her back to her table and the single
quilt remaining—the softly muted Nine Patch in the center.
"There, now, this'll make ya feel better."

"Denki," she eked out as she sat down, grateful to be off
her feet once again.

"You look altogether peaked." The woman eyed her. "You
got someone comin' for ya later?"

Quickly she nodded. "My husband will fetch me." She was
so thankful for the water as she took several small sips. Hoping to set her mind on other things, she considered the money
she'd made this day and the delightful new customers—pretty
Dottie and the two sisters, Julie and Wendy, and their friend
Bonnie. She pondered each face, each comment . . . all this to

keep her focus away from the fact that her darlings were here at market, in this very building.

If Elias hadn't arrived a few minutes later, Rosanna didn't know what she might have done. Created a scene, perhaps? She wanted to think she would have kept her emotions in check. But oh, the powerful tug on her heart toward Eli and Rosie.

For now, though, Elias was folding up the single quilt and looking at her curiously, asking if she was any better than she'd been earlier this morning. He supported her elbow as they made their way over to the small window to pay the percentage owed the establishment.

Then, as they walked to the exit, she told him she'd seen Eli and Rosie, and he slipped his arm around her and said not a word. All the while, she hoped against hope they would *not* run into Kate and Lizzy and the babies, she was so wrung out with emotion. *Help me make it home in one piece.*

Elias held her hand nearly all the way. The gentle sway of their old covered carriage lulled her into repose, and she leaned her head on her husband's strong shoulder.

When they arrived home, she went to lie down and rest, and Elias tenderly tucked her into bed, looking mighty concerned as he sat on the bed next to her, stroking her arm.

In spite of feeling quite comfortable now, Rosanna could not erase the memory of the babies snuggled happily in Kate's and Lizzy's arms. And she knew, without a doubt, she could not consider "adopting" another woman's wee one just now. *Maybe not ever.*

———

Chris Yoder couldn't wait to drive the back road leading to his Amish cousins' spread of land. He liked the openness and the farm activity on both sides as Amish and English alike were busy moving sludge around in their barnyards, creating shallow ditches for runoff to accommodate the spring thaw. Chris recalled seeing David Yoder and his older sons do the same thing, years ago.

Recently Caleb had said their driving horses had begun to shed—another sign of spring. Chris found himself looking for such things more closely since coming out to help. While Caleb and Abe were usually around working somewhere, occasionally Gideon or Jonah would come for a few hours at a time, too. Thankfully, the other brothers took his helping in stride, though only Caleb really seemed comfortable talking with him.

When Chris pulled into the drive, he was surprised to see the bench wagon parked there. He couldn't imagine David and Elizabeth hosting church this Sunday, not the way David had to be assisted. But then, he had no idea how this community operated. They seemingly continued to do the things they'd always done, even though the head of the family was so seriously injured. Really, the whole situation boggled his mind, this family subsisting without the help of an in-home nurse or therapist. When he'd talked with Caleb about his father's desperate condition, Caleb had merely said it was their way. *"Life goes on, no matter."*

Shifting into Park, Chris turned off the ignition. When he looked up, he was shocked to see Caleb's father being lifted out of the bench wagon on a makeshift stretcher lined with a narrow mattress and hoisted by the four brothers.

He hopped out of the car and caught up with them, walking slowly behind as the entourage lumbered toward the back door. Not wanting to interfere, he waited on the back stoop, puzzled by what he'd witnessed. When Leah opened the door and asked if he'd like to come inside, he told her he would wait there for Caleb.

"My brother might be a while yet."

Until today, he had not been invited inside the house since

he was a child. "I'll wait, thanks," he said. He'd gotten the impression from Caleb that it might be best if he didn't stir up the waters.

Soon two older men with long brown beards emerged from the house, talking slowly in Pennsylvania Dutch. The men nodded their heads when they caught his eye but kept walking. He stood there awkwardly, overhearing snatches of someone talking rather loudly inside. Actually grumbling— then a holler—and he assumed Caleb's father was having difficulty getting situated in his wheelchair again.

Quickly Chris moved out of earshot. Not knowing where to go to avoid catching private exchanges, he headed to the barn and watched the determined parade of cows as they moved into the milking parlor, amazed again at how each animal independently moved to its own stanchion.

While he waited, he wondered if maybe David Yoder had just returned from a doctor appointment. *Had to be.* And he instantly knew how he could help lessen such an ordeal for his father's cousin, the poor man.

He heard voices and turned to see Abe and Caleb coming into the barn. Swiftly the brothers began to secure the stanchion bars into the locked position while the cows fed on hay. Chris could have helped do that in their absence, but Caleb had said last week that the cows were still getting used to him, and Chris did not want to spook them.

He didn't have to ask about his suspicions. Once Abe got to milking, Caleb mentioned how hard it was for his father to go to his weekly rehabilitation sessions in the bench wagon.

Right then Chris offered his dad's van, the vehicle they used to make deliveries for the nursery, for the trips.

Caleb turned, stunned. "You'd do that?"

"Sure, why not? I can easily drive your father back and forth, as long as it's after school hours. I know Dad won't mind. I've already talked to both my parents about what I'm up to here."

"Well, his next appointment's set for Tuesday morning," Caleb said. "I'll see if it can be moved to the afternoon. I'm sure Daed'll be willing to go with you—beats his other option all to pieces. He complained today he'd never go back if he had to lie on that stiff board again."

"Do you think you could make a ramp for his wheelchair?" Chris suggested.

"Good thinkin'. We'll look into it." Caleb nodded. " 'Tween you and me, it pains me to see my father suffer so. Denki, Chris."

Caleb's eyes held a mix of pain and gratitude. *I hope I'm helping to ease the stress around here—not adding more,* Chris thought, wondering what else he could do without infringing on his cousin's life.

CHAPTER 15

All afternoon, Mamma kept talking about scurrying off to see Martha, hoping to also run into Rhoda, but she was still there working in the bakery shop near closing time. Nellie, presently waiting on customers, was eager to talk privately with Nan, if Mamma *did* actually leave. Either that, or Nellie would have to wait till evening. She and Nan had enjoyed several nighttime discussions about scripture while curled up on Nan's bed. Together they'd nearly memorized the first five chapters of the gospel of John.

Moving toward the door, Mamma said a quick good-bye and hurried toward Dat and the waiting horse and carriage.

"Honestly, I thought Mamma might up and change her mind and stay home today," Nan said, looking out the window.

"Ach, funny. I was thinkin' the same thing."

"So, you've got yourself a secret to share, is that it?" Nan's eyes twinkled.

"Well, I've been thinking 'bout all the times you've asked me to go along to the New Order barn Singings."

Nan leaned near, a droll expression on her face. "Are ya sayin' you might be ready?"

"Nee."

"Then what?"

"It's just that I'm anxious to see your beau . . . if only from afar."

Nan laughed. "Oh, you're the sneaky one, ain't so?"

Nellie tried not to grin. "How much longer must I wait, sister?"

"He is mighty good-lookin', I'll say that much."

"But lots of fellas are."

"He's not as bold as some, though, so I doubt he'd ever meet me at the barn door . . . just so *you* can catch a glimpse of him."

"All right, then, you'll have to tell me who."

Nan crossed her arms in jest. "I don't have to tell you any such thing."

"Ain't that the truth."

Brightening again, Nan teased, "But if you guess his name, I will."

Nan had her but good. "It'll take far too long to name off all the youth in the new group. And I doubt you'll give me another hint, knowin' you."

"Not a one!" With that, Nan again burst out laughing.

"Well, if you're getting married come fall, I s'pose he'll be a baptismal candidate, jah?"

"Now you're gettin' warmer."

Nellie Mae considered all the young men who were the right age to join church. Mostly their second and third cousins came to mind. "You're not in love with a Fisher relative, are ya?"

Nan's eyes bugged out, and she tried to compose herself. This was fun. "Dat's cousins have quite a few courting-age sons. . . ."

"Never mind. I won't tell you even if you do guess."

"Aw, Nan."

"Best not say, for now."

"Oh, and I was that close, too."

Nan had that twinkle again. "You only think so."

"Ach, you're the feisty one, ain't? Guess I'm just going to have to go to Singing with you, then."

"Wonderful-gut! That's what I was hopin' you'd say."

Nellie Mae shook her head. *What am I getting myself into?*

———

"Life's full of twists and turns," Caleb told Chris as they entered the milk house. "I never expected my father to end up in a wheelchair. I figured he'd still be out cutting tobacco when his time came."

"Must be hard, seein' him that way."

"One thing's for certain," Caleb said. "It makes you think twice."

"What does?"

Caleb shrugged, knowing that a discussion about sickness and death was like opening a barn door to Chris's undoubtedly strange ideas. At the moment, though, he didn't care. "We deal with so-called tragedy differently than Englischers, you might know."

"But you're human. You still suffer."

"Usually in silence," Caleb said quietly. "Sometimes I wonder . . ." He paused, shaking his head, unwilling to voice his frustrations. He stared out the window, wondering how they'd gotten to this.

Chris cleared his throat. "I don't blame you. You might think you know how you'll react to something as terrible as your father's accident, but until it happens, you can't really know at all."

Turning away from the window, he was surprised at Chris's response. He'd become accustomed to seemingly prideful

159

statements from some of the New Order folk—*the saved folk.* But Chris seemed different. Why?

As if in response to Caleb's questioning stare, Chris bowed his head for a moment, running his hands through his thick blond hair. "I'll tell you . . . Suzy Fisher's drowning was the worst thing that's ever happened to our family. The hardest thing on Zach and me."

"Did you know her very well?"

Chris paused, as if wanting to be careful how he put this. "For the short time my brother dated her, I'd say I knew her fairly well, yes."

Caleb searched Chris's face. "You were there when she died, weren't you?"

Nodding, Chris stepped away from the bulk milk tank, and Caleb cautiously opened the lid to check on the stirring mechanism. "I'll just say that it shook our faith—my brother's more than mine," said Chris. "Why would God allow such a wonderful young girl to drown? We'd heard debates on suffering, but . . ." He hesitated. "Until it hits home, all the talk in the world is simply that . . . talk."

"So what happened? I mean, how did you keep on, you know . . . believing like ya do?" asked Caleb.

Chris shrugged. "We decided to take God at face value, so to speak. It's hard sometimes, but in the Bible it's clear—what's waiting for us . . . after this life, is impossible to understand or fathom. But most important for us . . ."

Caleb waited.

"We knew we'd see Suzy again."

Caleb swallowed hard. He wouldn't let on how he felt—downright helpless. Even alone. "My father says we can't know for certain where we're goin'. But we can hope for heaven, come Judgment Day."

"Well, I disagree."

Chris seems so sure. "Why's that?"

"Because God's Word tells us differently."

"Since Daed's accident, I admit to thinkin' things that might shock the bishop." Caleb forced a nervous laugh.

"Well, I'm not your bishop, Caleb."

He turned slowly, taking a long look at his modern cousin. "Maybe that's a good thing." Caleb smiled.

They continued to work together like close brothers. And, later, when it came time for Chris to leave, he mentioned a boy in his church class who might benefit by spending a few hours at the farm.

Caleb agreed to ask his father about having Billy Zercher visit sometime with Chris. But what Caleb really wished for was to invite Chris to stay on for supper. *Anything to keep him here longer.*

Caleb sat whittling in the corner of the tobacco shed after supper. A gray barn cat sauntered through the open doorway and nuzzled her head against his leg. Dusk closed in around them, and Caleb found some tranquility in the stillness of night-fall. Peace was something he longed for, especially now.

He'd left the house for a reprieve from watching Daed in his wheelchair at every meal. His father was so determined to cut his own meat or reach for his glass, but needing help from Mamm to steady him. He seemed to be losing more muscle tone and mobility even in his arms and upper body as the days passed. But he remained at the head of the table—where a crack in the wood reminded all of them of his fierce temper. Now the paralysis had pushed Daed's ire to a frightening rage over his weakness as he still strove to control his household with a strong hand. His willingness to allow Caleb to help out was purely practical, Caleb knew, and nothing more.

"My father's not getting better," Caleb told the cat. She

turned her head sideways, looking at him with yellow-green eyes. And he sighed. "I must be desperate if I'm talkin' to you."

He leaned back against the shed wall gingerly, muscles sore after a long day of unloading stored hay for the neighbors. Lately, he seemed to meet himself coming and going—getting up before dawn and staying up too late, contemplating his lot in life.

It hadn't been more than a few weeks ago that his father and brothers had been pressing the cured and stripped tobacco leaves into a bale box, packaging it for auction. Daed had always sold his "Pennsylvania 41" to a broker from the Lancaster Leaf Company. The dark-colored, gummy leaf made for good cigar filler, according to his grandfathers, and some fine chewing tobacco, too. He'd tried the latter, but only on the sly, as a rite of passage when he turned sixteen.

The worst thing about raising tobacco was all the labor. When Caleb's older brothers were busy with harvests of their own, a whole group of farmers had to drop everything to help Daed cut the "leaf." It was backbreaking labor to hand-cut the stalks one at a time, leaving the cut leaves on the ground for the sun to soften, before stabbing them onto the long laths and stacking them on the cart for hauling to the curing shed. It was a great deal of work for the return, he knew, having heard his father complain through the years.

Caleb yawned, staring up at the empty rafters. He did not miss hauling the forty-pound laths required to hang the tobacco leaves on the long rails here in the shed. Nor did he miss the insufferable temperatures beneath the tin roof. Late summer's heat was a true test of a man's endurance, he knew firsthand. He never had trouble falling asleep during that season.

But these days sleep was slow in coming, if it came at all. He'd struggled with maddening insomnia since his father's return from the hospital. The minute Caleb closed his eyes, no matter how exhausted he was from the day's work, his brain kicked into high gear. Even now his brain whirled with Chris's kind offer to drive Daed to rehabilitation.

Sighing, Caleb forced air through pursed lips. He ought to be well rested before he approached his father on this. He wouldn't speculate how that conversation might go.

Truth was, everything had changed since his father's head got in the way of that ornery mule. There were days when Caleb felt he might suffocate. Had the Lord God reckoned to punish him?

Ironically, Caleb actually missed working alongside Daed—filling silo, helping birth calves. And soon there would be plowing and planting. His father would not be present in the fields all day, muttering his ongoing grievances and whatnot. But Abe would be. And Gideon and Jonah and some older cousins, each taking shifts. Everyone but Daed.

Probably not for the rest of his life.

Caleb whittled harder, taking out his frustrations on the piece of wood as twilight fell. He considered the hour difference between the People and the modern folk who moved their clocks up a full hour each April, lengthening the end of the day, instead of the beginning, when work was best accomplished. The fancy practice was called "fast time" amongst the Amish because it pushed everything forward. *"Not at all the way God intended,"* Daed had always said.

Fast time meant more daylight hours for not only work but for play and courting, too, even though most fellows waited till twilight to go out riding with their girls.

He wondered if Nellie Mae was looking ahead to the weekend and the Sunday Singing. No doubt she was pairing up with a new fellow by now. There were plenty of New Order boys to make for a nice choice of a mate, if a "saved" husband was what she was after.

His knife cut deep. Looking down at the misshapen wood, Caleb gave up trying to whittle it into a small horse. Flicking the strips of wood off his lap, he realized anew that he would never have the chance to talk with Nellie Mae again if she met up with one of those "redeemed" fellows. And come Sunday, the new church would have another minister and deacon, too. Apparently Preacher Manny's group was thriving, not dissolving as he'd hoped.

He reached down to rub the mouse-catcher's neck. "My girl's gonna end up marryin' some preacher-man . . . you just watch and see." The cat leaned into his hand, purring hard. "Well, she *was* my girl. Now she's free as a bird. . . ."

It still hurt, though he doubted a single soul knew just how badly.

CHAPTER 16

A gentle rain fell as Nellie Mae sat with Rosanna at the kitchen table on this gloomy Friday afternoon. At Mamma's urging, she'd left the bakery shop to visit her dearest friend, who still looked so pale, Nellie was sure she'd caught a springtime bug.

Nellie stirred the freshly made peppermint ice tea. "Sure is soggy out there," she said.

"Elias said the fields were startin' to dry out, so this shower's nice." Rosanna glanced out the window.

Nellie watched it rain, enjoying the peaceful sound. "It's makin' down pretty good."

Getting up for a plate of oatmeal raisin cookies, Rosanna said, "Before I forget, I want to show you an old quilt pattern I found." She set the cookies down and left the room. Soon she returned with a tattered magazine. "Lookee here." Rosanna pointed to a picture of a turn-of-the-century cradle quilt. "Perty, ain't so?"

"What's the pattern?" Nellie had never seen this one, but she wasn't up on the older patterns. Mammi Hannah would know, though—she was a walking dictionary of quilt patterns—sometimes comically referring to herself as having "quilt pox," she loved quilting so much.

"It's called Grandmother's Dream and was made from twill-weave wool."

"And a Lancaster County pattern, yet." Nellie looked at the picture more closely. "Will you try to copy it?"

"If all goes well, I'll make three of them—as thank-yous."

It dawned on her what her friend was up to. "Oh, that's so thoughtful of you, Rosanna."

"Well, I don't know 'bout that . . . but I *do* want to make something nice for Emma Sue, Rosie, and Lena. They were so kind to me."

Nellie Mae waited, hoping Rosanna might say which woman she was considering for her baby.

The steady patter of rain on the roof was the only sound as Rosanna reached for a cookie. She glanced at Nellie as if she had something on her mind but couldn't quite say it.

At last, Rosanna sighed and moved the quilt picture to the side. She kept her hand on it, breathing slowly. "If I told you something, Nellie Mae, would ya promise to keep mum?"

Nodding, Nellie ran her pointer finger and thumb across her lips.

"This is ever so hard," she whispered, locking eyes with Nellie.

"You can trust me with your decision," Nellie said. "Honestly."

"No, no . . . ain't that."

Nellie searched her friend's eyes, seeing the pain there. "Are you all right, Rosanna?"

"I'm with child again." Rosanna leaned into her hands, covering her face. "Not even Elias knows."

Nellie's heart broke for her.

"It'll disappoint him so . . . when I lose this baby, too."

Rosanna wiped her eyes. "Best not to get his hopes up again, ya know?"

"Oh, Rosanna . . ."

"Pray that I'll have the grace to bear this yet again." She wept uncontrollably. "Or for healing, if it be God's will."

Nellie fought down the lump in her own throat. "I'll pray . . . you can count on that."

"I mean now. Would ya?" asked Rosanna. "The Lord healed the woman with the issue of blood . . . what sort of disease was that?"

Nellie had also read the New Testament story. "All I know is she believed that if she could touch the hem of the Lord's robe, she'd be made well."

"Oh, I wish He could walk among us today."

"Well, He does," Nellie Mae said.

Rosanna brushed away her tears. "You sense His presence?"

"These days, jah . . . since He lives in my heart."

Rosanna nodded silently, unable to speak.

"We can show His love to each other—and to others—as we walk through the hardest valleys."

Rosanna searched for a hankie in her dress sleeve.

"Like the one you're walkin' in now." Nellie leaned closer. "Have you thought of askin' the elders to lay hands on you, like the Scriptures say to us?"

"But we're here now. And the Lord promises to be with us when we come in His name, jah?"

Nellie studied her. "You must believe that God will heal you if we pray together."

"It's mighty hard, I'll admit that." Taking a deep breath, Rosanna seemed to brighten a bit.

Nellie Mae didn't feel skilled enough to offer a powerful prayer, like the ministerial brethren might. She merely took a breath and did her best. "O Lord, my friend Rosanna here wants a baby with all of her heart—just however you might see fit for that to happen. And she wants to be strong enough to carry her baby till it's time for the birth." Nellie paused, hoping she was choosing the right words.

Only the Lord knows my heart . . . and Rosanna's.

Nellie continued, filled with a deep love for her friend. "But more than any of this, Rosanna longs for your will to be done. She wants it more than everything else. Amen."

———

Betsy wished to be in a prayerful attitude all during this gray and rainy day of working in the shop. She had been mindful of communion for a full month now, Sunday being one of its twice-yearly celebrations, with the ordination service following. In preparation for taking communion with the membership, she had committed to memory a good portion of First Corinthians, the eleventh chapter. But it was the twenty-eighth verse that convicted her most.

But let a man examine himself, and so let him eat of that bread, and drink of that cup.

She had no known sin in her heart, yet she wasn't perfect. Only the Lord was that. And there was this awful rift between Rhoda and the family. How she longed to somehow heal the breach. *Ach, the folly of worldliness . . .* Rhoda's selfish living still hurt terribly. Yet she chose to forgive her willful, wandering daughter.

Several times she had even made the trip to see Rhoda at James and Martha's, only to find her already gone.

What can I possibly do to smooth things over?

Nan held the door for her as they entered the bakery shop with the still-warm pies and cookies. Quickly she and Nan arranged the fruit pies and two coconut cream pies in the display case. The cookies were set out on platters with plastic wrap over the top to keep them nice and moist.

"I do hope Rosanna's all right," Nan said softly.

Betsy counted out a baker's dozen for each variety of cookie. "I 'spect Nellie Mae's visit will do her some good."

"Rosanna's a strong believer. I daresay she's been praying 'bout the women over yonder."

"Nellie must've told you, then?"

Nan smiled. "Anymore there isn't much Nellie doesn't share with me."

Both girls have lost close sisters . . . they've come to depend on each other.

"God's so good to give me Nellie Mae," Nan added.

Betsy couldn't have agreed more, and she reached for Nan, wrapping her arms around her girl. "Oh, I'm so glad you're all right, Nan. You know, I was awful worried after your beau broke things off."

"Well, no need to, Mamma. I'm fine now." Nan continued talking about the church and youth gatherings, how she couldn't wait to read Scripture with Nellie at night. "We go upstairs after Dat reads to all of us and memorize verses."

Oh, the joy! "I daresay the younger you are when committing Scripture to memory, the better you'll remember it . . . for a lifetime."

"I can see that. Ev'ry poem I ever learned when I was a little girl, I can still recite."

"Ach, see?"

"What poems do you remember from childhood, Mamma?"

Betsy raised her finger to her cheek. "Here's a sobering one I was taught from the *McGuffey Reader*: 'Tobacco is a filthy weed. It was the Devil sowed the seed. It leaves a stench wher'er it goes. It makes a chimney of the nose.' "

Nan was nodding her head. "Ain't that the truth!"

"And it rhymes, too."

They had a good laugh, and when she looked up, Betsy spied a tan car pulling into the driveway. Lo and behold if the selfsame blond fellow who'd come Monday didn't climb out, running through the rain, straight for the shop door.

Well, lookee here. . . .

———

Nellie wanted to stretch her legs, since Rosanna was resting. She pulled her raincoat up over her head and ran out to see Elias's new baby goats. She found one of the mothers, a beautiful brown-and-white doe, nuzzling her little one playfully. Nellie was taken by the gentle way the nanny goat had with this baby, who soon began to nurse. The kid still had its horns, so it was less than ten days old, which was when Elias would dehorn it.

An earthy scent hung heavily in the air, and she thought of David Yoder's herd of dairy cows, wondering how Caleb was managing since his father's accident. She caught herself. *He's at the edge of my every thought.*

She heard the creak of a carriage and the sound of approaching horse hooves and saw Elias pulling up to the barn. He jumped out of the buggy and quickly unhitched the horse in the midst of the rain. *He's lost some weight.* Rosanna had said he'd skipped meals recently for the purpose of fasting and prayer. Nellie had assured her that once *Gmee*—the big church gathering this Sunday—was over, he would eat again and gain the weight back. She'd seen Dat and her brothers do much the same when they went to their prayer closets, doubtless pleading in part for God to withhold the divine lot from them, so solemn a responsibility it brought. Yet praying for God's will, too.

After a time, Nellie returned to the house. She was relieved to see Rosanna had awakened and her color was some better. When Elias came inside, he headed upstairs, saying he'd come down after supper.

"God's called him to prayer for the future of our church," Rosanna explained, tucking a loose hair under her Kapp.

Nellie Mae had never heard of the Lord calling someone to pray for something specific. Always before, the bishop had been the one to admonish the membership to do so.

"Honestly, Nellie, I've never seen Elias so bent on something. And he's decided against seeding tobacco this year, too."

"Seems Preacher Manny's message is catchin' on, then."

"Jah, for sure, even though the crop's always been a good mortgage lifter, as the tobacco farmers like to say." Rosanna set a pot on the stove and then washed her hands.

"Some folk still cling to bringin' in the 'baccy, you know."

"Sure they do. It'll take some time before things change much round here, no doubt." She reached for her wooden cutting board and gathered up the vegetables intended for the evening meal. "All that talk aside, Elias and I've found a real home in the new church. We've had some good fellowship with two older couples who are like spiritual parents to us."

Since Elias's and Rosanna's families had remained in the old church, their being looked after by older believers was a blessing.

"Well, I can hardly wait for September," Nellie said right out.

"To join church?"

Nellie smiled, ever so anxious for her baptism. Until that day, she was exempt from the ordination process, so she and Nan and other non-baptized youth would keep the young children occupied outdoors while their parents chose a worthy man to nominate. If a man received three or more votes, his name went into the lot. Of those men, one would eventually draw the old hymnbook containing the scripture signifying he was God's man. *Just as in the old church on Gmee Sunday,* she thought, glad Uncle Bishop had decided to ordain a second preacher.

"Must be our church is growin'," she said.

"Oh, is it ever." Rosanna steadied the celery with her left hand, cutting firmly through the stalks with her right. "That's why this ordination comes at such a good time. And I'm not the only one who thinks so."

"Mamma says there's not to be any talk 'tween members 'bout who should be nominated," Nellie said.

Rosanna nodded. "We're to make it a matter of prayer."

"Nonmembers can pray 'bout all this, too?"

"Whether you're a member yet or not, you want God's will."

Nellie finished chopping carrots and reached for the onions. "How long before we'll have our own bishop, do you think?" She'd wondered this for months, ever since Uncle Bishop Joseph had lifted the Bann from the People, temporarily allowing those who wanted to join the New Order to leave with mercy.

"Elias thinks it'll take a few years to make us a bishop."

"It must keep Uncle Bishop busy, overseein' two church districts."

Rosanna nodded. "I daresay the ministerial brethren carry a love-burden we can't begin to understand."

"Dat's said much the same," Nellie acknowledged.

"Your father's a wise man—Elias often looks to him for counsel, as well as Preacher Manny. Manny's concerned we not 'go soft,' taking anything for granted concerning our salvation . . . lest our deeds deceive us." Rosanna stopped her chopping to look at Nellie. "I wasn't sure I should say anything, but your Aendi Anna came to see how I was doin' . . . you know, after Elias and I met with her bishop husband and John and Kate about . . . the babies. It was just so nice of her . . . considering everything."

Nellie was glad to hear this. "My aunt always loved you, Rosanna."

"She was so dear, comin' to check up on me. If Anna were younger, she could be like a mother to me . . . 'cept for one thing."

"Disagreeing that you can say you're saved?" Nellie asked softly.

"No matter what anyone thinks, the split is still dividing the People," Rosanna said.

For some it's more heartbreaking than for others, thought Nellie.

Together they dumped all the prepared vegetables into a big pot, and Rosanna added ample salt and pepper before setting on the lid and lighting the gas stove.

"You know, Anna did tell me, without a blink of an eye, that she and the bishop read the Bible out loud every day," Rosanna said.

Nellie thrilled to hear this.

"Something they've been doin' for a while . . . but she made a point of saying, mind you, that they wouldn't think of studying or discussing the verses." Rosanna wore a mischievous smile.

"Nor memorizing, either?" Nellie could hardly keep herself in check.

"I truly believe the Lord's at work in their hearts," Rosanna said softly.

Reassured that supper was well underway, Nellie gave her friend a quick kiss on the cheek. "Good-bye—and take good care." How she hoped and prayed Rosanna would not lose this baby. "I'll look forward to seein' your pretty Grandmother's Dream quilts next time, Lord willing."

"Be careful out on the wet roads," her friend called. "And come again soon!"

With a wave, Nellie hurried across the soggy yard to retrieve her horse from the stable.

CHAPTER 17

His mom's eyebrows rose and remained aloft when Chris carried the boxed coconut cream pie into the kitchen and, with a flourish, set it on the counter.

"Are we celebrating something . . . again?" She smiled, opening the lid and breathing in the luscious aroma.

"Do we need a reason to eat a delicious pie?"

"Must be you're sweet on a cook somewhere," Zach teased, sauntering over to peer at the treat. Then, his eyes darting comically, he sneaked a swipe at the creamy white peaks with his finger.

"Hey . . . watch it." Chris swatted him away.

Zach was nosing around, eyeing the plain white box. "Where *are* you getting these? Three pies in one week?"

Chris simply smiled. "Just eat it already."

Mom reached for the knife rack. "We'll have our dessert before dinner," she said with a smile.

Zach grinned and bent close to the pie.

"Oh, you . . . you're goin' to inhale it next." Mom pushed him back playfully.

Chris loved having his mom around. She'd never considered any job but that of homemaker. *Like Nellie Mae Fisher surely will be.*

Startled, he attempted to push away the thought while Mom cut thick wedges of Nellie Mae's mouthwatering handiwork. He'd sure missed seeing her at the shop today.

After Chris enjoyed every morsel, Zach followed him to their shared room and plopped down on his bed with a demanding look on his face. Chris knew he'd better come clean with his brother. After all, he'd already told their parents about his visits to their Amish cousins.

"Listen, the pies came from a country bakery," he said.

With an obnoxious smile, Zach raised his eyebrows. "And . . . ?"

"And . . . what?"

"You're not so big on pies," Zach shot back. "C'mon!"

Chris sighed. "There *is* someone. . . ."

Zach laughed. "I knew it!" Then he frowned. "Wait a minute. I thought you were flipped out over Sheryl Kreider. Weren't you at her locker the other day?"

"Well, I *did* ask her to the banquet."

"So, are you two-timing someone else?" Zach's eyes twinkled.

Chris sprawled out on his bed, across from Zach's. "Listen, man, can you be serious for once?"

"Oh, this is *good*." Zach leaned up on his elbow. "So . . . who's the other girl?"

Chris paused a moment. "Look, I don't want to get something all stirred up again."

"What are you talking about?"

"Suzy Fisher."

Zach shook his head, frowning. "Wh . . . I don't get you."

"The girl I like is Amish."

"Translation, please?"

Chris decided to just say it. "The other girl is . . . Suzy Fisher's sister."

Zach tilted his head, looking baffled. "No way."

"Nellie Mae. But I'm not sure what to do about her. I mean, you know how it is." He looked at his brother, who was nodding thoughtfully, evidently still taking all this in.

"Yeah," Zach said, "I know."

––––––

Rhoda slipped out of bed, having already slept for several hours. She'd come in plenty early last night, thanks to Ken's insistence. Now she crept to the kitchen for a glass of milk, careful not to awaken the children.

Sitting in the light of the moon, the sky having cleared since her date with Ken, she stared out the window. She felt awfully sad. Ken might think of it as having a pity party—she'd heard him say much the same regarding one of the real estate agents at his company, who complained when her sales fell short of making her Realtor of the Month.

But Rhoda's malaise was about herself and Ken. How had she managed to miss his disinterest in having children?

He was, after all, father material. Wasn't he? Perhaps he just didn't see it in himself. Maybe if he spent more time around his cousins, it would help him to discover his paternal instincts.

Moonlight fell on soon-to-be-planted cornfields, and Rhoda stared out at its beauty. She felt sure she could move Ken to her point of view, at least in time. That's when she decided maybe it *was* a good idea to rent the room from him.

James would want a decision soon—he wanted her things moved out by next Tuesday. There was no changing *his* mind on anything, unless . . . Maybe she could buy herself some time.

What if I went to church with them this Sunday?

––––––

Rosanna busied herself with the newly commissioned quilt projects acquired at market. But since tomorrow was communion and ordination Sunday, she was mindful to divide her time amongst cutting colorful squares for the quilt Dottie had ordered, reading the Good Book, and praying for guidance.

The nagging pain in her lower back had faded somewhat today. And her cheeks seemed a bit rosier when she'd looked in the mirror. Overall, she felt stronger than she had for some time.

The mail arrived and she hurried outside, though she was not yet expecting a circle letter back from either her aunts in Smoketown or her cousins down in Conestoga. When she spied a letter postmarked Bird-in-Hand, she was curious.

Eagerly she tore open the envelope, surprised to see it was from Lena Stoltzfus, the kindhearted New Order woman Treva had introduced to her. The expectant mother and quilting friend of Nellie's grandmother had written it just yesterday.

She began to read.

Friday, April 11, 1967
Dear Rosanna,

Greetings in the name of our Lord!

I enjoyed meeting you so much, knowing we share a like faith. Oh, but I would've liked to sit down with you alone when you visited here—to share my peculiar story.

Not long ago, while I was praying, I felt strongly that I was to give my seventh baby to the Lord, like Samuel of old. Of course my husband and I have dedicated all of our children to God, but this baby—I truly believe it's a boy—is meant to be raised in the house of the Lord.

At the time, I had no idea what that meant, but when it came to my ears that a young woman in Honey Brook had repeatedly miscarried, then lost her two adopted babies because of her newfound faith, I wondered if God meant for me to give him to you, Rosanna. To be raised in the fear and admonition of the Lord.

The more I prayed, mind you, the more I felt this child would be a great blessing to you and your husband. I believe that as strongly today as I did that day more than two months ago.

Bless you, dear Rosanna. I hope to hear from you soon, whatever you decide.

Your sister in Christ,
Lena Stoltzfus

P.S. The baby is due in mid-September.

Rosanna attempted to read the last couple of paragraphs again, but her eyes filled with tears. *More than two months ago.* So Lena had been in deep prayer around the time Eli and Rosie went back to Cousin Kate. . . .

She felt reassured that this woman had not acted impulsively. Because of that and this amazing letter, Rosanna knelt to pray for her, unsure how to respond to Lena's generous offer. Her heart beat a little faster, thinking what it would be like to someday hold Lena's son in her arms. *If it is your will, Lord.*

———

Following his father's afternoon nap, Caleb took extra care getting him settled in the kitchen, with assistance from Abe, who left quickly. His brother obviously struggled with Daed's helpless state. They all did, but Abe seemed to show it more than Mamm or the girls. Caleb, however, always stayed by to do his father's bidding, especially if Mamm was out running an errand or attending a quilting bee, as she was today.

Surprisingly, Daed's only request was for a full glass of cold water within arm's reach. He would sit while he waited for

Mamm's return. She had somewhat apologetically reminded Daed before leaving early this morning that this was the big month for quiltings. Caleb had even wondered if Mamm was suffering from cabin fever, although she'd been outdoors plenty to plant many of the garden vegetables with his sisters. She'd announced just last night that the radishes were up already . . . some lettuce was peeking out of the soil, too—"*a bit early.*" Mamm's eyes had shone at the telling.

She's making her own happiness. . . .

"Abe and I are buildin' a ramp for your wheelchair, Daed," Caleb said.

"What's that for?" Daed growled.

"You'll need it to get to your rehab sessions."

His father's eyes brightened briefly, like a light flickering on, then off.

"Your English cousin's son offered to drive you in a van, so you'll get there right quick . . . more comfortably, too." He held his breath, waiting as if for the next shoe to drop.

"Who do ya mean?"

"Christian Yoder."

Daed smiled faintly. "My cousin John's boy? Well, what do ya know."

Before Daed could change his tune, Caleb mentioned that Chris had been coming several times a week to help with milking and other chores. "He's workin' mighty hard. And just so good round the herd, too."

Daed nodded and closed his eyes in repose—either that or he was recalling former days.

Should he forge ahead and risk asking to have Chris's young friend, Billy, come for a visit? Slowly he went to sit on the corner of the table bench, facing his father. "Chris would like to bring a grade-school youngster out to see the farm sometime, Daed. Just for a few hours. What do ya think?"

"This here Chris is a good boy, ain't?"

Caleb was quick to nod. "A big help, jah."

"Well, I can't say I'm happy 'bout using outside help." He drew a slow, deep breath, eyes cast downward. "I just don't know. . . ."

Caleb's heart sank. "Chris Yoder *is* blood kin," he reminded him.

Another long groan. "That he is. I s'pose it's all right on both counts. After all, John Yoder and I go back a long ways, though I haven't seen him in years."

Stunned by how well his father had responded, Caleb allowed himself to breathe more easily.

"When can I lay eyes on this long-lost cousin's boy?"

"Chris'll take you to rehab next Tuesday afternoon. Gideon will help Abe cover the milking so I can ride along."

"Well, better hurry and get that ramp ready, then."

With that, Caleb headed for the back door, relieved. On the way out to the barn for the saw, he thought of going back and asking if Rebekah might also be permitted to help out during daylight hours.

Then, thinking better of it, he decided he best leave well enough alone.

CHAPTER 18

Nellie Mae couldn't wait to close up the shop today. She'd sent Mamma down to the house to relax while Nan made supper— fried chicken, noodles and gravy, and green beans with ham and onions. Pulling the shop door closed, she walked toward the house, drinking in the raw, damp smell of overturned soil. Farmers would be out plowing and planting soon, and that made her think of Caleb.

Inside the summer porch, she wiped her bare feet on the rag rug at the door and put a smile on her face. Then she rushed past Nan in the kitchen and made her way upstairs to her room. All day she'd had it in her mind to get Caleb's old letters out of hiding and reread them. *To help me move forward without him,* she thought. *Nothing more.*

Yet now that she had a few moments to herself, she feared she might open up an even deeper hurt, seeing his loving words . . . the strong slant of his handwriting.

Sitting on her bed, she reached for her Bible instead and began to read Psalm 89. *I will sing of the mercies of the Lord for ever: with my mouth will I make known thy faithfulness to all generations.*

"O Lord," she prayed, "I broke up with Caleb . . . for you. And once again, I give him—and our love—back to you."

Again and again, she thought, realizing it was still nearly a daily occurrence.

Heartened, she read half of the chapter, the phrases soothing her. Then, resisting the urge to ponder the past, she went to look for her mother. Seeing her parents' door ajar, she called softly, "You busy, Mamma?"

"Come in." Her mother held a piece of paper, the Bible in her lap.

"Didn't mean to interrupt—"

"I'm preparing for communion council tomorrow."

"Same way as the old church?"

Her mother nodded. "Some things are similar, jah. There's a time of soul-searching beforehand." She held up the page. "Come, look at what you'll be asked to think 'bout as a member next fall . . . before the foot washing and communion service."

She sat next to Mamma on the love seat, near the window. "I know the bishop always asked if the People were of one mind before communion Sundays."

"Unity's necessary for this most holy ordinance." Mamma showed her the five written questions, and the verse printed in Preacher Manny's own hand at the top: *For as often as ye eat this bread, and drink this cup, ye do show the Lord's death till he come.*

They discussed the bread and the "wine," which for them was grape juice, and read aloud the first question to be given prayerful consideration. " 'Are you willing to be at peace with God, wholly trusting in Jesus Christ and living a life without spot or blemish, by the power of the Holy Spirit?' "

Mamma smiled sweetly. " 'Tis my heart's cry." Tears sprang to her eyes. "Oh, Nellie Mae . . . it's the second question that hurts me so. And I've been considering it all month, seems."

Nellie soon understood as she read aloud, " 'Are you aware

of any unresolved relationship, where someone is carrying something against you?' "

"Rhoda is hurt, surely she is," said Mamma, sighing. "What can I do to make it right?"

Nellie patted her hand. "It was never your fault Rhoda left."

"Still, I must try to talk to her . . . I simply must."

They shared further—Mamma was convinced she could not partake of holy communion if she did not speak with Rhoda today. "To offer forgiveness, if nothing else."

"Well, I'll take you to see her, if that's what you want."

"Oh, would you, Nellie Mae?"

She gave her mother a hug. "I'll tell Nan we'll be havin' supper away from home this evening."

"Let Dat know, too."

Nellie hurried out to the horse barn, praying Rhoda might have an open heart toward their mamma. Swiftly she hitched the horse and buggy, thinking about someday partaking in communion—the emblems of the Savior's body and blood. She was touched deeply, tears falling down her cheeks.

"O dear Lord, if only Caleb could understand. If he could just realize what you did for each of us," she whispered as she stroked the mare's long neck.

———

As she waited for the cook to complete her order for table number four, Rhoda spotted her mother and sister coming in the restaurant door. Stricken by the solemn expression on Mamma's face, Rhoda wanted to hide in the kitchen. Instead, she determined to be brave and simply "face the music," as Mrs. Kraybill sometimes said.

Nellie caught her eye, waving shyly as the hostess showed them to an inviting booth. *Now what'll I do?*

She had no choice but to be polite, and she wanted to be kind. But really, *another* visit from her family—and this time Mamma, too? Was eating out just so appealing now that she was a waitress?

Putting on a smile, she breezed over to their table. "How are you, Mamma . . . Nellie Mae?"

Her mother looked up, her beautiful face alight. "Oh, Rhoda, dear . . . are you our waitress?"

"What would you like to order?" She flipped her order pad over to a blank page.

Nellie said nothing, and Mamma kept looking at her, as if she hadn't heard Rhoda at all.

"We have several specials tonight," Rhoda said, rattling them off. The sight of Mamma brought her final evening at home right back in one sweeping rush: The horrid way she'd talked to her father, her haughty attitude, and her impatience to leave the house. Doubtless Mamma recalled all of it.

"Would you mind terribly if I talked to you before we order our supper?" Mamma asked.

The weight of the world landed on her. Her mother was going to confront her about coming home, she just knew it. "I can't . . . well, I'm at work."

"For pity's sake, Rhoda, we came all this way," Nellie piped up. "Won't ya hear Mamma out?"

"Only a few minutes?" Her mother's eyes were bright with tears.

Reluctantly Rhoda slid in next to Nellie Mae. "What is it, Mamma? Is someone ill . . . or worse?"

Her mother lowered her eyes, and her shoulders rose slowly as she inhaled. "No one's ill physically, no. But I am heartsick, daughter. I've come to ask your forgiveness . . . to make things right 'tween you and me."

Surprised, Rhoda said, "You don't understand." She sighed

and continued. "This isn't easy to say, Mamma, but my leaving has little to do with you . . . or the family. It's nothing you've done at all."

"But why, then?" asked Mamma. "It's not natural for a single woman to live away from her father's house. Just ain't."

She'd expected her mother to feel that way. It was all she knew. "I'm fine. No need to worry."

Mamma reached across the table. "Will you forgive me . . . all of us?"

"For bein' Plain? That's something we—you—were born to. None of us had any say in the matter." She moved quickly out of the booth, perplexed. "It's not something I can forgive you for, Mamma."

Her mother bowed her head.

"It's all right, Mamma." Nellie cast a disappointed glance at Rhoda. "You did what you came for . . . now we best be orderin' our supper."

After a moment's hesitation, Mamma chose a meatloaf dinner from the menu, and Nellie Mae asked for the fried chicken.

Later, after they'd finished and she'd switched on her professional demeanor once again, Rhoda offered them a look at the desserts, but both her mother and sister said they were "plenty full."

Rhoda felt nearly sick as they paid their bill, unsure if she should accompany them out to the horse and buggy or remain inside at her post. But with the intense uncertainty came a familiar wave of frustration, and all she could do was watch them move toward the door.

What sort of woman refuses her own mother? Rhoda hurried into the hallway and to the washroom to check on her makeup, fearful her sudden tears had smudged her fancy face.

April sunsets were colorful, replete with reds and gold. And Nellie was particularly glad for the long light in the evening as she and her mother left the restaurant and headed toward home, the horse's *clip-clopp*ing helping to rid her of tension. "You're not sorry we went, are you, Mamma?" she asked.

"It was good to see Rhoda, even if she's not herself."

"You did all you could," Nellie said, holding the reins nice and steady.

"I hardly recognized her, really."

Nellie sighed. "Well, she has lost a little weight. And her hair's cut short . . . and styled right fancy."

"It's more the way she holds herself . . . her way of talkin'."

Nellie agreed. "More fancy than Plain." Rhoda had seemed resistant to their request, too, not wanting to sit down and talk. Was their company so unwelcome?

"The world's rubbed off on her." Mamma sniffled a little.

Nellie dared not glance at her mother or she, too, would cry. "Let's try 'n' think happy thoughts. Tomorrow we'll have us a deacon and another preacher."

Mamma perked up. "The church is thriving, that's for sure."

They rode along serenely for several miles, taking in the beauty of the fields and the ever-changing sky. But out near Route 10, a ways from town, where the road opened up with less traffic, two cars—joyriding, more than likely—passed by a mite too close, one after another, like they were racing.

Nellie steadied the reins and held her breath as the horse veered, causing the carriage to careen dangerously over the center line. "Oh, Lord, help us," she cried out as Mamma gripped her arm.

She struggled to control the horse, using the reins and calling to the mare, "Get over, girl!"

But the horse reared up and then began to gallop. "Come on, girl," Nellie said more softly, her heart in her throat. She'd heard of too many carriages being tipped over in the midst of a dangerous situation. *I can't let that happen!*

Attempting to slow the horse by repeated pulls on the reins, she finally managed to get the mare over to the side of the road. Her arms were limp with fright, and all she could say was "Thank the dear Lord. . . ."

She looked at her mother's face, white with near dread. "Ach, Nellie, you managed so well." Mamma folded her hands in her lap. "I doubt I could have done the same."

Nellie Mae felt some relief following the close call, yet she was still shaken all the same. She wondered when her heartbeat might ever return to normal.

She clicked the horse forward again and asked Mamma, "Do you ever pray for protection when you start out on the road?"

"Well, I do now . . . since I started reading the Bible ev'ry day."

"Not before?"

"We weren't taught to pray for the covering of protection when I was growin' up. There's plenty of scripture about calling on the name of the Lord for salvation, for guidance, for His loving care—changin' the tide of evil or preventing harm," Mamma explained. "So many passages, really. We just didn't know what was there before."

"Passages like some Suzy wrote in her diary?"

Mamma fell silent.

"Ach, I should've kept quiet."

Eyes serious, Mamma shook her head. "Actually, I'm glad you brought that up, Nellie, because I've been meanin' to ask if I could read Suzy's diary. To ease the grief that lingers in me."

"Well, it's only the last part of the diary that's of any comfort, truth be told. Even so, Rhoda has it now."

Brightening, Mamma said, "Better yet. Jah, such good news."

"I'm sure Rhoda's read it through by now, although she hasn't said so."

"No matter. I can wait."

Nellie recalled Rhoda's rather distant remarks earlier and wondered why Suzy's words had not seemed to soften her heart. Was her sister so steeped in the world of the English that she was deaf to the still, small voice of God?

———

Her time with Elias following supper was one of Rosanna's favorite hours of the day. Tonight they sat at the table discussing the communion-council questions, pausing when they came to the third one: *Are you willing to live in love, forgiveness, and peace with your brothers and sisters in Christ and with all people, as far as it is in your ability to do so?*

Rosanna felt a tug in her spirit. "I have absolutely no peace 'bout something."

"What is it, love?" Elias's eyes searched hers.

She sighed, trying not to cry. "To tell you the truth, I don't know what to do 'bout taking a baby from yet another woman. I just feel so numb." She found Lena's letter in her pocket and handed it to Elias. "This came today, complicating matters even more."

She waited as he read, watching his expression change from surprise to brief consideration, and back to astonishment. "I say we commit this to the Lord."

Trembling, she reached for his hand. "There's something else, Elias. Something I should've told you sooner."

"You're shaking, love. What is it?"

"I'm with child again," she whispered, scarcely able to form the words.

His eyes grew wide. "Ach, Rosanna . . ."

"I've known for a while, but I couldn't think of takin' communion without telling you."

He leaned toward her, kissing her cheek and then taking her hand in both of his. "Now, why would you keep such a wonderful thing to yourself?"

She pressed her lips together as she struggled not to cry. "I wanted to bear the pain alone, to spare you when . . . if . . ."

He rose quickly and crouched beside her chair. "You must promise me never again to suffer so, my darling. You're carrying our baby, created by God . . . by our love for each other."

Nodding, she yielded to his arms, resting her face against his. *Trust . . . trust,* she told herself. *Do not fear.*

"We'll pray every day for the baby's safety," he whispered.

She felt his chest heave as Elias drew her near—as though he, too, was terribly frightened.

CHAPTER 19

Caleb's bantam rooster began to crow, awakened not by the brightness of the moon moving out from behind a cloud, but by the noisy arrival of a carriage. Caleb had been up for nearly a half hour reading a few verses from the old family Bible, merely to start out the Lord's Day. *No other reason,* he told himself, although here lately he was intrigued by his cousin Chris's exuberant talk of the Good Book.

Caleb went to the window and saw a young woman emerge from the carriage, her head bowed. Was it . . . could it be his long-lost sister? He leaned closer to the window and realized it was indeed Rebekah. "What do you know!"

She had not darkened the door since leaving nearly three months ago. Quickly he headed down the stairs, to the back door, chagrined at not having kept in touch as he'd promised that miserable Sunday night in late January. Things had gone awry shortly thereafter, spiraling out of his control. There had been no time for his headstrong sister, with so many problems of his own.

"Well, look at you." He opened the door.

She smiled. "You're up early."

"I might be the only one awake in the house." He stood

near the cookstove, thinking he ought to fire it up to take off the chill. For Daed, especially. "What brings you here?"

"It's communion Sunday—at Preacher Manny's, that is. And even though I'm not a member just yet, I want to have a clean slate, so to speak." She eyed him hesitantly. "Caleb . . . I want to make peace here. If at all possible." Her light blond hair was still parted down the middle and combed back smoothly on top, the twisted strands on the sides pinned beneath her white netting Kapp. He'd thought his sister might have begun to look different by now, spending time with the defectors. "Are ya starin' at me?" she asked softly.

"You look exactly like you did before you left."

"Well, what did ya expect? Ain't like we're fancy folk. We dress Plain and still use horse and buggy." She smiled. "It's the spiritual teachings that are the big difference . . . and I daresay, Caleb, if you gave it a try, you'd find it wonderful-good, too."

He shrugged, put off.

"How's Daed since . . . the accident?" she asked.

"Go and see for yourself," he dared her.

She flung off her shawl. "Be serious, Caleb. It won't be that easy to make amends."

"With Daed?"

"Well, not with *you*." She poked his arm, mischief in her eyes.

"Ach, I miss seein' ya," he admitted. "You oughta come to see Mamm some. You have no idea how hard things are for her—Daed's unable to move without help and all."

"I'm here for that, as well. But do you think I'll be welcomed back?"

He shook his head sadly. "Truth is, I doubt it . . . not if you're bent on stayin' with the heretics."

Her eyes dimmed. "Why do you call us that? You can't condemn what you don't know firsthand, now, can you?"

It occurred to him that she was in touch with Nellie Mae every week at church, or so he assumed. He found himself straining to hold back, even inching away from her, not wanting to ask what he was dying to know.

"What is it?" Her eyes searched his. "You all right, Caleb?"

He forced a chuckle, waving away her question. "I'll see if Daed and Mamm are up yet."

―――――

Rhoda awakened to the sound of wood thrushes bickering loudly in the pasture. A sudden breeze rang the dinner bell hanging on the back porch from a rope high in the eaves. Stretching in the warmth of her bed, she remembered it was Sunday and thought again of attending church with James and Martha. She could help with the babies in the nursery, which might soothe her a bit. Oh, how she wished she could wipe Ken's offhand remarks from her memory!

Getting up, she washed and dressed in Plain attire for the day. It was impossible to push her short hair into a bun, so she merely parted it down the middle and secured it on the sides with bobby pins. Then, putting on her Kapp, which she had not worn in quite some time, she hurried downstairs to start breakfast for Martha before the rest of the family awakened. For herself, though, she would lay out only fruit—grapefruit, apple slices, and half a banana. She wouldn't take any sugar in her coffee, either, nor allow herself a single bite of Martha's scrumptious cinnamon rolls, baked yesterday evening.

A boring breakfast is my lot. . . .

Even Emma seemed to notice her Amish garb as the little girl came running into the kitchen to give her a good-morning hug. Eyeing her but good, Emma grinned shyly, her eyes drifting to the undoubtedly disheveled appearance of Rhoda's too-short hair. She quickly guided Emma to the drawer for her apron, tying it around her waist before her niece gave her yet another hug, as if to say, *I'm glad you look more like yourself today, Aendi Rhoda.*

Sitting at the table to await the rest of the family, Rhoda listened to Emma's chatter about going to "God's house" and wished Ken could allow his own heartstrings to be tugged by such an adorable child.

When James and Martha came to the table with the rest of the children, James's eyes lit up momentarily at seeing Rhoda dressed so conservatively, ready for church. And Martha's smile never once ceased all during breakfast.

The same noisy birds were still quarreling even after the morning meal, their song occasionally rising amidst the ruckus— *ee-oh-lay, ee-oh-lay*—as Rhoda walked to her car. Although she still hoped to stay on with James and Martha, she would not stoop to groveling, in spite of her church attendance today.

Her words were not the only thing she had to convince James. Though headstrong, he was quite responsive to Martha—unlike her brother Ephram, who paid little mind to what his wife ever thought.

So I'll play my cards right—for now, Rhoda decided as she drove to the Beachy meetinghouse, quite pleased with herself and her growing collection of wordly phrases.

She hoped her willingness to don a cape dress and apron— and to attend her brother's church—this beautiful Lord's Day morning might just soften his heart.

———

Rosanna couldn't help noticing the size of Preacher Manny's black sheepdog as she and Elias pulled into his yard Sunday morning. Sitting guard presently on the front porch steps, as if observing all the gray-topped buggies, the dog was a fixture. Nothing moved him, including the comings and goings of the teen boys who were busy leading driving horses to the stable to water them for the long day ahead.

Eventually she took her seat in the kitchen for council with other women church members. They turned in handwritten sheets of paper giving their individual answers to the communion questions, and clusters of the membership were asked to answer as Preacher Manny read the list of questions.

She was glad she'd shared openly with Elias last evening. As unworthy as she felt apart from God's mercy and grace, today Rosanna believed she was ready, indeed, to take communion.

It was during the time of congregational singing that she sensed a near-tangible sweetness in the room; tears of repentance shone on the faces of some. And following communion, during their traditional foot washing, she delighted in the miracle of unity displayed among the membership. She knelt to tenderly wash Betsy Fisher's callused feet, considering the many families separated during the span of time since they'd made their choice to follow the way of salvation. *So many of us heeding the prompting of the Holy Spirit . . .*

When it was time to dry Betsy's feet, Rosanna prayed silently that Ephram and Maryann Fisher, and Rhoda, too, might come to find the Savior in a personal way. With a warm smile, Betsy stooped to slip on her stockings and shoes again, and they traded places as Betsy, in turn, knelt to wash Rosanna's feet. Betsy wept as she did so, her head bowed for the duration of the foot washing. When at last she had finished, she looked up and nodded to Rosanna, her eyes gentle and kind.

Nellie Mae was happy to baby-sit a group of hushed small children. She used her white handkerchief to do clever tricks to entertain them—one minute making imaginary mice, then the next twin babies who slept side by side in a hankie cradle. The little girls' eyes were bright with glee, although they knew better than to make more than a quiet sound out here in the barn.

When at last communion was over, she took the children back to the house to reunite them with their parents. Happy to help further, Nellie offered to work in the kitchen to get the common meal laid on the table. Preacher Manny's wife was glad for the extra assistance and asked her to retrieve a variety of cheeses from the summer kitchen.

Going for the cheese, which needed some preparation yet, Nellie Mae happened to glance out the back window. There, near the barn, she spied Preacher Manny's nephew standing not so far away from Nan. The attractive young fellow was actually grinning and flirting in an understated way.

Well, now, is this Nan's beau? Curiously she watched as he stepped closer to Nan and slipped her a note.

Nan quickly pushed it into her dress pocket and walked away, head high, as if merely strolling to the outhouse. Out of respect for her sister's privacy, Nellie wiped the smile of delight off her face before continuing to the kitchen, still savoring her discovery.

Nan'll wonder how I know, Nellie thought as she sliced the cheese thinly on the cutting board. *I'll have such fun teasing her!*

"What're you lookin' so happy about?" Rosanna came over and hugged her arm.

"Oh, nothin' much."

Rosanna's eyes were puffy but bright. "Romance in the air? The possibility for a beau, maybe? New Order marrieds look awfully handsome with their neat beards."

Nellie blushed and laughed. "No, there's no beau. Not for me."

"Aw, Nellie Mae . . ." Rosanna leaned close. "There *is* a Singin' tonight."

She knew that all too well, thanks to Nan.

"Elias's handsome cousin Jacob will be attendin'."

"It just ain't fair for me to go, honestly," Nellie managed to say.

"Why's that?"

She sighed. With so many womenfolk milling around, it was impossible to explain. " 'Tis just best for now. That's all."

Rosanna smiled. "You'll know when you're ready. . . ."

Appreciating Rosanna's insight, Nellie nodded. "All in God's hands."

———

Ken should see me now, Rhoda thought as she snuggled a baby close. The morning service had lasted longer than was usual, yet she didn't mind. Feeding and changing the infants in the nursery was a joy, even though it had been some weeks since she'd attended the Beachy church. And she truly enjoyed being back. *Even more than I thought . . .*

The baby boy in her arms was fussy now. Rhoda began to walk, whispering in Amish to the wee one, realizing it had been months since she'd spoken her first language to anyone but family. She hadn't been able to erase from her mind Mamma and Nellie Mae's visit to the restaurant yesterday. Not for a minute.

Sighing, she sat down to rock the child, hoping that a change in his position might help to calm him. "I've hurt my mamma terribly." She muttered her woes.

One of the other women asked if she was all right. Rhoda

nodded and suddenly realized she was crying. Stroking his little head, she faced the wall, attempting to compose herself.

Not only have I disappointed my family, I've disappointed myself. . . .

———

Reuben was the last man to make his way into Preacher Manny's temporary house of worship this Lord's Day. His delay was intentional, as he had been outside pacing behind the barn. Several others had been there with him, all of them doubtless begging God to pass them by. So heavy was the burden of ministering to the People . . . the lot brought with it a lifelong pledge, one that came with no financial compensation for being on call at all hours. That, however, was not so much Reuben's worry as was his concern over wayward Rhoda . . . and even Ephram and Maryann, who still embraced the old tradition. He wondered if he shouldn't have asked not to be considered for either the office of deacon or preacher. Yet likely all his worry was for naught. Truly, the very idea of presuming that anyone would nominate him felt prideful.

He sat down on the backless bench next to his son Benjamin to wait his turn to nominate a man to fill the office of deacon. Once that man was divinely appointed, they would all line up and repeat the same process for the ordination of a preacher—whispering the name of an honorable man to Preacher Manny.

Reuben had always kept his mind trained on matters at hand, but today he noticed several of the men, including Elias King, fidgeting three rows ahead. *We're all restless till this is over. . . .*

He was somewhat reticent to nominate for preacher the man he felt was the most deserving of all the married men.

Naming a choice for deacon was another thing—while it was sobering to have the lot fall on you, that particular position did not carry the immense responsibility of preacher. *A near-crushing blow to most.* Some men lost sleep for decades after the lot struck them.

Bishop Joseph rose and stood before them, reading from First Timothy, chapter three. " 'Likewise must the deacons be grave, not double-tongued, not given to much wine, not greedy of filthy lucre; holding the mystery of the faith in a pure conscience. And let these also first be proved; then let them use the office of a deacon, being found blameless.' "

The bishop went on to admonish the wives of the prospective deacons: " 'Be grave, not slanderers, sober, faithful in all things.' "

Bowing his head, Reuben pondered the verses of instruction, praying for God's will to be made known in this place.

Women members formed a line on one side of Preacher Manny's farmhouse, while the men did the same on the opposite side. Betsy watched as their neighbor, the newly elected deacon, Abraham Zook, stepped forward. "Whisper only one name for preacher at the door," he reminded them. For womenfolk it was one kitchen door; for men, it was the other. Neither the bishop nor Preacher Manny could have a vote, but Manny would be standing there in the kitchen to hear the name, which he would pass on to Bishop Joseph once he closed the door. The bishop, for his part, would write each candidate's name on a piece of paper. Any name that was whispered three or more times would be included in the lot.

Betsy's heart pounded as she approached the kitchen door, which was slightly ajar. She dared not look ahead but kept her gaze on the floor. Her mind was on Reuben, hoping he would not be in the preacher's lot. He had enough on him already, what with his sons scattered to the four winds, or so it seemed. *And with our wandering Rhoda. A big worry,* she thought.

She put her hand on her heart and stepped forward. Softly she spoke the name of the man she believed most praiseworthy and then she meekly moved away, returning to the house by way of the front door.

Inside, she joined the others in the large front room who'd already offered their *Stimmen*—votes. No one, except the bishop, would ever know how many votes each man had received.

When Bishop Joseph, solemn as night, came at last into the room and offered a prayer of blessing upon what they were about to do, Betsy squeezed her eyes shut. Afterward, the man of God chose five exceptionally worn *Ausbund* hymnals and placed a single piece of paper inside only one of them. Each hymnal was then secured with a matching rubber band, and the books were arranged on the table.

Bishop Joseph asked, "Does either Preacher Manny or Deacon Zook want to reshuffle the hymnals?"

Silently Preacher Manny stepped forward and made a stack of the books before laying them out on the table to reorder them. He moved aside, allowing the new deacon to do the same. When the ministers appeared satisfied the books had been sufficiently shuffled, the bishop announced the names of the five men in the lot. Elias King was the first named, and Rosanna gasped, a reaction repeated by the next three wives as their husbands' names were called.

Not my Reuben, Betsy hoped, her hands moist.

Bishop Joseph stopped to wipe his eyes. Then, looking at the congregation, he said gravely, "And last . . . Reuben Fisher."

Betsy reached to clasp her daughter-in-law Ida's hand next to her. *Ach, dear man.*

She swallowed hard, fully conscious of the seriousness of the hour . . . and the weight of duty about to befall their soon-to-be chosen servant. The men whose names had been called could no longer refuse the lot, because they'd already promised at their baptism to serve as ordained ministers, should the divine lot strike them.

Betsy was aware of her own heartbeat as the bishop reverently spoke the familiar words, "Are those in the lot here, seated before me, in harmony with the ordinances of the church and the articles of faith?"

Each man answered, "Jah," and then knelt to beseech the Lord to use the biblical process to show which one was to be the minister.

Betsy bowed her head and recalled the day Reuben's cousin Manny had been struck by the lot. His wife and many of his immediate family had wept, their grief something that no one among the People would dare to slight.

When the prayer was finished, Reuben bowed his head as the oldest of the five men went to the table to select one of the hymnals. After a time, he heard that man shuffle back to the bench and sit down.

The next two men each took turns choosing one of the hymnals, but the lot was still not cast.

Only two of us remaining. . . .

Holding his breath, Reuben walked forward to the table. He thought of the added responsibilities ahead should he be chosen by the Lord, and an enormous weight seemed to press on him as he picked up a book.

When the bishop removed the rubber band, Reuben reverently searched the pages for the slip of paper bearing the telltale Bible verse. The lot was not there.

His breath returned and he made his way back to his seat.

Then, realizing the outcome before Elias ever rose to take the remaining hymnal, Reuben heard the sound of weeping as it swept through the room—the ritual mourning. His heart went out to Elias and Rosanna—both so young to receive this divine call, and already so brokenhearted. . . .

Elias's shoulders heaved as he returned the book to the bishop and stood for the bishop's charge. "In the name of the Lord our God and this church, the ministry of preacher has been given to you, Elias King. You shall preach God's Word to the people, and encourage and instruct them to the best of your ability." The bishop went on to list other expected duties before concluding, "May the almighty God strengthen you in this work, with the help of the Holy Spirit. Amen and amen." Bishop Joseph then shook Elias's hand and greeted him with a holy kiss.

Immediately following, the members were instructed to pray and "to encourage Elias and his good wife, Rosanna," and the half-day gathering swiftly came to an end.

Reuben searched the congregation for Betsy and noticed how relieved she looked. He couldn't help wondering how they both might be feeling now had the lot struck Reuben instead of Elias, who was expected to give himself—his time, energy, and insight—for the good of the flock. *All the days of his life.*

————

Elias and Rosanna spoke not a word as they rode. Silence reigned except for the clatter of the buggy wheels on the pavement, punctuated by the steady *clip-clop-clipp*ing of their horse.

Fully aware of her husband's humble heart, Rosanna wiped tears away. *Dear Lord, give Elias the patience of Job, the wisdom of Solomon, the faith of Abraham. . . .*

When Elias reached for her hand and offered a meek smile,

she made an unspoken pledge to help her husband however she could, for as long as she lived.

A sudden and sharp pain shot through her stomach. She started but suppressed the urge to cry out.

"What is it, love?" Elias turned.

"Ach . . . the baby." She cradled her middle, trying not to cry—refusing to allow fear to overtake her.

Elias drew her near. "O Lord, protect our child. And if it be your will, strengthen . . . and heal my wife. I call upon your name, Lord Jesus Christ," he prayed.

Rosanna was comforted by her husband's confidence, yet her own doubts threatened to assail her. *Don't let me lose the baby today, Lord,* she pleaded, thinking of Elias's ordination. *Please, not today. . . .*

Chapter 20

On the way to the Sunday night Singing, Nellie noticed tire tracks in James and Martha's cornfield. "Sure seems odd that James uses his tractor for fieldwork instead of just in the barn like some farmers," she told Nan from the front seat of the family buggy. "Guess he wants to do more than fill silo."

Nan nodded, holding the reins. "It's hard gettin' used to all the modern equipment round Honey Brook."

Nellie noticed the stubble from last year's cornfield covering the ground, keeping the green from springing up. *Less need for horses anymore, it seems.*

Her thoughts turned to the Singing. She half wished she'd stayed home and planned the flower beds with Mamma instead.

I'm thinking like a Maidel, *for sure.*

Crows were *caw-caw*ing in the underbrush, and redwing blackbirds cackled out near the pond behind the new deacon's place. How quickly word would spread of Abraham Zook's and Elias King's ordinations. She wished she might have been sitting next to Rosanna when the lot fell on Elias. She would have cried right along with her.

When the youth had finished with the evening's songs, more than half the fellows sought out girls, moving swiftly across the barn floor. Nellie caught sight again of Ezekiel Mast, Preacher Manny's dark-headed nephew. He strolled confidently to Nan and discreetly touched her hand, his engaging smile and the way his whole face brightened when he spoke to her revealing his intentions. Nan seemed to make no attempt to hide her own brilliant smile, either.

Now that the organized part of the event had concluded, Nellie assumed she would be returning home in Dat's carriage, leaving Nan to ride with Ezekiel in his open buggy. Waiting to let her sister know she was about to leave, Nellie stood there until Nan glanced her way. She motioned toward the barn door and Nan nodded. Satisfied, Nellie turned to depart.

She reached to slide the rustic barn door open, and Jacob King slipped in next to her. Elias's tall and good-looking cousin offered an enthusiastic smile, his big brown eyes intent on her. The heat rushed to her face when she realized how close he was. Rosanna had undoubtedly put a bug in his ear, and for that Nellie was even more mortified—although it wasn't the first time someone had tried to matchmake. *He is awfully cute,* she thought as he heaved open the barn door with one easy shove.

"Goin' out for some air?" He fell into step with her.

"Thought of heading home."

He glanced up at the sky. "But the night's mighty young yet, jah?"

She'd heard that before. All the fellows said it with a new girl when they were at a loss for words. He was definitely going to ask her to go with him in his courting buggy.

Should I? How would Caleb feel?

Jacob glanced down at her, still smiling encouragingly. She felt so uncomfortable walking this way with a new fellow— like she was betraying her former beau.

Suddenly she said, "Jacob, please wait just a minute." She ran back to the barn, motioning for Nan to come quick.

Nan hurried over to her. "I thought you'd left."

"Well, I did, but . . ." She hesitated. "There's someone waitin' outside for me. Ach, Nan . . . this is just so awful."

"You'll be fine. The first date after a breakup is the hardest." So Nan had guessed Nellie might have an opportunity to go riding. "I'll tell ya what, if our buggy's still sittin' out there when I'm ready to leave, I'll drive it home and walk to meet . . . well, my beau, somewhere later."

"No need to be secretive 'bout Ezekiel Mast, ya know."

A smile spread across Nan's face. "Well, don't be goin' and telling anyone."

"Like who?"

"Like anyone," Nan said, eyes twinkling. "And I'll keep mum 'bout Jacob King, too, jah?"

"So you saw him." Nellie sighed. "Now, listen: I haven't decided what I'll do tonight. Honestly, I shouldn't be here at all."

Nan frowned and then leaned closer. "Why not go with Jacob just once? See if he makes you forget Caleb."

Nellie squeezed Nan's hand, wondering if Jacob had given up on her by now. But when she stepped outside again, he was still in the vicinity, talking to his horse, petting the animal's long neck—waiting for her.

———

Nearly afraid to move from her comfortable position in bed, Rosanna lay as motionless as a log, her breaths coming in shallow sighs. She let her body sink into the mattress, embracing its consolation. Aside from her many miscarriages, she had never endured such gripping pain, pain that caused her to clench her jaw to keep from crying out, curling her toes beneath her pretty, handmade quilts. But she must not allow herself to relive those terrible, wrenching times. *Try to think on the Lord,* she told herself. *The Lord and Elias.*

Her dear husband had been so kind to her, it nearly made her cry. She remembered how he'd sat on the bed, holding her hand tenderly as he prayed, entrusting her and their baby to God's will.

Eventually she fell into a deep sleep, dreaming of holding the twins once again, and waking to find Elias near, his arm draped over her protectively.

Rosanna awakened hours later and realized her pain was somewhat lessened. Yet she couldn't trust that it was over, even though she longed for this frightening afternoon to pass.

Elias brought up some tea for her to drink and helped her to sit up slowly, murmuring loving words . . . taking such good care. Truly, she loved him all the more. "There, now, you're goin' to be all right." His lips brushed her forehead. "The pain's subsiding, jah?"

"How'd you know?" she asked.

He reached for her hand. "Your eyes are free of it, love."

"Perhaps a false alarm." Tears sprang to her eyes. "Ach, Elias, I've never heard you pray so earnestly."

He nodded, looking down at their entwined fingers. "I believe the Lord heard the cry of our hearts, Rosanna."

She sipped the tea, letting the warmth fill her slowly as she relaxed in the presence of her husband . . . the newly ordained preacher.

———

It was already dark when Chris headed for home following the Sunday evening meeting with the Mennonite Youth

Fellowship. They'd discussed plans for their annual Lord's Acre fund-raiser coming up this summer, deciding which vegetables to grow for sale.

Zach and a few of the kids from MYF had decided to go out for sodas, including Sheryl, who'd glanced Chris's way as if wondering why he, too, wasn't going. He'd smiled at her as he left, but now, thinking about it, he must have seemed aloof. With all the hours he was putting in at the landscaping office and David Yoder's farm, he was finding it tough to stay focused on his studies and eventual academic future at Eastern Mennonite School in Harrisonburg, Virginia. He was especially interested in their cross-cultural study programs. He was glad they'd added seminary courses less than two years ago, since he hoped to enroll in those once he had his four-year degree.

Chris had been driving only a short time when he noticed in the distance an Amish buggy parked off the road, not many blocks from the ice cream parlor in Honey Brook. He tapped on the brake. He hadn't seen many Amish courting couples milling about yet; the evenings were still too cold. Most of the time they kept to themselves anyway, staying on the back roads, far from prying eyes. He was curious about their secretive dating customs, which Caleb had alluded to in passing. How strange that no one was supposed to know whom you were seeing until the preacher "published" your wedding date and time just a few weeks before the actual wedding.

Slowing down even more, Chris could see a young Amish couple on the shoulder of the road, surveying their broken-down carriage. Without thinking twice, he signaled and slowed to a stop, parking a safe distance behind. The last thing he wanted to do was startle them.

Hopping out, he walked up to the young man, who looked about his own age. "Anything I can do to help?" asked Chris.

"Well, it ain't somethin' that can be fixed tonight. Denki anyways." The boy tipped his straw hat, seemingly frustrated. "I'm goin' to unhitch the horse and lead him home over yonder." He pointed toward the farmhouse in the middle of a vast meadow to the south.

Chris assumed that meant the girl was going to walk with him, but a chilling wind was picking up now. "You sure I can't give you two a lift?"

The young man glanced at his date, whose face was veiled by the shadow of her black bonnet. "Nellie Mae, would ya want to catch a ride home with this Englischer?"

Nellie Mae? Chris was struck cold.

"Nellie Mae Fisher?"

"Jah, how'd ya know?" asked the boy, scrutinizing him.

She held her hands stiffly in front of her. But now that she had turned, he could see that she was definitely the very girl he'd been unable to stop thinking of since they'd met on the road in early February. "Hello, Nellie Mae," he said, suddenly unaware of her date.

She nodded. "Hi, Christian."

The Amish fellow eyed him suspiciously and then looked back at her. "You two know each other?"

"We've met before," Nellie Mae said, still looking at Chris.

"Well, I s'pose it's all right, if you know him," said the boy.

She seemed hesitant, glancing back at her date. "Jah, then," she said. "I'll go on home."

"You'll get there more quickly," the boy urged her.

"All right." She gave a halfhearted wave to her young man before turning to follow Chris, who was still trying to decide if this was just dumb luck or what.

He went to the passenger side and opened the car door,

waiting for her to gather in her long skirt before closing it securely. *Whatever you do, be cool,* he warned himself, not wanting to seem too keyed up.

"Your friend . . . he'll get home okay?" he asked Nellie as he started the car.

"He lives close enough, really. Just over there a ways." She pointed. "Not sure how we broke down. This happens lots on dates." She laughed softly. "You just never know with a horse. . . ."

"You'll have to help me find your house in the dark."

"Oh, ain't so hard. To tell ya the truth, I'm glad to be headin' home earlier rather than so late."

He glanced at her as she made small talk. "Your boyfriend seems like a nice guy."

She looked back at him shyly. "Well, Jacob's not my beau. Just a fella who . . ." Her voice trailed off. Then she continued. "He's nice enough—I don't mean that."

Nodding, he felt a surprising sense of relief. He continued to listen, figuring it was smart to let her do the talking.

"How'd you like the pies?" she asked out of the blue.

"Well, they disappeared real fast."

She let out a little laugh. "Ach, there are more where those came from."

He was pleased by her exceptionally friendly manner. But she was clutching the door handle, keeping her eyes ahead on the road.

"You're not afraid to ride in a car, are you?"

"I rarely ride up front, is all. When I go with paid drivers, it's usually in a van. And we often travel in large groups if we have to go anywhere that's not so safe for the team."

"The team?"

She laughed softly, a melody to his ears. "What we call the horse and carriage."

"Of course." Now *he* was laughing, and much too comfortable with her for his own good.

"Would you mind terribly . . . well, will you tell me more 'bout my sister Suzy and your brother Zach?" she startled him by asking.

His thoughts flew back to the times he'd been with them. "Zach thought she was it, you know . . . and Suzy seemed to think the same about him."

"Do ya think they would've ended up hitched, if she hadn't drowned?"

"I know that Zach was praying about a life mate right before he met Suzy." *Like I did not long ago.* He could see her out of the corner of his eye, sitting there demurely.

She turned to look at him. "Zach's faith led Suzy to Jesus." She sighed, releasing the door handle now and folding her hands. "Suzy wrote 'bout it in her diary, which I decided to read. I broke my promise to her on that, but I know she would forgive me. The scriptures she wrote and things she heard at a nearby campground—all of it—put a longin' in my heart for more. Ach, well, I'll be frank with you, Christian—I wanted to know what Suzy had found."

Stunned that she was so open to talking about the Lord, he listened intently. Nearly all the Amish he'd ever encountered, Caleb and his family included, spoke little of having a personal faith. And they definitely shied away from discussing scripture.

"I'm a follower of Christ," Nellie Mae said boldly. "So are my parents and Nan, the other sister you met." She mentioned several married brothers and their wives who were also saved. "But they're much less conservative—for the time bein', anyway."

He realized now why he was drawn to her, apart from her appealing and natural beauty. Nellie's love for the Lord shone on her face, and he must have known it subconsciously from the first day.

"When did *you* become a Christian?" she asked. "Besides the day you were named 'Christian,' that is."

He smiled at her little pun. "I was young when God called me. I didn't wait—I opened my heart and gave Him my whole life right then. Like my dad and mom did when they were also children."

"Your parents seem very nice, too."

Was she trying to say that *he* was nice?

"I'm glad my parents and Zach met you and Nan at the restaurant that night."

"Did your father like celebrating his birthday out in public like that?" Her voice was softer now.

He had no idea what she meant. "Do you and your family usually observe birthdays at home?"

"Oh, always. But we keep it very simple, with a special dessert only occasionally—no cake with candles, like fancy folk." She paused, perhaps catching herself. Then she went on, as if not fully realizing that a "fancy" person was at the wheel, driving her home. "There's usually homemade ice cream, and the children receive small gifts like at Christmas. And we sing 'Happy Birthday,' too. When we were little, Suzy once gave me a pretty little plate to put on our dresser on my birthday." She sounded slightly sad all of a sudden.

He waited, hoping she might continue, but she fell silent for the whole rest of the drive.

Later, after Chris let her out at the end of her driveway at her insistence, he replayed the whole evening in his head. He couldn't have planned it better. Glancing at the passenger seat where Nellie had sat, he shook his head.

What is it about her? Why is she so unforgettable?

CHAPTER 21

Chris wanted to arrive punctually at the Yoder farm Tuesday afternoon. He spotted Sheryl Kreider at the traffic light in town and, feeling bad about not talking with her Sunday evening, he waved, perhaps a bit too enthusiastically.

She smiled and returned the gesture. *Good.* At least she wasn't ticked off. He didn't want to be without a date for the banquet.

One thought led to another, like dominoes cascading down, and Nellie Mae came to mind as the light turned green. He still was amazed at the strange turn of events, meeting up with Nellie Mae and her "fella." If any aspect of the night had been altered at all—from Zach's decision not to ride home with him to Chris's choosing not to go out to eat after MYF—the chance of his driving her home would have been a big fat zero.

All the same, he'd be better off not daydreaming too frequently about a girl who was off limits to him. Reaching for the radio knob, he found his favorite station, 94.5 WDAC, "the voice of Christian radio." He hoped to play some of that soul-stirring music for David Yoder and Caleb while they rode together to Lancaster for rehabilitation.

Help me always to be a light for you, Lord. . . .

Nearing the outskirts of Bird-in-Hand on the drive back from David Yoder's rehab session, Chris heard David snoring.

217

He and Caleb had made sure he was securely strapped into the locked wheelchair, positioned toward the back of the van.

Caleb glanced over his shoulder from his spot in the front next to Chris. "These sessions take a lot out of Daed."

"And I'm sure they will for a while." At first Chris had sat in the waiting area and studied while Caleb and his dad were in the rehabilitation room, but then Caleb had returned to wait with him. They'd talked for a short time, until the magazines lying on the lamp tables seemed to catch Caleb's attention. So Chris had returned to his history textbook.

Now that they were able to talk more confidentially, out of the public eye, he wanted to ask Caleb about his father's prognosis. "Is there some hope your dad's condition will improve over time?"

"No updates lately. Daed might make some minor progress here and there, but . . ." Caleb shook his head. He looked out the window and then back down, as if unable to express something. At last he spoke in measured tones. "Like I said before, it's kinda impossible to prepare for something like this."

Chris nodded, wishing he could make a difference in his cousin's outlook. "Your father seems determined, though. That's positive."

"Jah, well, determination's always been one of Daed's strengths."

Caleb went on to speak of the many doctors involved in his father's care and "the helpful way the People give to families in crisis—like ours now." He talked up a blue streak as they headed toward Honey Brook.

When they were within a mile or so of the farmhouse, Chris asked, "Do you have extra help lined up for milking on the days we go to rehab?"

"Gideon and Jonah help when they can, and my sister Rebekah is comin' now, too, three days a week. Even Leah and Emmie are pitchin' in some with the farm work." Caleb chuckled. "Abe's got us all workin' hard, that's for sure."

"Your dad must be proud of how well his children are all handling things."

Caleb shrugged. "It's hard to say with Daed." He removed his straw hat, running his hands through his hair. "You know, I enjoy havin' you out for milkin', Chris." He paused. "Not sure how to say this, but . . ."

Chris glanced at him, wondering what Caleb might have on his mind.

"Truth be told, these days, my life's not about much 'cept work and sleep . . . and then more work. Same thing, day in and day out." Caleb fingered his hat on his knees. "Once my brothers leave for home before suppertime, that's the end of my day, pretty much . . . as far as someone to talk to."

"No time for friends . . . or a girl?"

Huffing, Caleb shook his head. "That's it in a nutshell . . . and there's no girl. Not anymore, there isn't."

Unsure what to say, Chris kept his eyes on the road, his ears open.

"She's in love with someone else—well, *something* else." Caleb lowered his voice, and Chris saw him look over his shoulder nervously. "But my father didn't approve anyways, so that's that."

"Sorry, man."

"Jah, so am I."

They were nearing the turnoff to the Yoder farm. "Listen, Caleb . . . anytime I can help so that you can get away from the house for a while, just let me know."

"No need for that," Caleb stated. "I have to admit I'm not quite ready yet to return to the Singings."

"Singings?"

"Two Sunday nights a month the young folks get together, sing for a bit, then pair up and go ridin' round the countryside in the dark." Caleb pushed his hat back onto his head. "When you find the girl you like best, you ask her to marry. Then, come fall, you get hitched durin' wedding season, 'tween November and December."

"You can marry only two months out of the year?" This came as a surprise.

"After baptism . . . jah." He said it so solemnly, Chris wondered if he was hinting at his own aborted plan to wed.

They turned into the driveway, and Chris heard Caleb's father rousing behind them.

"Oh, by the way, my Daed agreed to let you bring Billy out to see the farm," Caleb said quickly.

"That's great, thanks. I'll check when he can come with me." Chris was grateful, but Caleb's gloomy expression made him wonder if more might have been revealed about the former girlfriend Caleb seemed to still care about, if only there had been more miles to today's trip.

It boggled his mind to think he might be the one and only friend in this trying season of his Amish cousin's life.

———

Tired from hours spent breaking a strong mare but convinced the Lord wanted him to make another attempt to visit David Yoder, Reuben made his way toward the man's dairy farm in his old, rickety market wagon, since Nellie Mae needed the family buggy to visit Rosanna King. The afternoon had turned out nice, with the sun as bright as that of a summer's day . . . the sky clearing as far as his eye could see to the west.

He'd awakened early and tilled manure from the barn into their two gardens first thing, including the charity garden planted for the purpose of growing produce for their new minister, Elias King. Betsy had already planted Swiss chard, lettuce, onions, and horseradish. She and the girls would tend it, as well as an abundance of planted celery, *"just in case,"* Betsy had said with a smile. A creamed-celery casserole was standard fare at a wedding feast, and they would need plenty for all their guests. He assumed Betsy had Nan in mind; that daughter seemed to be out with a beau nearly every weekend now.

Reuben neared the Yoders' place, hoping not to be turned away this time. *The poor man needs to know we care!*

When he reined the horse to the left to make the turn into the driveway, he spied a large gray van parked there, blocking the way. Lo and behold, if David Yoder wasn't being brought down out of the van on a wooden ramp built for his wheelchair. "Well, I'll be." From the looks of things, he had himself some outside help, all right. Reuben took a good look at the tall, blond fellow, clearly English. Was this the young man Ephram and Betsy had mentioned? He certainly did resemble Caleb quite a lot.

Not wasting any time getting down from the wagon, Reuben tied up the horse, his curiosity getting the best of him. The process of getting David safely out of the van was painstakingly slow, and he walked over to see if he could be of help to Caleb and his fancy sidekick.

"Hullo, Reuben," Caleb greeted him.

Reuben nodded. "How are yous doing?"

Just then David himself spoke up, tilting in his wheelchair. "I'm all tuckered out, Reuben."

"My father's just returned from his rehabilitation," Caleb explained politely. His eyes held the full story. The session had apparently been grueling.

"I'll come another day, then," Reuben said, but before he turned to leave, Caleb quickly introduced him to "Christian Yoder, my second cousin."

"Good to meet you, Christian." He shook the English fellow's hand.

"And, Chris, this is Reuben Fisher. . . ." Caleb's voice drifted off. Reuben wondered if he'd been about to add *Nellie Mae's father.*

Christian studied him. "Fisher, you said?"

"That's right."

"You wouldn't, by any chance, know of a bakery shop called Nellie's Simple Sweets?" Christian asked, eyes fixed on him.

"Why, that's my daughter's little place—well, she does most of the bakin', anyways."

Christian's face beamed, but he quickly became more subdued.

"Nice meetin' ya," Reuben said as Caleb pushed the wheelchair around the side of the house.

"Very nice to meet you!" Christian called over his shoulder. *Such enthusiasm.*

"What the world?" Reuben muttered on the way back to his horse and wagon.

"You must've stopped in at Nellie's shop," Caleb said once they'd gotten Daed back inside and resting in his room. He handed his cousin a glass of lemonade.

"I've been a couple times, yeah. I bought some pies to surprise my family," Chris said, taking a seat out near the woodpile. "The best I've ever tasted."

Caleb wished to goodness Chris hadn't brought up Nellie's wonderful-good baking. Nobody's compared, that he knew of. Not even his own mother's tasty desserts held a candle to Nellie's. "Ever have her peach pie?" he asked, making small talk.

Chris shook his head. "Not in season right now."

"Jah . . . long out of season." Caleb knew he shouldn't have said it like that, as if he were trying to reveal more than he really cared to.

Chris rose, still holding the lemonade glass—empty now. "Well, I'd better let you get back to your family," he said. "I need to return my dad's van."

"I sure appreciate it—and I know Daed does, 'specially."

"Not a problem," replied Chris. "Maybe sometime your dad and mine can get together again."

"I think Daed might like that." Caleb walked with him toward the large van.

"I wonder if Nellie's bakery shop is still open—do you know?" Chris looked at his wristwatch.

Caleb used to know the minute Nellie closed her shop, but that was another time. Things might have changed. "Can't say I do."

"Well, maybe I'll stop by and see."

Caleb couldn't help but notice the unfamiliar glint in Chris's eye, and he wondered just how well his cousin knew Nellie Mae Fisher.

———

"Ach, why don't you stay for supper?" Rosanna pleaded.

Nellie Mae didn't want to overextend her welcome. "You sure I'm not imposing?"

Rosanna smiled sweetly. "Maybe we can get in another hour or so of quilting afterward. All right?"

She'd come to help Rosanna stitch up the three baby quilts meant for the expectant women in Bird-in-Hand. "I'll stay if you want," she said. "But only if you let me cook supper."

"No, no . . . I'm not an invalid," laughed Rosanna. "I can help."

So they agreed to make supper together, and Rosanna chattered about how much better she was feeling. "I wish you could've heard Elias pray after I had such pain on the ride home Sunday afternoon."

Nellie smiled. "I put your name and the baby's at the top of my prayer list."

Rosanna sliced four hard-boiled eggs to make deviled eggs, grinning. "Seems to me, with all of us prayin', just maybe this time I'll keep my baby."

"The Lord knows how you long for a son for Elias."

She removed the golden yellow yolks and began to mash them with some homemade salad dressing. "I honestly don't have my hopes up much at all, Nellie," she said softly.

"It's normal to be cautious."

"S'pose so . . . which is why Elias and I've decided to accept Lena Stoltzfus's baby." Rosanna looked up at her. "Well, that's not the only reason."

"What do you mean?"

"The main reason was the content of her letter. Elias pointed out to me that it was rather prophetic." She mashed some mustard into the mixture and then added salt.

Nellie waited to hear more, stunned at her friend's change of heart.

"Lena seemed to know—maybe the Lord showed her as she was writing—that the divine lot would fall on Elias last Sunday."

Nellie Mae stopped peeling potatoes to look at her. "You don't mean it!"

"She wrote about wanting her babe to be raised in 'the House of the Lord.' "

"Well, how on earth did she know?"

Rosanna shook her head, shrugging slightly. "Would ya like to read the letter?"

"No, that's all right." A little shiver ran down her back. Truth be known, Nellie was stunned. Why was Elias hoping to raise Lena's baby while praying so hard for Rosanna's and his own child, asking God to help her carry it to term?

CHAPTER 22

It was prayer-meeting night at the Beachy church in Honey Brook. But Rhoda sat in Ken's comfortable living room in Strasburg, her feet up on the plush ottoman as she sipped a thick vanilla milkshake she'd made for herself, against her better judgment.

"You prefer that shake to, say, some dessert wine?" Ken teased, winking at her. He placed his wine glass on the coffee table and slid over next to her on the sofa.

She pouted. "I've all but busted my calorie count for today, so I might as well stick with what I've got here." She'd already indulged in a juicy steak, grilled out on the balcony by none other than "the chef," as Ken playfully referred to himself.

"Aw, honey, you'll get back on the wagon again."

She didn't ask what that meant. Truth was, she was miserable, and when she was this blue, she ate. Not healthy fare, but fatty foods like this thick milkshake made with loads of ice cream, extra sugar, and topped with oodles of real whipped cream. Not to mention the two cherries.

He slipped his arm around her. "Why the sad face?"

Dare she tell him? He was altogether thoughtful and wonderful tonight. *Even so* . . . Taking a deep breath, she knew this was not the time to talk about her desire for a family.

"I'll be all right," she whispered, her face close to his. *When we're married and planning our first baby . . .*

He kissed the back of her hand. "Are you worried about moving away from your brother's? Because the room I showed you will be vacant by Friday. Just say the word and it's yours."

She wanted far more than to be Ken's tenant.

"We'd see each other every day." He smiled.

Sitting up straighter, she pulled away gently. "Ken . . . please, can we talk this over?"

"What's to talk about? You need a place to live. How hard is this?"

She nodded but inside she felt tense. *What would my family think?*

"I'm falling in love with you, Rhoda. We'll have more time together . . . to get to know each other."

I'm already in love with you. She faced him, letting him kiss her gently. "I don't want to do anything that would look . . . well, questionable," she said.

"How can it be wrong to rent a room from your soon-to-be fiancé?"

Her heart beat faster. Was he nearly ready to propose? She couldn't help but smile up at him.

He'll change his mind about a family once we're married, she thought, wrapped up in his arms.

———

His cousin seemed restless when Chris arrived after school Friday with Billy Zercher in tow. Billy had been rather quiet on the first part of the drive, as he usually was in the junior boys' class, but as soon as the Amish farms came into view and the road opened up, Billy became more talkative. Then if he didn't hit it off surprisingly well with Caleb, who seemed to brighten as he took Billy on a tour of the place. In no time, Billy was calling him Cousin Caleb.

Rebekah caught up with Chris in the barn once Caleb took Billy over to the milk house to show him where the milk was cooled and stored. "I hoped I'd have a chance to talk with you again." She wiped her hands on her long, black work apron, her hands still dirty from her work in the vegetable garden. "I wanna say how glad I am for Caleb that he has you to talk to."

Chris smiled. "I enjoy talking to him, too."

She seemed to study him. "You know, back when we were little kids, I always thought you and Caleb could pass for brothers. And I still think that sometimes when I see you two workin' together." She tilted her head, her eyes thoughtful. "You've prob'ly heard about our church split. It's been hard on all of us, but on Caleb more than most." She paused, looking down. "I guess I shouldn't be sayin' anything, 'tis such a private subject, but Caleb and his girl got caught in the middle of that. It really hurt to see him end up, well, single again . . . even though I understand why they broke up."

He didn't know how to respond, or even if he should. Fact was, he'd only heard bits and pieces from Caleb, who was guarded about church talk . . . and his former girlfriend.

"She is the most hardworking, pleasant girl I think I know," Rebekah was saying. "I was lookin' forward to having her as my sister-in-law."

Just then Caleb returned with Billy, who was holding a glass of fresh cow's milk. "Look what Cousin Caleb gave me," Billy said, eyes shining.

Chris couldn't keep from grinning at this usually forlorn boy. "Did you get to see how the lines carry the milk to the big tank?" he asked Billy, who nodded his head, still smiling bigger than Chris had ever seen him.

He's definitely out of his shell!

Chris suddenly wondered if Billy might like one of Nellie's delicious cookies to go with his milk—he hoped she would be at her shop this time. Chris could feel his own smile widen at the thought.

———

As April gave way to May, the lengthening days became ever busier. With the help of James and Benjamin, Dat prepared the cornfield for planting, and Nellie and Nan took turns helping Mamma with early morning weeding in the family vegetable garden and the charity garden pledged to Preacher Elias. Keeping up with the necessary baking was a challenge without the help of either Suzy or Rhoda, but somehow the three Fisher women managed. Life was a flurry of action since spring had sprung, yet with warmer days finally enticing them outdoors, Nellie made time for after-supper walks with Nan. The plentiful wild flowers reminded them of Suzy.

Nellie wondered how Rhoda was getting along over in Strasburg. Martha had said she'd moved last month into a big house owned by her beau, a real estate agent. *"I hope this worldly man doesn't break her heart,"* Martha had whispered to Mamma. Nellie also was concerned. She knew all too well how difficult breaking up could be.

As for Nan, her face literally shone whenever Nellie Mae looked her way. Even right this minute, all smudged with dirt from the garden, Nan was glowing.

"We could be in for a hot day." Nellie stopped to catch her breath and observe the blazing gold of the sunrise beyond the potato field.

Nan paused, too, staring down at the long rows of celery before them. "Why do ya think Mamma insisted on planting so much celery?"

"Isn't it obvious?" Nellie smiled.

"She must guess I'm serious about a beau."

"Well, aren't you?"

Nan blushed. "Oh, Nellie . . . Ezekiel's just the best ever. I love him so."

"You wear your happiness on your face," Nellie said. "I daresay you've been through the mill and back."

"Well, and so have you." Nan started to hoe again. "But I think there's someone who's more than just a little interested in you these days."

Nellie was afraid of this—worried, really. Christian Yoder had become a regular customer of the bakery shop, a fact not lost on Nan or Mamma.

"You'd think Chris Yoder's mother doesn't know how to bake at all." Nan looked at her askance.

She had to respond. Truth was, she'd felt Chris's interested gaze more than once. She'd also contemplated the time he'd driven her home, when Jacob King's buggy broke down. "As nice as he seems, he's surely got himself a girlfriend," Nellie said casually.

"Jah, I would say so." Nan was grinning to beat the band. "If only in his imagination."

"Oh, now, I hope you don't mean what I'm thinkin'."

"Well, what *do* you think, Nellie Mae?"

She didn't honestly know, and the more she tried to dismiss his weekly visits, the more peculiar they seemed. To compound things, Dat had mentioned some time ago that he'd met up with Chris over at the Yoders'. Word had it he was working in the barn and milking with Caleb, for goodness' sake.

"You ignoring me?" Nan asked.

She laughed nervously. "I think Chris is just a friendly fella. And he knows good bakin' when he sees it . . . well, *tastes* it."

That brought more laughter from Nan, and they finished weeding the celery and then headed for the lettuce rows, knowing Mamma was keeping an eye on the baking pies. Nellie was thankful the awkward conversation was over.

———

Nellie sat on her bed that evening, all wrapped up in her bathrobe and wishing she'd taken Rosanna up on reading Lena Stoltzfus's letter. She simply could not understand why Elias and Rosanna were willing to take another such risk, accepting Lena's baby as their own. *If Rosanna were thinking clearly, she wouldn't. Not after the nightmare with her own cousin.*

But Nellie had no choice but to trust her friends' judgment, and since Elias had evidently said the letter was discerning, she shouldn't question that. Especially now that Elias had been ordained by God for the new congregation. Still, she would keep praying for protection over Rosanna's fragile heart.

She opened her Bible to find the picture of Suzy she'd slipped between the pages of John, in chapter three—the chapter that had been the turning point for Dat and Mamma last fall. Looking now at Suzy's face, she sighed, wishing she knew what her sister had known about Christian and Zachary Yoder.

What a strange thing, Chris's visit to the bakery shop each week. Every Thursday afternoon now he came happily to purchase a pie or two—"for my family," he would say, looking right at Nellie Mae with his endearing grin. She couldn't help but wonder when Mamma might make something of it like Nan had today.

Surely Suzy would have felt uneasy at first about going with a boy outside the Amish community. Yet according to her diary, she had been drawn to the Yoders. Quite strongly, in fact. Perhaps because she was fed up with worldly Jay Hess. Nellie remembered having read the final section enough times to know that Chris and Zach were honorable and good. *As fine as any young men I've ever known,* Suzy had written.

Did being honorable and good mean Chris would seek her out, just as Zach had pursued Suzy? Why should Chris look outside his own church for a girlfriend? Perhaps he was only curious about the Amish family that might have been Zach's in-laws had Suzy lived.

She pondered this as she reached beneath her pillow for the snipped-off Kapp strings—the ones from the last head covering Suzy'd ever worn. Holding them as she gazed fondly at the face of her blue-eyed sister, so full of God's love in this picture, she breathed a prayer for wisdom.

———

The clink of china and silverware and the muted talk of couples and their youth group leaders and sponsors blended into the background as Chris held a chair for his date. Their being seated at the head table had come as a surprise to him, although he should have expected it, since his scholarship was going to be announced.

"How's this for front and center?" he joked with Sheryl, who, in a floor-length soft blue dress, looked prettier than he'd ever seen her. Nearly all the other young women were dressed just as conservatively for their church's version of a senior prom, though there would be no dancing here.

"Did you think we'd be sitting here?" she asked softly.

He offered a quick yet heartfelt apology when he saw how ill at ease she was. To distract her, he pointed out the attractive program beneath her napkin and fork, and together they looked at the order of events. There would be a delicious dinner and dessert, then a guest speaker, a cappella singing by the attendees, and special remarks by key youth advisors. All in all, it made for a big night.

They bowed their heads for the blessing when the minister took the podium. Throughout the meal and awards, Chris felt like he had to carry the conversation, what little there was of it between him and his date. He'd known painfully shy girls before, but he'd never spent an entire evening with someone as quiet as Sheryl. Somewhat frustrated, he imagined for a moment what the event might have been like had Nellie been sitting to his right. It was nearly impossible to picture her at this white linen–covered table. Not a single young woman present wore the traditional garb of the Amish.

For everything that was good, even sweet, about Sheryl, he looked forward to next Thursday, when he planned to stop in at the bakery shop again and surprise his mom with yet another tasty dessert. Of course, she was on to him, even though he'd played down his interest in the "young Amish cook."

When his name was called from the podium to announce his academic scholarship to Eastern Mennonite School, Chris forced himself to focus on the present. Sheryl was smiling at him, clapping with all the others.

Gratefully he rose and made his way to their senior pastor, who, smiling, gripped his hand and said, "Well done, Chris . . . the Lord bless you."

He thanked him and returned to his seat, excited about his college plans.

The rest of the evening was a blur of conversations with friends from the youth group. He did his best to include Sheryl, who stood at his side throughout.

When he arrived home later, Chris was exhausted. Such an important evening should have been joyful, yet it had turned into an endurance contest. By comparison to his graduation banquet, the mere twenty minutes he'd spent taking Nellie

Mae Fisher home seemed more thrilling—and all because of the company.

I've got to get Nellie into my life, he thought, taking the stairs two at a time.

CHAPTER 23

Reuben strode through his cornfield on the last day of May, the day before another Lord's Day. Having two preachers and a deacon for the New Order church had boosted the morale of the congregation. Not that it needed boosting, as the house church was packed each Sunday. All of the witnessing they were doing was certainly seeing a gathering in of souls. Even so, the Old Ways still held an iron grip on many of the People, including David Yoder, who was either too weary to visit with him or eating "in private," according to Elizabeth, whenever Reuben stopped by. He had felt like he was making some slight progress toward a connection with David the day the man had spoken directly to him after returning from rehab—but no longer. Reuben felt like a weekly intruder, but he also believed the Lord wanted him to persist, regardless of any frosty reception.

Not one to shy away from a challenge, Reuben took a minute to pray again for David. After all, it took determination to do anything worthwhile, including breeding and breaking horses to sell to other farmers. That attitude had made him a reliable source for driving horses all around Lancaster County and to the east. Farmers came from as far away as Maryland and New Jersey to talk turkey with him about his horses, many of which were bred from lame racehorses he had restored to health and trained for buggy driving.

Jah, persistence is the key to anything worth doing. But the last time he'd gone to see David, even young Rebekah had turned him away, adding quietly how sorry she was that her father did not wish to see him.

"I'll keep offering my friendship," he'd told her.

"Now, I'm not tellin' you to quit comin', mind you," she'd said, a glint in her eye. "Just relaying what my father said." Rebekah had even followed him out to the buggy, waiting till he was inside before adding, "God will bless you, Reuben Fisher. You have been a faithful friend to my father, which hasn't been true of some of his own kin."

Reuben hadn't known what to make of that, but he assumed it had much to do with the demanding and likely ticklish task of caring for David.

The accident had undeniably taken its toll on the whole family. But with this continuous barrier to his attempts to visit David, there was little he could do, except pray. And hope.

He leaned down and pulled up a tall weed, carrying it along with him through the furrowed rows of corn on either side of his feet. As he walked, he prayed over that vast field and the potato field up yonder, asking for a bountiful harvest, after last year's drought. "We sure could use a good crop, Lord. But good or bad, may your will be done."

The sky was devoid of color now, as white as the eggs laid by the purple martins in the two new birdhouses he and Benny, his six-year-old grandson, had built together last winter. Reuben had sent the birdhouses home with James's boy, who had nearly burst his shirt buttons with pride.

Now if Reuben could just find some time, he would ask if his father might not enjoy building a few with him. *For old time's sake.* He rarely saw his parents anymore, but he made a point of writing every week, though he never received a letter back. *They're still miffed, no doubt. . . .*

Thus was the way of things, he was discovering. You stake your claim with Christ and risk the loss of family and friends. He breathed in the familiar earthy tang of dirt and manure at the far perimeter of the field, near the edge of the forest, and tossed the weed from his callused fingers into the wood.

Narrow is the way.

But Reuben was not to be defeated, even though he was somewhat discouraged—a good, long reading of God's Word should cure that. *Surely David is discouraged, too, day in and day out in that wheelchair,* he thought, wishing he might share the encouragement of scripture with the man.

"Help me have patience, Lord," he prayed. "Soften David's heart."

———

Rhoda made a flourish of counting her tip money, raising her right hand high as she placed each bill on the pile. She was ever so glad she'd worked all of Saturday at the restaurant. Glad, too, her boss had noticed how conscientious and helpful she was, often offering to do things that other waitresses weren't as willing to do, like sweeping the floor before closing time. Her customers appreciated her diligence, as well, and her attention to detail was paying off in better tips.

Now if she could only get her checkbook to balance. She glanced up, looking around at the room she'd managed to furnish with a bit of help from Mrs. Kraybill, who'd given her a small sofa and several lamps she'd had stored in the attic.

Even James and Martha had come through with an old bedstead, although it hadn't come with a mattress. She'd had to purchase one outright, borrowing a small sum from Ken, which she hated to do. He was more than happy to help, but that fact didn't make her any less discouraged. Truth was, she was in debt to the hilt. "I need a rich husband," she said to herself with a little laugh.

Opening her notebook, she checked off each bill she was able to pay right now, too aware that the beginning of June was just around the corner.

I'm slowly going under, she thought, adding up her obligations, including her rent to Ken. The hand-to-mouth existence was getting the better of her, and she wondered if she might manage to add more hours at the restaurant. Or better yet, get another housekeeping job.

She sighed. Adding more hours to her workweek meant less time to spend with Ken. He'd already begun to complain. "If I'm to persuade him to marry me, I need to be available to court," she murmured.

To think I gave up a free room at James and Martha's. Goodness, I did the same at my father's house, too.

She pictured Nan and Nellie Mae out tending to the garden, working the soil and running the shop. Dat's corn would be ankle-high by now, and there would be nights when her sisters fell into bed nearly too tired to put on their nightgowns. She had also known such fatigue. She was even tired now, but her weariness stemmed partly from a sense of great concern—even fear. Yet all was well, wasn't it? She had her car, she'd gotten a man, and she had two good, albeit part-time jobs. But there seemed to be scant happiness to accompany all of that, and not a single dime had been saved toward her dreams of travel.

She found herself lying awake at night, thinking about Nan—had she gotten over the loss of her beau? Was Mamma still in deep mourning for a sister Rhoda rarely thought of anymore?

Sighing, she closed her notebook, going to the drawer where she kept Suzy's journal. Opening it to the page she'd marked, she read: *"Be not faithless, but believing."* She'd turned to the line more times than she cared to admit.

Suzy had been fascinated with doubting Thomas, as some referred to the disciple who couldn't believe until he pressed his hand into the Lord's wounded side. Evidently Suzy had been curious about the verse, too—enough so that she'd copied and underlined it.

Rhoda did wonder how Suzy had managed to go from dating a very worldly fellow to a nice Mennonite boy. She pondered her sister's steps and missteps. The way she saw it, Suzy's final months were a series of choices that made little sense.

At least she wasn't broke like me.

Rhoda slipped her stash of money into an envelope for depositing on Monday, conscious of the sudden lump in her throat.

———

Nellie Mae meant not a speck of harm when she decided to open her heart to Nan and show her Suzy's picture.

Nan blinked her eyes. "Ach, where'd you get this?" she gasped, leaning close to look.

Nellie plunged ahead, telling Nan that, at Zach's insistence, Chris Yoder had given her the photo back in February, along with Suzy's bracelet.

"He wanted you to have Suzy's picture?" Nan regarded her like she'd done something sinful.

"He thought we might want it to remember her by," she explained.

Nan refused to touch the picture, but she continued to look at it longingly, like it might disappear. "She seems so happy, doesn't she?"

Nellie Mae couldn't disagree. "I think she was." She went

on to say what Chris had told her about his younger brother and Suzy's close relationship. "They loved each other dearly."

Nan bit her lip, frowning. "I'm glad you showed me, but I almost wish I hadn't seen it."

"I never wanted to upset you. That's why I've kept it secret till now."

Nan scratched her head. "I honestly don't know what to think."

They both knew photographs were prohibited for the Old Order, but nothing had been said about whether or not they were allowed in the New Order church. "I'd rather not bring it up to anyone else," Nellie said, still holding the picture. "I'd hate to part with it. I have to confess it's become precious to me."

Nan nodded, glancing at it again. "Maybe that's why pictures weren't allowed . . . before."

"I'm not sayin' that I couldn't do without it."

"Even so, do you wish you'd never seen it?" Nan leaned back on the bed, her head resting against the footboard, arms folded across her chest.

"It's not an idol to me, if that's what you mean." She clasped the picture to her heart. "I'm sorry, Nan. I don't mean to be short with you."

Nan's eyes were sober. "Maybe there's more to it, sister." She sat up quickly. "Hear me out before you jump to conclusions, all right?"

Nellie pushed a pillow behind her. "I'm listening."

"Is that picture more dear to you because of Suzy . . . or because of who gave it to you?" Nan asked.

She should've seen that coming. "Well, if you're accusing me of liking an Englischer just because he gave me Suzy's picture—"

"I didn't say that."

She huffed. "In so many words, you did. You can't deny it."

Nan rose and stood at the window; then she slowly turned to face her. "Are you sayin' you don't care for this fancy fella?"

Nellie was hurt. "How could you think that?"

"I think it, sister, because I see it on your face."

Nellie was stunned. Did Nan see or know something she herself did not realize? *Am I falling for Chris Yoder, of all things?*

———

The Lord's Day was a tiring one for Nellie Mae. And today Rebekah Yoder had returned home with the Fishers after the common meal, as she sometimes liked to do. Nellie was happy for Nan, who'd missed seeing her friend regularly now that Rebekah was helping her family during the day when she wasn't working for the Ebersols.

Glad for some time to herself, Nellie curled up on her bed to answer circle letters as Nan and Rebekah's happy chatter filtered down the hall.

She was most eager to write to Treva, and as soon as she finished her other letters, she started one to her Bird-in-Hand cousin.

Sunday, June 1, 1967
Dear Treva,

It seems like a long time already since you visited here for Sister's Day. I'm so glad we've had letters to stay in touch. Are you keeping busy? I surely am, what with the bakery shop and tending to the vegetables this year—our gardens are larger than ever. Hopefully, the Lord will see fit to bring them and our crops to a plentiful harvest.

Elias King has settled into his new role and is preaching

some mighty fine sermons. I wish you could hear them! Speaking of the Kings, you might already know this, but Rosanna has told me to share with you that she and Elias have accepted Lena's offer of a baby. He's due in the middle of September, the Lord willing. (They and Lena speak of him as a boy.) Rosanna and Elias have already named him Jonathan, which means "God's gift." It seems fitting, since it was my father's cousin Jonathan Fisher who first shared the Good News over here in Honey Brook.

As for me, I am praying that Lena's baby will be a strong and healthy child, whether a boy or a girl.

She stopped writing, careful not to share too much. Except for the midwife, Ruth Glick, Rosanna had told only Elias and Nellie that she was with child. Ruth had urged Rosanna to see a medical doctor, and Rosanna had agreed, not surprised when the doctor called for bed rest if further pains persisted. Her friend had confided to Nellie her daily fear that she might lose this baby after carrying him or her for four months—indeed, the longest time yet.

Nellie wondered if Elias viewed Lena's baby as a cushion of sorts, so he and Rosanna would not be too devastated if they lost their own. Yet surely Rosanna would tell Lena at some point that she was also in the family way. And what then? Would Lena follow through with her offer?

Finishing her letter, Nellie placed it in her top drawer to mail later. She touched the small blue plate on her dresser, looking fondly at it. *Is Suzy's picture—and everything I love of my sister's—an idol?* She pulled the ever-present Kapp strings from her pocket. "Are these, too?"

She roamed about the room, going to the window to look out on the emerald fields as far as she could see, out to the lush rolling hills along the bright horizon. Had she fooled herself in believing she was past her grief?

Feeling restless, she went to ask Dat if she might take the family buggy out for a ride. As she hitched the horse to the carriage, she pondered what Nan had said about the expression on her face when she spoke of Chris Yoder.

She glanced at the bakery shop and recalled his last visit—if one could call it that. He had been all business as he chose a pie and then paid for it. But he had also looked her way more than necessary and lingered momentarily, as if there was something else on his mind.

She couldn't deny how much she'd enjoyed their conversation in his car back in April. Sometimes she even wondered if he hoped to have another such chance.

The afternoon was perfect for a ride out toward the old mill to the east, and even though she should have known better than to drive down that particular road, she felt compelled to seek out the millpond and the treed area, in all of its green and resplendent beauty.

She hadn't expected to see people walking along the millrace or near the old stone mill, but there was one couple holding hands, veiled a bit by the dense underbrush and leafy trees. Surprised that the sight of them didn't upset her as it might have months ago, Nellie urged the horse along. Always before she'd felt so sad at what she and Caleb had lost . . . how separated they were by their beliefs.

Am I resigned at last to not having him in my life?

It did seem that things remained unsettled between her family and the Yoders. Her kind, caring father had been trying for over two months to visit with David—she'd heard Dat and Mamma discussing it enough times in the kitchen to know Dat had yet to meet with any success. Caleb's father was hard to understand and seemingly unmovable. Was he so stubborn as to continue in his hardhearted ways even when dependent upon others for his daily needs?

Deep in thought and allowing the horse to lead her, Nellie was startled to see Caleb's house coming into view. In a sudden panic, she slowed, searching for a quick turn to the left or to the right, but there were no crossroads. It was not a good idea to try to make a turn on this narrow road, although she recalled Caleb's having done so one night last fall, both to her amazement and to Caleb's obvious relief when he completed the dangerous maneuver.

"Ach, not good," she muttered, wishing for her winter bonnet to hide her face as she approached the lane leading to the Yoders' house.

Elizabeth or one of the girls had planted bright red and white geraniums in the front flower garden, along with pink coralbells and white Shasta daisies, too. The lawn was well manicured and edged along the walkways, showing no sign of neglect. She glanced toward the house and felt a twinge of sadness for David Yoder's terribly altered life. She wished to tell the whole family just how sorry she was.

Yet I'm cut off from them. . . .

She thought not only of Caleb and his family but also of Rhoda and her strides into the world . . . and Ephram, holding fast to the Old Ways, much like the Yoders.

If only all the People could know the truth that ruled her own life: *The Lord's dying breath has given me life.*

She burst into tears, so great was the tenderness she felt toward those who still clung to tradition. With all of her heart, Nellie wished she could sit down and share with each one what the Lord meant to her. *Especially Caleb and his poor hurting family.*

CHAPTER 24

The days dragged on in one sense yet seemed to fly by in another. Caleb and his brothers weren't needed nearly as often to move their father to the wheelchair, since Daed mostly stayed in bed. Even with continual treatment, their father's and the doctors' efforts seemed futile. And the realization that Daed's health was declining struck Caleb mighty hard as he and Chris prepared for milking on this mid-June afternoon.

He and Chris had become good friends but, although there was much he wanted to tell his cousin, Caleb held back, lest he be misunderstood, especially where Nellie Mae was concerned. No matter how fond he was of Chris, his regrets over Nellie Mae were no one's business. And anyway, his cousin smiled much too broadly for his liking whenever Nellie's Simple Sweets was mentioned.

"My dad wants to visit your father," Chris told him before leaving for home, after milking was done. "We could drop by this Sunday after church, if that's okay."

Caleb shook his head. "Well, I'd hate for you to make a trip out here for nothin'. You know how it is . . . Daed's not so keen on visitors."

"Well, we're not talking about Reuben Fisher here. Wouldn't your dad be more willing to see his own cousin?"

"Jah, prob'ly. Though it's been a long time."

"Wonder why they drifted apart."

Caleb shrugged. He didn't know but could guess—likely something to do with the ongoing debate over the *hope of* versus the *assurance of* salvation. But Daed wouldn't mind so much what his fancy cousin believed. John wasn't trying to change his colors like Reuben and Manny's other followers had attempted to do.

Since Daed's accident, Caleb had personally had to turn away numerous folk from the New Order church, none of them having been received even once. Daed had made his stand and wasn't budging. Of course, with John Yoder being kin and all, who was to know? "Well, if you just drop by, maybe he would be more agreeable."

Chris opened his car door and climbed in. "Then that's what we'll do." He waved as the engine roared to life.

"See ya Sunday!" Caleb called, watching the car make the turnaround before heading down the lane toward the road. All the while, Chris's arm stuck out of the window, held high in a sweeping gesture similar to Caleb's own way of waving good-bye.

Sure hope Daed doesn't turn them away.

Heading for the house, Caleb sat on the back stoop, staring down at Mamm's handiwork there in the small garden near the walkway. Years ago, they'd pressed some of their old shoes into the soil, making little plant holders for petunias and marigolds. The shoes were holding up just fine, withstanding the wintry elements each year.

The sight of his outgrown boyhood shoes brought back memories of better days. *Before Daed's accident.*

At times, when anger threatened to overtake him, he wished they'd sold away the offending mule. But Daed had been the one to insist they keep the animal. Far be it from Caleb to say otherwise.

Not aware of the hour, he looked up and saw Rebekah coming up the driveway on foot, carrying a cake holder. "Hullo, *Bruder!*" she called. "It's almost suppertime, ain't so?"

"You brought me some dessert?" He chuckled and rose to meet her, always glad to see his most cheerful sister. "What kind of cake?" He leaned down as they walked, comically trying to nose his way in for a peek.

"Now, you just wait and see." She hurried toward the back door and then paused, a worried look on her face. "Tell me . . . how's Daed doin' today?"

He winced, dreading to say. "Not so good, I'm afraid."

"The cake might perk him up."

"It'll take more than that."

She grimaced. "I wonder if he'll listen while I read my favorite Bible verses."

"Well, *I* can read to him." He caught himself, not wanting to reveal that he'd been curious to read for himself the chapter in John so many of the New Order folk had talked about at the outset of the split. Truth be told, Chris's fondness for scripture had him thinking a bit.

She eyed him. "What'd you say?"

"The Good Book—anyone can read it to Daed. That's all."

She grinned at him, reaching for the door. "Well, what's keepin' *you*, then?"

Her words haunted him all during supper. But each time he glanced toward the head of the table, it was all he could do to keep smiling, for his mother's sake. And for his sisters', too, surprised that Rebekah was permitted to partake of the meal with them.

Yet there was no getting around it: Daed was failing—weakening physically and emotionally—before their eyes.

————

Rhoda was delighted at the tenderness of the pork chops she'd made for Ken. There were mashed potatoes, gravy, and buttered carrots and peas. She'd baked dinner rolls, plump and flaky. More often than not, they ate supper by candlelight in his third-floor suite, where they enjoyed the view from the large windows and each other's company.

Ken mentioned reading in the paper about a midair crash of two airplanes reported over the radio. Rhoda wondered, *Is he trying to discourage my dream of traveling by plane?*

"Many people were killed." He picked up his knife to cut his meat.

"That's dreadful," Rhoda agreed, "but it doesn't scare me away from wanting to fly. Maybe if I had children, I would think differently, but—"

He looked up at her sharply. "Old Order Amish girls don't fly . . . it's against their upbringing."

"But I'm finished with that life," she said.

"Are you?" He narrowed his eyes. "Finished with the God-thing, the apron strings, the brats, the whole nine yards?"

She felt her lips part but was shocked into silence. She was only leaving the Old Order. She'd never said she had given up God or her dreams of a family.

He searched her face. "Well? Are we through with all the hints about kids?"

She felt as frustrated as she'd ever been in her life. Getting up, she walked to the sliding-glass doors, staring out at the grill and the plush patio furniture. Everywhere she looked, things were colorful, pretty, neatly arranged. Ken had plenty of money, certainly. Why didn't he want plenty of children? At least a few? She struggled not to cry.

She felt his gaze on her and glanced back at him.

"You look like you're going to be ill," he said.

"When I think of the life my family would have me live, I do feel sick. But when I think about the kind of life you seem to want . . . with no little ones, I feel just as ill. If not more so."

Hadn't Ken been the one to say life was what you made it? Well, she was determined to make a life with him. She straightened her shoulders and took a deep breath. "I want to have a family someday." She turned to face him. "A big family."

He frowned. "It's a dead issue, Rhoda. There is no room for debate on kids, I can assure you."

Now she was crushed. "What's so terrible about babies?" Her neck was hot. Why did he feel so strongly about this?

He sat tall and still at the table. "I thought you wanted to leave all that outdated tradition behind you. Be a modern woman."

"I never said that. Sure, I wanted to make a new life for myself . . . and then I met you, Ken. It seemed like our friendship was meant to be. Providential, as my people say."

He scrutinized her; then he shook his head in disgust. "Come on, Rhoda. There is no such thing as 'providential.' God is just a comfortable myth. We've talked about this before. Your family really brainwashed you, didn't they?" He crumpled his napkin and tossed it down.

"No." Tears filled her eyes. She knew he wasn't fond of their long Preaching services, but how could he not believe in God himself? No matter how hard she had tried to embrace Ken's views, she simply could not dismiss the reality of the Creator.

"What did you think? That you could change my mind?" She cringed at the cutting tone of his voice. "Change *me*?"

She wouldn't confess she'd thought that very thing. She wouldn't tell him she'd been sure, once they were married, she could convince him what a wonderful father he'd be. Or that she'd imagined the two of them and their children attending church together. How stupid she felt now. How deceptive. "I'm sorry, Ken. It was wrong of me to let things go so far between us."

"No," he said quickly. "I was wrong . . . to think this could ever work out." He sighed loudly. "I just don't seem to understand women—ever!"

She groaned audibly, and Ken glared at her. But she had no more to say, so she walked to the door. "I'll let myself out."

He didn't follow to see her leave, or ask if they could talk further. He just let her walk away, and all the while she wanted to kick herself for believing in a pipe dream, another one of Ken's English expressions. Well, now it was hers, too.

What a ridiculous thing to move to Strasburg, only in hopes of getting married. She hurried to her room and closed the door. *Now what?* She went to sit on her bed. *Am I stuck here, with this lease to Ken?*

She buried her face in her hands.

"I'll put all the jam away." Nellie Mae stacked several glass jars and stored them in the utility room cupboard while Mamma went and sat next to Dat. It was nearly time for Bible reading, and already her father was thumbing through the Good Book, looking for the spot where he'd left off last evening.

"Mamma, you've been pushin' yourself too hard lately." Nan glanced over her shoulder as she washed dishes.

"Well, picking strawberries is always the biggest chore," Mamma said.

"I can't believe how much jam we've put up," Nan said.

"Don't forget the pies," Dat joked, smacking his lips.

Nellie wondered if Chris had ever tasted strawberry-rhubarb pie. *Just delicious.* She reprimanded herself for thinking of him so familiar-like; then she grinned.

"Maybe you should take one of my pies over to the Yoders' tomorrow, Dat," she said, knowing her father still hadn't gotten a foot in the door. "Maybe a strawberry pie will do the trick."

"Something's got to give." Mamma touched Dat's arm gently.

Nan placed Mamma's big kettle on the rack to be dried. "Rebekah says her mother cries a lot," Nan told them.

"Aw, Nan . . . did she now?" Mamma said, a frown marring her face.

"Well, word has it David's goin' downhill," Dat added.

This news deepened Nellie Mae's sorrow for the family. "What'll happen if . . . ?" She couldn't bring herself to finish.

"I say we pray right now." Dat motioned to them.

Nan dried her hands quickly, and the four of them joined hands while Dat, who could scarcely speak for his tears, asked the Lord to extend David's life—so he might find Jesus before it was too late.

Silently Nellie Mae prayed the same for Caleb, hoping her former beau would not follow in his father's stubborn footsteps.

Reuben excused himself to go upstairs after Bible reading. Betsy said she'd stay down in the kitchen with the girls, which was just as well, as he found he could beseech the Lord better when praying alone.

He pulled out his prayer list, beginning with his own father, who was up in years. How he missed talking to . . . learning from, gleaning lost wisdom from the man. Then he prayed for each of his sons, their wives, and their children—those born and yet to be born.

Last of all, he whispered Rhoda's name. "Bring my daughter to her senses soon, O Lord."

So many needs. He wiped his eyes and continued to kneel like a trusting child at his side of the bed.

After a time, when his burden had lifted some, he went to the dresser and found his writing tablet. Tearing out a sheet, he began to write to his father.

Friday, June 20
Dear Daed,

Hello from Honey Brook. Here I sit, writing to you and missing you. I think of you and Mamm so often, hoping you're both well.

The thought popped into my head that we might build a martin birdhouse together, you and I. Benny and I did just that not so long ago. We had a wonderful-good time, and I couldn't help but recall how you and I did the same thing when I was but a boy.

I'll be glad to bring all the necessary materials—get me a hired driver to haul everything over to your place. Betsy could bring a hamper of food and visit with Mamm, if it suits her. What do you think of that?

I'll wait to hear from you. And if you don't reply, I'll simply write again next week.

May the Lord be with you over there in Bird-in-Hand.

> *Your son,*
> *Reuben Fisher*

Folding the letter, he was not ready to give up on either his father or his old friend David. Nor would he turn his back on daughter Rhoda, although it seemed she'd done so to them.

Expelling his breath, Reuben rose and slipped the letter beneath the gas lantern on the dresser. Thankfully, the dear Lord had not given up on him.

Or any of us.

————

Caleb had been waiting for his English cousins to arrive, trying not to be too anxious as he glanced out the front-room window every few minutes. He tried to picture his father's first cousin John. It had been years since he and his wife and their five boys had come to visit. There was no apparent reason for them not to have further fellowship . . . none that he knew of, other than their obvious differences. He'd never once heard his father speak ill of his Mennonite relatives. If anything, Daed held them in high regard; otherwise Chris would not be allowed to work here alongside Caleb and his brothers.

He looked across the expanse of the front room toward the door that led to Daed's small room. The door was slightly open, and Caleb could hear his father muttering to himself, something he'd begun to do more recently, definitely disturbed by his circumstances. *Who can blame him?*

Caleb often tried to put himself in his father's shoes, but it just wasn't possible. He was quick on his feet, strong, and energetic, and youth was on his side.

Seeing Chris's car pull into the driveway, he went to his father's bedroom door, peering in through the crack. *Good, he's awake.* Caleb hurried out the back way to greet Chris and his father, hoping Daed might agree to see them. If he refused, he hoped at least that he would not shout as he had the other day when Preacher Manny had dropped by after Nellie's father, Reuben Fisher. The man had to have some grit in him to keep coming back for more rejection.

Chris and his dad were getting out of the car as Caleb

went to meet them. He was immediately taken by their Sunday attire, the dark suits and ties they'd probably donned to attend church. In fact, they were so fancy looking, he worried it might be off-putting to Daed. *Either that or he'll view it as a compliment.*

"Hi again, Caleb." Chris offered the same friendly smile he always did when he arrived. "You remember my dad, don't you?" He motioned toward his father, a tall, slender blond man who stretched out a hand to firmly shake Caleb's.

"Good to see you again," Caleb said, leading the way toward the house. "My father's awake . . . but I should warn you—"

"No worries. I've already told Dad," Chris interjected.

Caleb felt some relief. "Mamm's upstairs resting. So are my sisters." He opened the back door. "It's just the three of us downstairs . . . and Daed."

Chris offered a sympathetic nod, hanging back to let his father go first as they headed through the kitchen. A plate of sandwiches was laid out on the table in anticipation of their arrival.

"Would ya like anything to eat or drink first?" Caleb asked, mindful of his role as host.

"Thanks for the offer, but we'll wait till after we've spoken to your father, if you don't mind," John said graciously. Chris's father seemed calm and poised, and Caleb thought unexpectedly of Nellie Mae, who had always been so hesitant, even frightened around Daed.

Moving toward the small bedroom, he paused, glanced back at Chris, and then pushed the door fully open. His father was staring at the ceiling, eyes glazed from boredom and pain. "Daed . . . your cousins are here," he said.

Daed lay propped up on the bed with an abundance of pillows, thanks to Mamm, who'd gotten him situated before heading upstairs. Caleb expected his father's booming voice of disapproval to erupt at any moment. Instead, Daed eyed his cousins before smiling faintly. "Have yous come for my funeral?"

John lost no time moving toward the bed. He leaned down to shake hands. "We came directly from church," he said. "That's why we're wearing monkey suits."

"Well, pull up a chair." Daed motioned with his hand.

Caleb was shocked. No tantrum today? By the looks of things, it seemed Daed might even enjoy this visit. He was listening peacefully as John began to reminisce about the old days and their childhood visits to Uncle Enos's. "Remember that old fishing hole, out behind the rickety barn? We cut our way to ice-fish one winter."

Daed blinked his eyes in response. "Gut days, jah. Mighty gut."

The two older men did most of the talking, and Caleb could sense that Chris was pleased at the way things were going.

Daed's voice suddenly grew stronger. "It's awful kind of you, John, to loan that fancy van of yours . . . for my trips to rehabilitation."

"Glad to do it. Just give Chris a holler."

Daed breathed in long and slow, looking now at Chris. "And your boy's been a big help here. I owe ya both."

"Nothing doing." John moved his chair closer.

"Well, I'm glad you came today, so I could say Denki in person." He drew another long breath before continuing. "You see, I won't be needin' your vehicle any longer, John. Won't be goin' in for treatments anymore, neither."

Caleb perked up his ears. *What?*

"But they're essential, right, David?" John frowned, folding his hands. "They'll strengthen you over time."

Daed shook his head weakly. "Well, there ain't much time

left for me, so I won't be pushin' myself out the door any longer. They can carry me out when I'm dead and gone, that's what."

Caleb was embarrassed. Even if Daed believed he wouldn't live much longer, it wasn't right to say so in front of company.

"Surely you don't want to throw in the towel, do you?" John asked, gesturing to Chris. His cousin took the hint, glanced at Caleb, and rose, stepping out of the room.

Caleb followed quickly behind, not knowing what Chris's father intended to say to Daed. But obviously it was personal.

He caught up with Chris out in the kitchen, and he reached for two apples in the bowl on the table, handing one to his cousin. "Here, help yourself to a sandwich, too," he said before heading toward the back door.

Chris complied and followed. "Your father's dejected," he said soberly. "He's made a bad turn since his last rehab session, hasn't he?"

"Haven't seen him like this before today, to tell you the truth." Caleb directed Chris toward the tobacco shed, where they could sit on some old stools in back. "Maybe it's time I slipped Reuben Fisher in to visit my father . . . if they're to see each other again before—"

"So Reuben and your dad were friends at one time?" Chris looked surprised.

"They go back a long ways."

"And now? Evidently Reuben's very anxious to see your dad." Chris took a bite of his sandwich.

Chris could always be counted on for a line of questions, always wanting to get to the bottom of things. "Well, there's a lot of history there. Daed's upset because Reuben's Fisher cousins—Jonathan and Preacher Manny—got an upheaval started when they decided the Good Book was not only to be studied but memorized and discussed, too. Every which way."

Chris's eyes grew wide. "Are you sayin' you're not supposed to do any or all of the above?"

"Scripture isn't s'posed to be fussed over, no."

"Not even talked about?" Chris's face registered disbelief.

"The ministers do that at Preaching service, every other week. Mostly they expound on the Sermon on the Mount." *Why should I have to defend the church fathers?* "For the rest of us, scripture is only meant to be read."

Chris seemed appalled. "But it's inspired by God—every word. Isn't that what you believe, Caleb?"

Uncomfortable now, Caleb welcomed the sound of a large flock of birds flying low overhead, and he craned his neck to look. All the while, he wondered why John's father had left the Amish decades ago. As curious as he was, he wasn't going to ask. Another day, maybe.

Chris had never been so pointed before. Even so, Caleb did not feel antagonistic, not as he might've had someone like Reuben or others from the new group come tooting the dangerous horn of salvation through grace. No, the way Chris talked typically wasn't threatening. And now he suddenly felt as he had when his own "saved" sister, Rebekah, had mentioned reading the Bible to Daed earlier. "There are times when I'm befuddled," he confessed, " 'bout what to believe."

Chris nodded, shifting his weight on the stool. "I hear you. But there *is* something to hang on to—something that doesn't change. *Someone* who can be counted on, no matter what's going on in your life."

This sounded too much like the way Nellie Mae had talked. Caleb could still picture her standing so prettily behind the display counter in her bakery shop, her face glowing—why?—

his arms gentle around her despite his fierce desire to protect her from being swept up in the fanciful talk.

And here he was again—his own cousin about to spout off more of the same.

Yet Chris was respectful. He didn't just forge ahead with what he was surely impatient to say. He waited for Caleb to nod or say something, to give consent. But Caleb was determined to be true to the old church, aware of the pull on him. Above all, he must be loyal to the only church he knew, or cared to know. For this reason, he budged not even an inch.

But long after Chris and his father drove away, Caleb could not escape his cousin's words: *"Someone who can be counted on . . ."*

CHAPTER 25

A few hours before suppertime, Daed asked Caleb to call Mamm so he could talk with her alone. Caleb nodded and left the bedroom his father had claimed as his own since the accident. *He needs a doctor,* he thought, wishing Daed hadn't decided to abandon his treatments.

Ever since Daed's cousins had left earlier today, Caleb had wondered what Daed and John had discussed. He didn't understand how Daed could simply give up and not want to get stronger.

I won't think about this now!

He knew the cows would be lined up at the gate, waiting for their feed—and for milking. Today being the Lord's Day, it would take him at least twice as long, since his three brothers usually stayed put at home Sunday afternoons.

Rebekah hadn't arrived yet, either, so he'd have to get Leah and Emmie to help, unless the neighbors wandered over to pitch in, as they sometimes did on weekends.

Caleb set off to the pasture to open the gate for the cows, glancing toward the cornfield, still watching for any extra help. He wondered if Daed and Gideon had already discussed what would happen if his father were to die. Would Abe continue to run things? Would Jonah? Which of his siblings would care for Mamm in her old age? Perhaps Daed was talking to Mamm about that even now, holed up as they were in the small main-floor bedroom.

To keep from fretting, he pondered the bishop's sermon— the longer of the two sermons this morning. Not a single time today had he dozed off. The bishop was changing his way of preaching, repeating scriptures that seemed foreign to Caleb. Had anyone else noticed? There was no getting Mamm's or Leah's opinion, since they'd taken their turn staying at home with Daed. And anyway, for the most part, he didn't discuss church-related matters with his mother and sisters. Only Rebekah had ever shown any interest in such things, but he couldn't talk to her now, not since she'd gone to live with the Ebersols. *Since she'd gone off the deep end* . . .

Caleb was washing down the fifth cow in the first row when here came Leah, Emmie, and Mamm. He looked away when he saw how puffy and red Mamm's eyes were. "I don't want to be gone long from Daed," she said quickly, which created even more apprehension in him.

What's happening? Is it possible my father's dying?

After milking, and before a light supper of sandwiches, red beet eggs, and celery sticks with peanut butter, Rebekah sat down with Caleb at the far end of the table. As was her way, she smiled freely.

Placing a plateful of cookies in front of him, she said, "I baked your favorites yesterday."

He reached for a chocolate chip cookie, eyeing the peanut butter ones, as well, but she slid the plate back quickly. "You'll spoil your supper, Caleb Yoder."

"Where have I heard *that* before?" He glanced at Mamm, worry slapping him in the pit of his stomach each time he noted her serious demeanor. She was even more solemn than earlier. *Why?* He wanted to fool himself into thinking it was merely her usual response to the Lord's Day; she'd always been a stickler for observing Sundays reverently. But something told him her glum spirits had more to do with Daed's deteriorating condition. That and whatever they'd discussed alone.

Mamm sat with them for the silent prayer, which Caleb offered as the only male present at the table. Then she rose and dished up food for Daed. "I'll be helping your father with his meal tonight" was all she said before leaving the kitchen.

Once the door to Daed's room was latched shut, Rebekah leaned forward. Her smile faded. "I don't mean to frighten yous, but Mamma's told me Daed believes his days are numbered."

Leah gasped, covering her mouth with her hand, and Emmie shook her head, mouthing, *No.*

"He's settin' his house in order," Rebekah continued, looking toward Caleb now.

"What's that mean?" Caleb managed to ask.

"Well, I know you may not understand this, but if I may be so bold . . ." She paused, her eyes on Leah and Emmie. Then she faced Caleb again. "The way I see it, God's beginnin' to answer the prayers that have gone up for our family . . . and for Daed, 'specially."

Unable to grasp her point, Caleb stared at her. "Meaning what?"

"Evidently Daed's makin' peace with God . . . in his own way." Rebekah reached for her sandwich.

"But he did that at his baptism," Leah said, "back when he joined church as a youth."

Rebekah glanced at Caleb. "Well, if you go walkin' with me in a bit, I'll tell you more 'bout what I mean. And the reason for the break in the old church, too, in case you don't know."

"Had something to do with a big debate," Caleb said. He hadn't meant to sound so dismissive.

Rebekah's face lit up—the same glow he'd seen on Nellie Mae's face the day they'd said their good-byes. "Jah, the split was about saving grace," she said. "And makin' a public confession of it."

"I'll take a walk with ya, Rebekah," said Leah, her voice surprisingly bold.

Caleb wasn't interested in Rebekah's views of the church split. He already knew far too much about all of that.

———

Rosanna saw the tobacco farmer first as the man turned into their lane. *Coming for counsel with Elias, no doubt.* She touched Elias's hand as they lingered at the table, having a piece of strawberry pie.

"Mind if I go out and talk to him?" Her husband rose quickly.

"Supper's through," she said softly, and Elias got up from the table and headed for the back door. No question, he was taking his ordination seriously, even to the detriment of his own work, just as Preacher Manny and others of the ministerial brethren did. Elias not only embraced his divine calling, but his was truly a caring heart for the congregation.

The Lord knew what He was doing when He chose him. . . .

Rosanna carried the dishes to the sink, surprised again at how much stronger she felt lately. *Will I keep this wee one, Lord?* It was the question she dared not ponder too much, for she was so much in love with this baby, conceived in the midst of her great sadness over the loss of the Beiler babies. Little Eli and Rosie were growing like weeds now—she'd seen them again from afar, all bunched up with John and Kate and their other children in their carriage, on the way to Preaching service this very morning. She hadn't winced at the sight of them sitting on Kate's and her oldest daughter's laps but waved as they came up closer on the road. Elias had done the same, and after the two buggies passed, neither he nor she had mentioned the twins or John and Kate. In fact, they'd said nary a word, which seemed odd to Rosanna now, thinking back on it. Yet what a blessing to realize her darling also held no animosity.

Washing the last dish, she reached for a tea towel. She glanced out the window, observing her husband. Perhaps he was discussing tractors and what they could and could not be used for in the fields, the subject of much talk these days. Now that fieldwork was going on all over Honey Brook, this fellow probably assumed he could make some time by using his tractor for transportation on the road, as she'd heard of others doing. Such was not permitted by the new ordinance, and several families had left the New Order church over this issue, joining up with the Beachys, who allowed more liberal use of tractors.

For herself, she much preferred to think about all the pretty yarn she planned to purchase this week with the money from her quilts. She wanted to begin crocheting baby afghans for Lena's baby, whom Lena intended for the Amish midwife to bring directly to the Kings', following his birth. Lena had started referring to herself as the "baby carrier," declaring Rosanna the mother appointed by God. Because of her own secret pregnancy, Rosanna felt rather sheepish reading Lena's touching letters, even though she cherished each one and saved them in a pretty wooden box Elias had built for her as a recent birthday gift.

Another glimpse outside showed Elias was still engaged in conversation, his arms folded—likely he would be busy for a while longer. Perhaps Rosanna should take this time now to reply to Lena.

With a prayer in her heart, she sat down to pen her most private thoughts, words that might completely change Lena's mind.

Sunday, June 22
Dear Lena,
> *I can't tell you how often I've been in prayer here. I truly believe with you that your baby is to become Elias's and my own. And we will care for him as lovingly as we would a flesh-and-blood son.*
>
> *There is more for you to know and to understand, though—something ever so dear to me. You see, I, too, am with child. It is my hope and prayer that I will carry the baby in my womb to term, something that has never happened before. Yet, if things continue as they are—and oh, how we pray they will—I'll begin to show soon, and there will be talk wending your direction that I am in the family way.*
>
> *I have only a small hope that this little one, who lies so close to my heart, will be born alive. Our baby's sisters and brothers all reside in heaven now, with our Lord, whose will we desire in all things. Elias says he likes to think the angels are caring for them till we can get there to do that ourselves.*
>
> *In the meantime, I am being ever so careful, seeing a doctor and taking bed rest, too, praying that this time these things will make a difference. Will you keep me in your daily prayers, just as I pray for you, dear sister in the Lord?*

Thinking about Lena's possible reaction, she dared not write for much longer. It might have been wiser to wait to tell this news to Lena in person, but the doctor had put the nix on any travel right now for more than twenty minutes at a time. And she needed someone to go along with her for even those short trips, which meant she'd be asking Linda Fisher to go with her to the yard-goods store this week.

Hoping Lena would not be disheartened by word of the pregnancy, Rosanna finished her letter and signed off, deciding to put her feet up while she awaited Elias's return inside. In her heart of hearts, she hoped this revelation would not change Lena's mind. But why should she worry about that, when it was the Lord who'd prompted Lena to offer her child in the first place?

I must remember the scripture to not be anxious.

———

Caleb paced near the window and waited in the kitchen for his mother to emerge from Daed's room, hoping she might tell him more about Daed's conversation with his cousin John. Could Daed be softening? Knowing his father, Caleb didn't see how that was possible.

Even impending death wouldn't deter Daed from his life course. The Old Ways were stamped on his heart. *"You're either in the church or out. There's no betwixt and between,"* his father had always said.

In a few minutes, Mamm came into the kitchen, her face tearstained. She motioned for Caleb. "Your father's askin' for ya."

He steeled his heart and made his way to the small room, where he stood in the door before entering. Daed looked to be sleeping.

Silently Caleb sat on the cane chair across from the bed, watching his father's chest rise and fall. He sat there, hands folded, and understood for the first time something of the misery Nellie Mae and her family had endured when they lost Suzy.

Chris had said a person couldn't prepare for something like a death in the family. No matter how you thought you might react, you never truly knew till the time came.

Has it come already? He leaned forward, checking to see if his father was indeed breathing. *Slowly, jah . . . mighty slow.*

But lest he become fearful, sitting in a room with death nipping at his father's heels, he let his thoughts fly away to his cousin Chris. Truly, he was the happiest person Caleb had ever known, and he found himself comparing him to Rebekah.

So what was it they had that he lacked? They both claimed to be saved, he knew that. They also talked of a freedom they experienced. Nearly everything they did or said was somehow linked to God's Son, their "Lord and Savior."

From where he sat, he could see Rebekah and Leah through the window, returning from their walk. He wondered what things Rebekah was filling Leah's head with now. Since her return visits, Rebekah had gone out of her way to attempt to influence each of her sisters for the new church.

Caleb smiled, allowing a speck of momentary pride. *She'll have a hard time cornering me.*

Closing his eyes, he shut out the image of his helpless father. The last thing he wanted to hear today was a deathbed appeal.

After some time had passed, his father whispered, "Caleb."

Jerking to attention, he sat up. "I'm here, Daed."

"My cousin came to set me straight. . . ." His father's voice faltered, then began again, stronger now. "He showed me what a stubborn soul I've been."

Caleb didn't know how to respond. Never before had his father admitted his wrongdoing, his too-stern ways. Such odd behavior—was it a result of being confined to this room and a wheelchair?

"Today I'm puttin' my house in order, before it's too late. And I want to start with you, son." Daed smiled sadly. "You've endured unnecessarily harsh treatment over the years. You did nothin' to deserve such severity. And I'm sorry."

He's apologizing? Caleb was stunned. The words sounded out of place on his father's lips. And yet, the old temptation to be resentful, even bitter, reared its ugly head.

"You must surely think I've gone ferhoodled." Daed drew a slow breath, his eyelids fluttering. "But it was hellfire that put the fear of God in me. I want you to hear it from me. Otherwise if it's secondhand, you might doubt it."

"No need to, Daed. You get some rest now, ya hear?"

"Caleb . . ."

"You're not yourself," he insisted. "You've suffered terribly."

"No, son, listen to me."

He clenched his jaw. All of Nellie Mae's arguments for her faith came rushing back. The strange and ridiculous way she'd behaved, throwing away their love, breaking their engagement for Manny's church. Caleb chafed against the "alien gospel," as he'd heard it called by his Daed and others. And now had his own father succumbed to it?

Daed continued. "I know it goes against the grain . . . to say I've been granted salvation." He reached for a glass of water and his hand shook as he sipped through the straw. "John finally got me to see the truth. Ach, what a persistent soul . . . for so many years."

How can this be?

"John said if I asked the Lord, He would make me a new creation, givin' me His gift of grace and makin' me fit for heaven. I know God's forgiven me . . . and I'm hoping I might ask the same of you."

Caleb shook his head, still uncomprehending. "Daed, I . . ."

"You don't have to say anything now, Caleb. But I would like ya to do somethin'." His father inhaled slowly. "I must speak to Reuben Fisher. Go fetch him and bring him here to me . . . straightaway."

Such a strange request on top of even stranger words—nothing like Caleb had prepared himself to hear. "Jah, I'll go."

With that, he left the room.

———

Shocked to see young Caleb looking mighty grim at the back stoop, Reuben immediately believed David had passed away. Mighty thankful to learn he was mistaken, he reached for his straw hat, agreeing to ride to the Yoders' in Caleb's courting buggy, oddly enough.

All Caleb had said was his father had asked to see him—nothing more. But as they rode, Caleb described his Daed's declining health, as well as the man's firm belief his end lurked just around the corner. Caleb was forthright, saying he had no idea what his father wanted with Reuben.

At first Nellie thought she must be dreaming where she sat at the window, reflecting on the day's sermon.

When she heard a horse and carriage come rushing into the drive, she turned and looked out, amazed. She gasped at the sight of Caleb Yoder sitting tall in his courting buggy. *Well, what on earth?*

She remembered the last time he'd come unannounced. But knowing how fragile his father's health was, she worried.

Moments later she heard Dat's voice downstairs. Then, of

all things, if Caleb didn't whisk Dat away, driving lickety-split back down the drive, toward the main road.

She had no reason not to assume that David had passed away, but if that were true, why was Caleb taking Dat back with him? At this, Nellie was beyond befuddled, and she dropped to her knees in prayer.

———

When Reuben arrived at the Yoder farm with Caleb, Elizabeth greeted him somberly and led him to a downstairs room, where David lay on the bed, flat on his back, eyes shut. "He's resting," Elizabeth reassured Reuben and then left.

Reuben considered the situation. Here he was finally at David's bedside, after months of repeated rebuffs. *Why has he called for me?*

David's wrinkled eyelids fluttered open and he fixed his gaze on Reuben. "Denki . . . thank you for comin'."

"Glad to, David." He nodded.

"I daresay I don't have long for this world," David said in low tones. "I've been given a warning this day . . . by an English cousin of mine." He drew a labored breath. "I'm in danger of eternity without God unless I repent." He closed his eyes, and a tear squeezed out and slid down his ruddy face. "I'm guilty of callin' you a fool, Reuben Fisher. . . . I've looked down on you for chasin' after this new faith, thinkin' you and the others were bent on destroying the People with prideful ways. Turns out . . . I was the one in the wrong."

Reuben was dumbfounded.

David reached out his hand. "I plead for your forgiveness."

Reuben gripped David's hand, the lump in his throat crowding out his very breath.

"You're entitled to your way of thinkin', Reuben—if it's

assurance of salvation you want, then so be it." David's face was ashen; he was spent.

"I forgave you months ago, David. Truly, I did."

David blinked his eyes open, then shut, then open again. "I was the fool."

"We're brothers."

"That we are . . . I've laid down my will for God's," David said softly. "At long last." A tear trickled down his cheek. "I wanted you to hear this directly from me."

Overjoyed, Reuben clung to David's hand.

David went on. "I'll die in peace, whenever the Lord wills it."

"Maybe He'll raise you up . . . make you whole."

"No need for that now. Dying has brought me life, Reuben. Tell all the People, won't ya?"

If Reuben had not heard this with his own ears, he might not have believed it. "I'll tell the brethren first."

"And ask your cousin Manny to stop by. I need to be speakin' to him, too." David went on, his voice a throaty murmur. He was saying he wanted to ask both the bishop and Preacher Manny to preach at his funeral. Reuben took mental notes, not questioning whatsoever as David uttered his last wishes. This was a man who had always known what he wanted, and he was going to have it. Reuben would see to that.

———

Betsy stroked her husband's hair as they rested together later that night. "What you're tellin' me is nothing short of a miracle," she said.

"I've been thanking God for His mercy," her dear husband said.

She kissed his face. "Wouldn't it be somethin' if David lives for longer than he expects?"

Reuben smiled. "I hope that, too."

"Meanwhile, what'll Elizabeth do? Surely she knows from David's lips what he's told you."

"Oh, she knows."

"Will she follow in her husband's footsteps?"

"Who's to say?" Reuben looked up at her. "The Lord is at work."

And Caleb . . . what of him?

She realized how such a fork in the road for the Yoder family—which would certainly include the Bann—might change things for Nellie Mae, as well. Betsy assumed Nellie had started attending Sunday Singings again with the New Order youth. It was also rather apparent from his frequent visits to the shop that Caleb's cousin Chris Yoder was sweet on their dear girl, though probably that would prove a passing fancy.

It wasn't as if Nellie was sitting around waiting for her first beau to catch up to her spiritually. All the same, Betsy couldn't begin to know what was in her daughter's heart.

CHAPTER 26

Nellie Mae was alone in the bakery shop when Christian Yoder inched his car right up to the front and parked. She couldn't have planned the timing any better if she'd had a thing to say about it. Actually, she was surprised at her happiness to see him . . . and he was right on schedule, too. After all, this was Thursday afternoon; she *should* be expecting him.

Watching him get out of his car, she suddenly questioned if his afternoon visit was the reason for Nan's and Mamma's disappearance earlier. *Well, surely not,* she thought, a bit bemused.

He strode up with confidence, as though on a mission. And for the first time, he lacked the look of adolescence evident in most fellows his age. His hair was neatly combed, as always. *As fair-haired as Caleb,* she thought.

For a moment, she wondered what it might be like for the three of them to be friends. Naturally, that was no longer possible, in spite of the amazing news Dat had shared of David Yoder's embracing salvation. Even so, she thought of Caleb and experienced a fleeting envy at Chris's weekly contact with him.

The door opened, and Chris smiled his way inside. "Hi again, Nellie Mae."

"Hullo, Chris."

He took in the small shop with a glance and was not subtle about noticing she was there by herself. "What pies do you have today?" he asked.

"Well, if it's pies you're interested in . . ." She caught herself for being so bold. "I do have several kinds of cookies, too."

His eyes searched hers. So much so that she felt nearly ill at ease; yet she did not look away as she might have with a stranger. "Nellie, I've been thinking." He paused, as if weighing his words. "And please be honest with me . . . if I'm overstepping . . ." His voice trailed off. He seemed unnerved.

What's he going to say?

His smile reappeared. "What I mean is, how would you like to go for ice cream sometime . . . with me?"

He was obviously ferhoodled, so she wanted to make this easy for him. "When were you thinkin'?" she asked, realizing too late that she should've said something less forward.

His smile spread clear across his handsome face. "So, you *do* like ice cream. . . ."

She tried without success to keep her own smile in check. "Ach, who doesn't?"

"When would you be free to go?"

"Well, only after dark . . . of an evening. That's *our* way, though. Is that what you had in mind?" She felt terribly odd taking the lead this way, but she had no choice—not if they weren't going to be found out. *And, oh, we will be.* Surely they would, the way Nan had talked about Chris while weeding the garden with her that day in May.

Nearly staring a hole through her, he pressed his hands on the counter. "I'd like to get to know you better. But I also want to respect your . . . customs."

She nodded. "After dark, then."

"Is tonight too soon?" His gaze softened, as if with hope.

"Tonight's just fine." She told him that she would meet him up the road. "I'll come on foot," she said. He agreed . . . and left without choosing a pie or cookies or any sweets at all. She refused the giggle that threatened to burst out as she watched him hop into his car again.

Mamma mustn't find out what I'm up to, Nellie thought, deciding she'd only go with Chris Yoder just this once.

————

Adding a few extra hours of waitressing each week would be precisely what Rhoda needed to help get out of her financial bind. After a little over a week of not seeing Ken Kraybill—not even encountering him in the hallways of his own house— Rhoda had realized their dating relationship was most likely finished. *Time to move on,* she decided as she returned a smile to the two fellows at one of her restaurant tables.

One of them seemed quite nice, and she imagined what it might be like to have dinner with him. She found it surprising that she didn't miss Ken as much as she thought she might. Of course there were moments when she missed talking with him, especially last Friday night, after getting off work. Still, she was convinced there was a fine, good-looking man for her somewhere out there. Someone who wanted to marry and start a family.

I wouldn't mind if he likes to watch television, too, she thought. She'd acquired a taste for *The Lucy Show* while baby-sitting the Kraybill children once the little ones were tucked into bed.

When she'd asked about working more than her regular hours, Mrs. Kraybill had agreed to put her at the top of her list for baby-sitters— *"but only if it doesn't interfere with your social life,"* Mrs. Kraybill had said. Her employer seemed aware that Ken was no longer in the picture, which was interesting to Rhoda. She wouldn't have pegged him as the type to talk to his aunt about matters of the heart.

Rhoda considered whether she might somehow scrape together enough money to buy a small TV set, so she'd have something entertaining to do on the evenings she wasn't working late. That is, if she didn't land a new beau soon.

"Would you like to order dessert?" she asked the men at her table.

"What's your favorite?" asked the blond man.

"Maybe we'll order something for you, if you'd like to join us." The taller man patted the seat.

She blushed. "Do I look like I'm off work?" Then she laughed.

They nodded enthusiastically. "C'mon, don't you want some pie or ice cream?" asked the first fellow. "You know you do."

As appealing as a break sounded, she wasn't going to while away her time and get herself fired.

Trying to be more professional, she asked, "What would the two of you like?"

The more handsome of the two leaned forward, eyes twinkling. "A banana split sounds good," he said. "And bring an extra spoon, just in case." He winked at her and then pulled out a card from his shirt pocket. "Call me anytime."

She accepted the card, noticing his name—Ted Shupp— and that he owned a welding shop on the outskirts of Honey Brook. Come to think of it, she'd seen it. "We don't have banana splits on the menu," she told him.

Ted pretended to pout. "Aw, can't you go and whip up something, Rhoda?"

She was surprised he knew her name and then realized it

was pinned on her dress. She laughed at herself, but the flirty Ted must've thought she was laughing at him, because he waved her over closer. "Tell you what: I'll take you out for a banana split later, okeydokey?"

She gave him a careful look, trying to decide if this attractive fellow could be trusted. She didn't want a repeat of her dreadful night with Glenn Miller last winter. "I'll meet you at the ice cream parlor at nine o'clock," she said, thinking it wiser to drive herself tonight.

———

Nellie Mae thought of any number of reasons she might have given Chris Yoder to refuse his ice cream date. Yet here she was, scurrying up the road, hoping neither Nan nor Mamma suspected where she was going. And how could they not suspect something? After all, she'd waited till dusk to slip away without saying good-bye—a telltale sign she was meeting someone.

I can hear Nan now, when she corners me. She smiled, knowing however prying her sister might be, no amount of teasing would keep Nellie from meeting Chris tonight. *Caleb's cousin, no less.* The thought had clouded her thinking during supper. Was she only willing to spend time with Chris because he was related to her former beau?

She recalled how comfortable she'd felt around Chris the evening he drove her home—she'd nearly forgotten she was with an outsider. Maybe it was because she, too, was on the periphery, by Old Order standards.

She noticed the field grasses in the warm twilight. When had they grown to nearly waist-high? She hadn't gone to the woods at all since last fall, although she'd promised herself she would. Was she so hesitant to see the uncoiled ferns of deep summer . . . the rainbow of wild flowers? The sweetly scented air would be filled with the sounds of crickets at this time of day. All happy reminders of Suzy.

She sighed, realizing her nightly dreams of Suzy had ceased. And worse, she hadn't noticed, till now.

Suzy's description of the last weeks of her life was still clear in Nellie's mind, though—weeks that Chris's brother Zach had helped to make some of her very best.

Jah, there are plenty of reasons to have ice cream with Christian Yoder tonight, Nellie told herself.

The ride to Honey Brook was as pleasant as the last time she'd ridden with Chris. He'd greeted Nellie with an infectious smile, as he always did at the shop. Then, once she was settled inside, he hurried around the front of the car and jumped in behind the wheel, fast as a wink. Maybe to set her at ease, he asked if she minded listening to his favorite radio station, which turned out to be one that played fast hymns. At least, he said they were church songs, but the fancy-sounding melodies could've fooled her, despite lyrics that seemed drawn from the Bible.

The music got them talking for a while about the kinds of songs he sang as a member of his church. "You've already joined?" she asked.

"When I was sixteen. Our church allows baptism when someone professes faith, but most parents, like mine, want their children to be older before they become voting members."

"Sixteen's not too young, really. I know lots of girls, 'specially, who take the baptismal vow as soon as they're allowed to court."

He seemed to understand. "Our church requirements are different from yours, I'm sure."

She found it interesting he knew something of Amish practices. Perhaps it was due to his father's family tree.

The more Chris talked, the more she realized he was very settled in his church and seemed to have a deep sense of purpose.

Why *had* he asked her out?

When they arrived at the ice cream shop, she wondered if they would go inside to eat or if he would prefer to stay in the car. After all, she was wearing a Plain dress, unlike Rhoda, who she'd heard flounced all around town in her worldly getup.

No, I must not think more highly of myself.

When Chris came around to open her door, she smiled, pleased. *He's not embarrassed at all.*

It was a chore to rein in her smile as they headed to the sidewalk leading to the little shop. This being a weeknight, she hadn't expected the place to be so busy. But then, school was out for the summer. She'd nearly forgotten to ask Chris about his graduation last month and made a mental note to mention it later.

"What's your favorite flavor?" he asked, his eyes intent on her as they waited in line.

"Mint chocolate chip." She could almost taste the rich, creamy ice cream made on the premises—as delicious as the homemade kind she and Nan took turns cranking in their old ice cream maker on hot nights. "What's yours?"

"Coffee," he was quick to say. "I don't drink it, but I love the taste of coffee in ice cream."

She inched forward in the line with him. "It's funny, but coffee brewing smells just wonderful-good, yet the actual drink tastes bitter to me."

He nodded in agreement.

"I use coffee in my Chocolate Christmas Cookies, though. And they are delicious, if I do say so myself." She felt her cheeks grow warm. It wasn't like her to boast.

He smiled down at her. "I don't doubt it. How many recipes do you have?"

She shrugged. "I don't know. Oodles. I've even started writing out some of them."

His eyes lit up. "That's great. Are you making a cookbook? Recipes from Nellie's Simple Sweets?"

She shook her head, pleased but embarrassed by his enthusiasm. "Ach no. Just jotting them down for the customers who ask." She quickly changed the subject. "Suzy wasn't much of a baker, but she loved to make all kinds of ice cream. Nearly as soon as the bumblebees flew, she'd want to make it—around the time we started goin' barefoot in the spring."

"Suzy was keen on bare feet," he said.

"Oh jah, and she was always pushing the time for when we'd shed our shoes. Suzy loved the feel of barnyard mud squishing 'tween her toes." She caught herself. "Sorry . . . I don't mean to chatter on so."

"Isn't talking the best way to get acquainted?"

Her face reddened again. Goodness, but she liked him.

They were having such a laughing-good time already, and Rhoda scarcely even knew Ted Shupp. He walked over to her car after she'd pulled up and waved to him, opening her door. "Nice wheels," he said admiringly.

"Thanks," she said, blushing a little as she stepped out.

"This place is sure hopping tonight," he commented.

She noticed several Amish courting buggies toward the back of the lot and wondered who was out on a weeknight.

"Ever ride in one of those contraptions?" Ted asked.

She already liked Ted, but she wasn't ready to go into the whole story of her family background. "I sure have." She laughed. "I have friends who are Amish."

"Hey, me too." He grinned, and she was struck again by

how comfortable she felt around him, which must surely be a good sign. "Who do you know that's Plain?"

She pulled a name out of her head, that of one of their former preachers. "Oh, the Zooks."

He chortled. "Aren't there a hundred and one Zooks around here?"

She nodded slowly, stepping back on the slippery path of pretense. "More Zooks than you can count, prob'ly," she said, walking beside him as they headed into the pink, red, and white ice cream shop.

I best watch myself. . . .

Jazzy, upbeat music wafted through the ice cream shop. Nellie felt like bobbing her head, as Chris was doing.

He caught himself and smiled apologetically. "I have to admit to liking cheerful music." He began to describe the appealing gospel-style music he'd heard at the Tel Hai Campground tabernacle.

"Suzy went there," she said suddenly. "Last summer."

"She loved that little place." He glanced upward, as though thinking back. "Suzy walked to the altar there, in fact."

Nodding, Nellie admitted she'd read Suzy's account of that happy day.

"How would you like to go with me sometime?" he asked, blue eyes shining. "I'm sure you'd enjoy it."

She'd wanted to attend the open-air services ever since learning of her sister's fondness for the rustic setting, but she'd never dreamed she would have the opportunity. Not with Chris, the very person who'd first invited Suzy, of all people!

Then she remembered she'd promised herself only one date with him. It made no sense to encourage Chris. Green though she was around English fellows, she was not so naïve that she couldn't see how fond he was becoming of her.

"A revival meeting's beginning in a few weeks—we could get in on the start of it, Nellie Mae." The way he said her name, part pleading, part admiration, startled her.

She wanted to ask Chris if he felt strange being seen with her, but maybe she was jumping ahead too quickly, becoming too personal.

"Would you like to go?" He was pressing for an answer between spoonfuls of ice cream. "We could come here afterward."

"But we hardly know each other."

He stared at his dish. "Well, I don't know about you, but it seems to me we've been friends for . . . well, quite a while."

She couldn't deny that, or the fact she felt drawn to him, as well. "Even so, I'm Amish. Surely this must be a problem."

She found herself holding her breath.

What'll he say to that?

"My grandparents were Amish, so it's not like I'm a fancy, worldly man, or whatever it is your People might think of me." His eyes were solemn but tender. "Just a few decades ago, my father's father was Amish. My father and David Yoder are first cousins."

Wanting to ask, yet cautious, she said, "How's David doin' since his accident?"

He bowed his head; then slowly he raised his eyes to meet hers. "My dad and I went to see David last Sunday afternoon. He's struggling . . . he's giving up."

"Ach no." Her heart sank.

Chris nodded sadly. "Caleb's worried—all the family are. You can see it in their eyes, the way they move around the house, taking care of him. Elizabeth rarely smiles," he added.

"Hopefully Rebekah can bring some joy to them," she said. "I've heard she's helpin'. She's my sister Nan's closest friend."

"I've seen her sometimes—she comes by during the day."

"It's just so sad." She didn't want to dwell on this topic, although she cared deeply for the Yoders. She wondered, too, why thus far Chris had made no mention of David's recent conversion.

Chris began to share about his church youth group and the Wednesday night Bible studies. Nellie lost herself in his words. How she enjoyed spending time with a date who loved the Lord.

She wanted to ask him about the passage in Romans she and Nan had discovered recently—one all about grace, which was still becoming a reality to her. And she would have brought it up, but at that moment she heard a familiar voice. Glancing at the door, she was surprised to see her sister Rhoda coming in with an Englischer, both of them laughing.

Is this her serious beau?

Then, just as quickly, she was more concerned about the possibility of Rhoda's seeing her with Chris Yoder. She turned to face Chris again, her back to her worldly sister.

They were sharing an enormous banana split, the two of them dipping with long fountain spoons into the mounds of ice cream topped with whipped cream. Rhoda thought it dear of Ted to sit beside her in the booth. He had a great sense of humor and, now that he wasn't hanging around the other guy, was much less a flirt—not that she minded the occasional wink or playful comment. So many nice qualities about him—he was polite and complimentary—and he was even better looking than Ken Kraybill.

Funny I should think of Ken.

She again marveled at Ted, sure she had found the perfect

way to forget the pain her former beau had caused her. "Do you like kids?" she asked, spooning up her next bite.

"You bet I do. The more, the better." He leaned close, like he might kiss her cheek. "How many babies do you want, honey?" He was so near to her, she could smell his cologne.

"As many as the Good Lord sees fit, I'm guessing."

He laughed. "The way I see it, the Lord doesn't have much to do with all of that."

She smiled back at him, puzzled, thinking that sometimes there was a secret code to the Englischers' way of talking. Even so, something told her he might be just a little fresh, sitting this close. Yet she didn't budge. She'd been lonely since she and Ken split up, and having Mr. Ted Shupp be so attentive was just as nice as it could be.

The couple at the table behind them got up and left, and she leaned back in the pink booth, Ted's arm around her shoulders now. That's when she spotted her sister Nellie Mae with a fancy fellow. "Well, I'll be snookered," she said, excusing herself.

Boldly, she approached them, eyeing Nellie suspiciously from behind. She leaned over and smiled. "Why, goodness' sake! Nellie Mae . . . what're you doing here?"

Her sister instantly turned pale. "Oh, hullo, Rhoda . . . how're you?"

Then, as if remembering her manners, Nellie sputtered out an introduction. "This here is . . . Christian Yoder, a friend of mine."

"Hi there." Rhoda offered her hand. "I'm Nellie's sister, Rhoda Fisher."

Chris nodded, smiling politely. "Weren't you our waitress for my father's birthday dinner?"

"Oh, so *that's* where I first saw you. Christian Yoder, you said?" The name seemed familiar to her . . . but then, there were an awful lot of Yoders in these parts.

"Mostly it's Chris." He glanced now at Nellie Mae, who seemed to be shrinking on her side of the table.

"Are you eating alone?" Nellie asked her.

Rhoda realized what she'd done—setting herself up to be questioned later by Ted. She sure didn't want that. Talk about spoiling things for herself, and mighty fast! "It's my first date with someone, so I'd better get going." She inched back, dying to return to Ted but still very curious about what Nellie might be up to. "Just wanted to say hi. Great ice cream here, ain't?"

"Nice to see ya, Rhoda," said Nellie. "I'll tell Nan I saw you—it'll make her ever so happy." Nellie Mae looked forlorn as she mentioned Nan, and it made Rhoda feel lousy for abandoning her dearest sister. *I wonder how Nan is, really,* she thought, pasting on a big smile for Ted as she scooted in next to him once again.

First date? Nellie didn't quite understand, unless perhaps Rhoda meant this was a new beau. She wasn't about to turn and gawk, but she would have liked to meet her sister's friend, just as she'd introduced Chris to Rhoda.

She and Chris fell back into conversation, discussing everything from Chris's college scholarship to his youth group fundraisers. As nice as he was, suddenly she felt terribly uneasy. Her parents would be upset, and Nan, too, if they heard she was out with an Englischer. How long before news of Nellie's "fancy beau" would find its way to the Amish grapevine?

Across the way, she noticed Rhoda and her friend moving through the maze of tables, heading for the door. Nellie expected her sister to look over and wave, but Rhoda was preoccupied with her new boyfriend, laughing loudly as she held his hand.

"I'd love to go to the tabernacle with you, but I better

not," she told Chris after he'd brought up the revival meetings again.

His face drooped. "Well, it's hard to describe, but I think you'd really like it. Lots of youth attend."

Nodding, she knew intuitively that if Suzy had loved it, so would she. But she refused to break her mother's or her father's heart. There had been far too much sadness amongst the People for one year, and her seeing Chris was sure to raise eyebrows and bring unnecessary anxiety. "I should be getting home now," she said, torn between the lovely idea of seeing him again and knowing their relationship had the potential to lead to yet another parting.

He rose quickly and gently escorted her to his car, not pressing the matter further.

Chris had witnessed the marked change in the tide. Somewhere in the space of time between Rhoda's coming to their table and when she and her boyfriend exited the ice cream shop, something had changed drastically in Nellie Mae. Hard as he tried, he could not determine what had happened to alter her openness toward him.

He knew of a longer route back to Beaver Dam Road and chose that way, wanting to get things back on better footing before the night was over. But how? If he brought up Rhoda's lack of Plainness, how would that serve to get Nellie talking again?

"I really wish you'd think about going to the tabernacle with me," he ventured.

She gave a small sigh. "It's kind of you." Then she surprised him by saying she didn't want to bring sorrow to her parents. She spoke more softly now—gone was the confident, talkative girl he'd brought to town. Was it her encounter with Rhoda, who apparently was no longer Amish, that upset her?

They drove without speaking for a time. Then, when he thought he might not get her to talk again, she looked over at him. "Besides your family history, how is it you know so much about . . . the Amish church?" she asked.

He was glad to explain. "David Yoder and my dad always liked to sit around after dinner at their house when I was a kid. They loved debating the rules of the Amish ordinances and my father's belief in the grace of the Lord. My dad often said he knew what his Amish cousin believed nearly as well as David did himself."

"Ach, really?"

"When David started to talk about dying last Sunday, my dad shooed Caleb and me out of the room and laid out the Gospel to him one more time."

She shifted herself to face him, as if eager to hear more.

"Dad told his cousin that following the rules of a church or a bishop wouldn't get him past the pearly gates. 'You need Jesus,' Dad told him flat-out."

"What did David say to that?"

Chris hesitated, not wanting to sound critical. "I don't know how well you're acquainted with my dad's cousin, but—"

"Quite frankly, most folk know he's stubborn."

"That's putting it mildly. Even with death starin' him in the face, at first he was as closed-minded as he's always been." Chris thought how ironic it was that a mule's kick to such a hardheaded man hadn't softened him up much. "But God can crack the hardest heart, and David cried out to Him . . . and repented."

"Too bad it takes a calamity to get a person's attention." Nellie's voice quivered. "Suzy's death brought my family to their knees, I know that for sure. I'm so thankful God was able to use this accident to get David's notice . . . and his heart."

Hearing her express herself so sweetly made Chris want to reach for her hand. *I have to be out of my mind.* By tomorrow, he guessed, he'd be glad if he kept his hands firmly on the steering wheel, where they belonged.

CHAPTER 27

Nan was waiting for her in the hallway when Nellie Mae tiptoed up the stairs. "Did you go out with you-know-who?" She was smiling, clad in her long cotton nightgown.

"Well, it won't happen again, so you don't need to fret."

"So, you *were* with Chris Yoder!"

Nellie hurried to her room. "Is this the same sister who made me wait for weeks to know the name of my future brother-in-law?" She nearly closed the door on Nan's nose and then opened it right quick to pull her inside. "I'll just say this much—Chris told me more about the day David Yoder opened up to Christ. We mustn't quit praying for him or the rest of the family."

Nan agreed, waiting for more information—Nellie could see it in her too-eager eyes.

"Other than running into Rhoda, who looked to be in good spirits, there's nothin' else to tell." She yawned and stretched her arms. "Now I'm tired . . . and so are you."

"Jah, s'pose it is bedtime." Before Nan left for her room, she grinned and said, "If you need advice 'bout, well, just anything, I'm willin'."

"Good night, sister," Nellie said, reaching up to undo her hair.

The weekend passed quickly for Rhoda, who couldn't believe how nice it was to have a new beau with a flair for romance. He stopped by the restaurant with flowers for no reason, and the day after waited till she was off work to take her to dinner.

Since meeting Ted a week ago now, she'd already stopped in at the welding shop twice to talk to him and simply "hang around," as he put it, with a twinkle in his eyes. Today, though, when she arrived, hoping to surprise him before heading to work at the restaurant, she noticed a couple of pretty girls already doing just that, and Rhoda wondered if they were there to see Ted or one of the other guys. Watching from her car, she felt a pang of jealousy when she saw Ted go over and put his arms around both of them. *Like he does with me!* One of the girls leaned against him flirtatiously.

Deciding not to stay, she drove away, as offended as she'd felt the day Curly Sam Zook had dropped her like a hot fried potato.

Best not be counting my chickens before they're hatched!

Seized by an overwhelming desire for a milkshake and salty French fries, Rhoda drove straight to the nearest fast-food place.

Just this once.

———

The dream began as the dearest Rosanna had ever dreamed. A covering of radiant leaves showered around her as she strolled merrily through the golden wood. She savored the earthy scents of autumn and cradled her swollen stomach, where her darling babe grew.

A gentle gust swept across her face, making her apron billow out around her ankles. She felt the sun . . . ah, the sweet, warm sunshine. The day of her baby's birth was drawing closer. *Elias will be ever so happy.*

At first she didn't see her—the wee baby curled up in the blood-red leaves. Then she stopped to look and cried out, "Oh, surely not!" No . . . *not my precious little one. My baby, on the ground, lifeless* . . .

She awakened with a start and, sitting up, realized she must've made a sound.

"Rosanna?" came Elias's sleepy voice. "You all right?"

"I had a horrid dream."

"Ach, you're crying, love." He sat up with her, drawing her near, and she buried her face in his warm embrace.

"Shh . . . it was a nightmare . . . jah?"

She dared not say just how awful the dream had been . . . how frighteningly real. No need to burden Elias, whose own pillowcase was sometimes wet with tears in the morning, so heavy was the burden he faithfully carried for the People. And now here she was waking him.

Is it a forewarning?

Lena's thoughtful letter had arrived earlier that Friday, the looked-for reply to Rosanna's. Lena had seemed overjoyed to hear of Rosanna's pregnancy, calling it "wonderful-good news" and thanking the Lord for this "gift," praying Rosanna would have the health to deliver a full-term baby. Yet Rosanna's own baby news had not changed a single thing in Lena's thinking.

In the distance, the crack of fireworks from the town's Fourth-of-July celebration punctuated the present silence.

"I'm here, love." Elias pulled her gently down with him, cradling her in his strong arms. "Just rest."

She nodded, trembling at the vision of the beautiful baby girl . . . dead on the forest floor.

O Lord, please let it not be so. . . .

Caleb stayed at home with Mamm on the Lord's Day to help with Daed while Leah and Emmie attended Preaching. Though both the bishop and even Preacher Manny had dropped by, nothing more had been said about his father's wishes for the funeral. And Caleb remained chagrined at Daed's sudden change of heart, as well as Mamm's reluctance to discuss the events of the Sunday two weeks ago.

He'll come to his senses, Caleb told himself. *He's off-kilter.*

To Caleb's surprise, today Daed seemed able to hold his head more erect and wanted to come to the table for the noon meal. And strength did seem to be returning somewhat to his upper body as they all sat at the supper table presently. Caleb also noticed how much longer his father bowed his head for the silent blessing . . . and when he asked for various dishes to be passed, his words were unexpectedly soft and kind.

Was Daed experiencing a miraculous turnaround, just as Chris Yoder had prayed? And where would all this talk of miracles lead them, anyway?

When Daed asked to be wheeled back to his room, Caleb rose quickly. Alone together in the bedroom once again, he sat waiting for Abe to drop by and help move Daed back into bed.

Motioning for Caleb to close the door, Daed said, "I have something to say to you, son."

Caleb braced himself, not ready for another confession. His father looked so feeble in his wheelchair.

"I've said before that I've been a hard man." Daed raised his eyes to Caleb's. "I was bullheaded to force you away from your girl. Wasn't my place."

All the anger Caleb had felt—all the pain and loss—came flooding back. He didn't want to talk about Nellie Mae now, least of all with a man he scarcely knew anymore.

"I rejected your choice of a mate, somethin' mighty sacred." Daed stared down at his rough hands. "You should've been allowed to marry the girl you chose. The one you loved."

Caleb gritted his teeth, unable to make heads or tails of this. After thwarting his longed-for plans at every turn, did Daed hope to gain his forgiveness so easily? This wasn't the time to inform Daed of Nellie's choice. That *she*, not Daed, had cut things off in the end. Caleb breathed deeply, studying his father—still shocked at the words coming out of his mouth. Was the new belief Nellie embraced—that tore their love apart—truly now Daed's own?

Daed continued. "I've talked with your brothers—each one. And you can rest assured there'll be no hard feelings from them." He made no attempt to restrain his tears, which ran down both sides of his wrinkled face. "Son, my land is yours for the taking."

Caleb felt the air leave him. Had he heard correctly? "Ach, I wasn't expecting this."

"I know, Caleb . . . I know. But there's a big difference now. There are no strings attached. You're free to farm it for as long as you live."

Caleb was speechless. He'd never seen such benevolence in his father. Truly, something deep had altered in him.

With much effort, Daed offered his hand. "I failed you, son," he said. "Can you ever forgive me?"

Without giving it a second thought, he clasped his father's hand. "Dat . . . this is all so sudden. . . ."

Slowly, Daed nodded his head, his beard bumping his chest. "But I believe you'll see . . . in due time . . . what I'm talking 'bout." With those puzzling words, his trembling hand suddenly dropped, too weak to grasp any longer. "You'll see."

The land he'd always wanted, even coveted, was to be his—if Daed was in his right mind, that is. Caleb would be foolish to refuse the very thing he'd longed for, yet he felt mighty distrustful as he sat staring at this father who'd changed nearly before his eyes.

"I love you, Caleb . . . whether you forgive me or not."

Once again, Caleb was bewildered, unable to recall ever having heard his father declare such a thing.

———

For sure and for certain, Nellie enjoyed Rebekah Yoder's Sunday afternoon visits almost as much as Nan. Today she'd stayed for supper, and since it would be daylight for a few more hours, Nellie suggested the three of them go walking in the woods. "The red columbine should still be blooming," she told Nan, knowing her sister would remember the brilliantly scarlet blossoms that had always been Suzy's favorite.

It was a hot and muggy July day, the first Sunday of the month, and blue sky was divided by a buildup of clouds to the west. All three girls had worn their winter bonnets to shield their faces from the sun.

"How's your father doin' today?" Nan asked Rebekah as they hiked through the paddock, toward the meadow.

"Well, it was a bit surprising when I stopped in to see him earlier. He seemed some better, actually." Rebekah glanced at Nellie Mae. " 'Tis such a blessing to be welcomed by him again. Ya know, he's offered to let me move back home, if I want to. Caleb says I should take him up on it before he changes his mind." She chuckled.

Delighted as she was to hear this news, Nellie tensed up at the mention of Caleb.

"I was out walkin' with my sister Leah just two Sundays ago, talking about Daed's makin' peace with God and explainin' the reasons for the church split," Rebekah continued. "Ach, such a thorny thing. Most of the youth have little idea what went on, or what even caused it."

"I daresay 'twas a mighty confusing time for all of us," Nan said.

"My father's saying he wants as many of the People present at his funeral as will come—everyone from the New Order and the Beachys, too," Rebekah said.

"I wonder why." Nan stopped to pick a black-eyed Susan and spun it between her fingers.

"Has the bishop been to see him?" Nellie asked, curious what David Yoder was cooking up.

"Jah, the bishop and Preacher Manny, both. The two of them met with my father." Rebekah shook her head, removing her bonnet and fanning her face. "To think Daed is willing to talk to a New Order preacher, of all things. Only the Lord could make that happen."

Nellie wondered if David had softened at all toward Caleb. She still felt dreadful when she thought of him giving up his treasured inheritance, grasping anew what Caleb sacrificed to prove his love for her. The whole thing made her stomach tie up in knots.

Quite by surprise, Chris Yoder came to mind. She liked the fact that he shared her faith—ever so appealing—in contrast to Caleb's disapproval of her new beliefs. She found much to admire about Chris, although they should limit their conversation to his weekly visits to the bakery shop from now on.

Even so, Nellie couldn't help but think how exciting it would be to go with him to the very tabernacle where Suzy had first encountered the Lord.

———

Caleb carried a glass of water into Daed's room, placing it on the lamp table near the bed. As usual, he'd brought a straw to make drinking easier, since his father wanted to hold his own glass—in some ways, his father was as bent on being independent as ever.

Going to the window, Caleb noticed a long V-shaped line of birds fly over the house, and he watched them travel east till they were black specks in the distance. The evening sun remained high in the sky at nearly seven o'clock, and Caleb reached up to pull down the green shade.

"Come . . . sit with me, son." His father's eyes were open again.

Caleb reached back to raise the shade slightly, surprised at the request. "Thought you might want to retire for the night." He set a chair next to the bed.

"Not yet, no. There are still things I must say." His Daed was quiet for a moment, and Caleb wondered what on earth his father had in mind. He had been avoiding him some, hoping not to be cornered with another request for forgiveness. *It's too late to put everything right.*

Weak as his father appeared, his gaze held steady, and Caleb had an uncomfortable sense that he suspected the fight within. "Don't follow in my obstinate ways. Give your life over to the One who died for you . . . and for me. Nothin' else you do is worth a lick otherwise."

"Daed . . . I just don't understand what's happened . . . this way of thinkin'. You were so opposed to talk of grace and salvation before."

His father's breathing seemed shallow now, and his eyes were closed once more. "Don't wait to believe, Caleb," he whispered, folding his hands over his chest. "Preacher Manny was right . . . all along. Honest, he was."

Unable to sit any longer, Caleb rose and went to the window again. Did his father expect him to abandon the Old Ways as quickly as he seemingly had?

"None of this adds up," Caleb muttered.

He didn't know how long he remained there, but some minutes had passed and he sensed something amiss—even absent—in the room. Daed's arduous breathing had subsided. And when he turned to look, he saw the pallor of death settle over his father's face. Gone was the fight for each lungful of air; his eyes were closed with the sleep of the ages.

How easily he passed. . . .

Caleb felt like an intruder suddenly—shouldn't Mamm have been the one present to hear Daed's last words? Moving to the bedside, he looked more closely and saw a slight smile on Daed's lips. A good death, as some might say.

Standing there, he felt a sense of peace, followed by his own regret. He had withheld forgiveness from his father . . . and now Daed was dead.

He stared down at the folded callused hands and laid his own there lightly.

"Don't wait to believe, Caleb. . . . Preacher Manny was right."

Caleb shuddered at the memory of his father's final request and went to tell his mother.

———

By the time they returned from the woods, carrying handfuls of red columbine to give Mamma, Nellie was spent. After the long church service this morning and with Rebekah's visit, she'd missed sitting down to write her circle letters and her weekly letter to Cousin Treva. She felt tired for some unexplained reason. Unless, was she somehow allowing herself to be burdened by Caleb's concern for his father? Connected in grief?

She'd enjoyed the walk to the woods, where Rebekah had revealed her hope to marry in November, during wedding season, as Nan smiled knowingly at Nellie Mae.

With a happy sigh, Nellie looked forward to spending the evening hours with Mamma. Nan and Rebekah would soon be heading together to the Sunday Singing.

It was some time later, after Nellie had taken down her hair and was brushing it before bedtime, that someone came riding into the drive, bringing word that David Yoder had died not but a few hours ago.

CHAPTER 28

The morning of his father's funeral, Caleb found his mother weeping over the kitchen sink. Her hair was still flowing past her waist, and it appeared that she'd come downstairs for some juice. Still wearing her nightclothes and bathrobe, she must have thought she would be alone.

Not wanting to startle her, he went to stand near, unsure how to comfort her. "I'm mighty sorry 'bout Daed's passing," Caleb managed to say.

She looked at him with pleading eyes. "Did he make his peace with ya, Caleb?"

He nodded slowly.

A sad sort of smile crept across her lined face. "It was the most peculiar thing." She drew a long breath. "I believe your father must've had heavenly visions—did he tell you?"

"First I've heard it."

She glanced nervously toward the doorway. "He asked me several times the day he died, while I sat with him, if he was 'in glory yet.' I didn't know what to make of it. And then, closer to his time of passing, he seemed ever so joyful."

He wondered if she'd noticed Daed's small smile when she came in right after his passing. Or had he only imagined it?

She put a hand to her trembling lips, her eyes filling with

tears. "He changed so, toward the end. Honestly, I hardly knew . . ." She couldn't go on.

"Maybe the medicine was the culprit," Caleb was quick to say. Certain drugs could alter one's thinking. Had that been the case for Daed?

"Your father asked forgiveness for bein' *Hochnut*—all puffed up. He regretted treatin' folks as he did. Ya know what a stickler he was for the ordinance."

This jolted Caleb. So his father had apologized to Mamm for the very thing he'd accused the new church believers of? He'd told Caleb many times that the New Order and Beachy people seemed to think they were better, because they "knew the Lord." That had irked him no end.

Footsteps on the stairs brought their conversation to a close when Leah and Emmie came into the kitchen to prepare the pancake batter. The milking was already done, thanks to Jonah and several sympathetic neighbors. Caleb had been glad for the help, not wanting to awaken his sorrowful sisters on a day that would undoubtedly stretch on for all of them. And as distraught as she already was, he didn't see how Mamm would make it through the three-hour funeral and the burial service.

Just three short days ago, Daed was alive and sitting at the head of their table. He'd had a momentary reprieve from some of his physical weakness . . . enough to carry him through to his passing. The body required energy to die, or so Caleb had once heard.

Where was his father's spirit now that his body was soon to be committed to the ground of the nearby cemetery? Was he indeed in heaven?

Caleb made his way upstairs to clean up, pondering Daed's abnormal behavior. Was it possible he'd found a personal connection with the Lord, like Cousin Chris claimed to have? *Like all the supposedly saved folk . . .*

———

Word had spread rapidly, and Caleb's father's wish was granted. The Yoder farmhouse was packed to standing room only with those faithful to the old church, as well as many who'd gone to the New Order and the local Beachy Amish church. Because he sat close to the front with his Dawdi, brothers, and nephews, Caleb was not able to see how many English neighbors were present, nor if Chris and his family were in attendance.

He put mental blinders on, narrowly focusing on the casket before him. Here, in the front room of his father's own house, where so many Preaching services had been held all through the years.

Bishop Joseph gave the first and shorter sermon, as Daed had evidently requested. But soon it was clear that the service was a departure from the norm, as one long scripture after another was read, and not from the old German Bible, either. Hearing such sacred words in English jarred Caleb—and others, he was mighty sure.

Why had Daed asked for this? And why had the bishop agreed?

After a full hour, Preacher Manny rose. The second, longer sermon was to begin.

Immediately it was clear that this portion of the service would also depart from tradition, the very thing Daed had defended for so long. "Coming to Christ means you are no longer in denial," Preacher Manny commenced.

Denial of what? Caleb froze in his seat.

"David Yoder lived a life pleasing to himself. He requested that I speak to you all today to the best of my ability about

the kind of faith that became his before the end." Preacher
Manny held a piece of paper in his hand, his dark hair shiny
and clean for the occasion. "David told me to my face that
he never knew why he balked so hard at the reality of saving
grace, till it struck him between the eyes. He said God had to
use a mule to get his attention."

A low stir rippled through the room.

"Truth is, David laid down his will for God's. And although
he didn't live long enough to personally share his newfound
faith with each of you, his belief in the saving power of Jesus
will resonate from his grave."

Caleb wanted to look and see how his mother was holding
up, over there with Rebekah, Leah, and Emmie, and all her
daughters-in-law, too—cushioned by the womenfolk.

Preacher Manny continued speaking to the congregation
in conversational tones, another departure from their usual
way. "If David Yoder were alive today—and strong enough
to speak here—he'd want you to know that life is too short
to bicker over church ordinances, or to think more highly of
ourselves than we ought. Doing so is an abomination in the
sight of God."

Caleb's neck ached with tension, and he wondered how
soon Preacher Manny would get back on track, if he would
at all.

Preacher Manny looked out at the congregation, his eyes
moving slowly over them before returning to his notes. "With
tears of joy, David made a profession of faith two weeks ago.
He believed, in the final days of his life, that God's grace was
a gift from the Father's hand—not something to be spurned,
but to be received as the loving blessing it was intended to be.
These are the words I read to him when I last saw him, words
he openly laid claim to: 'Not by works of righteousness which
we have done, but according to his mercy he saved us, by the

washing of regeneration, and renewing of the Holy Ghost.' "
Preacher Manny wiped his eyes with his handkerchief, composed himself, and went on. "So, beloved family and friends of our brother David Yoder, it is only through God's mercy we are made new, a precious gift indeed."

Caleb wanted to escape, but he had no place to go. He was compelled by his upbringing and his mother's would-be shame to remain . . . to endure this unimaginable sermon. *What will the brethren think?*

It was talk like this that would get his family shunned . . . and yet, the bishop himself was allowing it. Why should a son question the wishes of his dying father?

Thinking now of his English cousin, Caleb knew Chris would be in full agreement with a sermon like this. And Nellie Mae might well be whispering amen, too.

He stared at the long handcrafted coffin, narrow at both ends. Daed was nestled in there, wearing his for-good clothes. Mamm and her sisters—and other womenfolk—had bathed and dressed him in all black, but for his best long-sleeved white shirt.

He remembered his father's outstretched hand . . . the humble way he'd asked for forgiveness. And the bequest of land— what Caleb had once so coldly rejected had been unexpectedly offered anew with no conditions attached. Was this the very sort of mercy Manny spoke of?

Sitting straighter now, he returned his attention to the preacher, who opened the German Bible to John chapter eight, verse thirty-six. Then, following that short reading, he moved to the English Bible and read the same words. " 'If the Son'—meaning our Lord and Savior—'therefore shall make you free'—this is the salvation our hearts yearn for, beloved— 'ye shall be free indeed.' " Preacher Manny's eyes brimmed with tears, and he took out a white handkerchief to wipe his eyes. "Our brother David is no longer trapped in a broken body. He is present with the Savior . . . the very One whose words he denied for most of his lifetime." He breathed deeply, clearly moved. "And our brother is free in ev'ry way now. He worships the living God even as we gather here to mourn his passing."

Caleb recalled his father's good death. Was Mamm right about what she assumed? Had his father experienced glimpses of heaven before dying?

"If the Son shall make you free, ye shall be free indeed. . . ."

The verse echoed in his mind . . . the selfsame words he'd read on his own several times now. According to this verse, in some inexplicable way, Daed had found a spiritual freedom in the last days of his life.

This was the first funeral Nellie Mae had ever attended that seemed more like a Preaching service—certainly the messages being delivered were quite unfamiliar to a third of those in attendance. She felt strongly that David Yoder's death might either unify or further divide the People.

She looked toward the back of the room, where Chris and Zach sat with their family. A few other Englischers were there, as well, including a couple regular customers of the bakery shop.

But today it was Caleb she found herself drawn to, utterly sad for him. A tear trickled down her cheek, and she glanced his way again and saw he was looking at her, his countenance pained. She wondered if he'd had any previous warning about what would be said today by either Uncle Bishop or Preacher Manny. Had David Yoder shared any of this directly with Caleb? If not, how was such a service setting with the family—

Caleb in particular, who'd adhered to his father's tenacious beliefs even when it meant the death of their relationship.

All in God's hands now.

Aware of the apprehension in the room, she closed her eyes, pleading for divine mercy to settle over the congregation. Nellie added a silent prayer of thanks for the miracle of salvation in David Yoder's heart, grateful to Chris and his father for their part in this wonderful turn.

Chapter 29

Nellie Mae was determined to be a good sister, even if it meant appearing to be meddlesome. She had to know if Rhoda was aware of David Yoder's death and felt the need to go and visit by herself. After all, Rhoda was surely as lost as David had been, and she was still her dear sister, no matter how far into the world Rhoda wandered.

With this in mind, she left Mamma in charge of the shop and went on foot to the Kraybills' house midmorning, hoping to see elusive Rhoda there.

She spotted a black-and-white car parked off to the side of the driveway and guessed it was Rhoda's. Seeing this reminder of her sister's fancy life, she wondered what David Yoder might share with all of them about that, after four days in Glory.

"Hullo!" she called to Rhoda, who was carrying trash out the back door.

"How're you, Nellie Mae?" Her sister shielded her eyes from the sun. "What brings you here?"

"I hoped you might have a minute to talk."

Rhoda frowned. "Well, Mrs. Kraybill's expecting me to finish cleaning."

Nellie followed her to the kitchen door. "I won't keep you

long. I just wanted to know if you'd heard that David Yoder passed away last Sunday."

Rhoda shook her head. "Ach, I hadn't." She opened the door, and for a moment, Nellie wondered if their conversation was to be cut short. Then Rhoda kindly held the screen door, motioning for Nellie to go inside first. "Maybe we could sit at the table for a bit." Going to a tall refrigerator, Rhoda opened it and brought out a pitcher of orange juice, already made.

"I'll make it snappy," Nellie said. She couldn't help noticing the modern kitchen, with its shiny dishwasher and double oven—ever so bright and cheerful, too. "Ya know, David Yoder turned to Jesus before he died . . . made his peace with God." She paused, wondering if she'd make matters worse if she said what was on her mind. "I sure hope you're happy with your . . . um, fancy life."

"Why, sure I am." Rhoda sipped some juice. "How'd David die?"

"He was kicked in the head by one of his mules some time ago."

"Oh . . . that's just terrible." She shook her head. "So many dangers on a farm."

"So many dangers in the world, too," Nellie said softly.

Rhoda gave her a sharp look. "Are you here to ask me to come home?" she said. "Mamma has, you know—a couple times. I wondered if she'd sent ya, maybe."

Still hesitant to speak her mind fully, Nellie Mae turned the juice glass around, staring at it. "It'd sure put a big smile on Mamma's face, I know. Nan's and Dat's, too. But since you haven't joined church, that's all up to you."

"Honestly, I couldn't go back even if I wanted to." Rhoda explained she'd signed a year's lease with her landlord.

Dat had taught them well—there was no sense in talking

about breaking a legal promise—or any promise, for that matter. "So, after a year's up, would ya consider it?"

Rhoda shrugged and glanced away, toward the vast green meadow visible through the window. " 'Tween you and me, I hope to find me a nice husband by then." But she looked ever so glum now. "Though I haven't had much luck with that yet, either."

"I could say the same." Nellie offered a small smile as she rose from the table. "Denki for the juice. Sorry to keep you from work."

"Tell Nan I think of her a lot." Rhoda touched her arm. "Tell Mamma, too."

"Well, you're not a stranger—you could tell them yourself."

There was a faraway look in Rhoda's pretty green eyes, and Nellie wanted to throw her arms around her. *If only she wasn't so stubborn . . . bent on her own way.*

Together the two sisters walked out the back door and down toward the narrow road. Nellie buttoned up her lip, finding it mighty curious that Rhoda had clearly forgotten about the cleaning she was being paid to do.

———

In spite of having declined yet another date from Chris, Nellie hoped he might stop in at the bakery shop that Thursday afternoon. Just as before, Mamma and Nan made themselves conspicuously scarce near the time he usually appeared.

Chris strode up rather comically, offering his familiar grin. "How's the prettiest baker in Honey Brook?" he asked, his eyes serious.

Blushing, she looked away.

Chris pointed to the notebook on the counter. "Are these your recipes?"

"Jah. I was just adding to them." She was relieved his intense gaze was no longer focused on her. "S'pose I should just put together a little book as you said, since so many customers have asked."

"If you want to, I could help you print and bind it. I know someone who could help us."

Us? He wanted to include himself in the imaginary project? There was no question that he was thoughtful . . . even sweet. And she felt more certain than ever that he liked her—he wouldn't keep coming by every week if he didn't.

"Denki, Chris . . . that's nice of you."

He smiled, pausing before continuing. "Have you thought any more about going to the tabernacle meeting?" Before she could respond, he added, "I'd like to take you—considering I was the one who first invited Suzy there last spring." He explained how he'd given Suzy the flyer, inviting her to the meetings. "But maybe your sister wrote about that, too."

Nellie nodded. *Should I give in?*

The whole time he stood there, Chris never once looked at either the pies or the delicious cookies. And when he didn't ask again, she hoped she hadn't miffed him. Sure, she wanted to go. Despite all the reasons she'd talked herself out of another date before, she was secretly glad he'd come by to ask again.

"Thanks for invitin' me," she said softly, unable to avoid his clear gaze.

"Then, you'll go?" His eyes twinkled with irrepressible delight.

Nellie couldn't keep from smiling her joyful reply.

CHAPTER 30

The days following his father's funeral were heavy with heat, humidity, and strenuous work—threshing small grains took up the hours from dawn to dusk, as well as hoeing the tobacco patches. Caleb's extended family pitched in and helped with both as Amish and English farmers up and down the road continued cultivating their potato fields and cornfields.

Stifling hot evenings were spent outdoors with picnic blankets spread on well-trimmed lawns. Amidst the creak of rocking chairs and hushed chatter of teenagers, Caleb's nephews and nieces chased lightning bugs, putting them in canning jars. An occasional harmonica tune wafted over the dense midsummer air as the family sat on the porch, trying to escape the heat and longing for sundown. Nights were nearly as muggy as the daylight hours, bringing little relief. Those sleeping in upstairs bedrooms were sometimes forced to shed their nightclothes, hoping for the slightest breeze.

Caleb found the absence of his father surprisingly difficult. Daed's last words still stirred in his memory. More than once, while sitting in his room next to the open window late at night, he had reached for a pen and paper to start a letter to Nellie Mae. He wanted to share his keen understanding of her loss of Suzy more than a year ago. He longed to tell her that his love for her remained, that he missed her more than his words dared communicate.

Each time, though, he realized again how futile it was to attempt to link across the short distance to her. And with that knowing came the wadded-up paper and the aggravation of realizing the gulf between them was much too wide now. Besides, according to the grapevine, Nellie had already moved on—attending Singings with the New Order church youth. He'd even heard she'd been seen out with an Englischer. Was she taking the same path as Suzy? After all, she was every bit as pretty. *And truly delightful in every way* . . .

But it was past time to forget her. And there was no time at present to think of courting anyone new, not till after the laborious tobacco harvest was past . . . if even then.

———

Nellie Mae walked beside Chris up the narrow aisle to take seats on the rustic benches at the little tabernacle at the Tel Hai Campground. The wooden platform was low and smaller than she'd envisioned from Suzy's account, but it was the fervor in the singing that captured her attention as many young couples and other folk crowded into the open-air meeting. She was happy to be outside on such a warm Saturday evening, although thunder rumbled in the distance.

The sermon text was the nineteenth chapter of Job: " 'Oh that my words were now written! Oh that they were printed in a book! That they were graven with an iron pen and lead in the rock for ever! For I know that my redeemer liveth, and that he shall stand at the latter day upon the earth: And though after my skin worms destroy this body, yet in my flesh shall I see God. . . .' "

As the evangelist explained the verses, she realized his conversational style was similar to Preacher Manny's. Nellie was grateful to be in a church where the preaching was vital for daily living. Thinking of the verse just read, she thanked the Lord once more for bringing David Yoder to the knowledge of salvation . . . just in time, too.

Sitting next to Chris, she imagined what Suzy might have felt, coming here the first time . . . the evening she'd felt so uneasy. Thankfully, she had returned a second time and answered the Savior's call at the altar up front.

After the final prayer, people began to rise and Nellie noticed quite a few Amish couples, the girls in their long cape dresses and aprons. There were Mennonites, too, some of the girls wearing the formal head covering, others without the Kapp, their hair pulled back in a loose bun.

Later, on the drive to the ice cream shop in Honey Brook, Chris asked if going to the tabernacle had made her sad . . . because of missing Suzy. He mentioned that he'd seen her cry several times.

"I wasn't thinkin' so much of my sister as I was David Yoder's family. Elizabeth, 'specially . . . and poor Caleb."

"Well, he seemed all right today when I saw him during milking. Grieving, yes, but not openly."

She sniffled at the mention of her former beau. "It's just that . . . well, Caleb's been through a lot this year." She didn't know how much Chris and Caleb talked. Did he even know Caleb had been sent away by his father?

"He's shared a few things."

She wondered if Chris knew about her and Caleb's breakup. "We were once engaged," she admitted. "But then our church broke apart."

Chris's smile vanished. "So you're the girl. . . ." His voice sounded pinched, even pained.

She felt uncomfortable—she wouldn't be rude and go on

about how they'd met or how long they'd courted. Chris was her date tonight.

"What happened . . . after the church split, I mean?" he asked.

"Well, Caleb wanted me to keep to the Old Ways."

"So you came to the Lord after the church folk scattered?"

"Jah, and strange to say it, but the Lord came between Caleb and me. That's all I'd best say."

Chris became uncommonly quiet as they drove the moonlit back roads. She realized she'd upset him somehow.

Some time later, he said, "I'm sorry for Caleb—losing his father . . . and his girl." Chris looked over at her, his gaze lingering.

"I'm glad he has you for a friend, Chris." She went on to say that she prayed daily for Caleb to know the Lord.

"So do I," he admitted.

When they arrived at the ice cream shop, she hoped they might talk about other things. She didn't want the evening to end on a sad note, especially after having enjoyed the service so much—and Chris's company.

"What flavor will it be tonight?" he asked as they approached the counter.

She eyed the many choices on the board behind the counter. "Strawberry sounds good. Denki."

"Branching out a little, I see." He placed her order and then paused. "I'll have what you had last time—it looked so good."

They found a table in the back, more private than before, and she was quite relieved when he made not a single further mention of Caleb.

Later, when Chris drove her home, Nellie noticed he took the long way, as he'd done before. She enjoyed the starry sky and the moonlight on the fertile fields while soft music played on his radio. It was impossible to justify accepting another date from him, but goodness, he looked her way nearly as often as Caleb had when they rode out on nights like this in his open buggy.

"I'd like to see you again, Nellie Mae," he said as he parked along the wide shoulder, near her house.

"You mean next Thursday at the shop?" She couldn't keep her smile in check.

"Yes, that too." He got out and came around to open her door. "I'll walk you down the road a ways, okay?"

"Nice of you, Chris . . . but it's a plenty bright night."

"Well, is it all right if I want to?"

She wouldn't think too far ahead. She'd simply relish this moment. How she'd enjoyed this special night filled with memories of Suzy and her faith . . . and ice cream with Chris. Somewhere, in the back of her mind, was the constant thought of her former beau, but she pushed it away. Feelings for Chris Yoder had grown in her heart in such a short time.

What does it mean? Am I finally over Caleb?

———

Rosanna King sat alone at the kitchen table, looking out at the glow of the moon on waist-high corn that ran in long, even rows beyond the side yard. To keep the insects from flapping and fluttering against the window, she'd decided against lighting the gas lamp. Besides, it was ever so late to be up.

She had painful cramping again tonight, although she couldn't tell if it was due to the baby or indigestion. The midwife had suggested saltine crackers at such times, so here she sat nibbling on one—snacking and praying.

Visions of a funeral and burial threatened her peace. If she were to have a stillbirth now, she would have to endure

315

both, being so much farther along. But on the brighter side, if all went well, in just ten more weeks, their baby would be safe in her arms.

Will you allow me this miracle, Lord?

Lena had written another very encouraging letter, including a prayer she'd composed just for Rosanna. So touched was she by it, Rosanna had tucked it into the pages of her Bible to reread whenever she felt the panic lurking.

Here lately she did not suffer from panic as much as she did fatigue. So far she had spent nearly half the day in bed and was becoming quickly weary of it. Even so, she was willing to do more than that for her precious babe.

If Elias wasn't so busy with tilling potato fields, she might mention the need for a short trip to the doctor again. But making even that drive frightened her. Perhaps she'd ask Linda Fisher to use her telephone to call the midwife tomorrow when Linda stopped by with lunch. Or, better yet, stay to pray with her yet again. Truly, the Beachy woman who'd first introduced Rosanna to the idea of salvation full and free was as dear as any believer she knew.

Meanwhile, she ate crackers, letting the salty blandness soothe her stomach and hoping . . . praying these alarming spasms might cease.

CHAPTER 31

On his way to Elias King's, Reuben passed three vegetable stands and a child's deserted bicycle with its small wicker basket dangling from the handlebars. Today he would till Elias's twenty acres of corn with a team of eight mules. He knew by the warmth of the dawn that this next-to-last day of July would be a scorcher. *Should be done by sunset.*

He'd awakened earlier than usual to finish up some of his own chores before heading to Elias's. Knowing he'd have little time to rest today, he leaned back in the buggy seat as he rode, taking in the fields, verdant and thriving, in all directions. It sure looked to be a good year for potatoes and corn . . . even tobacco for the old church farmers who were still growing it. Thus far, God was answering prayer for a bountiful harvest.

When he came within shouting distance, he was glad to see lights in the Kings' kitchen windows, which meant Rosanna might be up and feeling better.

Soon, though, he discovered it was Elias who was making himself some oatmeal and toast. "Rosanna's plumb tuckered out," Elias told him. "Doctor wants her in bed till the baby comes."

"Must be awful hard on her, seein' how the summer's been so hot."

Elias nodded, finishing up his breakfast. "Still, we're not nearly as bad off as we were last year round this time."

Remembering the severity of the drought, Reuben finished the coffee Elias had poured for him. "Looks like this year could be different, Lord willin'."

"Let's be mighty thankful for that." Elias wiped his mouth on his sleeve. "Best be getting to work, jah?"

Reuben carried his coffee mug to the sink before he followed him outdoors. On the way up the earthen ramp to the second story of the bank barn, Elias asked if he would remember Rosanna in prayer. "Truth be told, her health—and the baby's—are in the back of my mind all the time."

Reuben promised to pray. "The Lord sees the desire of your heart—yours and Rosanna's."

"I'll try to keep that in mind." Elias nodded. "Denki."

"Anytime, preacher."

———

They were driving home from the nursery on a day Chris had worked in the landscaping office.

Zach yawned loudly, leaning back on the headrest. "I helped Dad put together a knock-out landscaping plan today. He seemed pleased," he said. "Looks like I've got my focus back."

"Great to hear it. Would you mind if I asked you something about you and Suzy?" asked Chris.

"Fire away."

"Did you guys ever talk about your future—how to make it work if you were to marry someday?"

Zach's head popped back up. "Where'd that come from?"

"The culture clash, you know. Wondered how that would fly."

"Easy. Suzy was finished with Amish life."

"You knew this?"

"Sure." Zach stretched his right arm out the open window, yawning again. "She was all geared up to leave. Just didn't know how to switch from wearing Plain clothes to more modern ones without causing an uproar at home." Zach frowned, facing him. "Why are you asking?"

Chris didn't want to say.

"Hey, fine, go ahead and clam up." Zach folded his arms across his chest.

Chris was surprised Zach was so sure about Suzy's plan for going modern. He couldn't imagine Nellie Mae as anything but Amish. Oh, he'd tried, but he was sure that wasn't happening— not in his head, and not in reality. She was so Plain, in fact, it was a waste of time to think of her otherwise.

So, if I'm to keep seeing her, I might need to grow a beard. . . . He grinned at the image of himself decked out like an Amishman, but he had no interest in joining the horse-and-buggy crowd.

If only he'd thought all this through before he'd fallen so hard . . . but then he might have missed his chance to get to know her at all.

Frustrated as Chris was, he wouldn't deny his feelings. He needed to figure things out—the sooner, the better.

——

Betsy was surprised and elated to see her mother-in-law at a pickling bee over at Martha's the first week in August. Several women had gathered to put up dills and bread-and-butter pickles, with Martha and the two younger women making and stirring the hot brine, while Betsy and Hannah prepared the cucumbers. Little Emma and her younger brothers got underfoot in their efforts to help, creating lots of chuckles all around.

It had been such a long time since she'd seen Hannah. She sat right next to her and they chattered nearly all morning. Glad for a bit of a break from the bakery shop, she asked Hannah what had brought her here today—it was rare that she or Noah ventured this direction anymore.

"Oh, I've been missin' Honey Brook, is all. Seemed like a good time to take Martha up on her invitation." A small, sad smile played across her wrinkled face. "And Noah and I wanted to offer our sympathy to Elizabeth after we heard of David Yoder's passing."

Betsy didn't want to get her hopes up, but she was glad to see her mother-in-law accepting an invitation from family to visit again—from a Beachy home, no less. She wished they'd move back. *Where they belong.* After all, the Dawdi Haus was still vacant. And even if Reuben's parents wouldn't consider living with them, there was always Ephram and Maryann, who'd remained firmly planted in the old church.

She contemplated again David Yoder's conversion and had a strong belief that Elizabeth might soon follow in his footsteps. Elizabeth had asked her meaningful questions following the burial service, and Betsy had shared with her some of the verses that had touched her so deeply in the third chapter of the gospel of John.

God's Word will accomplish the good pleasure of the Lord, she thought, recalling another favorite passage she'd discovered recently in Isaiah. She trusted it would be true for dear Elizabeth and the rest of her family.

———

Food, and lots of it, brought her such comfort here lately, despite the fact that she'd already gained a good five pounds—pounds Rhoda had dropped with great effort and satisfaction in the previous months. But with bills pouring in, including the latest, for the small television she'd impulsively purchased, she'd immediately turned to food, especially the grease-laden fast food she craved. In any case, eating kept her from crying . . . over the loss of Ken and Ted and all the uncaring Amish boys who'd ever looked her way, only to reject her.

She sobbed about being stuck in Strasburg, with the long drive to work at both the restaurant and the Kraybills', and she cried because she had no one to talk to, missing her cozy sisterly chats with dearest Nan. When she was wholly honest with herself, she even admitted missing Dat's long, drawn-out nightly Bible reading.

Leaving the restaurant after work on this blazing afternoon, Rhoda was tempted to make a left-hand turn and head out east, toward Beaver Dam Road. *For old time's sake.*

But did she really want to return there?

The thought of having to let her hair grow back—that miserable middle part and tight bun—made her squirm. And the unstylish dresses and the long black aprons she'd worn whether cooking or not. What was the apron for, anyway? She wore one at the restaurant and at the Kraybills', but there was a reason for it when she was working. Even then, she could scarcely wait to untie it and toss it into the hamper the minute she was finished for the day.

Thinking of Mrs. Kraybill, she had a hankering to stop in and talk to her. After all, the woman had encouraged her flight to the world in every imaginable way. Without her influence, who knew where Rhoda might be today. Most likely not living in a second-floor room, hearing her former beau clomp around overhead while he played his music too loud—

up there living his happy, single, and childless life, content to be without her.

All this time I thought he cared. . . .

Sighing, Rhoda fought back tears and drove straight to the house where she'd once hidden this beautiful car she drove. Where all of her fancy ideas had gotten their start.

———

His mouth parched from a long day in the sun, Caleb went to the well and pumped several cupfuls of water, gulping them down. Hungry for supper, he headed to the house to rinse the rest of the grime off his hands.

Leah and Emmie were setting the table, carrying food over from the cookstove. "Where's Mamm?" he asked, going to the sink.

Emmie glanced his way, a worried expression on her face. "She's in Daed's old room."

Concerned, he dried his hands and tossed the towel onto the counter. He found her kneeling at Daed's bedside, weeping.

Placing a hand on her shoulder, he stood there silently. He'd never seen her cry like this before, and it convicted him for his own lack of sorrow. He was sorry about his father's death—it wasn't that—and he missed Daed's presence in the house. But he hadn't wept. Not at the burial, where he'd helped shovel heavy clumps of dirt into the gaping hole for Daed's coffin, nor at the surprisingly unorthodox funeral service.

He waited while Mamm dried her eyes and rose to sit on the edge of the bed. Patting the spot next to her, she gave him a smile.

"You all right, Mamma?"

She sighed. "I'm glad you're here. There's something your father told me. . . . I can't get it out of my mind."

Had his own mother also endured sleepless nights with Daed's words turning continually in her head?

"Your Daed kept sayin', 'Preacher Manny was right,' until I didn't know what to think." Profound grief was evident in her eyes, and deep lines marked her face. "But it was his tears, Caleb—he couldn't stop lamenting. He urged me to attend the new church . . . said I would find what he'd been missin' till the last few weeks of his life."

Caleb understood her confusion. He, too, still struggled to grasp that his father—the man who had forbidden him to marry Nellie Mae—had embraced the very faith that had once made Nellie and her family unsuitable in his eyes. How could it be? How could a hard, stubborn man like his father change so drastically?

"I'm honestly thinkin' of going this Sunday," Mamm said.

Startled by this, he wished he might persuade her differently. "What'll the bishop say?"

"Well, I've talked to his wife, Anna, already. Seems the bishop has taken to heart much of what Preacher Manny shared at the funeral."

This made not a smidgen of sense. How could it?

"Anna and the bishop have been reading together every night," she whispered.

He held his breath. "Reading what?"

"The Good Book, of course." She referred to it in reverent tones, just the way Nellie Mae had . . . the way Chris did.

"Well, I read it, too, but I'm not thinkin' of switching churches. Are you, Mamm . . . truly?"

She covered her mouth, trembling.

"Ach, don't tell me . . ."

"I just know if your father hadn't been injured—if he was robust and healthy and alive today—he wouldn't have talked

that way. God used his paralysis—and his impending death—
to lead him to accept new life . . . eternal life."

He looked at her. "You believe this for truth?"

Nodding, her eyes glistened again. "Never more than
now."

Sitting here in the room where his father's life had ebbed
away, Caleb wished he'd at least made some attempt to confess
his deception during the latter days of courting Nellie Mae.
And the shifty way he'd handled things, willing to do anything
to get his father's land. But he'd let the moments tick away,
not heeding the inner nudging.

*And I let Daed die without knowing that I freely for-
gave him.*

"Daed confessed his shortcomings toward me. I should've
done the same," he said quietly. "I just never thought he would
slip away so fast."

She listened, reaching for his hand. "I'm ever so sorry."

"Should've made things right when I had the chance."

She leaned her head on his shoulder. "That's exactly what
your father told me, Caleb. 'Make things right with the Lord
while time's on your side. . . .' "

In the solemn stillness, Caleb was keenly aware of his own
lack of time. Did he dare wait for the light of truth Nellie Mae
had told him about, there in her shop? Did he know without a
doubt—*who could possibly know?*—he would survive a mule
kick to the head? Or any other freak farm accident, for that
matter, and not be plunged into eternity without God?

*"If the Son therefore shall make you free, ye shall be free
indeed."*

Was it possible? Could he, too, have the assurance of eternal
life, just as Daed had so urgently declared?

"I oughta think good and hard 'bout this," he whispered.

CHAPTER 32

Nellie Mae suggested Mamma sit out on the front porch with her, wanting to just relax and look out over the neatly trimmed front lawn. Down on the road, market wagons traveled back and forth, and there were several young children on scooters.

Dragonflies settled on the pond across the way as dusk played hide-and-seek with the sun. And dark, rich soil peeked out between the rows of corn to the north. Far to the horizon, the ridge of hills turned slowly gray, then black, as the sun made its slide to earth.

"I've been wantin' to show you something, Mamma." Slipping her hand into her pocket, she pulled out the secret picture. "It's Suzy," she whispered.

Mamma gasped. "Oh, goodness!" Her mother held it away from her eyes, squinting a bit. "Well, doesn't she look happy?"

"Her beau took this picture before she drowned," said Nellie quietly.

Mamma sniffled. "Did ya ever see such a sweetness in her eyes?"

Nellie clasped her mother's hand and they were still for a long moment, sharing the secret that had troubled Nellie so.

"Oh, I can't tell you how nice it is seein' her face again," Mamma said.

"What must I do with this—now that you know I have it?" Nellie asked. "Does the New Order prohibit such things? I'll be starting baptism instruction next week, ya know."

"Well, if it was just me, I'd say if you don't sit and stare at it, or let it come 'tween you and the Lord"—Mamma smiled now—"you might keep it in your Bible, maybe. A good reminder of what Suzy's dyin' brought us." Mamma reached into Nellie's dress pocket and pulled out Suzy's Kapp strings. "As if you need another souvenir, jah?"

Together they smiled knowingly, and their laughter rose and scattered on the wings of twilight.

———

Chris was heading for the car after finishing up the milking with Caleb.

"Hey, don't leave just yet," Caleb called to him. "I'd like to show ya something in my room."

"Sure, but I have some college paper work to do with my dad, so I'll need to get going."

"It'll only take a minute."

Upstairs, on his dresser, Caleb showed him the deed to Daed's land. "Man, is this some relic or what!" Chris said, noticing the yellowing around the edges.

"Passed down through the generations." Caleb's smile extended from ear to ear. "My father wanted me to have it— Abe just brought it by."

Chris looked out the window and whistled. "Wow—what do you plan to do with all the land?"

"Well, grow cash crops, for certain, and have plenty of grazing land for the dairy cows. Maybe raise horses, like Reuben Fisher."

Like Reuben . . .

Chris caught the curious glint in his cousin's eyes. *He's still thinking of Nellie Mae.*

"What about tobacco?" He was curious, knowing that the crop had been the family's staple for generations.

"Well, tobacco harvest is comin' up fast . . . but after this year, I'm not sure." Caleb motioned for him to take a seat near the open window. "Mamm's urging me to raise other crops . . . hoping I'll make the right choice on that." He went to sit on the edge of his bed. "To be blunt, plenty's goin' to change round here . . . and right quick, too."

Chris wondered what he meant.

"I've made a hard decision," Caleb said. "My father seemed to change overnight . . . he became downright *niedrich*— humble—before he died. I have to say it got my attention."

Chris leaned forward, listening.

"My father not only willingly gave me his land, Chris . . . he gave me something else. Something better." Caleb got up and went to the dresser, picking up the deed again. "Our great-grandfather—yours and mine—owned this property. Did you know that?"

Fascinated, Chris looked at the old deed again.

Caleb pointed to the former owner. "Right there, see? Christian C. Yoder. Guess what the middle initial stands for."

Chris laughed. "No way."

"Kinda spooky, jah?"

Caleb handed it to Chris. "Yep, your name's on there, too—must've been your namesake." He spoke of all the blood kin who'd lived out their lives here in this house, on this land. "All of them following the Old Ways to the best of their ability, then dyin' and never knowing what my father experienced in the last days of his life. Never knowin' the assurance of their salvation.

"Before Daed died, he pleaded with me to make the faith he found my own." Caleb's face shone. "I'm glad to say I finally took him up on it. I'll see my Daed again someday. And I know now it's not a prideful thing to say I'm born again—since the Lord himself paid the price for me."

Chris gave him a firm handshake. "Now, that's the best news, cousin. Hey, we're brothers now."

Caleb smiled. "Sounds good to me!"

———

Thursday afternoon, on the way over to Caleb's, Chris stopped in at Nellie's Simple Sweets. He'd considered what he wanted to do and hoped Nellie Mae might agree to see him again. After all, revival meetings were still in full swing at Tel Hai.

Besides, he was anxious to see how she might react to his invitation. He recalled her lingering tenderness toward Caleb, even though Chris was certain she was happy to be in his company now.

At first, she seemed surprised to see him, since he usually came later in the afternoon. She was walking over from the house, carrying several medium-sized boxes—filled with fruit pies, he assumed.

He rushed to help. "Here, let me take those."

"Are ya back for more desserts?" Her quick smile gave her away. She *was* glad to see him.

"I was hoping you'd go again to the revival meeting this Saturday night."

She paused, like she might be thinking it through. Then she said, "All right. Sounds nice."

Filled with a growing sense of excitement, he carried the pies to the bakery shop. He tempered his grin when he saw Nellie's mother behind the counter in the bakery shop today.

He greeted her, and Mrs. Fisher held his gaze, smiling. "Can I interest you in two pies today, Mr. Yoder?" she teased.

Deciding to try something new, he bought a peach cobbler. Then, waving good-bye to both Nellie Mae and her mother, he headed back to his car. He noticed Nellie standing in the window. He waved again and was tempted to memorize the outline of her, carrying it in his mind all the way to Caleb's.

———

After milking was done, when they were washing up in the milk house together, Chris mentioned the surprise he had out in the car. Caleb perked up his ears, and Chris went to get the peach cobbler, still warm from the sun.

Coming into the kitchen, he placed it on the table, and Caleb's eyes widened. "I see you've been to Nellie's bakery shop."

Chris could hardly contain his pleasure. "This is just one small thank-you for letting me hang around with you here, in the country." He dished up ample portions and served the dessert first to Caleb, then to himself. "I also thought you might like a tasty reminder of someone's baking skills."

"Well, believe me, this here's somethin' you don't soon forget."

They exchanged banter about their favorite foods—pies and pastries included—and Chris's plans to head to college soon.

Then Caleb said, "You know, I used to be able to talk with Nellie 'bout most anything. She has no idea what's happened to me."

"That you're saved, you mean?"

Caleb nodded. "Honestly, it's still hard to think of it just that way."

Chris listened.

"Even so, I know I've already lost her." Caleb reached for another scoop of cobbler. "And rightly so."

Seeing the look of longing in Caleb's eyes, Chris inhaled deeply. "Listen, Cousin—"

Caleb's laugh was hearty. "Hey, it's *brother*, remember?"

"Brother it is." Chris stared at his Plain cousin, who so closely resembled himself in so many ways. "You know, Caleb, you've shared some personal things with me about you and Nellie Mae. . . ."

Caleb's head jerked up, his fork poised in midair. "Jah?"

"Well, I've been thinking . . . and I realize it's time I leveled with *you*. . . ."

————

Rhoda parked her car up the road and walked along the shoulder, down to the house. The horse pasture on this side of her father's house was shaded with cottonwoods, all lined up in a straight row. She'd leaned against the trunks of those very trees, counting slowly to one hundred, while her sisters ran and hid, back when they were all little girls.

Breathing in the sweetness of honeysuckle, she dared to let her eyes roam over the rambling paddock and the neatly trimmed front yard. It looked to her like the picket fence had been newly whitewashed, and she was struck by a pang of sadness, not having been around to help with a chore she'd always enjoyed.

She tried not to look at the house directly as she made her way up the drive, as self-conscious as she'd ever been in her pretty blue skirt and blue and yellow floral-print blouse, her short hair free and floating against her cheeks.

What'll Dat say when he sees me all fancy like this? She could only imagine the jolt to his heart.

Hoping she would not cause more pain for her parents,

she hurried through the grass and crept into the barn. The acrid sting of manure mixed with the sweat of the horses overwhelmed her—she'd forgotten the smells of her father's beloved trade.

She moved past the stable toward the little woodworking shop, where she spied Dat bent over his wooden desk in the corner, poring over his logs of birthing schedules and training programs.

Pausing at the threshold, she leaned against it. *This is it . . . the end of all my so-called fun.*

She pushed up her glasses. "Dat . . . it's Rhoda," she said softly.

He turned, his startled expression turning into a full smile. "Well, well. Gut to see ya, daughter."

"You too." She felt the lump in her throat. "You have a minute?"

He rose and pulled out a chair. "For you, Rhoda, I'd say far more than a minute."

She found courage in his reaction to her being here. "I'll get right to the point." Struggling not to cry, she looked down. Oh, she needed his acceptance, his love. And she needed the openness of fields and pastureland once again—even the woods appealed to her now that she'd been gone so long. Being cooped up in a one-room apartment wasn't at all what her heart craved. "I was terribly wrong, Dat. . . ."

"Rhoda, whatever you've done—"

"Truth is, I'm just plain miserable." She looked at him, this man who worked harder than anyone she knew. He'd never asked for anything special or unreasonable—only that his children yielded to his covering as their loving father. "The worst of it was breaking your heart," she said. "Yours and Mamma's. For that, I'm most sorry."

He tugged on his beard, his eyes piercing hers. "Would you like to come home, daughter?"

She wanted to laugh. No, cry. "Where would I park my car?" She knew it sounded ridiculous, even prideful to think she could live here again, yet have much of her own way.

A slow smile reached across his tan face. "Well, last I looked we've got a nice big woodshed."

She could tell by his sincere, steady gaze that he wasn't kidding. "You'd let me come home and still be . . . well, a bit fancy?"

He leaned forward, resting his elbows on his legs. For a moment he stared at the floor filled with sawdust and chips of wood. "Just how fancy do ya mean?"

She'd thought it all through. "Well, I'd like to attend the Beachy church—if they'll have me back—and dress more Plain than I am now, of course." She stared down at her favorite skirt and pretty white sandals. *Willing to give an inch so you can have a mile, Dat must be thinking.*

"I'll keep working hard for the Kraybills'. If you want me to quit the restaurant, I'll do that. And, once I get back on my feet, I'll start paying you room and board."

He waved his hand and shook his head. "Ach, just help your mother and sisters all you can. How's that?" He got up with a grunt and walked with her all the way down the lane and out to see her new car. And before she opened the door, he asked, "Heard you've got yourself some sort of lease where you're stayin'?"

"Mrs. Kraybill's agreed to handle that with my landlord." She'd covered all her bases, at least for now. Her brother James liked the idea of having her television, and any other fancy cast-offs she wanted to sell him at a discount. That way she wouldn't have a pile of questionable items sitting out in a yard sale, making Dat and Mamma a laughingstock.

"I must confess that I've prayed for unity amongst the People till the cows come home." He closed the car door for her and leaned on the open window. "But charity always begins at home, ya know." She saw tears in his eyes, and her heart lifted.

"Denki, Dat . . . ever so much. You've made my day!" She couldn't believe she'd just said one of Ken's favorite expressions.

Waving, she pulled onto the road, waiting until she was out near Route 10 before she gave in to her joyful tears.

Nellie, Nan, and Mamma stood next to the bakery shop window, all bunched together, their noses nearly touching the pane as they watched Dat walk down toward the road with Rhoda. "What could they be talking 'bout?" Nan asked.

Nellie realized she had been holding her breath. "Ach, do ya think Rhoda might be thinkin' of coming home?" she nearly gasped.

Nan did a little jig next to her, sniffling and then pressing her lips together. "I won't cry . . . I just won't!"

Mamma, more serene, slipped a plump arm around each of them. "Don't ever doubt it, dear ones . . . you're seein' firsthand how God answers prayer."

Oh, please let it be so! thought Nellie, squeezing Nan's hand.

CHAPTER 33

Rosanna eagerly awaited the sound of Elias's footsteps on the stairs, especially during the noon hour, when he so kindly carried up a large tray of food for the two of them. The families from their church had been faithful in keeping them supplied with hot meals for both lunch and supper.

Such a blessing . . .

Elias had repositioned the bed from its original spot, so she could look out the window when she tired of reading or needlework. At times, she could even watch Elias out in the field, as the second cutting of alfalfa was in full swing.

She tired so easily anymore that sometimes it was all she could do to stay awake when Nellie Mae dropped by to read aloud from the Bible. Yesterday, Rhoda—who'd just returned home—had come to visit for a few hours, sitting upstairs with her and crocheting baby things right along with Rosanna. Such good company she was, and what stories she told on herself—ever so amusing. Sobering too.

Today, when Elias brought up a delicious meal of hamburger puffs topped with cream sauce, green beans, and a side of cabbage slaw, he sat and talked with Rosanna about the possibility of inviting Rhoda to stay with them, for pay, when Lena's baby was born. That way, she'd have someone to help with Jonathan—as they'd named him already, hoping he would in fact turn out to be a boy—while she waited for her own little one to arrive.

If all continues to go well . . .

"Will you want Lena to come for a while, too, maybe?" Elias asked, shoveling a bite into his mouth.

She cringed, thinking of her cousin Kate's coming too often last year. "As a wet nurse, ya mean?"

He nodded, his mouth still full.

"Maybe . . . I'll ask her if she'd feel comfortable staying for the first few days." But then she thought of all the children Lena had to care for at home.

Surely there's a wet nurse close by.

Once her own baby was born, Rosanna wondered if she might not have plenty of breast milk for two wee ones. But if not, she would resort to infant formula, just as she had with Eli and Rosie.

"Looks like the Lord's goin' to give us the desire of our hearts," Elias said, reaching for his glass. "With Lena's baby not much older than ours, Lord willin', it'll be nearly like having twins all over again."

She blew a kiss to him. "And I s'pose you'll be quite satisfied if we end up with two little girls, jah?"

Elias leaned over to give her a kiss. "You do have a way of makin' a man chuckle, love." He reached down and stroked her hair, still loose from the night. "I best be headin' back out. But I'll be in for supper later."

"Take plenty of cold water along in your thermos," she called to him, watching her darling go.

Rosanna planned to spend even more time praying for her preacher-husband, what with the church youth already having begun their study of the Confession of Faith and the New Order *Ordnung* in preparation for baptism. Elias was working alongside Preacher Manny to learn all he could, and right quick, too, as he instructed the young applicants about being in right relationship with the Lord and one another.

Nellie Mae's joining church, she thought with a smile, ever so happy about that. *Now, if you'll just see fit to send her a kind and good husband, dear Lord. . . .*

———

Her father's horses rhythmically moved their heads from side to side, lowering their noses into the tallest grazing grass in the high meadow. Dat had once told Nellie they did this to watch the insects spread out below them as they moved forward. She wasn't sure if he'd said that in jest, but she liked the idea all the same.

Nellie watched from her bedroom window as the horses nuzzled one another and then meandered forward, finding their way along, letting first one mare lead . . . then another.

She felt something like them as they drifted toward the barn for watering. First Caleb had led her, so to speak, and then Chris. Both young men were special to her, but neither was right. She knew this now; she'd spent long hours pondering her upcoming date tonight with Chris.

Having taken care to brush her hair fifty extra strokes, she pinned it back just so. Sure, she was enamored with Chris. Well, she had been until she'd really thought about the possibility of courtship. Which of them would budge, if they were to become serious? Was it even practical to think of Chris settling into the Plain community his grandfather had chosen to leave?

How's it possible for us to manage as a couple?

But even if he did decide to leave his modern life and join her here, she believed she still cared too much for Caleb. She wasn't ready to be wooed by a new love—might never be. So, when the time was right, sometime this evening, she would tell Chris the truth . . . that she liked him, and quite a lot, but she loved Caleb. And maybe she always would.

Thus far God had given her the grace to bear her sadness. Yet she wouldn't stay marrying age for too many more years. Even so, she must trust the Lord, who does all things well, as Mamma so often reminded her and Nan. *And now Rhoda, too.* Such a delight it was to see her sister settle quickly—and happily—into James's former room down the hall, the very spot she'd asked for and been refused. But something had changed in Mamma . . . in Dat, too. They were more tolerant, and Nellie had noticed the number of necklaces hanging on the edge of the old dresser mirror was fewer than before. Rhoda had placed Suzy's bracelet front and center, however, saying it was a big part of why she'd come home. Rhoda had also begun sewing new cape dresses and aprons, and Nellie secretly wondered if she might someday up and sell her car, too.

Just that morning Rhoda had returned Suzy's diary, and Nellie Mae had passed it right off to Mamma.

"Where're you headed?" Nan poked her head into Nellie's room.

"Over to the little tabernacle at Tel Hai—ever go there?"

Nan nodded. "Ezekiel's talkin' of going sometime."

"This is my last time to go . . . with a fella."

Snickering, Nan covered her mouth. "Ach, you're always talking 'bout the last you'll do such and so."

"Well, I mean it this time."

A frown crossed her brow; then she reached for Nellie's hand. "I hope what I have to say won't upset you." Nan sighed. "Ezekiel and I've set our wedding date for the first Thursday in November . . . the sixth."

"What's to be sad about?"

A smile broke on Nan's face. "I'm hopin' you'll consider being one of my bridesmaids. You and Rhoda."

"Oh, Nan, I'd love to!" She gave her sister a quick hug. "You and Ezekiel will be such a cute married couple, ya know?"

They stood smiling at each other, arms still entwined. "Only one thing could be better 'bout that day for me, Nellie . . . that's if you had a best beau there for you to fellowship with during the wedding feast."

The feast would last long into the evening and be followed by a special barn Singing with the wedding party and all the youth in attendance—a right good and happy time, for sure.

She nudged Nan to the window. "Look out there. Watch the horses . . . see how they trust the one in the lead?"

Ever so still, they watched. At last Nellie said, "They're not in any hurry to get where they're goin'. And neither am I."

"Dat always says essential things can be learned from nature, if we pay attention. Journeying with the seasons the Lord set into motion."

Jah, journeying with the Lord . . .

After a time, Nellie moved toward the door. " 'Tis nearly dusk, so I best be goin'."

"Is it Chris, then, tonight?" Nan whispered.

Nellie Mae gave her a nod. "Pray for me . . . it won't be easy." She thought how much harder it would be to say good-bye to someone if they were further along in their courtship. Like she and Caleb had been . . .

There was such a stitch of sadness in her soul at the painful memory of their last conversation together. Her beloved's rejecting the dear Savior . . .

Nan walked her to the end of the hall. "*Da Herr sei mit du*—God be with you, sister."

"Oh, He is, Nan." She patted her heart. "Rest assured . . . He surely is."

————

The night was especially still and heavy with nature's perfume—a scent as sweet and pure as that of wild honey.

Nellie made her way down the drive, turning right at the road. She'd slipped through the redd-up kitchen to fleeting glances from both Dat and Mamma, though as was their way, they asked no questions. But from now on, she wouldn't be sneaking out anywhere. Her dates with Chris Yoder would soon be a thing of the past.

She guessed he might try to dissuade her—try to talk her into giving their friendship more time. He did seem interested in knowing her better, even though if they were to continue their friendship, it would have to be by letter. Soon he would be leaving for Virginia to attend college.

But she wanted to share with him the truth—what lay in her heart. *Oh, but I don't want to hurt him.*

She recalled the freshness heralded by the fragrant morning as she worked out in the blackberry patch early today, alone and talking to God. A red-tailed hawk had flown overhead and hung in the high current, its call sounding almost like the *mew* of a new kitten. And she'd wept, her tears falling to the soft soil. Even so, she knew this difficult deed she was about to do was the right thing.

At the bend in the road, Nellie looked for Chris's car along the wide shoulder—their appointed meeting spot. She noticed an open buggy parked there—at first glance, it looked like Chris sitting atop, holding the reins. She looked away, knowing she had to be mistaken. What would he be doing with a courting buggy? Unless . . . had he borrowed one for a joke? But no, she couldn't imagine that.

Certain she must be imagining things, she kept her head down, embarrassed, eyes still on the road. The crickets had begun their evening song, and Nellie listened, aware of the beauty to be found in the fragile twilight.

Love is ever so fragile, too. . . .

How could you open your heart fully to someone new when it already belonged to another? That very realization had overtaken her in the blackberry patch this morning.

She heard someone call, "Nellie Mae?"

Looking up, she let out a little gasp, startled to see Caleb sitting in the buggy, smiling down at her.

"Word has it a pretty girl would be walkin' this way at dusk." He leapt down from his perch. "I'd say that's right about now."

She couldn't help herself—she laughed. Chris and Caleb in cahoots. For how long?

But she didn't have to know. The surprise was purely delicious, like mixing favorite ingredients together and getting a blue-ribbon pie.

"I hear there's a wonderful-good meetin' over at the Tel Hai tabernacle . . . want to go with me, Nellie Mae?" he asked.

She saw the sincerity in his beautiful hazel eyes. Now she was crying . . . tears of greatest joy. Caleb was here . . . *here* where Chris had agreed to meet her, of all amazing things. "That's why I came," she said, overcome with delight.

He helped her into the left side of his shiny black buggy and then sat down next to her. "There's so much I want to tell you. . . ."

With that, he picked up the reins and clicked his tongue.

The laughter she'd first suppressed at this most unexpected reunion slipped out softly, mingling with Caleb's own. A welcome breeze swept across their faces as nightfall gathered in around them.

"You once said you believed in miracles," he said.

"Now more than ever." Oh, she could hardly wait to sing joyful praises that night, blending her voice with those of the other worshipers, and her darling's!

Only one thing mattered now: She was with Caleb as the horse pulled them forward, toward the little tabernacle beneath the stars.

EPILOGUE

——

February 1968

Just imagine my excitement when both Preachers Manny and Elias agreed to help my darling catch up with the other twelve baptismal candidates as we prepared to join the New Order Amish church. Once his father led the way, the truth of the Lord became real to Caleb, and it was impossible for him to deny it for long. Or so he's told me, all smiles. As a result, Caleb and I made our kneeling vows to God on the fourteenth of September last year, becoming church members together. After he was greeted by the ministerial brethren, his face shone with purest joy as he looked my way. Up until that wonderful-good day, there had not been a more sacred moment for either of us.

As the Lord planned it, Rosanna's adopted son, Jonathan, came into the world that very evening—and with little to-do, according to Lena Stoltzfus, who kept her word without hesitation. Bright-eyed and weighing nearly nine pounds, fair-haired Jonathan seemed to bond immediately with Rosanna on the second day of his life, when Lena herself presented him. And just as was her desire, Rosanna was soon able to nurse him, once she gave birth to her tiny blue-eyed daughter, who came a bit early. A true miracle, according to the midwife. Praise be!

So Jonathan and Lena Grace are only one day shy of three weeks apart. "Two precious gifts," Rosanna says as she holds one in each arm, cooing and carrying on. Ach, how it does my heart good to see it.

My oldest sister is the busiest mother's helper ever, according to Rosanna. She hopes to keep Rhoda around for a while longer—at least till Caleb's and my own little one is born in late September, marking the month two years ago that salvation came to my father's house.

Sweet Nan and her husband are in the family way, too, which isn't surprising, as my sister and I put our heads together and planned a double wedding. And, oh, it was the finest Indian summer day there has ever been, like a divine sign, truly. Even Mamma thought so. I stood up for Nan as her bridesmaid while she made her vows to Ezekiel Mast just moments before I made my own to dearest Caleb. It was only fitting, being that Nan's older than me.

As for Dat's ongoing hope for unity, Uncle Bishop has surprised the People—some more than others—by softening his stand on studying and discussing Scripture, departing from the typical way of the Old Order. Truth is, the words spoken at David Yoder's funeral shook up quite a few folk, including Ephram and Maryann. Dat says the Lord knew what it would take—that the rather pointed and sobering sermons were necessary to nudge the most reluctant of all my married brothers in His direction. It's safe to say that freedom in the Lord—with less emphasis on man-made regulations—is becoming rather contagious round here. More prayer meetings and Bible studies are cropping up all the time, and in the most unexpected places. There's no denying it: God is at work in all of our hearts.

I can't think of anything that would please Suzy more. Honestly, I think of her most often now when Caleb reads Chris's letters from college. I'll never forget how Chris and Zach played such an important part in leading my sister to faith. And I still find it curious that the Lord used my interest in Chris—and his in me—as a wonderful reminder of Caleb while we were apart.

Just recently Chris wrote describing his ministerial studies, and I recalled that he'd once shared wanting to do something big for God. To think that his and Zach's befriending Suzy started such a stir amongst the People, like a dewdrop falling into a vast sea, rippling out to touch so many thirsty souls.

At the close of Chris's letter, he mentioned having heard that a Miss Rhoda Fisher was signed up for college days weekend in April—two months from now. Evidently Rhoda is confident about passing her GED test—the class is the sole place she goes in her car anymore, preferring to take Dat's horse and buggy the rest of the time. Of course, if Rhoda does attend the Eastern Mennonite School, I won't have her wonderful-good help with Caleb's and my first baby. But Mamma will surely make up for that, if need be.

Meanwhile, I sew and crochet for our little one to come while reciting aloud my recipes to Elizabeth, my dear mother-in-law, who kindly helps me write them down. We're hoping to finish my *Nellie's Simple Sweets Cookbook* before it's time to plant my vegetable garden. Dat and Mamma closed the bakery shop after Caleb and I moved into his parents' big farmhouse, ending one more happy chapter in my life. Now I'd much rather cook and bake for my husband. Every so often, Caleb sneaks up behind me in the kitchen to reach around my ever-widening middle and whisper loving words, his nose tickling my neck.

He likes to talk to our baby, too, which makes me smile. Oh, the Lord is so good to bring us together as man and wife. To think we'll soon be a family of three!

Caleb's mother moved right away to the Dawdi Haus after our wedding, an unspoken way of showing her hope for grandbabies—Lord willing, one right after another. It'll be especially fun for Rosanna and me to raise our wee ones together, so close in age they'll be.

As for Caleb's sister Rebekah, she managed to keep her beau a secret longer than most brides-to-be, publishing the wedding date after church just one week before Nan's and my wedding day. She and her husband, one of Susannah Lapp's cousins, live within walking distance of Caleb and me. So my husband enjoys seeing his sister, and I'm becoming a close sister-in-law to Nan's dearest friend.

Last week, between quilting frolics, Cousin Treva wrote that she noticed two new purple martin birdhouses standing tall in Dawdi and Mammi Fisher's side yard. Dat has the most interesting way of turning his father's heart back toward Honey Brook. Mammi Hannah has also sent a nice batch of recipes in answer to my request, and she has been writing to Mamma quite a lot since seeing her at Martha's for the pickling bee last summer, recently hinting at moving back "home." Although now with all the religious stir amongst my married brothers—wanting more of Scripture, as well as fancier things—who's to say my grandparents might not just end up at the Dawdi Haus next door to my parents, after all.

Early in the morning, when I do my bread baking, I ponder my love for Caleb . . . and his growing love for the Lord.

For folks who say miracles don't exist, I've imprinted in my mind the happy day when my father walked Rhoda clear out to the road, to her pretty car. And I offer prayers of thanksgiving for Rosanna's tiny, full-term daughter, as well as the blessing of Lena Grace's brother, Jonathan—both miracles, indeed. What a joy that our young preacher and his wife have themselves a cuddly pair to raise and love—a farmhand in the making for Elias, and a cute little dishwasher and quilter someday for Rosanna.

But above all, I marvel at the change saving grace has brought to the lives of the People— 'specially David Yoder, whose transformation might have been the greatest of all. Word has it, if the Lord can save such an obstinate, hard-hearted soul—soften him before his family's very eyes—then why should any of us ever doubt God's power?

Yesterday evening following supper, while thick snowflakes fell, Caleb discovered a note his father had written and stuck inside the old family Bible. *God no longer sees me as a sinner. Because of His Son's blood sacrifice, He looks at me . . . and sees Jesus there instead.*

Caleb and I had to wipe away tears, and we clasped hands and looked at each other, amazed at this precious legacy of faith for our family. We decided then and there it must be framed. We'll hang it on the kitchen wall so all who sit at our table can see the reason for our enduring happiness. Even before we realized it, our deepest longing has always been for the Savior, our dear Lord Jesus—for sure and for certain.

Author's Note

THE COURTSHIP OF NELLIE FISHER is a work of fiction inspired by the intriguing events of 1966, when the Lancaster County New Order Amish church was birthed.

Among the many helpful individuals I've conferred with, I am especially thankful to Ike and Fay Landis and to my husband, Dave, who assisted with unearthing fascinating research, as well as by taking his red pen to my manuscript. I am also grateful to my wonderful editors, David Horton, Julie Klassen, Rochelle Gloege, and Janna Nysewander, along with meticulous reviewers Ann Parrish and Barbara Birch.

I owe the greatest debt of gratitude to my Savior and Lord, the Light to my path, and Joy to my journey.

> O the deep, deep love of Jesus,
> vast, unmeasured, boundless, free!
>
> —SAMUEL TREVOR FRANCIS, 1875

More From Bestselling Author Beverly Lewis

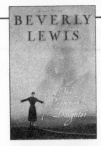

Annie Zook, the only daughter of an Old Order Amish preacher, desperately wants to please her parents and her Plain community. Yet her art is strictly forbidden, as is her friendship with the mysterious and handsome Englisher, Ben Martin. With a life-altering decision on the line, Annie must choose between her desires and the only life she knows.

ANNIE'S PEOPLE
The Preacher's Daughter, The Englisher, The Brethren

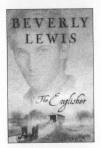

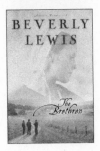

Beautiful Children's Books From Beverly Lewis

Beverly Lewis spins a delightful tale of a boy searching for answers about heaven. Complemented by beautiful illustrations and scripture verses on each page, *What Is Heaven Like?* also offers suggestions for parents and educators to use when talking with children about heaven.

What Is Heaven Like? by Beverly Lewis

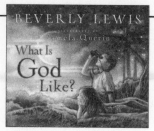

With Bible verses and inspiring illustrations, *What Is God Like?* tells of a brother and sister spending a fun-filled day and night remembering all they know about their heavenly Father. The last page also offers suggestions for parents as they seek to teach their children about God.

What Is God Like? by Beverly Lewis